For Josh!!

The Emerald Cloth

CLARE C. MARSHALL

Keep enjoying life!

_2023_

THE VIOLET FOX SERIES - BOOK THREE

The Emerald Cloth
Copyright © 2018 Clare C. Marshall
Cover Design © David Farrell
Editing by Samantha Beiko
Map Illustrations by Scott Henderson

FAERY INK PRESS
Calgary, Alberta
https://www.faeryinkpress.com
clare@faeryinkpress.com

Printed in Canada by Marquis.
Second Printing

Books by Clare C. Marshall:

The Violet Fox Series:
The Violet Fox
The Silver Spear
The Emerald Cloth
The Midnight Tablet

The Sparkstone Saga:
Stars In Her Eyes
Dreams In Her Head
Hunger In Her Bones
Darkness In Her Reach
Voices In Her Song

Other Titles:
Within
Gear and Sea

- CAST OF CHARACTERS -

Kiera Driscoll. *AKA The Violet Fox.* A sixteen-year-old Freetor-born folk hero who fights for her people's freedom. After a series of adventures, she has married the rightful prince of the realm, Keegan Tramore.

Keegan Tramore. The rightful Prince of Marlenia and son of Eamon Tramore. Married in secret to Kiera Driscoll. Currently cursed in a frozen sleep and in the clutches of the Frostfire family.

Laoise Mullen. *Pronounced LEE-sha.* Best friend and confidant of Kiera Driscoll. Fast runner, quick thinker, and devoted to the cause. She is Bidelia's daughter.

Bidelia Mullen. *AKA Mother Margaret.* Laoise's mother. Determined, stubborn, and cautious. She worked undercover for years as the head servant in the castle until she was exposed and tortured at Sylvia Frostfire's hand.

Monju Farin. Southern bard assassin who helped Kiera and Keegan find the Silver Spear. Once loyal to Dominique Castillo, he now fights loyally at Kiera's side.

Conal Driscoll. *AKA the Advisor, AKA Ivor Ferguson, AKA Kiera's father.* A Freetor-born man who pretended to be a Marlenian shopkeeper and rose to power as the Holy One's Advisor. Universally hated by Freetors—very few know the secret of his birth. Often duplicitous, he is devoted to Kiera, but equally devoted to the study of magic.

THE FROSTFIRE FAMILY
Rulers of the Eastern Province

Sylvia Frostfire. *AKA Daughter of the East.* The youngest child of Leszek Frostfire. Airy, arrogant, fond of large dresses, and blindly in love with Keegan Tramore. Despises Kiera. Would have married Keegan Tramore if Kiera had not interrupted the wedding, sparking the current Eastern invasion of the West. Currently betrothed to Marin Castillo.

Leon Frostfire. The second-oldest child of Leszek Frostfire. Boisterous and eager to prove himself worthy.

Boris Frostfire. The eldest son of Leszek Frostfire. Quietly imposing, stubborn, and usually boring. Currently betrothed to Dominique Castillo and heir apparent to both the Western and Eastern thrones.

Leszek Frostfire. *AKA High King of the East, AKA Emperor Leszek.* Invaded Marlenia City—the seat of power in the West—and declared himself emperor of the entire realm. Hungry for revenge, desperate to keep his newfound power, and greedy. Currently ruling from the occupied Marlenia City.

THE CASTILLO FAMILY
Rulers of the Northern Province

Dominique Castillo. *AKA Daughter of the North.* Ever since the Freetors kidnapped her and stole her identity, Dominique has pledged her life to eradicating Freetors everywhere. Kiera's chief nemesis. Clever, constantly scheming, and fond of cutting out tongues. Currently betrothed to Boris Frostfire and therefore set to become the next High Queen of Marlenia.

Marin Castillo. The little-seen nine-year-old son of the High King of the North. Dominique's brother. Sequestered away in the Northern capital of Ninyanas. Currently betrothed to Sylvia Frostfire.

Matís Castillo. *AKA High King of the North, AKA the Pauper King.* Frail and probably ill, he remains as always hidden in his castle in the Northern capital.

THE GARETH FAMILY
Rulers of Baile Gareth in the Western Province

Ansel Gareth. Ruler of Baile Gareth in Feenagh Forest. Historically loyal to the Tramore family, Ansel's allegiance has been called into question with the Tramore family scattered and the Frostfires now in power. His word influences other lessor lords. Currently harbouring Kiera and her friends from the Frostfire forces. Will do what is right for his small corner of the realm and nothing more.

Linnaea Gareth. Only daughter of Ansel Gareth. Quiet and timid, she is unmarried and living beneath her father's thumb—for now.

Joel Gareth. Ansel's second son. Rebellious and definitely hiding something.

Wallace Gareth. Ansel's oldest son and heir to Baile Gareth. Married and living in Gareth Manor with his wife.

OTHERS

Rordan Driscoll. Kiera's older brother. Member of the Extremists. Publicly executed.

Pascal Antony. Unofficial spokesperson for the Roamers. Former mercenary, usually spoiling for a fight, and slow to sway to any cause—unless you can afford him.

Alastar the Hero. A powerful magic-user who rose up against the royal class, creating the Freetor movement two hundred years ago. He cursed the Silver Spear.

Dashiell. The man-god worshiped by some surface Marlenians. "Creator" of the four artefacts.

Marlenia

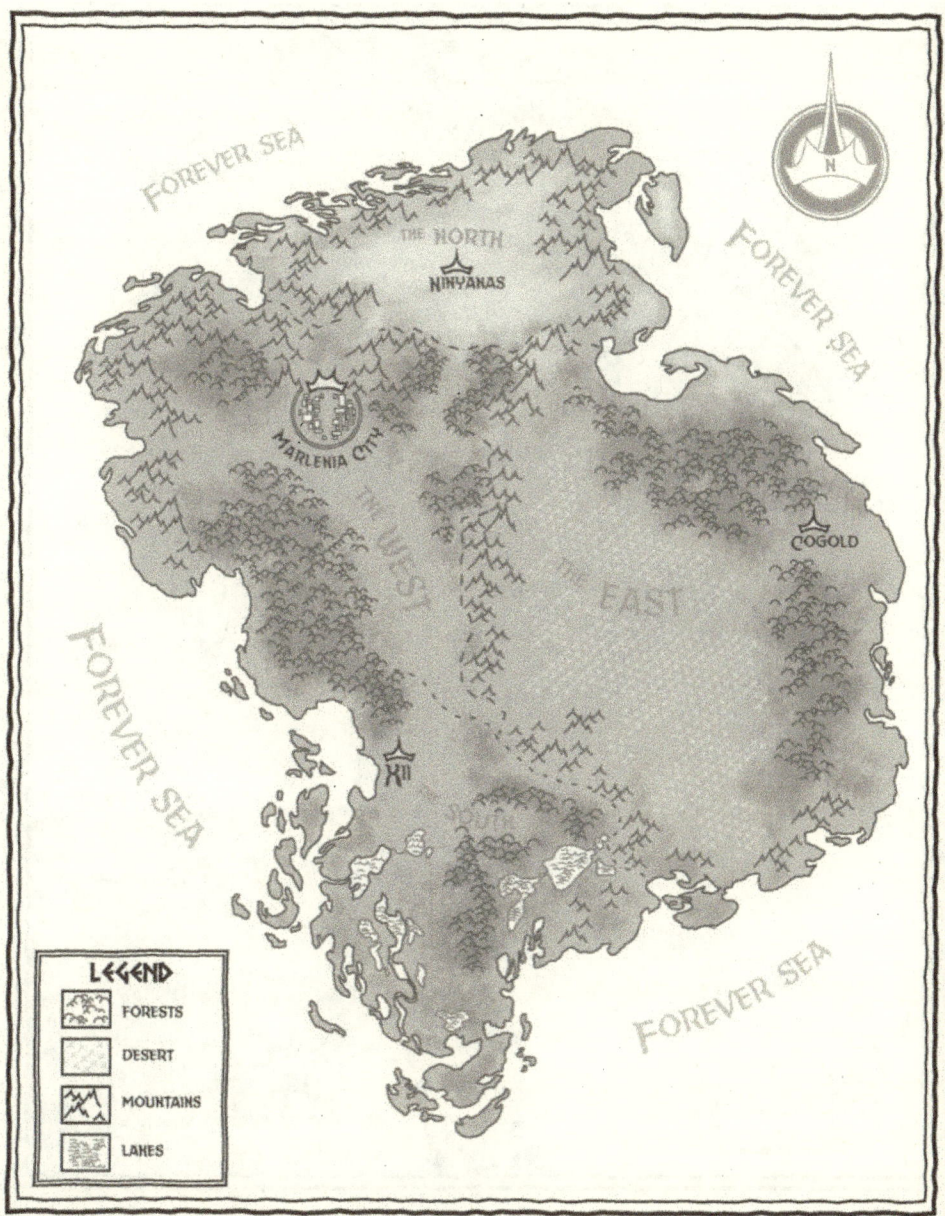

Marlenia
THE WEST

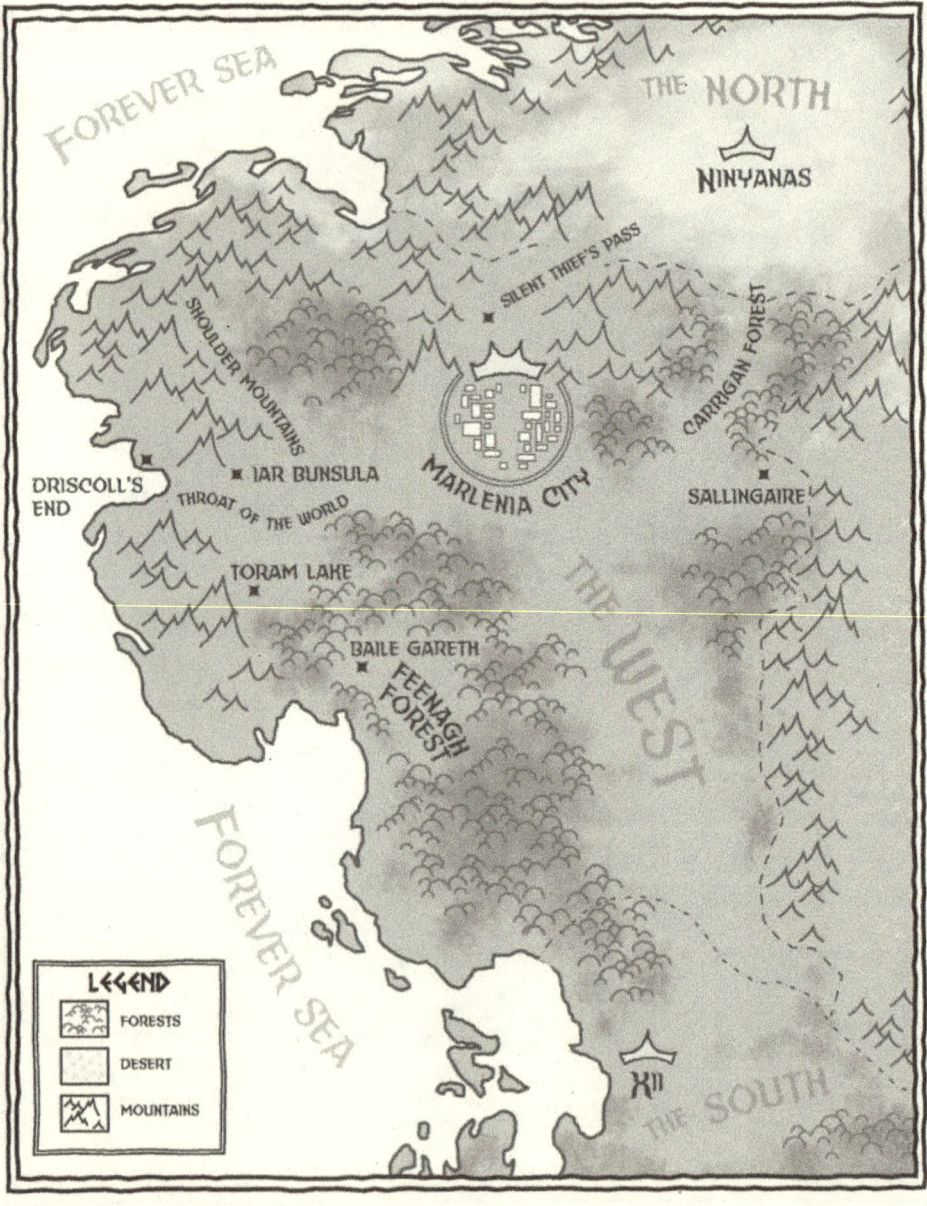

FOREVER SEA

THE NORTH

NINYANAS

SILENT THIEF'S PASS

SHOULDER MOUNTAINS

CARRIGAN FOREST

DRISCOLL'S END

IAR BUNSULA

THROAT OF THE WORLD

MARLENIA CITY

SALLINGAIRE

TORAM LAKE

THE WEST

BAILE GARETH

FEENAGH FOREST

FOREVER SEA

LEGEND

FORESTS

DESERT

MOUNTAINS

XII

THE SOUTH

One

Run. That was what my anger told me.

The men loyal to Lord Ansel Gareth, our gracious host, closed in fast three stone-throws behind me. I grinned as I gripped my rough-woven skirts and mustered more speed on the worn wooden floors of Gareth Manor. The men had the advantage of knowing the manor intimately. I had the advantage of running from soldiers like them all my life.

"Stop! Thief!"

Those words alone brought me back to my base instincts. Run. Hide. Survive. Give the spoils to those in need. My father would be furious if he found out I'd been sneaking around the manor, swiping treasures from the kitchen. Yes, I was a thief. I had to keep my skills sharp. Doing anything was better than doing nothing. I couldn't be idle.

Because if I was, even for a moment, I'd think of the man I loved in the clutches of my worst enemy.

Gareth Manor wasn't as large as the mountain castle in Marlenia City where, over two months ago, I'd disguised myself as Lady Dominique Castillo and gotten myself into this mess. In that time, I started a war between the two most powerful provinces in the world, crossed the West on foot with my love, Prince Keegan Tramore, and found one of the most powerful artefacts of Dashiell: the Silver Spear.

That was when things went horribly wrong: why Keegan was

no longer with me and why I was forced into hiding here, in Baile Gareth, with my friends and what little family I had left.

I rounded a sharp corner into a long corridor. At the end was the back exit to the stables and the henhouse, and beyond the grounds: the dark, thick trunks of Feenagh Forest loomed. Gareth Manor was considered the second most fortified structure in the West, as it was situated in the middle of a forest populated with dangerous, once-mythical creatures called the beatag. Once-mythical, only because Keegan and I managed to meet one, and survive.

"She's just a servant!" one of the guards shouted, close behind.

"No, she's a noble brat! We can't lay a hand—"

I raced on down the corridor and threw open the door. Fresh air. For the first time in nearly a fortnight, I stepped outside the manor and breathed in the crisp aromas of Feenagh Forest and the comforting smell of barnyard animals. I dashed through the knee-high grass hugging the manor. To my left was the henhouse, fortified by a scaleable fence. No good—Laoise had told me of the frequent patrols and the watchtower some distance to the south. Beside it, the stables. Better.

Horses greeted me from their stalls as I approached the stable at top speed. Some danced nervously at my sudden arrival.

A man much taller than me grabbed my upper arm and swung me around. "You're coming with—" When he recognized my face, his grip loosened, and with it, his resolve. "Aren't you...?"

Only a select few knew that I was in Baile Gareth: the former Advisor to the throne known publicly as Ivor Ferguson, my best friend Laoise, her mother Bidelia, the bard assassin Monju Farin, and the Gareth noble family. The face of Kiera Driscoll, the Violet Fox, was not as well known outside Marlenia City. She was also rumoured to be dead. A rumour my father wanted to encourage—for now. As far as the manor staff and the bannermen were concerned, I was but another lesser noble relative visiting after a long journey, who preferred to keep to myself. My friends were my servants, and the Advisor—well, his face was trickier to hide than mine, and his motives less trusted.

"I get that a lot," I said. "Got to run."

I hurried back the way I came, towards the manor. The guard was on my heels. Where had the second one gone? To warn the other bannermen patrolling the manor? The entire Gareth family? No, thefts would be trivial to them. I hoped. I slammed the hardwood door behind me. He couldn't stop in time: the door hit him with a heavy *thunk* on the forehead. He slumped to the ground.

First thought: Hopefully he doesn't remember me when he wakes.

Second thought: I just knocked a guard unconscious.

This wouldn't go unnoticed.

As for the second guard, he seemed to have given up. But if the Gareth men found their friend, then they'll likely report to Lord Ansel, putting our tenuous safety treaty in jeopardy.

I opened the door. The bannerman muttered incoherently.

"Sorry," I said. After checking for witnesses—just a few clucking hens—I grabbed the man by the underarms and dragged him to the wall. My belly wound screamed. Although my father's magic had sped along the healing process and probably prevented my untimely demise, lifting and moving heavy objects reminded me that I was not my old self. The bannerman was heavier than three packs of grain. My lower back ached and the bandages around my middle felt tight against the strain, but I managed to prop him against the rough stone.

He looked up at me, dazed. "You're..."

"Yeah, don't spread it around." I sighed. "I'll put them back. I promise."

I hurried back inside before he could further identify me and strode confidently down the corridor. At least my treasures were safe in my apron pocket. I scooped out a handful of berries and stuffed them in my mouth, feeling immediately guilty. Taking them had been too easy. The kitchen staff had wanted to prepare blueberry pies for tonight. My belly was sated, like everyone else living in the manor, and I knew no one that needed them more.

I turned right at the next corner and headed for the kitchen.

A small, startled gasp gave away her position. There was nowhere to hide in the narrow corridor. Even so, I pressed myself against the wall and lowered my head. One person saw my face today—I didn't need more trouble.

"Kiera? What are you doing outside your room?"

I let out a loud breath of relief at the sound of Laoise's voice. "How long were you following me?"

"Long enough." She hurried for me, her straw-brown bouncing around her ears, hand outstretched. I clasped it, worried why she wasn't on the third level scrubbing the floors. If anyone were to find me, it would be Laoise. Only the dearest friend of the province's most notorious thief and scoundrel could take her by surprise.

"I was...going to the kitchen," I said, gesturing down the hall. "Do you want to—?"

She wasn't fooled. She reached into my apron pocket and drew out a fistful of evidence. "Why would you put yourself at risk? If you were hungry, you could have just sent for me."

"It wasn't about that. And I'm going to put them back."

She put her hands on her hips. "Give me the apron. I'll do it."

"No, please, Laoise—"

"Shh! Just do it, okay? You're lucky it's me and not...you know."

Laoise still had trouble saying my father's name—especially his surface name. Advisor Ivor Ferguson had been responsible for the imprisonment of countless Freetors, all in the name of protecting his secret: that he was a Freetor himself and had climbed the social ranks to make a difference in the lives of all Freetors. But things hadn't worked out that way.

I untied the apron and carefully handed it to Laoise. She retied it around her waist. "I know you're just trying to add some variety to your life. I wish you could come wash floors with me. It's back-breaking work, but it's better than doing nothing in that closet chamber all day."

Such a Freetor statement if there ever was one. "I wish you would have been there with me. The confectionary was empty for just a moment. I waited for the two ladies to leave and then I reached up and snatched the berries and—"

She grabbed me before I could elaborate any further and pulled me down the hall, towards the cramped prison that was my quarters. "I already heard. You charged one of Lord Ansel's guards! Outside! Kiera, anyone could have recognized your face—"

"I didn't charge him, he chased me. And I'm pretty sure no one recognized me."

She stopped and rounded on me. I'd known Laoise my entire life. She was more than my best friend. She was my sister, and would have been for real, had my brother not been publicly executed for his Extremist affiliations. Her thin lips twisted with disapproval—so like her mother, Bidelia—as she shook her head.

"Pretty sure isn't good enough. Your father asked me to keep an eye on you."

"Oh please. Don't tell me he expects you to report all my activities to him."

"He does."

"And you're...not...right?"

She crossed her arms. "Just the ones that matter. I know you don't like being cooped up here like a prisoner. I don't like it either. But unless you want the Frostfires to know that you're here, and cause a whole bunch of problems for Lord Ansel, and eliminate that fragile alliance we've built with him..."

"I didn't mean to cause trouble." I really didn't. Lord Ansel's hospitality was the main reason we weren't rotting in the dungeons within the Marlenia City mountain castle—assuming there was enough of it left to rot in.

Two voices echoed besides our own in an adjoining corridor. I pressed against the wall instinctively until we realized they were standing still.

"We should go the other way," Laoise whispered.

I grabbed her hand and moved silently towards the voices. She didn't resist.

A high-pitched, wavering voice was pleading her case. "I was just—"

The deep, gruff voice with authority interrupted her. "It's too dangerous, Linnaea. Running around outside, as if you're a..."

"Laoise, is that the lord and his daughter?" I whispered.

We halted before the end of the corridor and peered around the corner. Indeed, it was Lord Ansel Gareth, patriarch of the manor and Baile Gareth itself, and his only daughter, Lady Linnaea. Lord Ansel had the face of a man who had seen war: grizzled, stern, with deep chasm lines on his cheeks and forehead. Lady Linnaea had no such stories embedded into her skin. I'd heard she'd never left the manor grounds in her seventeen years. Her long, fair hair had been braided down her back. She was dressed in one of her finer dinner gowns: unusual, as there was at least three hours until meal time—five hours until Laoise and I got the kitchen scraps.

"Please promise me you won't do this again," Lord Ansel said.

"I..." Linnaea was close to tears. "Can we speak about this elsewhere?"

"I found you here, so this is where you will answer me. Promise your father you will obey."

Laoise and I exchanged curious looks.

"Father—"

"I know how you feel about this," he said, not unkindly. His clothing rustled as he leaned over and kissed his daughter on the forehead. "If there was another way, I'd pursue it. Right now, our family stands to lose everything we have built over the past two hundred years if you do not yield and marry him."

Linnaea drew a sniffly breath and whimpered something in the affirmative.

"We can talk more about this—"

Laoise grabbed my arm and pulled me silently down the corridor, away from the arguing nobles. It wouldn't do us any good to be caught, not when Lord Ansel's patience with us was already stretched thin. There was another way to my quarters, a longer way around, that would give us time to speculate.

"I wonder who he's making her marry," I whispered.

"Probably some old noble in the East, or maybe the South. It doesn't matter. We'll be out of here soon."

"Why do you say that? Have you also plotted ten escape plans?"

"Just three. The servant girls are chatty. Doesn't leave me a lot of silent thinking time."

I grinned. "I bet your three are better than my ten. Well, nine now. The berries plan didn't work."

Thinking I was serious, she gave me an incredulous look, until I burst out laughing. She snorted, and I grabbed her hand, and together we ran like we used to, hand-in-hand through enemy territory, down the hall and up the winding servant staircase.

This was how it should be, when we were truly free. Once I had Keegan back, once my face was no longer feared, once we had a place to call home again...

Our laughter died as soon as we entered my cramped quarters. The Advisor stood at the window, arms crossed, staring out into the forest. His fingers tapped impatiently on his forearm. He didn't even turn to greet us; he knew it was me, returning from my forbidden journey outside.

"Kiera," he said. "Laoise, get back to the third floor. The scrubbing won't finish itself, and the other girls are far too curious about your frequent visits to the noble quarters."

"Yes, my lord," Laoise said flippantly. She squeezed my hand in a silent, well-wishing gesture and closed the door behind me, leaving me alone with Advisor Ivor Ferguson, or as he was known to the Freetors, Conal Driscoll.

The man who had abandoned me and my brother. And, also, the same man who had come for me when I had no one at Driscoll's End, and pulled the Silver Spear from my chest, saving my life.

"Father," I said, unable to avoid Laoise's infectious sarcasm.

He faced me then, unable to contain his surprise. It was hard to know what to call him, but maybe it didn't matter. I would have died at Driscoll's End if my father's strange magic hadn't plucked me from Lady Dominique's grasp. Thanks to him, I was alive. The wound from the Silver Spear had nearly healed under his care, although it would leave a nasty scar. Yet because of him, I was trapped here, forced to do nothing while he spun webs of deceit with Lord Ansel, instead of searching for Keegan.

My husband.

"What were you thinking, Kiera?"

Just when I thought we'd come to a mutual understanding—a respect, even—he had slipped back into patronizing me.

"I shouldn't be lecturing you." He let his arm fall to his side with a threatening snap. The garish clothes once afforded by his station were gone. Now he wore the guise of a merchant. Ivor

Ferguson in his most basic form, before he became the Advisor to the Holy One so long ago.

"Are you going to explain yourself?" His shoes scuffed on the stone floor. "If you're listening at all. That would truly be a miracle from the man-god."

My mouth was dry. A conversation with my father was like a sparring match. I had to be quick with a witty reply lest I become burned.

"I have no explanation," I said truthfully. Although I'd mostly recovered from Lady Dominique's fatal blow to the stomach, I barely slept. Keegan was out there somewhere, and every plan we conceived to recover him seemed more childish, reckless, or impossible to pull off.

"If this is a cry for attention, Kiera, you needn't continue. I'm here."

He meant to be comforting, but he sounded frustrated.

"I have to do something," I said finally, gritting my teeth. Staring out the window at the forest kept me grounded. Looking at my father now would send me spiralling, and I had a history of letting my anger get the better of me.

"I know you're worried about—"

"I'm beyond worried about Keegan. What if he's dead?" I thumbed the violet cloth wrapped around my forefinger, the symbol of our marriage. A union no one but his man-god had witnessed, and thus, could not be proved. "What if he never wakes up?"

The magic of the Silver Spear came with a steep price. Although the Freetors could handle the ancient weapon, it was deadly to anyone born on the surface. Something I wished we'd known before the enchanted frost overtook Keegan, causing him to fall into a death-like sleep. I glanced at the Spear, wrapped in brown tattered cloth, sitting on the desk as if it were a gift.

I caught the flicker of sympathy on my father's face. "We'll find him, Kiera. I promise. You're not making this easy on me. While I'm constantly searching for reasons for us to stay under this roof and keep Lord Ansel from bending the knee to the Frostfire family, you're acting like a child."

"I can't stay cooped up like this while he's out there, probably being tortured by her." I could barely bring myself to say her name. Lady Dominique Castillo. The woman whose face and name I stole to capture Keegan's heart. Now, she had his frozen body and the kingdom under her thumb, with Lady Sylvia Frostfire's help. "I have to keep my skills sharp."

"By stealing berries?"

"I was going to put them back." That was the point of the exercise, after all. How much could I steal from the kitchen without attracting attention? Now I knew the answer. Not enough.

"We have already stretched Lord Ansel's hospitality."

"He won't throw you out," I mumbled. Though that wasn't necessarily true. With Keegan being the last of his line and with his whereabouts unknown, Lord Ansel didn't have to adhere to the treaty his ancestors had formed with Keegan's family. It was only because of my father's influence—and possibly because of Lord Ansel's distaste for the Frostfire family—that we were safe at the moment. But there were still people suffering directly under the Frostfires' hands within occupied Marlenia City. It pained me to think of those who had died because they remained publicly loyal to Keegan and me, instead of submitting to the invaders.

"Lord Ansel has called a gathering tonight," my father said as he shuffled for the door. "I want you to stay here until then. Perhaps I can convince him to hear your apology."

"My apology?" I blurted. All I wanted was to keep my skills sharp. To not sit here in this room and rot with the artefact that had stirred up this mess. "I didn't mean to cause trouble. I... really do...appreciate your help."

"Thank you," he said. "But saying it to me doesn't do you— nor any of us—any good. You must kneel before Lord Ansel. You don't have to speak in front of the entire court. You can speak after any visiting lords, merchants, and servants leave. We don't want to raise any more suspicion."

I sat on my cot and nodded. My father was right. He was almost always right. I just hated admitting it, especially to him. "Maybe if you were better at magic, you could give me a different face. That would solve some of our problems."

He smiled, and for a moment, I saw my deceased brother, Rordan. "Perhaps I..." Pausing at the door again, he turned. "Kiera, are you asking me to teach you magic?"

I hadn't thought of it that way. "No."

"You have no desire to learn?"

I shrugged. "I thought I had no aptitude for it. I wasn't chosen by the Elders when I was young."

"Yes. But you manage the artefacts just fine. The Elders strictly controlled magical knowledge, for good reason. Perhaps, if you wanted, I could...attempt to teach you."

My father had been trying to help me ever since I discovered he was alive. For most of our relationship, I didn't know his true intentions until after he executed his plans. Now, he was offering me a chance to control the force that defined the Freetors as a people.

"All I want is for my people to be free. All of my people." I stood, gripping the desk against the wall. "Many of our people fear magic. I don't oppose it, but every time a powerful magic wielder tries to do good, it seems like their desires become twisted. So...I can't say I'm that interested. No."

"Hmm," was all my father said. He opened the door to my prison. "I was hoping you'd say something of the sort. Perhaps you are more ready to learn than I thought."

* * *

Unlike the slippery tile floor that made heeled shoes loud and soft toes ideal, the gritty stone floor in the narrow mezzanine above the throne room left a thief no room for error. Every time I shifted my weight, the stone scraped beneath my feet, revealing my position to anyone who would care to look up. If I were down with the rest of the manor, it would only cause more problems. No, I had to remain up here, alone, watching the Gareth family conduct their weekly gathering until the time came for me to perform my apology.

The gathering room below was more like a converted dining hall than the ornate show of wealth that was typical of manors and castles. Instead of tapestries depicting the surface people as saints squashing the Freetors or slaying mythical animals, the Gareth family hung green and black banners over their drab stone walls, depicting their family crest: a large, shadowy beast surrounded by red thorns and twisted green vines.

Thirty-odd merchants, distant relatives of the Gareth family and other subjects living in the baile, chatted in low murmurs and filed into the room, stepping on a narrow, frayed red carpet leading right for the Gareth seat of power. Gatherings typically covered petty matters of state and allowed the lord to dole out justice for crimes and disputes, yet tonight tension thickened the air. How many of them had seen the ghost of the Violet Fox? How many of them knew that the former Advisor protected her, had risked his life to save her? How many of them believed that Keegan was alive?

There was only one throne and a green pillow on the seat, worn flat beneath Lord Ansel himself. He scrubbed his chiseled face, scrutinizing his approaching subjects. As they drew nearer to him, each one bowed, and he nodded curtly in acknowledgement to their loyalty.

Linnaea stood at her father's right side, her hands clasped nervously in front of her. Her braided hair had been pinned around her brow, making her innocent face seem more severe than usual. On Lord Ansel's left stood his eldest son, Wallace. Although twenty-seven, he looked far older, especially for a newly married man. His wife, Jemma, had entered with the merchants and the small lords. Her ringlets masked most of her face, though she looked young and content to stand next to her mother-in-law, Lord Ansel's wife Isabel. I didn't understand why Lady Isabel couldn't stand next to Lord Ansel. Did they not rule the baile together, even if it was Lord Ansel's namesake? The politics of baile lords had never been my specialty, though I'd patiently sat through my father's lessons, knowing it was important. I drew back into my hiding place, but not so far that I couldn't see the happenings.

"Where is Joel?" Lord Ansel asked.

Joel Gareth was Lord Ansel's second son. I smiled beneath my hood. Rumour had it he was trysting with a Roamer girl. That would not be an ideal match, even for a second son to a small but prestigious baile. Laoise and I had speculated wildly about how long it would be before Joel ran away and joined the travelling band himself, before realizing what a hard, dangerous life it was.

Wallace Gareth muttered something to Lord Ansel and the old lord waved his hand respectfully. "Very well. We'll start. Thank you for gathering here today. I'll keep this short. The rains are supposed to come tonight and I know many of you are looking forward to the coming harvest."

The crowd chuckled politely. I glanced at my father, freely leaning against the far wall for all to see. He smiled good-naturedly at Lord Ansel and the crowd before him, as if the gathering had been in his honour.

Lord Ansel glanced at my father. "We have had a guest for the past fortnight. An unusual one, at that. Advisor Ivor Ferguson."

My father bowed his head politely. "My title is likely forfeit, my lord, though I appreciate the gesture."

"As the Frostfires have not formally revoked it, I see no reason to stop referring to you as such, as you have kept me apprised of the situation, past and present, within Marlenia City." The lord looked suddenly grim. "Many of you have raised concern about my harbouring him here. Your words have not gone unheard. I have done my best to uphold the treaty my great-great grandfather signed with Killan Tramore.

"Advisor Ferguson has spent time in Marlenia City to determine if the last Tramore royal holds influence over the Frostfire family and requested their aid with the Freetor threat, or if the East's arrival in Marlenia City was, in fact, an invasion."

The Frostfires were so powerful; to admit that they had invaded would warrant punishment for sure. The crowd murmured at Lord Ansel's candour. I held my breath. Lord Ansel was acting cautiously. It was hard to know the truth when messages could be intercepted so easily. The Frostfires and the Castillos had burned Marlenia City's castle. They had murdered people in the street for their loyalty to the Tramores. At least, that was what we had heard. The fact that I had to sit here out of sight only made me more anxious.

I had to find a way back to the capital. To find Keegan, to defeat the Frostfires, to set things right for my people.

"After much discussion," Lord Ansel continued, "I have concluded that Keegan Tramore holds no sway over the Frostfires and that it is Emperor Leszek Frostfire, first of his title and name, along with his sons and Castillo family, who hold the true power in Marlenia City."

My father pushed off the wall. His face, normally a mask of self-assured smugness and secrecy, had faded. This situation was no longer in his control. "My lord..."

Lord Ansel held up a hand. "You have said enough, Advisor."

At least he knew when to fall silent, unlike me. My finger-nails drove into my palms as my father drew back against the wall like a wounded animal. Rage boiled inside of me.

"Keegan Tramore is indeed alive," Lord Ansel admitted. "And it seems he is safe within the capital, according to reports from the castle. Though from Lady Sylvia's parade, we know he is not in optimal health. He may go the way of his father."

There were several sympathetic murmurs from the crowd. My heart pounded. The Holy One, Eamon Tramore, had been well respected and had reigned a long time.

"The Frostfires claim they took the castle to prevent it from falling into Freetor hands. Be that as it may, the Tramore colours no longer fly. Whether we enjoy having the Frostfires as our overlords or not, they are here, and no army is strong enough to oppose them. I am not concerned with such matters of resis-tance and Freetor raids. My duty is to protect my baile and ensure the continued survival of its inhabitants."

Many of the small lords shouted questions mixed with jubi-lant cheers.

"Oh no," I whispered.

My father glanced at me. We were thinking the same thing.

"In that light, I have an announcement," Lord Ansel pro-claimed. He lifted a heavy hand towards Linnaea, whose fiery, tearful gaze was downcast at the scuffed wooden floors.

"It is with great joy that I announce my intention to formally join the Gareth family with the Frostfires. My daughter, Linnaea, will marry Leon Frostfire this coming spring in Marlenia City." He cast a grave look in my direction, daring me to challenge him. "This will ensure the continued prosperity and safety of all those living in Baile Gareth."

Two

LORD ANSEL'S PROCLAMATION remained with me, obscuring all other thoughts, as he conducted other baile business. No wonder Linnaea had been so distraught earlier. I shouldn't have dismissed her so quickly. Having your family select your marriage partner was bad enough—that she had to marry Leon Frostfire was a death sentence. I had narrowly escaped Leon and his band of men in Iar Bunsula. Not only was he a brute, but a staunch mouthpiece for the anti-Freetor movement within the noble class.

Eventually, the Gareth bannermen, merchants, and the other subjects of the baile left through the double oak doors to the promise of a communal supper in the dining hall, a tradition long established by a now-dead Gareth man. Only my father remained in the back of the room, half hidden in the drapery. Lord Ansel, Linnaea, and Wallace remained on the platform at the head of the hall. Apparently there was more business to conduct, and it more than likely concerned me.

"You can come out now."

I resented his tone—so cold, unfatherly—but I didn't have the luxury of acknowledging him as my blood, not here. I briefly considered swinging over the railing and falling like a limber cat onto the wooden floor; an impressive entrance fit for the Violet Fox. I settled for hurrying along the mezzanine to a covered, winding staircase that opened in the foyer and stepped into the throne room properly through the doors, like a regular cloaked lady without the reflexes of a feral creature and bones of steel.

My strides were long and purposeful as I approached the sitting lord. I drew back my hood to reveal my face and mess of curls. Laoise had tried to tame my hair, but neither of us could sit still long enough. What resulted was a frizzy, half-curled mess gathered around my fair face. Nothing on my face was painted so as to not attract attention. I was also not wearing a dress, but my freshly washed trousers, a large belt, and my nicest chemise.

My father evaluated my appearance quickly. The slight quirk of his lip expressed his disapproval. I bowed before Lord Ansel. Wallace frowned. To him, I probably looked like a stable hand. I smiled at him but my father cleared his throat.

"My lord. I have come before you today to..." The words were there, on my tongue, within my mind. I'd even practiced them, to please my father. But Lord Ansel's words had been heavier, stronger, and I couldn't say what I'd prepared. "My lord, if the Frostfires are truly in power, then we are all in grave danger."

My father sighed audibly behind me.

To my surprise, Lord Ansel smiled. "Having a liege lord always carries some sort of danger. However, by promising Linnaea to the Frostfires, I am alleviating some of that."

For you. "Surely there must be—" I stopped short of insulting them. Surely there must be a better match for Leon Frostfire, was what I was going to say. He was High King Leszek's second son, and while the throne would go to Leon's older brother, Boris, I couldn't see how Linnaea, the daughter of a mere baile lord, would be a better match than a daughter of the High King in the South.

"Surely there must be a better way for you to protect the baile than delivering your only daughter into the hands of treachery?"

Linnaea inhaled sharply, but didn't look up. She'd been silent as her father doled out her fate. I couldn't imagine living like that.

"I'm listening if you have a better idea, Fox," Lord Ansel replied drolly, exchanging an amused look with his eldest son.

Unfortunately, I didn't have a better idea. If I were in Linnaea's place, I'd be halfway out of the baile by now. I'd only dealt with Leon briefly in Iar Bunsula, but he'd been drunk and brutal, fanatically hunting down Freetors in the countryside.

The lord took my silence as answer enough. "I must send her to the castle as soon as possible. The Frostfires were...eager to have her safe within their walls."

Their walls. Eager. Their lies made my blood boil.

"Then you plan to send a carriage within a few days, my lord?" my father asked cautiously.

"I do," Lord Ansel said, matching my father's tone.

The idea struck my brain with such fury that I had no time to filter it. "Let us be part of the escort to Marlenia City."

Lord Ansel frowned and leaned back in his chair. "And why would I allow that?"

"We are a liability. Mostly me. It's safest for everyone in your baile if we aren't in it. But if we hide amongst Linnaea's escort, it would give us transport to Marlenia City. Which is where I want to go."

My father cleared his throat. "My lord..."

"I cannot guarantee your safety in my daughter's escort," Lord Ansel replied.

"You don't have to. I'm the Violet Fox. My friends and I can defend her if necessary."

At this, the old lord smiled slyly. "You are as brash as the stories say. Brashness does not make a warrior. It is, however, the quality of many thieves."

My face heated. I couldn't stop now. "And I apologize again

for any misunderstanding that may have occurred today. I... shouldn't have disobeyed my guardian, Advisor Ivor Ferguson."

Linnaea's gaze lifted from the floor. I had hit a nerve and not only with her. Lord Ansel's amusement faded into serious contemplation.

"You wouldn't be the only escort for Linnaea."

"Of course."

"Did you really kill the Freetor queen in the capital?"

White-lipped, I nodded. "Elder Erskina wanted me to kill Keegan. I refused."

"So you are truly in love with him?" Linnaea's voice, sudden and high, startled me.

"Yes," I replied with conviction. "And once I'm back in Marlenia City, I'm going to find out what the Frostfires and the Castillos have done with him, and I'm going to..." I glanced at my father, considering my words. "I'm going to rescue him. What we do after that, I don't know. All I want is to have him back."

Lord Ansel seemed unimpressed, but nodded anyway. He didn't care about my personal vendetta. He had a baile to run. "Very well. I will let my bannermen know that there will be an extra contingent riding with my daughter."

A ghost of a smile appeared on Linnaea's face. "I feel safer knowing I will ride with a legend."

The heavy doors behind me creaked open and a young man, a few years older than me, burst inside. Seeing the emptiness of the room, he swore under his breath, and doubled down on his oaths when his gaze fell upon me. I had only seen Joel Gareth in passing—as he was leaving the grounds, as he was leaving the kitchen—and he seemed ready to leave once more until his father's deep voice stayed his nervous feet.

"You missed the gathering."

Joel ruffled the red carpet underneath him as he scuttled

forward. "Uh, is she supposed to be...?" She glanced behind him, towards the exit. "Do people know now...?"

"If you keep talking they will," I muttered.

Lord Ansel ignored or otherwise didn't hear my remark. "Where were you?"

"I was sleeping, Father." He ran a hand through his bedridden head sheepishly.

"I walked past your chamber and knocked," Wallace said, lifting a brow.

"Well I wasn't in my chamber. I was in the library." Embarrassment rushed to his face, made only more apparent as he kept glancing between his father and me. "I'm sorry, Father. I'll take whatever punishment you deem fit, but I'm hungry, if you'll dismiss me."

Lord Ansel pushed to his feet, but before he could confer any kind of punishment on his unruly second son, Linnaea touched his arm gently. Her voice was clear this time. "Father. I ask for forgiveness on Joel's behalf. This gathering didn't concern him. And if I only have days left here, as you said..."

His face softened as he placed a large hand over hers. "Your heart is too kind. You must steel yourself to such matters. The Frostfires do not have such regard for their siblings."

Lowering her gaze in submission, her face noticeably paled. I couldn't imagine being forced to marry someone against my will, just to secure peace. Keegan had nearly surrendered to such a marriage, before I'd stood up in the cathedral and revealed my identity, just to stop it. I wished there was something I could do.

Joel trudged forward, hands outstretched and head bowed. "Am I forgiven, Father?"

Lord Ansel's cheeks coloured. "I will think on an appropriate punishment as I fill my stomach. Come with me to the dining hall."

It wasn't a request. Joel gulped and nodded, throwing me a

desperate glance. I didn't know what to say to him, so I gave him a weak smile as he turned and headed for the large doors from whence he came.

Lord Ansel stepped down the dais and, without gesturing, Linnaea and Wallace followed him. He barely acknowledged me as he passed. I bowed appropriately. "You are dismissed, Fox. Advisor, join me in the feast—it will be expected."

"Of course, my lord. I shall meet you there presently."

Unconcerned, the Gareths left the throne room without ceremony, leaving me and my father alone. We held each other's gazes as we listened for their footsteps to fade. We had similar instincts.

"I'll take you back to your room," he said, once we were sure they were gone.

"Doesn't he expect you to follow?"

He took my arm gently and led me back up the stairs, keeping his head low so we could continue our conversation. "He expects me to keep you out of sight and quiet."

"Just like he keeps his daughter under his thumb."

My father grimaced. "He certainly does a better job than I do."

"Well, if I were Linnaea—"

"You aren't, thank goodness. That girl will have to learn how to navigate the Frostfires on her own. We have larger issues to contend with. I thought for a moment you were going to admit that you wanted to restore Keegan to the throne. That would have made our situation more difficult, especially now. Better he think you brash and lovesick than a competent schemer."

Yes, I'd almost lost all my sympathy from him there. "It's not completely a lie. I want to see him safe. But I don't want to see the Frostfires on the throne."

"Neither do I. I have invested too much in Keegan for him to die now." While the words were cold, his tone wasn't, and I felt a sudden jolt of jealousy towards my husband. My father had been a second parent to him since age eleven, when he'd saved the young prince's life. "He will be a great Holy One someday. With our help."

"Once we rescue him," I said.

"We will." His hand, still guiding me, squeezed my shoulder. My father wasn't prone to physical displays of affection, and as odd as it still was to receive them from the former Advisor, a man hated and feared by all Freetors, I found great comfort from his support. So much so that my throat tightened.

I pushed my fears for Keegan deep down. I didn't want to appear weak in front of my father, even though I'd almost died in his arms a fortnight ago. I had to be strong for him, for Keegan—for myself.

My father continued. "Unfortunately for us, I think the Frostfires want this match with Linnaea as much as Ansel does. Ansel gets immunity from Frostfire attack, theoretically, and the Frostfires get the keys to Ansel's baile."

My eyes widened. "You mean...they'd send soldiers here to look for us?"

He nodded. "I believe so. Us, or anyone they believed to be disloyal to the Frostfire family. The only reason they haven't is because the forest is dense and filled with dangerous creatures. But once they have Linnaea, it wouldn't be easy for Lord Ansel to disobey, shall we say, a forceful request. Lord Ansel has already lied about harbouring me here. And they thought you were dead. We can no longer trust the lord once this marriage is sealed."

I hadn't considered that. I didn't trust him anyway, but to think that he would betray us once Linnaea was in enemy hands? "But you said the Frostfires wouldn't attack because the forest is dangerous."

"Linnaea knows her way through it."

They would definitely force Linnaea to lead troops through

her father's forest if it meant finding the slippery Tramore advisor, or me, a pretender queen, hero to the Freetor people. "Can't they hire someone to do the same...?"

"Sometimes blood is more reliable than silver." We stopped in the middle of the stairs. "That was a brave move you pulled. Foolish, perhaps, but...necessary. There is no guarantee that the carriage bringing us to the capital won't be escorted by Frostfire men or searched at the gates, however."

"Like I told Lord Ansel. We can handle it."

"Don't underestimate the enemy."

I didn't want to think that way. I had survived so much already. My father's caution took root. "I guess we should prepare for every contingency."

"Agreed. But not right now. I have a feast to attend."

We had arrived at my quarters. My stomach growled at the thought of food; likely Laoise and I would share scraps once she had finished her duties. "Should we meet tonight, with everyone?"

My father nodded. "I'll let them know."

As my father turned to leave, the sounds of hurried footsteps revealed Monju and Laoise as they rounded the corner. They skidded to a stop before us, nearly knocking over my father.

"There is the Lady!" Monju hissed, relieved.

Both were nearly out of breath, which was unusual. They must have rushed across the entire grounds just to get here.

"What's wrong?" I demanded.

"Monju intercepted a message—" Laoise began.

"—urgent, from Marlenia City," Monju cut in. "Private, in Frostfire handwriting. Messenger was careless, read message, broke the seal, made it easy to—"

"Kiera, there's a plague spreading in the castle. People falling into a frozen death-like sleep," Laoise finished.

I drew a deep breath. "Just like Keegan."

Three

"How do you know this isn't a deception?" I asked.

"It is the High King Leszek Frostfire's hand. Or, Emperor Leszek, the people are calling him now." Laoise shot Monju a *get on with it* look. "Monju knows the man's hand well. The slopes and curves, the quality of the paper and the wax seal—it is certainly real, Monju can swear on his life."

I nodded, averting my gaze. Monju Farin had a flare for handwriting and deception. He faked Keegan's hand to lure me into believing that he wanted Lady Sylvia Frostfire, and not me, as his wife. He'd helped Lady Dominique and Lady Sylvia mastermind our whole quest to find the Silver Spear on the hope that they would help him in turn to save his father's life. At Driscoll's End, when he'd revealed the truth, my trust in him had shattered. As it turned out, the bard was nobler than the two noblewomen, and though he helped save my life in the end, I didn't know if I could trust him ever again.

My father didn't seem to have the same dilemma. "You read the message, but you did not take it?"

"Correct, Lord Advisor. Monju ensured the wax was resealed."

He seemed amused by Monju's Southern vernacular. "Good. We don't want Ansel to suspect we've been snooping."

I drew a deep breath. "Wait. You said that the messenger also read it?"

"Not uncommon for pages. Someone else's hands are always in their pockets," my father said.

"You're not concerned?" Laoise asked. Her question mirrored my feelings. I hated how my father could be so calm when so much was at stake.

"Trouble in the castle can always be used to our advantage. Although, if this trouble is magical in origin..." He didn't have to finish the thought. The four of us knew all too well what happened when magic fell into the wrong hands.

I cleared my throat. "If Lord Ansel received the letter...he might call off the wedding!" This would be good news for Linnaea. Bad news for us—we'd have to find another way to the castle. I couldn't help but feel relieved. Linnaea needed to be protected from Leon Frostfire.

"We can speak more on this tonight. For now, I must consult with Ansel. I will see if he has heard the news and determine his next move." My father fixed his blazer and slipped easily between Laoise and Monju. Without looking over his shoulder, he added, "Don't expect to lay siege to the mountain castle just yet."

Once gone, the three of us exchanged uncertain glances. The thought of returning to the castle burned like hot coal in my stomach. I could still smell the flaming banners in the dark corridors, and as I balled my fists, the imaginary grit of the stone dug deep into my palms as I crawled hand-over-hand through the thick smoke.

"This means Keegan could be in the castle. Just like we suspected," I said, shaking off the creeping fog of the past.

"The Lady plans to mount a rescue mission?" Monju asked.

Monju and I had barely said twenty words to each other and we'd never been alone since I discovered he'd survived his sacrifice and double betrayal. I wasn't in a hurry to mend that bridge.

"It's something we'll have to discuss tonight." Every fibre of my being wanted to rush into the capital, into the heart of our enemy's den, and retrieve Keegan. I didn't know how we'd wake him yet—and my father had not yet revealed any useful information on that front—which meant he probably didn't have a plan, either.

Laoise smiled at me and then at Monju. "I won't be sorry to leave Gareth Manor."

"Is preferable to have a roof over Laoise's head, though, no?" Monju asked.

She squared her shoulders as he said her name, drawing herself up to her full height. "I've slept outside before. I...don't mean to demean the Gareth's hospitality. Just that being here, away from the Undercity, all those who are suffering..."

Monju shot me the briefest of glances, as if afraid to stare at me for more than an instant, and focussed his full attention on Laoise. "That is understandable. Being away from the battle, though, does not mean Lady Laoise has abandoned her people." He averted his gaze to the floor, stepping away soundlessly as if he was trespassing. "Monju should return to his duties."

"Oh?" Laoise said, one hand on her hip. Her cheeks looked rosier than before, and she did not correct Monju's use of Lady. "I suppose I should too. I have an entire corridor to wash. Since I didn't finish earlier."

He bowed to me, but when he rose, he was still looking at Laoise. "Until tonight."

She watched him go, her eyes shiny with a secret delight that illuminated her whole face.

A strange kind of fear passed over me, as though I'd missed something important, made more potent by Keegan's absence. I'd been locked away, so caught up in my own plans—finding Keegan, escaping Gareth Manor, restoring freedom to my people, removing the Frostfires from the castle—that I hadn't seen what had been blossoming right in front of me.

I shrivelled in my own skin, remembering that it was barely three weeks ago that Monju had looked at me in that way.

Opening the door to my room, I gestured for Laoise. She followed, her footsteps light and bouncy, as though the floor were made of clouds.

"Why were you looking at him like that?"

Laoise made a face as she shut the door. "Like what?"

I fell onto my bed in a huff. "Don't tell me. You like him?"

"No. I don't know." She leaned against the desk with a revealing, stupid grin on her face. "He is handsome. And charming." Her smile faded. "I know what you're going to say. What you're thinking. Having any kind of feelings for him is...dangerous."

"He did betray us."

"He was in too deep."

"Now you're defending him?"

"He saved your life. He could have taken that cure and walked away. He didn't have to stay."

It would have been easier if he'd died at Driscoll's End. The thought made me even more nauseous. I didn't want him to die. I just wanted this wound from his betrayal to fade. Or to have never happened in the first place.

Then there was the matter of Monju's kiss in the Roamer camp. Did Laoise know he'd had feelings for me?

I could hardly blame Laoise for her feelings for the bard assassin. His voice was silky and rich, his accent, while foreign, had an innocent charm that belied his deadly skills.

I had to tell her. "Laoise—"

"I won't let it interfere with anything," Laoise said, cutting me off. She hovered near the door, wringing her hands, nervous with the kind of energy I've seen in her before, when we used to talk about Rordan.

"I'm not...it's all right. I don't wish him ill." I looked up at her. The truth was on the surface, ready to be spoken. "I just want you to be happy."

"My feelings make you uncomfortable." She ran a finger along the desk absently.

"No. Yes."

Even admitting the possibility of my disapproval seemed to upset her. The desperate look in her eyes—she needed this. If I told her about Monju's kiss, I'd be taking away something precious. Not just the throes of new love, but the distraction she needed to get through. The kiss didn't mean anything to me. What it meant to Monju, I wasn't sure. He held great affection for me. I hoped it wasn't romantic affection. I couldn't destroy my best friend's hope—not now. I'd confront Monju before she could act on her feelings and ensure that he didn't mean to hurt her.

"I know what you're thinking," she said finally.

"You do?"

"He's not Rordan."

The mere mention of my brother's name brought the love and the pain he'd caused me to the forefront, banishing thoughts of Monju entirely. "I know he's not."

"I mean...not like that. Rordan was an Extremist. Monju is an idealist. A romantic." Another smile, another pause. "I've thought about this a lot."

"I can tell."

"Just try to forgive Monju, all right? Or at least, trust him a little more. We can't afford to have any more enemies."

My mouth twisted. I was still angry. If it weren't for him, Keegan wouldn't be in a cursed sleep—but mostly, I blamed myself. I had wanted to trust Monju in the first place. I still wanted to trust him. My heart told me it would take a thousand years for that to happen, no matter what Monju said or did, which only made me more frustrated.

"I know," I said sincerely. "And I'm not mad that he's not

Rordan. I want you to know that. That's important."

"I still think about him sometimes."

I sat up. "Me too."

"I don't think there's anything...wrong...about that."

"There isn't. He sacrificed a lot to keep me safe. To raise me, after my parents were gone. He was there—for both of us. I think being part of the Extremists must have given him some sense of hope." My brother had championed a dangerous cause, one that preached freedom at the expense of the destruction of innocent lives. It hurt to think about. It hurt more to think that he would never know that I forgave him.

"If he had lived...we would be sisters by now."

Laoise took my hand and the corners of her lips lifted in a small, knowing smile. "We don't need anyone to make us sisters."

My throat was tight. I grinned. "Yeah."

She squeezed my hand, then released it. "See you tonight."

* * *

"You're late."

Ignoring my comment, my father shut the door carefully to the kitchen. He darted around Laoise to inspect the different areas of the large, stately room. Although not as impressive as the kitchen in the castle in Marlenia City, Gareth Manor had the trappings of a good lord's house: a confectionary, a butchery, the copper, and of course, the vegetable prep counters. Each area was in a separate room, joined with wide archways for easy access for kitchen servants, the head cook, and the noblewomen who worked in the confectionary. It was nearly midnight. Five hours from now, at least twenty-five men would be preparing the morning meal, not to mention the women who would be bring the water for boiling and the wood to light the fires.

My father searched each room thoroughly before joining us at the main preparation counter, which was more like a wood-chopper's block the size of a dining table. I leaned against the head while Bidelia, Laoise's mother, sat patiently to my right, hands folded, waiting for my father to stop being paranoid.

I'd be waiting forever for that to happen.

"Checked the area already. No one else is here," Monju said. He paced before the only window on my left. The only light came from the candles we'd lit in front of us, which made our shadows stretch eerily.

My father stood next to Laoise, close to the entrance. He looked to Bidelia. "Why here?"

"Why not here? We certainly can't meet in Kiera's quarters, or yours, or mine. I've spent the last two weeks sleeping in a room with twenty other servants in the dampest, lowest part of the castle."

"Lucky, then," Monju said. "Beatag do not go underground."

I frowned, wondering where Monju had spent the past fort-night resting his head.

"Sorry for my tardiness," my father said finally. "Had to ensure I wasn't followed or spotted. And I was busy verifying the letter from the capital."

"It's true, isn't it?" Bidelia asked.

He nodded. "The frozen curse of the Silver Spear has spread within the capital. Only a handful of people have fallen so far, though the letter does not say who. When Keegan touched the Spear, how long before he became incapacitated?"

"Only a few seconds. The freeze started at his hands, and worked its way up his body." I dug my thumbnail into my palm. I could have stopped it. If only I had known, if only I had never gone on that quest...

"But how could these other nobles become frozen? The Spear has been with us the whole time. Right?" Laoise asked.

I nodded. "Maybe the Spear...infected Keegan. And the nobles touched him."

"Lady Sylvia touched the prince at Driscoll's End," Monju pointed out. "She shrieked from the cold, yet did not fall frozen. Neither did Lady Dominique, though she kept her distance."

"Sylvia only touched his clothes," I recalled, frowning. "And this frozen plague wouldn't be carried by air, or else the entire city would have been affected. It must be skin-to-skin contact." I blanched at the thought of scholars, soldiers, and Sylvia examining my husband while he was powerless and immobile. "Though...I'm not frozen. Maybe the curse only affects the surface-born Marlenians, just like the Silver Spear."

"We can't be completely sure that's the case," my father said, "but I would say it's a reasonable assumption. Curious nobles who got too close to Keegan, touched his forehead, his hand, and became frozen themselves."

"And then what?" Laoise asked. "Do these newly frozen nobles have the ability to spread the curse as well? Or are they simply frozen?"

"I don't know. The letter didn't say," my father replied. "It was a warning, likely sent to potential allies of the Frostfire family. The castle is under attack. Not by swords, spears, or flame, but by Freetor magic. For them, this is the Marlenian-Freetor war all over again."

"If we do nothing, all surface-born Marlenians could fall prey. And the Freetors would have their largest obstacle removed."

I massaged the worry lines burrowing deeper on my forehead. I could already see the frozen piles of bodies littering the streets, being carted out of their homes just so the Freetors could move in and resume some semblance of a normal life. The images were as real as the splinters driving into my hands, courtesy of the table I grasped in desperation.

The Extremists, assuming they still existed in some forgotten cave, would not hesitate to take further action. I could almost smell the fires. The burning flesh. My brother...

"Kiera?"

I shook my head, blinking away the memory. I didn't realize I was crying. I turned, wiped the tears away, hoping my friends would pretend they hadn't seen my weakness.

My father nodded at me. "This could be easily interpreted as a Freetor attack. An attack led by you."

If that were the case, I'd never gain the sympathy of the surface people again. "They're already exterminating any Tramore and Freetor sympathizers and enslaving the captured Freetors."

"If this isn't contained quickly, slavery would be too much of a risk," my father said grimly. "They might just kill every non-surface person they find."

The thought made me sick.

"If people are falling in the castle and within the city, that means Keegan is there. Or was, recently. I wonder which nobles have been affected. If Sylvia or Leon fell to the curse," I said. Sylvia's infatuation with Keegan and ignorance towards the commoners had been an annoyance in the few months I'd known her. If she fell to this mysterious, magical curse, I would shed no tears.

"It's possible," my father said. "Though I feel Leszek would use any calamity, real or not, to inspire sympathy for the invasion. No, I believe his three children are very much intact."

"I don't suppose you can return to the castle and try to get close to them as Advisor Ferguson?" I asked.

An old wound flickered like dying candlelight in my father's eyes. "I burned that bridge when I fled the capital." He glanced at Bidelia; her face was as his was, both of them trained to say and feel nothing, if necessary. The two of them knew more about the noble families than I'd ever know in a lifetime.

Before I could ask, Bidelia cut to the chase. "So, Kiera. I

suppose you have some ideas about our next move."

Our next move. The words scared me, though I was more afraid to show my fear. Or any kind of weakness. I was not just the Violet Fox anymore. I was a queen now. A leader for my people. I had to start acting like it.

"We have to rescue Keegan from the Frostfires," I said firmly. "The longer Keegan stays in the castle, the more innocent people risk falling to the curse. But we also have to deal with the genocide happening on our doorstep. The Frostfires have persecuted people loyal to the Tramore family as well as any Freetors and known Freetor sympathizers. The Frostfires have a large army and the silver to fund it. We need information. Resources. Allies."

"Information can be easily acquired," my father said. "Allies...not so much."

"You spent time with the Roamers," Laoise suggested. "Would they help us?"

After publicly punishing Keegan for a murder he didn't commit, I didn't exactly hold cordial feelings towards the travelling camp. I did gain the respect of one of their leaders, Pascal Antony. "It's possible they'd help us."

"Roamers never do anything for free," my father warned.

"They owe me, after what they did to Keegan," I said.

"Unsure if the Roamers will see it as the Lady does," Monju said respectfully. "The Prince did an honourable act, taking a punishment, though it was not his to bear. If the Lady expects a favour from this, it dishonours the Prince's act in their eyes."

I sighed. "Surely, though, they have no love for the Frostfires? The Roamer lifestyle isn't exactly looked upon as acceptable by most, right?"

My father seemed to share my frustration. "True, though the noble classes and the moneyed merchants see the Roamers as Marlenian travellers, and their lifestyle has been romanticized by literature and art. Unlike the Freetors, who are filthy and unnatural. Even though Roamers are made up of surface-born and cavern-born alike."

"We still have to reach out to them. The worst they can do is send no reply. Have we heard anything about the South?"

"They have kept quiet," my father replied. "It seems they still wish to remain neutral."

"Not unusual," Monju said remorsefully. "It is how Monju's culture has survived and thrived."

"The Frostfires aren't going to be content until they rule the entire world. Once they've married the North and placated the West, they will turn their gaze to the South!"

"The Lady is not saying anything Monju does not already know," he said defensively. "Just because Monju Farin is of the South, does not mean he represents his whole province."

"I know." It was easy to get mad at him. "Sorry."

"If they've gotten to a point where they are writing warning letters to the neighbouring bailes, we can assume the Frostfires are worried, which means they could be expecting an assault," my father replied. "They also may have sent Keegan out of the city entirely or destroyed his body."

"They wouldn't dare destroy him. Not while Sylvia is in the castle," I said.

"What has that to do with anything?" my father asked, sceptical.

"Sylvia would never let anyone near Keegan. She rebelled against her father and rode across the West to find him, convinced I had put him under a spell. I bet if she has him locked away under strict guard to prevent her father or Dominique from hurting him."

I hoped. If anything, Sylvia was predictable. So long as Sylvia remained at the castle, so would Keegan. "We could always try destroying the Spear. That may lift the curse."

"Absolutely not," my father said quickly. "The four artefacts of Dashiell are near-impossible to destroy. The Orb still retains its magic, even when shattered."

"Even if that were an option, destroying the Spear would forfeit our only chance of uniting the Freetors," Bidelia said. "No. We can use the Spear's magic on the Frostfires, trick them into touching it or Keegan, but we need to present the Spear to the Freetor people first."

"We don't even know if this sleep curse is permanent, or if he's slowly dying," I said. "How can we use magic against our enemies if we have no idea how to control it?"

"All the more reason to acquire more of the artefacts," my father said. "To study them. To give us the edge."

"We don't have that kind of time. Or have you not been listening? A curse is spreading. People are dying. Going off on another artefact adventure isn't going to solve our current problems."

"And what if I told you that it could?"

My mouth felt dry. "No."

"What are you talking about?" Laoise asked.

He loved this. Knowing what others didn't. Explaining only the necessary bits, holding the rest back. That had been his job in the castle and even though he'd lost his position, nothing had really changed. My father paced around the table smugly.

"The orb. The spear. The slab...and the cloth," he said. "Every Freetor knows the story of the Silver Spear, but are you familiar of the tale of the Emerald Cloth?"

Laoise and Bidelia shook their heads.

"Yes," Monju piped up. "An old one. A favourite of the South, told in many songs."

My father smiled. "Kiera, do you know it?"

I knew enough. The man-god imbued power in ordinary objects to remind the people of his presence, even if his physical body had died. "I don't think it matters, since you're going to tell us the story anyway."

"It's one of my favourites." He cleared his throat. "Perhaps the most tragic of the Dashiell myths was the story of the Emerald Cloth, for it showed Dashiell's human side, a side often hidden by the Church, despite them holding him up as a man-god.

"It began with a woman."

"You don't need to be dramatic, Conal," Bidelia said stiffly.

"But that is the fun of a story," Monju said. He nodded enthusiastically at my father. "Please, Advisor, tell the tale in a grand fashion."

Laoise was trying not to laugh, and despite being annoyed, I was, too. I had spent two weeks reading tomes, fantasizing about escape, and stealing berries. I missed being part of something larger than myself.

"Dashiell was a man of humble origins, who, because of his charming, resourceful, and kindly demeanour, became a successful merchant," my father began, smiling.

I realized why he liked this story. It was his own.

"He fell in love with a woman from an old, but small family—whose name and land has been lost to time. They were determined to be together, as she was just as bright and kind as he, but her family did not approve of Dashiell, and forbade the match. Despite their objections, Dashiell married the young woman in secret, and together they ran away to his small plot of land to begin their life together.

"Where this land is has been the subject of great debate, though Church excavations and study place it on the Western border with the South. Each province has a different study and a claim to Dashiell's lands. I posit"—he held up an authoritative finger—"that the reason it's so difficult to pin down the man-god's location during his time, is because his land stretched from near the current-day city of Xii to Maairem

Zar, bordering the East, perhaps reaching as far north on the map as Sallingaire."

He cleared his throat, realizing his story had become a lecture. "In any case, word of Dashiell's prosperity grew. And with it, tales of his generosity and kindness. Small lords and merchants flocked to him, and Dashiell's power—and his land—grew. Nobles and merchants swore fealty to him, and worked his lands, and Dashiell ruled over them. All who swore fealty became successful and prosperous, which only made Dashiell's popularity swell. All was well. For a time.

"But with Dashiell's power came many who despised and envied him, though none so much as the Rival. The Rival had lands bordering Dashiell's, and though his lands were identical, the Rival's fruits were never so juicy, his grain never as plentiful, and his flowers never quite as sweet. The Rival was a powerful, charismatic lord himself, and he planned to one day take Dashiell's lands by force.

"I should note," my father said, interrupting himself, "that stories of the Rival only became popular two centuries ago, during and after the Marlenian-Freetor war."

"Anything to justify Freetor persecution," I muttered.

My father nodded, then continued. "One afternoon, the Rival came to Dashiell's lands, as he often did, to see all that he believed would one day be his. Dashiell found the Rival walking through his busy streets. Believing kindness to be the most effective weapon against hatred, Dashiell invited the Rival to dine with him that evening. The Rival refused. He was too envious to eat the fruit and the grain he coveted. Instead, he spat on Dashiell's good name and rallied the townsfolk to his side. Why, the Rival demanded, should Dashiell reap all that was sowed, when the people did all the labour?

"Dashiell said, in typical Marlenian fashion, that the land belonged to him, he was a gentle lord, and all who lived on his land had plenty and never went hungry. If the Rival forsook his jealousy for the spirit of cooperation and swore fealty to Dashiell, the Rival would also reap the benefits of a fertile, well-tended land.

"The Rival found this most distasteful. Tempers became heated as the Rival planted and grew seeds of hatred within the townsfolk. A riot broke out and Dashiell, despite his strength, was overrun by his own people, and beaten terribly. Although he endured great pain, he did not weep.

"His wife heard the commotion and ran into the streets," Conal continued. "She saw her love, and wept. Tears running down her face, she braved the crowd to rescue him, without regard for her safety or her finery. The people saw her, and parted for her, because of her strength of will and gentle nature. Even those with hate in their hearts saw her tears, her love for him, and were filled with regret for what they had done."

"Even the Rival?" Monju asked, enraptured.

"Even the Rival," Conal replied, nodding sagely. "Dashiell was badly injured—near death. His wife tore a piece of her silk dress, spun from the finest of threads the colour of forest emerald, the colour of her house. Or, some would say, the colour of her eyes. First, she wiped the sweat from her brow, then her tears, and then, dabbed at his wounds. For because they were husband and wife, his blood was hers, as was his pain. The scrap of fabric held no mystic or magical properties. It was simply a gesture of their love."

The memory of the vows I exchanged with Keegan at the God Tears returned as a punch in the gut. I wondered if he felt pain in this moment, and if he did, would I know? What if our bond was not as strong as the one shared by Dashiell and his wife?

I forced the thoughts away. Months ago, my brother Rordan would have scolded me for such romantic notions, especially any involving the Marlenian man-god. The story felt like a fire-lit cave in the shadow of a cold night.

"The townspeople helped him up," Conal continued. "But it was his wife herself that carried him back to their home."

"Is that how the man-god died?" I asked. "At the hand of the people he was trying to help?"

"Some Church scholars say yes, others say he recovered and lived much longer. I can't say he would have survived, even with magic or divine intervention, if you consider the pummelling his body had taken." He cleared his throat again: he was getting off-track. "And it was at Dashiell's deathbed that he was visited by a force Pure and Good, and inspired by his acts of kindness and bravery throughout his life, the artefacts were created and Dashiell ascended to the heavens, becoming the man-god he is today. And despite magic being demonized centuries ago during the Marlenian-Freetor war, the Cloth remains the most coveted of the four artefacts."

Conal bowed his head, and then glanced up at me, as if expecting applause. Monju more than indulged him, springing off the wall and swinging his hands together, delighted.

"A tale for the ages! Love, sacrifice...the greatest love story ever told. Erm, except for the story of the Lady and her Prince, of course," he added, quickly. "His wife, carrying him. A strong woman, for a strong man. That is a version Monju has never heard! Truly, a wonderful detail."

"Isn't it? I borrowed it from Hova Erasher, one of the first female scholars on Dashiell, who went on to write many volumes on the role of Dashiell's wife. None of them truly sanctioned by the Church, though they never spoke against her either. Anyone writing on the subject of Dashiell nowadays is welcomed with open arms, given the Church's decline. I wonder if those volumes survived the—"

"Hold on," I said. "That story doesn't tell us where the

Emerald Cloth is, or what it can do. And you could have at least given Dashiell's wife a name."

"Kiera's right. Dashiell's wife must have had a name. He has one, why couldn't she?" Laoise said.

"With respect, the idea of doing so would ruin her mystique!" Monju said, beaming at my father. "The Advisor spun the tale well."

"Oh, stop feeding his ego. As if he needs it." I took a deep breath. "I assume that there's a clue within the story that tells us the location of the Emerald Cloth? Let me guess. It's in Xii. You're going to suggest we up and travel to the Southern capital. The opposite direction of where we should be going—which is Marlenia City."

My father was a patient man, as I had learned, but my directness seemed to test that quality. "That might be the core of the story, but there is an epilogue. After the creation of the artefacts, Dashiell called his four most trusted followers to his deathbed, and entrusted one artefact to each person. They were known as the Loyal Four, and would be the spark that ignited the Marlenian religion we are familiar with today. The legend insists Dashiell had the Loyal Four spread his artefacts across the flat face of the world, so that no one man could have all the power to himself. Or herself," he added with a sly smile. "The Silver Spear went to the far reaches of the west, the Orb was ensconced within the Cathedral of Dashiell in Marlenia City, and the Slab, or the Tablet as it's sometimes called, is said to be cracked and buried in the Northern mountains.

"You aren't wrong, Kiera. Traditionally, the Cloth is associated with the South. Many fakes have appeared over the years, over all four provinces, catalogued by the Church and tested to no avail. It is out there, somewhere. And yes, we should retrieve it, for it is Keegan's only chance." He seemed pleased with this decision. "In fact, now is perhaps the first time in a millennia that one group of people has obtained two of the artefacts. Soon to be three, once we retrieve the Cloth."

"And why would we do that?" I demanded. "What about it could help us wake Keegan? Do you think I'm going to re-enact Dashiell's wife's brave act? That by wiping his brow with it, I will save him?"

"Yes," my father replied. "Because as the legend goes, the Emerald Cloth was imbued with a great power. It can cure any plague, any disease, including grief."

My gaze narrowed. Grief wasn't a disease. Without it, how would I honour my brother? My mother? I still held grief for my once-gone father, even as he stood before me.

Although the fabled Silver Spear was in my possession, no non-Freetor could touch it without falling into a deep, death-like sleep. And the Orb? Smashed to pieces. My father had spent many nights burning dozens of candles, hunched over the desk in my closet-sized room, trying to reconstruct the delicate magical artefact with little success.

"No. No more artefacts." I crossed my arms defiantly.

"It could be the only thing that will save him," my father replied. "An artefact did this to him. An artefact will fix this."

"No. More. Artefacts." I slammed my hand on the table to punctuate the point. "They've only brought us trouble. It's not magic that we can control."

Laoise, startled at my outburst, stood and attempted to calm me down. "Are you sure that the Orb can't help us? Even in pieces, there's no legend or story about its healing properties?"

My father shook his head. "No. It was always the Cloth."

"We don't know the extent of the Spear's abilities, either," Bidelia added. "Perhaps it could reverse its own magic?"

"The four artefacts have great magical power that few understand. But after he killed Holy One Peadar Hightower's son with the Spear, Alastar the Hero cursed it to prevent it from falling into Marlenian hands. That is not a curse I can counteract." Conal paced around the table. "We have seen what it can do. What it is doing. If we do not find the Cloth, this curse will spread. Is that what you want?"

All I could hear was: *it's your fault, Kiera. We have to clean up your mess.* I'd dropped the Spear. Keegan picked it up to save me. It cost him dearly.

We had to do something. Yet relying on an artefact to save me—especially after what the Elders and the apprentices put me through—seemed foolish. The former leaders of my people had died for their lust for power.

I was sixteen now. A queen, even if my prince had been taken from me. A queen, especially the Violet Fox, protected her people. I couldn't go off on another quest based on a story with no clear evidence of where the Cloth might be when my husband was unintentionally spreading the curse throughout his former home. Was going on another quest, far from where I was needed, really the answer?

"Lord Ansel must be desperate if he's sending Linnaea to Marlenia City, even knowing about this...plague," I said.

"Despite my best efforts, Lord Ansel isn't convinced that the message is legitimate," my father replied. "That's why the caravan leaves not in two weeks, but tomorrow."

"Tomorrow!" I exclaimed.

"Are we prepared? Is that enough time?" Laoise asked.

"This is a good thing," I said. "You convinced him to send us sooner rather than later, didn't you?"

My father smiled. "He felt it was better to expedite matters with the Frostfire family now and get us out of his baile more quickly, despite the spring date for the wedding."

"We'll find Keegan. Get him out of enemy hands. Contain the curse. Then we'll figure out how to wake him and the others up," I said.

"Think about what I've said, Kiera. His life is not the only one on the line, not if this frozen plague continues to spread."

"That's why we need to get him out of the castle. Put him underground, under our protection, so no one accidentally touches him, or uses him for their sick, political games. As for stopping the spread, maybe we need another kind of magic to help solve our sleeping problem. The kind of magic that is standing right in front of me."

He appeared surprised. "Me?"

"You can travel great distances in minutes. Wield magic as a weapon. Surely you can wake a couple of sleeping Marlenians. Including my husband. Once we have him."

"I have power, you're right. But this is ancient, angry magic, beyond my abilities. I've already given you a solution to this problem."

"Yes. You want me to go on a quest. Again. To abandon the city that's in danger. Again." I balled my fists. "I'm not making the same mistake twice."

"I understand your reluctance," my father said solemnly. "I simply believe it's safer to find the cure, rather than rush into the heart of the disease."

The weight of all that had happened these past two months rested on my chest. I couldn't give in: I'd tried finding the Spear, and it had brought only sorrow. My father was like the stone wall surrounding Marlenia City. Impossibly tall, but not insurmountable. I just had to dig beneath the soft soil.

"I can't place faith in a story that's nearly a thousand years old that can be modified, picked apart, and retold by anyone with a quill and an audience. I've seen you wield magic. If you could...teach me...if we could gather the remaining Freetors who are adept, and if we all put our minds to it, maybe together we could find a way to reverse Alastar's curse. We are his descendants. If there is anyone that can stop the curse, it's us."

Amused, my father smiled. "You told me yesterday you wanted nothing to do with magic."

"If it's the only way to wake everyone—"

"I already told you the way. And it's not with my magic. The Elders are dead. The most powerful apprentices could barely think for themselves." He blew a sad sigh. "I want to believe that there's someone with a deeper mastery of Freetor magic than me. If that person exists, by all means, I would suggest that we ask for their help. But I don't think they do. I'm sorry, Kiera." He held out his hands, covered with the fading calluses of his younger days. "This is what we have to work with. I've presented my case. Whether we go after the Emerald Cloth, or contain Keegan's infection before more sleepers pile up in the capital, you can decide. You are the High Queen. I trust you will choose with the people's interests in mind." He nodded at Bidelia. "Ensure you're well rested. The journey out of the forest is likely to be perilous."

Without a goodbye, he left, cloak fluttering and nearly catching in the door behind him.

He always did this. His help never came when I wanted it, how I wanted it.

But always when I needed it, a small voice reminded me.

I served the people. He was right about that. Whether they were born on the surface or underground, they were all my people, and I had to act in their best interests.

"We can't keep relying on artefacts to save us," I said again.

Laoise moved towards me. "I'm not eager to trek across the world, but...if the man with the most magical knowledge in the land believes it's the only way to wake Keegan and the others..." She smiled sadly. She didn't have to finish.

"Spent the last year of peta's life searching for a cure to the incurable," Monju said quietly. "If the Lady wishes the advice of a humble bard?"

"I do," I replied earnestly.

"Time is precious. Fighting with the Lady's peta is a waste. Finding the Prince, keeping him and the other cursed safe...do this. This bard risked much for the promise of a cure that never came."

His words weighed heavily on me. He had the most to lose if the curse spread, as he was the only one of us born on the surface.

"We'll contain Keegan and any other sleepers we can find, quietly and quickly," I decided. "Maybe we'll learn something about the curse, try and figure out a way to stop it, or at least, put a stop to the idea that the Freetors are actively causing it, until another, non-artefact related solution presents itself. We'll take the Spear and the Orb and keep them hidden in the Undercity, where they can't cause trouble."

"It is a solid start," Bidelia said, rising to her feet. "I have no advice for you, Kiera. I know you. You will do what your heart tells you, even if you don't understand it." She touched her collar. It hid the awful scars Sylvia had bestowed upon her. "As long as the Frostfires and the Castillos pay for what they have done. A frozen sleep is too good for them."

"I haven't forgotten," I said to my friends. "We'll put up a good fight. Together."

Four

IN THE EARLY hours of the morning, I rose from the lumpy mattress and frayed sheets. Laoise was already awake, sitting in the desk chair, ripping pieces from a day-old roll, stuffing them in her mouth as she stared out the sliver of a window. I hadn't heard her come in. The cold air wafting in gave me gooseflesh, but neither of us minded. It was better to wake to that than to Lady Dominique's cold blade.

"Did you sleep?" I asked her.

"Not really." She passed me the half-eaten roll. "Mother is still resting. I should go get her. I'll see if Monju is ready, too."

"All right." My fingernails dug into the hard roll.

Today I would return to Marlenia City in the first time in a fortnight, to where I never should have left in the first place. I touched the fabric around my right forefinger. I will find you, Keegan. I promise.

The courtyard was solemn in the early hours. Three armoured Gareth bannermen guarded the large wagon as a pair of stable hands prepared it for the treacherous voyage through Feenagh Forest. Linnaea had rooted herself some distance away, near the treeline, staring wistfully to the east.

She likely wouldn't see her home again. Once married to Leon, the Frostfires were not likely to allow her to return, out of fear of losing their hold over Linnaea's family. The last time I'd stood in my cave in the underground was with Keegan, before the Silver Spear had plagued us. The cave hadn't really been home, though. Home had been with my brother. Then, Keegan had become my home.

I hoped I would see my home again.

I approached Linnaea cautiously. "Looks like the wagon is all set. Are you ready?"

"I suppose." Her voice was very quiet, but not unsure.

I glanced at Gareth Manor, suddenly small compared to the surrounding dark forest. "Your family isn't here to say goodbye to you."

"We said our farewells last night."

"Uh...that's good." She kept her gaze firmly in the trees, as if looking for the terrible beasts of Marlenian bedtime stories. The silence tormented me. I was anxious to get a move on. "If you're worried about animals or beatag and bandits, that's natural. If something does happen—and I don't want to lie to you and say there's not a chance—we'll handle it."

Linnaea lifted her gaze to me then. She was almost a head shorter than me. "How fast can you run, Fox?"

"Faster than some." In truth, Laoise was much faster and more agile than me. I was caught off guard by her truncated use of my street name. "You can call me Kiera, if you want."

She turned and headed slowly for the wagon, and I followed her. She nervously wrung her hands, though her face was the picture of calm. "Kiera. It feels strange to call you that. I've... heard your stories. Many times."

I smiled, face warming, which was welcome in the cold air. "Some of them are probably exaggerations."

"Like of your death." It was the first time I saw her smile. "Prince Keegan. You really do love him?"

"That story is true."

"I hope you are able to find him."

"Oh. Thanks."

She nodded and said nothing else. Wishing me to restore him to the crown would diminish her position, after all; I couldn't blame her for that. To have her support did mean that I had an ally in her—which could prove useful if we ran into trouble at the castle.

Bidelia, Laoise, and Monju appeared in the courtyard moments later. Bidelia and Laoise came around from the south side of the castle, Monju soundlessly emerging from the western woods, as if he had been a tree standing sentry this entire time.

Noticing my surprise, Monju grinned. "Brisk morning, Lady Kiera. Wind will be in the wagon's favour. It won't spread smells to any waiting beatag."

"That's reassuring," I replied.

My father was the last to arrive, and by then, nerves were thin. He rushed out the front entrance of the manor, dipping his head to the stable boy going about his chores, muttering apologies to the waiting Gareth men by the wagon, and, finally, grabbing me by the arm and practically throwing me into the wagon bed. "We'd best be off."

Linnaea sat with the driver. Normally, a royal lady would ride within the carriage, but I suspected the Gareth family wanted to show off their daughter as she drove right into the arms of the enemy—to prove they had nothing to hide. The wagon bed was cramped quarters otherwise, with me, Laoise, Bidelia, Monju, and my father hiding within. Unlike the ornate, four-person carriages used by the Tramores, the Castillos, and the Frostfires, this wagon was designed for eight people or more—the kind I'd only seen transporting servants. I supposed this model was efficient for rough forest travel. Two Gareth bannermen acted as footmen in the rear—I wondered if they were really there to protect Linnaea, or to keep an eye on us. Probably both.

"If they search the carriage, how are you going to hide yourself?" I asked my father.

He smiled. "I believe you mean *ourselves*. I've been working on that, while hiding in the shadows of Gareth Manor." From a hidden pocket inside his vest, he produced a round, flat tub the size of his palm. "A bit of Freetor magic I concocted. Took a few tries, since I had to do it from memory. Unscrew this"—he removed the lid, revealing a sparkling light blue cream—"and rub it on your face. It will temporarily change the perception of your appearance. Not drastically, but just enough to fool some-one who is familiar with your likeness."

An earthy, medicinal smell filled the inside of the wagon. Laoise and I wrinkled our noses. "How temporary is this?" I asked.

"I tested it the other day within the manor. Seven hours at most, then the effects start to wear off. There's enough here for you and I, Kiera, if we have to be in public for any length of time. Perhaps for a couple of days, if we are conservative."

"How did the Advisor find the herbs to create such medi-cine?" Monju asked.

"There are many plants scattered within Feenagh Forest that can be coaxed to show their underlying properties." He held out the container to me. "The cream doesn't change your face to appear as another. It merely distorts your features. Those who know you well may look twice, and claim you look familiar. It cannot change your hair, your eye colour, or your physical shape or size. You should put some on now."

I drew back instinctively. The smell was overpowering. "If it only lasts for seven hours, we should wait until we're closer to the city."

"Frostfire men could be on patrol. Or worse, Northern shadow killers. If they recognize either of us, our journey will end here in this wagon."

He was always right, wasn't he? I took the container from him and stuck a finger in the light blue cream. It was smooth and cool, like pudding, but had bits of green herbs that got under my fingernails. I streaked it down my left cheek. The left side of my face went numb briefly, then tingled.

"Odd," Laoise said as she searched my face, grimacing. "I see you in profile—and it's like I know you, but when you face me..."

"Is a strange sensation," Monju agreed. "Did it take the Advisor long to create?"

"Long enough," my father muttered. "I wish I'd had the time to make more. Alas, one never has enough time nor the proper tomes for anything when faced with an invading force and a daughter wanted for high treason."

I studied my father as he applied the cream liberally, willing myself to resist the magic effect. I'd only known his face as family for such a short time, and though the cream was temporary, I resented it as my mind recognized him less and less.

We spoke little as a result. Even an hour out from Gareth Manor, I could barely look at him as I tried unsuccessfully to match the face of the father I knew with the familiar man before me. Laoise dosed restlessly against her mother. Monju hummed random notes, composing a new ballad, and writing the music neatly in a notebook.

I caressed the purple fabric around my forefinger. With every turn of the wheel, we rolled ever closer to my love.

Except the wagon was slowing down.

There were no windows to see out of. My hand went to the knife at my belt as I expected the worst. Laoise stirred and sat up, momentarily confused. Monju was calm; though he exchanged his notebook for a blade.

"It might be nothing," Bidelia said. Her tone belied her concern. "We may want to relieve ourselves in the woods before we get too close to the capital."

I pressed an ear to the wagon bed. Linnaea and the driver

were exchanging words. Someone—possibly the driver—jumped from his seat to the ground. The wagon jostled as the footmen joined him.

"We should find out what's going on." I lifted from my seat, unable to stand to my full height, ready to make for the exit.

My father—or rather, the man who reminded me of my father—caught my arm. "Wait."

I wrenched my arm from his grip, but I did wait. The three men exchanged short words muffled by the carriage. Boots scraped against dirt. In the distance, a bird call. Grass rustling.

"Bandits," Laoise said, reaching for her weapon.

I stayed her as she leaned for the door. "This forest is full of creatures. Keegan and Monju and I had to fight one on our way to Driscoll's End. A beatag."

"Could the Lady defeat one again?" Monju asked.

Personally, I was willing to let Linnaea's men deal with it. They had more experience navigating these forests and slaying the beasts within. Feeling my father's eyes on me, though, I tried to show my best self. "Do you think the Gareth men need our help?"

"We best stay in the wagon. Less chance of being recognized," my father said.

Then: the whir of an arrow, followed by a telltale *shlump*.

"Ambush!" yelled a Gareth bannerman.

The next few moments were chaos.

Laoise and I, ignoring our parents' cries, jumped from the wagon. Monju, already wielding his blade, ran out after us into the fray.

No beatag. Laoise had been right—bandits. We were surrounded. In the treeline, six—no, nine men and women dressed in green and brown to blend with the forest engaged the three Gareth bannermen. Even the wounded man with an arrow in his arm drew his blade and charged the nearest woman, who scampered nimbly up a rough birch tree and resumed her target practice with her bow.

These were no ordinary bandits. Although most brigands spread across Feenagh Forest and beyond were made up of Freetors and down-on-their-luck Marlenians, they were rarely organized or wealthy enough to afford the same attire, much less fight with any kind of skill.

Laoise and I glanced at each other, thinking the same thing: we had to even the odds.

Yet as we rushed closer, the arrows stopped. Another bird call. Two bandits in the treeline, weapons drawn, ignored me as I rushed towards them. They were not afraid: they simply acted as if I did not exist, and went for the nearest Gareth bannerman instead, who was already engaging two other opponents.

"Hey!" I yelled at one as he whizzed by. I swung my blade, intentionally missing, hoping to draw his attention.

It was only when he spun towards me, grinning like a child at play, that I noticed the symbols.

Each bandit had red paint somewhere on them: their faces, their hands, their neck. The symbol was crude and hastily drawn, yet it struck a buried, healed nerve: two pointy brackets facing each other like open mouths, waiting to devour a squiggly, vertical line.

I nearly dropped my blade. Not bandits. Extremists.

An old fear wrapped around my heart, cold as a harsh wind. For two hundred years after the Marlenian-Freetor war, our people were hated and feared because of the magic our Elders and apprentices wielded. Yet there was a small group within the Freetor population that was feared by Freetors and Marlenians alike: the Extremists. Their hatred of the surface-born was so strong that they believed in taking drastic action against anyone that walked above ground—royal, soldier, or innocent child. They were dangerous, secretive, and destructive, for they often sacrificed themselves to kill others. I'd fought them before—in the Undercity and remote corners of the Marlenian capital. But what were they doing in the middle of Feenagh Forest?

Laoise and Monju engaged three of the Extremists. Bidelia wore the same determined look as her daughter as she protected her flesh and blood, striking any down who would dare to lay a hand on Laoise. Monju moved like a dancer, cutting down his opposition, around Laoise. The two of them worked together: Laoise taunted the man, jabbing and ducking and laughing with her short blade, and Monju came from behind and finished him off. None of his blows were fatal—Monju had a strict moral code that he'd broken at Driscoll's End—yet once the Extremist fell, it was clear he wouldn't be well enough to get up for some time. I'd never seen my father in hand-to-hand combat before; his magic had taken care of his previous enemies. His approach now was cautious and tentative, preferring to lead the attacker away from the rest, whipping around, and delivering a finishing blow from behind.

I moved to join my friends—my family—yet a scream from the front of the wagon spurred me in that direction. The other four, too distracted by the other Extremists, couldn't get away if they'd heard it at all.

Linnaea.

I ran towards the sound, rounding the nervous horses as a tall, thin young man wearing a green cloak pulled Linnaea off the wagon. She landed with a dull thud, but the Extremist grabbed her and dragged her to the treeline. At first, she screamed as he lifted her and drew her away from the fray. But as she looked up at him, a flicker of recognition passed over her face, and she stifled a relieved smile.

She wasn't being kidnapped. She was going willingly.

Why would the daughter of a noble house agree to be kidnapped?

She arranged this.

"What do you think you're doing?" I demanded.

Startled by my seemingly sudden appearance and my aggressive stance, he set Linnaea down and shielded her with his arm. He seemed vaguely familiar to me: I think he was friends with Rordan, a lifetime ago. "Don't come any closer. Or the noblewoman dies."

Linnaea gasped, pressing her hands to her mouth.

"You're not going to kill the hand that feeds you," I said. I kept my gaze on Linnaea. "I know that you're desperate. But hiring the Extremists, staging all this..."

She pressed into the Freetor. "I don't know what you're talking about."

"You're a bad liar, Linnaea. At least under duress." Arranging all of this and nearly pulling it off couldn't have been easy. "End this. Call them off. We can talk about it."

"No," said the Freetor. He drew up to his full height. He was the tallest Freetor I'd ever seen. "You have no right to take her!"

"Neither do you. This is a rescue."

"It's not a rescue!" With a surprising burst of anger-fueled strength, she pushed me backward, and I barely managed to retain my balance. "I'm not going to the castle. I can't."

"You can. We need you."

"You don't need me to marry Leon Frostfire. Haven't you heard the stories about that man?"

My heart sank into my stomach like a heavy stone. "I've fought him."

"Then you know I can't marry him."

"If you don't, the Frostfires will come after your family. Don't you care about that?"

Guilt twisted her features, but she shook her head. She turned to run, but I caught her by the arm. "It's more dangerous for you if you—"

"Let me go!"

"Your father's men are laying their lives down, suffering wounds at the hands of Freetor Extremists! You're just going to forgive that?"

All the while, the young man stood beside us, watching, his weapon at his side. He made no move to help Linnaea, nor did he stop me. He seemed torn.

"You don't know them!" she pleaded, glancing at the young man. "You have the blood of the underground in you, and you don't even understand the lengths they are willing—"

"I understand more than you think," I said, rising my knife. Thinking of Rordan, how he'd been willing to cause harm to innocent surface-folk just to further the Freetor cause made me sick. He would have killed Keegan, too, if my father hadn't stopped him.

The young man placed a firm hand on her shoulder. "It's all right, Linnaea."

Realization bloomed in my mind like a fearsome, bleeding wound. "This isn't just about escaping your betrothal."

Linnaea glanced up at the young Extremist man and squeezed his hand tightly. I recognized the look on her face. It was the same as when I looked at Keegan.

There were so many things I could have said. The Extremist cause is wrong. My brother died for them. Don't throw away your life.

But she was right. I, of all people, couldn't stop her from loving someone from a different world. I would be no better than those I was trying to fight. I lowered my knife.

With a wordless nod of gratitude, she turned and fled into the arms of her beloved. Gathering her close, he whistled sharply. The Extremists crawled from the fray and slithered between the dark trees. Linnaea and the young man, hand-in-hand, slinked together into the dark, unforgiving woods. I couldn't take my gaze from them. I wanted to follow. Escape was easy. Staying was hard. Explaining myself was harder.

The hurried, desperate bootsteps of my father rounded the carriage behind me. "Where's the girl?"

I couldn't face him. Did I...do the right thing?

I glanced to my left. Further off, Bidelia's iron grip supported Laoise as Monju tended to a wound on her arm. My heart clenched. She looked pale as she winced, and Bidelia seemed concerned, but Monju spoke in hushed, rolling tones as he bandaged her up.

"Kiera? Did you hear me?" My father rounded into my line of sight and gripped me by the shoulder. "Where is Linnaea?"

I swallowed hard. "She escaped."

My father searched my face as his fingers loosened their grip. "You let her go!"

Apparently I was a terrible liar as well—even under this false mask. I set my mouth in a hard line. "She's in love with—"

"I thought you were smarter than this, Kiera!" He jutted an angry finger towards the foreboding woods. "We have just lost our ticket into the castle. To where your husband is kept."

My knees buckled as I realized what I had sacrificed, all because I had listened to my heart instead of my head.

I'd been so caught up in getting out of Baile Gareth that I'd failed to see what Linnaea was plotting. I'd underestimated her, just as many men had underestimated me.

But she was with the Extremists now: a hard life, hated by all sides, but at least she was with someone she loved. She had the chance to be happy. How could I deny her what was denied me?

"I did what was right," I said finally.

"It's not about right and wrong. It's about saving our people. Which you have made difficult on this day."

His words burned me. I swallowed my pride—an impossible task. "What should we do now?"

My father let out a long, slow sigh. "Everyone in the wagon. Monju"—he walked towards them as Bidelia and Monju guided Laoise into the carriage bed—"ensure the horses haven't been completely spooked. The longer we stay in the forest, the more of a target we become."

"Yes, Advisor. But with Lady Linnaea and her men gone, where should Monju tell the horses to head?"

"We're still going to the castle," I said, just as my father said, "Marlenia City."

At least we were on the same page.

Bidelia helped Laoise into the carriage, both of them sharing equally worried looks. Monju rounded the carriage to carry out my father's instructions.

I relented, climbing into the carriage. I searched the forest floor. The ground showed the signs of battle, or to the untrained eye, a flurry of footprints and disturbed dirt.

"Where are the Gareth men?" I asked, sitting in the carriage bed.

"The Extremists took them," Laoise replied. She sat across from me, upright, but gripping her left arm. "I tried to stop them, but got hit pretty bad. Two were unconscious. One may or may not be dead."

"You shouldn't have tried," Bidelia muttered as she fussed with the torn black cloth that Monju had wrapped around Laoise's arm.

My father climbed into the carriage bed and shut the door, shaking the entire wagon. Laoise gasped as Monju jostled the reins and we sped down the forest road once more towards the castle.

Taking a seat next to me, my father minced no words. "We were lucky. With the Gareth men taken care of, Lord Ansel won't know what transpired here, at least for some time."

"Unless they escape from the Extremists," I said.

"Yes, that is a possibility," he said, his tone laced with anger.

"Why would they attack us?" Laoise asked, gripping her mother's hand. "For supplies, maybe, but surely they would have recognized you, Kiera—"

I took a deep breath, preparing to admit the truth.

"Linnaea played us," my father said. "It was a set-up. Ran off with her Extremist beau."

Both mother and daughter wore equal expressions of surprise and terror. "Foolish girl," Bidelia muttered, shaking her head.

The carriage fell silent. My father gripped his knees tightly in thought. "If a woman with Linnaea's name doesn't stand before Leon Frostfire in a few hours, our fragile alliance with Baile Gareth ceases to exist. Moreover, so do the people of Baile Gareth."

Laoise frowned. "I thought he wouldn't dare attack Baile Gareth, not with the beatag roaming the forest—"

"I'm sure he would find a way to make an example of a family who dared defy the Frostfire authority. They are doing it now in the capital, with Freetor and Tramore sympathizers and Freetors themselves. Kiera wasn't there for the slaughter, but you both were." He glanced between Laoise to Bidelia, face haunted. "We must honour the meeting."

The true meaning behind my father's words dawned on me.

Oh no. Not again.

I was about to voice my concerns, when my father nodded at Laoise. My best friend squared her shoulders, hiding the pain of her wound well, and rose to my father's silent challenge.

"I'll do it," she said.

My eyes widened. "You, as Linnaea?"

"Well, it can't be you," she replied, tucking a stray hair behind her ear. "There's not enough cream, and even with it, it's possible they may still figure out who you are. We don't know how long we'll have to carry out this charade."

She had a point. I'd already pulled that trick with them once. Although Laoise had lived in the castle and worked as a servant with her mother, it was unlikely they'd recognize her face, especially if she was done up in Linnaea's clothes.

"It would only be for a few days," my father said, partly to Bidelia, who was giving him a sour look. "Enough time to search the castle, gauge the situation in the Undercity, and at least determine Linnaea's safety and whereabouts. Then, we can extract Laoise from the castle, and if Linnaea is recovered from the forest, we could spin the story that she was captured by Freetors or Roamers and replaced by Extremists. They may be sympathetic to that. Otherwise, the rest of the plan still stands. Bidelia, Monju, and I will scope out the underground and find Linnaea, while Kiera can accompany Laoise to the castle."

"So you'll shift the blame for Linnaea's disappearance from her to the Extremists? As if our people haven't suffered enough, as you have already pointed out," I said.

A dark look crossed my father's eyes. He looked away. "In any case, it won't matter. We get in, we search for Keegan, we get out. Let Lord Ansel and the rest of the surface-born Marlenians worry about the details of Linnaea's disappearance. While they are busy tending to her, we'll have bigger things to worry about."

Bigger things. I had more than one mess. I was responsible for cleaning them all up.

"Why can't Monju come with us?" Laoise asked.

"Monju's face is too well known by the Frostfires, and by Lady Dominique, if she's in the capital. He sticks out in the West, and no magic cream can fix that," I said, nearly tripping over my words. "Likely he's not too eager to go to the Undercity, either." After what Monju did to the three reigning apprentices, I'd be surprised if the Fighters didn't slaughter him on the spot. If they had discovered what he'd done. If they could beat Monju at his own game.

My father considered this. "Kiera, you could come with us to the Undercity instead. Your presence may help us sway the remaining apprentices to our favour."

"No. I'm not leaving Laoise alone," I said.

"Agreed," Bidelia said firmly. "My face is too well known in the castle, now that the Frostfires know I'm a Freetor. Laoise must not be alone with them. Not even if it's just for a few days." She squeezed her daughter's hands.

"Right," he said. "Then the task falls to you, Kiera, to not only protect Laoise's identity, but to search the castle for Keegan, and any other information that might give us an advantage over the Frostfires and the Castillos. Military movements, key plans, their plans for the Freetors, as well as anything they know about the sleeping curse and who has fallen prey. We go in quickly and quietly, and we leave the same way, with or without Keegan. Do you understand?"

I squared my gaze on my father. I got us all into this. With their help, I could get us out.

Five

WE STOPPED THE carriage an hour outside the city to let Bidelia and Monju out. My father applied extra face cream and took up Monju's spot as the driver. He would see us into the castle bailey, then take off into the city to dredge up support from old contacts. Bidelia and Monju had the harder task of contacting what Freetors remained and presenting them with the Silver Spear: proof that the Violet Fox had retrieved the fearsome, legendary artefact, and that she still served the realm in secret.

"It'll be all right," Laoise kept saying to her mother as she finished fitting into one of Linnaea's gowns we'd retrieved from the tied-down luggage above the carriage bed. "This is just like any other mission you've done. Hopefully much shorter. Kiera and I will stick together as much as we can."

"You'll stay far away from her," Bidelia said, pointing a finger at me. "The less time you spend with Laoise, the less suspicious you'll be. Freetor magic or not, they will suspect some kind of sabotage. The same trick never works twice, even on Marlenians."

"I'll make sure her cover is safe," I said.

Bidelia's tough exterior cracked momentarily and she threw her arms around me. "I know you'll do what you must."

Monju watched us from a distance, his gaze never wavering from Laoise. As Laoise said her goodbyes to her mother, I noticed him muttering to himself, as if trying to get up the courage to say something to Laoise before he disappeared into the forest.

"Good luck, Monju," I said, somewhat restrained, trying to seem more confident than I felt.

"Lady Dominique and her men, they are smart. But Lady Kiera and Lady Laoise, they are smarter," Monju replied. He pressed a hand against a nearby tree trunk, as if swearing a solemn oath. "Will try to rally support for the Freetor Queen on Mountain High."

With the bundled Silver Spear in hand, Bidelia gave us both one last, hopeful smile, then she and Monju took off into Feenagh Forest. From there, they'd make their way into one of the many tunnels that led to the Undercity.

My father held the reins and waited in the driver's seat for us to give the all clear. I helped Laoise into the carriage and then trudged to the front. His gaze remained fixed on the horizon, where even from half a day's journey away, the towering walls of Marlenia City loomed.

"We should leave," he said simply.

"I know," I said. My feet dug into the ground like roots. "I don't want you to be mad at me. You know why I did what I did."

He leaned back in his seat. "Yes. But I also know what it's like to be sixteen-years-old. You don't think. You just act."

I crossed my arms defensively. "I do think. I just do it quickly. So people don't die."

"You might find yourself in a situation where you have to consider more than the short-term consequences, as well as the effects your actions will have on you." He glanced at me. "This is a longer conversation for a different time, Kiera. Get in the carriage."

His words stung. Didn't he know we might not get the chance to speak again? What if our mission failed—what if they realized Laoise was a Freetor? What if the cream didn't work? Before, I'd had a support team of Freetors. I'd had Rordan.

Now it was going to be just me and Laoise, alone in the castle, searching for a frozen body that may not even be there.

I whirled around, stewing in a mix of emotions that I didn't know how to deal with. It was so much easier when I didn't have a father who'd abandoned us for a better life.

Once inside the carriage bed, my father commanded the horses to move, and I slumped in the cramped bench seat.

"That bad, is it?" Laoise asked.

I sighed. "I wish he'd talk to me like..."

"...you were his daughter?" she finished, quirking an eyebrow.

Laoise always had a way of putting words to my untouchable feelings.

She took my hand, squeezing it as we wheeled over the bumpy road. "Once this is all over, you'll have time. We just have to survive until then."

* * *

As we rolled closer to the capital, the nerves in my stomach multiplied like ants on a morsel of food. I applied more of the face cream in silence, glancing periodically at my best friend. The first time I'd arrived in disguise at the doors of the Tramore castle, I'd worn Lady Dominique's face, her clothes, her title. Laoise seemed calm: calmer than I felt. Beneath Linnaea's gown, however, I knew the scared Freetor remained, ready to run.

I considered bringing up Monju to brighten her spirits—but then I'd be too tempted to tell her about his kiss. I couldn't have him swimming in her head, not when the lives of an entire baile rested on her performance as Linnaea Gareth. I burrowed the face cream into my apron pocket atop my servant dress and secured a bandana firmly around my head, tucking stray hairs beneath the faded fabric. Young servants in the service of important noblewomen often wore them to denote their status as handmaids. I played with the fabric of my makeshift ring around my forefinger. I should take it off. But who was to say that a young servant couldn't have gotten married? I covered my hand, hoping Keegan was blissfully asleep and not just frozen and terrified.

The carriage rolled to a stop. Right—inspection at the walls of the city. "Ready?"

She cast a frightened gaze at me just as the carriage door was forced open by a Frostfire bannerman. She grasped my hand, stifling her surprise.

"Lady Linnaea Gareth?" the man asked gruffly.

Laoise cleared her throat and adopted Linnaea's high, tinny voice. "Yes. I am she."

The man gave her the once over. "You brought only a driver and a handmaid? This is a large transport."

She didn't miss a beat. "Our carriage was attacked by Freetors. All my father's bannermen were killed in the fight, except my driver."

The Frostfire guard's brow furrowed. He bowed his head. "I am saddened by your loss, my lady. We will ensure your father receives word of the incident."

"Yes, please do so." She pressed her lips firmly together. Telling the truth was risky, but it was the only way to explain Laoise's wound and our lack of bannermen. There was no going back.

"Your papers, my lady?" the guard continued.

"They're here." Laoise presented the pieces of parchment. They'd been buried at the bottom of Linnaea's luggage. New procedures, implemented after my time pretending to be Dominique. Every noble entering Marlenia City now had to prove their identity. Usually this meant a statement written by their liege lord, or in Linnaea's case, her father. A green seal blotted the bottom of the parchment. She'd barely travelled out of the baile, protected from outside influence by her father, and that made her a target for replacement by the Freetors. Hopefully Lord Ansel's seal and letter confirming Linnaea's engagement was enough.

A full two minutes passed as the guard studied the papers and glanced intermittently at Laoise. "Hmm."

Laoise glanced at me nervously. "Is there something wrong?"

He started to walk around the carriage. "I'll have to inspect your luggage, my lady. Driver?"

Linnaea had two brown trunks. I had only the clothes on my back, as did my father. I wondered if he'd used magic to conceal any other baggage. The Gareth bannermen, they'd had two black bags, also secured to the top of the carriage.

It took a full ten minutes for my father to untie the knots and unload the trunks. The carriage shook every time he struggled. After thoroughly shaking our insides, he threw one of Linnaea's trunks to the ground, where it fell open. Linnaea's clothes scattered all over the road before the guards.

"No!" Laoise cried. She started for the door, but I gripped her arm tightly to prevent her from leaping from the carriage. This was a servant's job.

I rushed out, hurrying to gather the two errant gowns and white shifts and stuff them back into the trunk. Even the guard seemed frustrated with how long the inspection was taking.

"All right, all right," he said. He rifled through Linnaea's things daintily, embarrassed. I stood over him quietly, hoping there weren't any Extremist literature or symbols in her luggage that would give us away. I covered my ringed hand. I didn't need them asking who my husband was...

You're just a servant. No one cares about you, a deeper voice said sadly.

The lead guard's thick hands pressed the dresses and the other fabrics back into the trunk. Once properly secured, he passed Linnaea's things back to my father to re-secure on top of the carriage. I kept my head down, hands folded in front of me.

It took another ten minutes and the help of a Frostfire bannerman to re-secure the bags. None of the three guards even acknowledged me as they engaged in small talk with Linnaea about her day, her journey, and her expectations of the city. Laoise performed the part of Linnaea with grace and serenity, being equal parts apprehensive and enthusiastic about her new future as the wife of a now-major lord. As she chatted, I noticed two guards at the wall speaking with a castle page. At this rate, by the time we rode up the mountain, a delegation of lords would be expecting us.

I felt sick to my stomach. No doubt these new measures were Lady Dominique's idea. I'd slipped into the castle with only her name, her looks, and her carriage.

My father wordlessly returned to the driver's seat and the guard climbed down to resume his post on the wall. Laoise gracefully brought the conversation with the lead guard to a close, leaned over and spotted me, still standing outside.

"Come along now"—she hesitated, realizing I didn't yet have a name—"Rorda. We mustn't keep my future husband waiting any longer."

The guards chuckled politely as I climbed back into the carriage bed. Waving goodbye, the guards shut the carriage doors. The grinding of gears and the creaking of old wood hid our sounds of relief as the gates to the city opened, and with a jolt, my father urged the carriage forward.

Laoise grabbed my hand. "That...that wasn't so bad, right?"

I smiled. "Did you really have to name me Rorda?"

"Sorry. I just, there was a moment when..." She didn't have to explain. "I hope Mother and Monju made it to the Undercity."

"They'll be all right," I said. I was more worried about us. They had the Silver Spear, a weapon of legend. We had two wanted criminals wearing false faces and only our wits as we strode into the most dangerous castle in the realm.

My nausea only grew as we winded up the mountain road, closer to the castle. My astute Freetor nose picked up the remnant smell of smoke and ash. A reminder of all that I had lost. Then, as we drew closer: people shuffling in the dirt, men barking orders, and pickaxes denting stone. The castle had burned long and furious—it would be a great effort to restore it to its former glory.

"This is it," I said as the carriage levelled out. There were no windows in the carriage, but we were coming to a stop. "Time to stop being Laoise Mullen and fully become Linnaea Gareth."

"Yeah," Laoise replied, taking a deep breath. "I can do this."

I nodded, smiling at my best friend. "I know you can. Just remember—"

A Frostfire bannerman, an older, gruffer man this time, pulled open the carriage doors roughly. He looked at me, then at Laoise, and then back to me again. He didn't offer a hand to help either of us out. "You are expected. My lord is waiting for you."

My stomach felt like a stone. Thankfully, my fear held me in place as Linnaea navigated gracefully from the carriage. I kept my head down as I scrambled after her. It was customary for a member of the royal family to greet an arriving noble, though I hoped it would be a Frostfire lord I didn't know. Perhaps Boris Frostfire, the eldest son of Leszek. He had never seen my face. Maybe it would be like when I'd arrived as Lady Dominique, and no one would be there to greet me.

My hopes were dashed as my flats touched the dusty ground, and a gust of wind blew up around us. I coughed and shielded my face. The bailey was crawling with men—and some women—all wearing blue and red sashes around their forearms over dirty white tunics and dark trousers. Frostfire workers, all of them. Some carried pickaxes, others written orders and ran as if chased. Where there were once merchants, quarry masters gathered in fluttering tents, evaluating construction plans and instructing labourers under the watchful gaze of several men. So the great mountain castle of Marlenia City would be rebuilt—to the Frostfire image.

I grabbed Laoise and pulled her out of the way just as six workers hand-carrying a large stone lumbered by, swearing and sweating beneath the rock.

They were not wearing red and blue sashes: each one was scarred with an "*F*" somewhere on their face. The mark of a Freetor slave.

Keegan and I had outlawed the slave trade, but Leszek Frostfire was quick to repeal that. It was a lucrative business for both the North and the East. So while their coin purses and bodies grew fatter, my people were once again sold and shipped like products across the land. If the rumours were to be believed, one didn't even have to be born underground to be sold anymore. As long as a rich merchant believed you were a thief or a liar, you could find yourself stripped of your rights and halfway across the province.

"Watch where you're going!" the guard barked at them. On his hip was a curled-up hip. He reached for it.

I drew in a panicked breath. "No!"

The Freetor slaves, suffering beneath the weight of the stone as they hurried past, threw me worried glances. The guard looked sharply to me. "What did you just say?"

"It's quite all right," Laoise said, throwing me a warning look. She held out a placating hand to the guard. "I've had enough of this awful, dusty courtyard. Please escort me inside."

"Yes...of course, my lady," he said. He narrowed his gaze at me once more as I bowed my head. "Follow me."

I watched the slaves disappear with the rock around the corner of the large edifice as we followed the guard towards the tall doors, newly constructed. Though it had been nearly a month since the castle had burned, from where we were it was hard to spot the damage. Likely enslaving the Freetors had sped up the building progress tremendously.

I glanced over my shoulder at my father, but he was already driving away, around the bailey towards the back of the castle, to the stables. He didn't even acknowledge me, or say goodbye. As Freetors, it was what we were taught. While on the surface, every person for themselves. While infiltrating the enemy, do not give yourself away. The mission was the most important thing.

I just wanted him to break the rules for me.

More slaves carrying stones moved like spiders around us to the western side of the castle. So that was the weakest side—for now. I tried to find familiar faces and failed. They moved sparingly as the sun beat down as hard as a whip. I tried to memorize their faces, so I could free them. Somehow.

But I wasn't there to rescue them today. I drove my bitten-down nails into my palms. The Violet Fox's work was never done. Not while people sought to divide the realm.

A guard stood on each side of the doors, though they made no moves to open it for us. They watched the slaves, as if the Freetors' tired bones were about to revolt at any minute. Banging on the door with a large, flat palm, the guard who led us kept an ear and an eye on the proceedings, including me.

The door opened a crack and a timid page peeked out. Upon seeing the large guard, the page pushed the door open further. The guard had a few choice words for the lad as he gestured for Laoise and I to enter.

The hall was as dimly lit as the underground. Burning sparsely, the covered lanterns hung several stone-throws above our heads. I imagined the annoyance of the servants who had to keep them lit: likely they were another preventative measure. The Frostfires probably didn't want another inferno on their hands.

When I had first arrived, the tapestries in the halls had told the brutal, one-sided history of the Marlenian-Freetor war: how the Freetors had been driven underground because of their seemingly vile, uncontrollable magic. I had most of the violent ones removed and placed in storage. Keegan and I had discussed new tapestries to hang in the entryway—or at least, updated ones with a more balanced perspective—but during the month I'd lived in the castle, we'd never gotten around to commissioning them.

Now, only two tapestries hung, one on either side of us in the tall, imposing corridor. The first, tattered and burned, was one I recognized. A man stood atop a pile of disfigured Freetor bodies, planting a flag in them, claiming ownership over their deaths. The second, however, was new: two faceless blond royals, so depicted by their shining silver crowns, stood atop the mountain beside a disproportionately small castle. Below, a crowd of cheering, armed Marlenians celebrated and bowed before a large crest of the Frostfire family: a white hunting bird with a crooked beak hovering over twin flames.

How I wished the nearby lanterns would suddenly and deliberately explode.

Six guards—three on each side—lined the wall, armoured and armed. Further down, a party waited for us. I squinted: it was difficult to tell who they were in such poor lighting, but my heart sank as Laoise, the guard, and I came to a standstill three stone-throws from the delegation.

The gruff Frostfire guard cleared his throat. "May I present Lady Linnaea Gareth, of Baile Gareth."

I kept my head down, willing everyone in the room to look at anything, anyone except me.

The last time I'd seen Leon Frostfire was in Iar Bunsula, the last bastion of civilization before the Throat of the World. He'd been spreading lies and half-truths about me to the populace and urging citizens to come forward with information about Freetors in hiding. Monju, Keegan, and I fought him in a tavern and we'd been forced to flee on horseback.

My hand curled around the fabric of my skirt. I itched to finish that fight.

Leon, however, did not seem in the best of shape for a fight. He paced aimlessly before his three attendants. They wore knives, and had the similar fair colouring as Leon. Unlikely to be Northern shadows, though they covered themselves head to toe in black. Armed pages, then, tasked with supervising Leon. The attendants wrinkled their noses: even they could smell the bluesberry wine on him. Had the man drank an entire vineyard? His footing seemed uneven, he was muttering, and as the attendants weren't engaging him, the conversation appeared to be one-sided. Dressed in a blue silk blouse, I noted the faint stains on his trousers, and while his dark blonde hair had been styled around the silver circlet haloing his head, the hair itself was flat and stringy. This was a lord pretending to be a prince, pretending that he cared about the formalities of rulership.

The urge to fight bubbled within me. The odds were not in our favour, especially with Laoise in noblewoman attire. I imagined grabbing Leon and shaking him, forcing him to tell me where they kept Keegan as the guards advanced on me.

A fight would have to wait.

With a loud bang of the door, our escort left, probably to deal with the tired slaves.

"You're here. Finally," Leon said. He struggled to keep his words coherent as he bowed deeply. He remained in that position for a few seconds too long before swooping back up again, one hand on his circlet to keep it from falling off. I tightened my jaw to keep from laughing.

"Apologies for the mess in the bailey. Repairs are still underway. Thankfully, the church was not as damaged as the castle, and the wedding will proceed as planned."

"That is fortunate," Laoise replied.

"But where are my manners?" He grinned, revealing his blue-stained teeth. Although Laoise had not offered her hand, he took it anyway, and smacked his lips against it. Laoise was a statue, unblinking, unflinching before this smelly mess of a man. "I am Leon Frostfire, son of Emperor Leszek Frostfire, the ruler of this great realm."

"Very pleased to meet you, my lord. I am Linnaea Gareth, daughter of Lord Ansel of Baile Gareth," Laoise said in a clipped tone. She withdrew her hand, carefully wiping the spot where his lips had been. I hoped Leon would be too drunk to notice her flippant behaviour.

Leon drew upright. Laoise's appearance pleased him, for he could not take his eyes off of her, but his eyebrows lifted in question. "Where are the rest of your attendants?"

My heart pounded wildly but Laoise did not miss a beat. "My family sends their regrets. We've had to let go much of our serving staff as many of them were Freetor sympathizers or rats themselves."

"I see." If anything, Leon looked more interested in Laoise's bosom than her explanation. "Perhaps we can continue this conversation in a more private—"

The hard sound of heeled boots on stone and rustling skirts dominated the large corridor. Leon rolled his eyes in exasperation and grabbed Laoise's hand. "I'll show you to your room before—"

"Is that the Gareth girl?"

I stiffened and turned my face away, adjusting the kerchief

around my head, even though it would do little to hide my face. Lady Sylvia Frostfire and Lady Dominique Castillo rounded the corner with an attending guard—a shadow killer, by the look of him—and closed in on us. Sylvia appeared far more fresh-faced than her brother and uncharacteristically subdued in a dark blue gown with a respectable neckline adorned with garish jewels. My jaw clenched as I spied the large silver crown tucked in the mess of blonde curls. I wondered if that was my silver crown that she'd plucked from my room, or worse, if she'd taken it from Keegan's chambers as some kind of prize. As if having the prince himself wasn't enough.

"Your Graces," Laoise said, curtsying low. At least Laoise didn't have to put on an accent. Laoise and I had good ears, but I'd had far more practice with the Northern drawl.

Lady Dominique's venomous glare was enough for Leon to drop his grip on Laoise. Unlike Sylvia, she preferred earthy colours and practical garb: a weathered brown dress, a black belt wound tightly around her waist with pouches attached— likely hiding a number of poisons and other Northern secrets—and the same necklace she'd worn at Driscoll's End: the one that had housed the antidote that Monju had used to save my life.

I cleared my throat and dropped my voice an octave. "Please allow me to introduce, Lady Linnaea Gareth of Baile Gareth, here at the behest of the illustrious Emperor Leszek Frostfire, first of his name, of the Western Province and all of Marlenia." I used every bit of willpower not to sound insolent.

As I suspected, neither the Frostfires, Lady Dominique, nor her guard paid me any mind. Their attention was on Laoise, and whether or not she was another Kiera Driscoll, a flighty fox in their glittery den.

"I am honoured to be here," Laoise said to the ladies, with equal parts cordiality and apprehensiveness.

"You may rise," Sylvia said, smiling widely, and gesturing like a puppeteer.

Laoise obeyed, keeping her gaze steady and on no one in particular.

"You must be tired from your long journey," Sylvia continued. "We have arranged quarters for you. They're near to mine. I can't wait to introduce you to Mildie. Lady Milda, I mean. We can—"

Dominique held up a ringed finger, cutting off Sylvia's attempt to play host in a usurped home. "I y'am not yet ready to welcome dis estranger."

I kept my gaze downward. Of course Dominque wouldn't let us in so easily. Not after what I did to her. The Northern shadow shifted his weight; the hilt of his dagger protruded from a belt at his waist. No doubt he would stab Laoise's heart if Dominique gave the order.

"We can return another time, if that would please Your Grace," Laoise said, inclining her head at Lady Dominique.

"I y'am not *J'our Grace* yet," Dominique said bitterly. "My weddin' to Boris Frostfire will be y'in spring as well. J'ou may address me y'as de Lady Dominique, or my lady." Her gaze narrowed. "How else has j'our family failed to prepare j'ou pour life in de court?"

"Dominique!" Sylvia cried. "I apologize for—"

"Lady Linnaea may address me however she sees fit," Leon muttered, smiling savagely.

My heart pounded. I hadn't realized Dominique had been betrothed to Boris, yet with the North-East alliance as it was, it made sense. It also changed everything. Boris stood to inherit the realm if Leszek died. That meant Dominique would be High Queen—not Sylvia. We'd heard rumours she'd been betrothed to Marin, Dominique's much younger brother. No doubt that irked her to no end.

Laoise kept her composure. "My utmost apologies, my ladies. I have not spent much time outside Baile Gareth, and was fostered briefly in Ba'haram in the South, away from the court life of the West and the East. My father taught me to address my betters, but clearly I have much to learn. I look forward to brushing up on my etiquette as required." She smiled at Sylvia.

"I look forward to assisting you," Sylvia replied. "Now, come with me. Lady Milda has just arrived. We have to greet her, too! Then I will show you—"

Dominique waved away Sylvia's offer. "Of course, de Frostfires are so welcomin', dey forget de new protocol pour visitin' royals."

Leon spun around wildly. "Ah, my lady, that will not be—"

"Y'it will be necessary," she interrupted. "We can't take any chances. Freetor rats can disguise demselves in de cleverest of ways. We must outsmart dem at every turn if we y'are to drive dem out of our country and castle." Lady Dominique turned her sharp gaze to Laoise, as if it could bore through skin and bone to determine if she was begotten beneath dirt. "Tell me j'our family lineage. Go back four generations."

I stiffened, but I didn't dare look up. I had no idea how much Laoise knew of Linnaea's history. If only I'd paid more attention to—

"My father is Lord Ansel Gareth," Laoise began in a calm, cool voice. "His father was Wallace, the Silent Lord. Then his father was also named Wallace, and his father Angus. Then his father was Bazza Tel Gareth, the Treaty Lord, who signed Killan Tramore's—"

"Dat's enough. I don't want to hear dat name," Lady Dominique interrupted. She paced like her now-deceased tiger before Laoise. "J'our wagon was attacked on de way here. What happened?"

Eyes and ears everywhere. Word had travelled quickly from

83

the gate. "It was, my lady. Freetor rats descended upon us."

"And yet, j'ou escaped wit' j'our life?"

"Barely." Laoise raised her left sleeve, revealing her crude-ly bandaged arm. She winced—it was real enough to fool me. Perhaps my best friend was in more pain than she'd led me to believe.

"Oh dear!" Sylvia exclaimed, fanning herself. "I myself am a survivor of an onslaught, Lady Linnaea. You have my sympathies."

Dominique raised an eyebrow, swiftly approached my best friend, and pressed her forefinger into the bloodied bandage. Laoise recoiled, crying out. Leon and Sylvia were as taken aback as we were: both reached forward to save my friend from faint-ing, but it was unnecessary. Laoise was more sure-footed than me, and recovered quickly.

I did not move. If I, as a servant, interfered with the actions of a noblewoman, it would draw their ire.

Laoise regarded Dominique with a heated gaze I had never seen. "Why would you do that?"

"To y'ensure j'ou were trut'ful," Dominique replied simply.

"Please forgive her, she is terribly vile as of late, no doubt because of her imprison—" Sylvia trailed off beneath Dominique's angry gaze.

Laoise was quick to soothe. "All is forgiven, my lady. I under-stand these are difficult times and we must all do our part."

"Wise words," Dominique said coolly. "But words, dey're not'in'. Tell me, Lady Linnaea. Why come to de castle, marry dis man? Surely j'ou had better options."

"I..." Laoise swallowed audibly as she flicked her gaze down-ward, as the real Linnaea would, while Leon looked suitably offended. My stomach clenched. Did Dominique know the real Linnaea's secret? "My father made this arrangement. I agreed to please him."

Dominique looked unconvinced. "I see."

I held my breath.

"And..." Laoise searched for further ways to appease the mercurial lady. "We heard of the Freetor threat here in the city. Though we are isolated in Feenagh Forest, we have had our share of Freetor troubles. We wish to do our part to end this plague upon our families."

The word *plague* hit the three nobles differently. Sylvia, never one to hide her reactions, widened her gaze and glanced to her right, down the corridor that lead to the noble quarters. Leon snorted and shook his head. Dominique's eyes narrowed—in suspicion or in solidarity, I couldn't tell.

"If dis is true, den—"

Ruffling her skirts, Sylvia rolled her eyes, interrupting Dominique once again. "This charade has gone on far too long. I am tired of standing here, watching my new sister be inter-rogated by a...a..." She struggled to find a suitable insult, and eventually gave up. "Come, Lady Linnaea. Let me show you to your quarters. Then once you're settled, we'll greet Lady Milda. Unless you intend to interrogate my oldest friend, too, Dominique?"

"I do, j'es," she replied.

Sylvia made a disgruntled noise. "Even the nastiest of Freetor magic would not fool me into thinking that the Violet Fox was Lady Milda. Come, Lady Linnaea. Let Lady Dominique play her games. We have more lady-like duties to attend to."

Laoise gave her a polite smile, but glanced back at me. There was noticeable alarm in her eyes. She didn't want to leave me. "And my handmaid? Will she be sleeping in the servant quarters?"

Lady Sylvia barely gave me a passing glance as she extended a hand to Laoise. "Oh, probably. Come, leave those details to the servants. I can't wait to learn everything about you."

"Lady Linnaea, wait," Leon said. He had been quiet, nearly bored, during the exchange between the two noblewomen, but now he grasped for Laoise like a man dying of thirst. "If I may be so bold..."

No, you can't, you filthy Freetor-hating bastard, I wanted to say.

"Perhaps you might care to join me this evening for a private dinner in my quarters. With my sister, of course, and my father," he added quickly.

"Lady Sylvia and I y'already have plans," Lady Dominique said coldly. "Which will include de Lady Linnaea, y'of course."

"Yes. Well. As heir to the throne—"

"Second. J'ou y'are second in line, as j'ou y'are constantly reminded," Dominique said flatly. "J'our time in de cellar has dulled j'our mind."

"I don't need a—" Leon balled his hands into fists, momentarily forgetting himself. The attendants shifted in their places awkwardly. Leon glanced from them, to the guards lining the walls, and even to me, before twisting his hands behind his back. "You are right, of course, my lady. I will re-evaluate where I spend my time, indeed."

"See dat j'ou do." Dominique hurried away with Sylvia and Laoise down the long corridor, deeper into enemy territory. Laoise did not look back.

So all was not well within the Frostfire-Castillo alliance. I could barely suppress a grin. This would make it easier. Plant some seeds of doubt here and there and the alliance would crumble. Then I'd grab Keegan, and....

Then what? My father's words echoed in my mind. Would I try to restore him to the throne? That would be what Keegan would want. He was born to rule. And I was born to fight.

Leon lingered by the wall, as if he wished to become part of the tapestries. He stared at me curiously, as if trying to suss out my identity. His gaze heated my face, like the fire that had destroyed my brother and the castle.

Fortunately, one of the three attendants sprang into action. "We will show you to the servants' quarters. What is your name?"

I glanced sidelong at Leon. I wondered if we'd soon be rid of him. "I'm Rorda. Are the servants' quarters far from my lady? I...I hate to leave her alone."

"She will be well looked after, I assure you. You will be given castle duties in addition to your work for Lady Linnaea. Do you understand?"

"Yes. Thank you."

"Good, follow us."

The three attendants turned left, heading towards the eastern part of the castle, which housed the servant quarters and the kitchen. As the servants rattled off my new list of duties, a cold, sickening feeling settled in my stomach. I wondered if the Frostfires had replaced all of the castle workers. It was probably the only way to ensure complete loyalty. We passed by Leon, and his stare followed us, though he remained.

Once again, I was in the castle under a false name, for a mission to save my people, with only my best friend to guide me.

I'd wanted it to be just like old times. Seemed like I'd gotten my wish.

If only it hadn't come at such a high cost.

THE SERVANT QUARTERS were beside the kitchen, consisting of three large rooms: the largest was for the young women, the bunks piled three beds high from floor to ceiling. The second was for the senior servants—I suspected that was where Bidelia had slept when she was Mother Margaret, head of all castle servants. The third was for the male staff who worked and lived onsite: mainly the line cooks, errand boys, and pages.

There were only a few girls in the largest room, sleeping. Likely they had night duties. None of them were branded as slaves, as far as I could tell. The slaves likely slept in the most uninhabitable place in the castle: underground, in the dungeon.

The three attendants deposited me in front of a mountain of a woman. I shivered as she passed her unflinching gaze over me. She was just as inhospitable as the cold rocks we'd encountered in the Throat and at Driscoll's End. Unsurprisingly, the three attendants quickly abandoned me to my fate.

"I am Mistress Alwina El," she said in a harsh, clipped tone, as though she had better things to do. She spoke so fast that her names ran together: *Alwinael*. El was a surname given to orphans in the care of the church, a practice that had fallen out of favour when the Church's numbers dwindled and the clergy could no longer rear unwanted children. I hadn't realized the East had shared this tradition.

I bowed my head slightly.

"Can you speak, girl?"

"I can," I replied.

"A silent servant is useful to the nobles, but not so much to me. Your name?"

"I'm Rorda," I hadn't thought of a surname for myself yet and I had to suppress the urge to use "Fox."

She regarded me suspiciously. She had the tongue of an Easterner, but her dark hair and eyes betrayed her Northern blood. I could see why the Frostfires and the Castillos put her in charge. Even the girls lying in their bunks trembled. I could see now they were pretending to be asleep so as not to attract her ire. "I'm assigning you to the bottom bunk close to the door. Know that this is a privilege and not a permanent arrangement. You will have many duties as handmaid to the bride of our lord leading up to the wedding. After your lady's wedding, your duties will be reassessed, as will your sleeping arrangement." She gave me the once over. "You aren't a girl who has wandering eyes, are you, Rorda?"

I curled my fingers, pressing them against my dress, hoping she wouldn't notice my cloth ring. "I'm only here to serve my lady and the crown."

"A fine answer. One that has yet to be proven. Do your work quickly and quietly. Don't talk to the male servants or nobles unless instructed. I cannot stress enough the importance of this rule. Emperor Leszek himself will punish you if he discovers you have shirked your duties for dalliances. This is not a nursery. You become pregnant, whether it be within a lawful union or not, you will be dismissed from this castle's service."

My face heated. Don't talk to men? I highly doubted Leszek Frostfire took an interest in the daily activities of lowly servants. The East had a reputation for efficiency and candour, but I hadn't expected this blunt of a conversation on my first day. "I understand."

"I understand, *ma'am*. There is a protocol here. Keep up, learn fast, and you'll do well. I trust you haven't been briefed on the new security measures?"

"No, ma'am." Best not to speak unless absolutely necessary—the meeker I appeared, the less suspicious I would be.

"There is a sickness going around. Do not attend to anyone sleeping alone in a room. If you're on cleaning duty, clean only when the room is unoccupied. The underground well was damaged in the liberation. It will be a while before the repairs are complete. If you're fetching water, you may go as far as the stables and ask them for assistance. They usually leave buckets outside for cleaning. Do not give me the excuse that the river is part of the royal hunting grounds. I don't want anyone venturing out that far."

That wouldn't be a problem, considering I'd nearly drowned there. Keegan had saved me.

"Don't enter the royal gardens, the stables, or any of the Western hunting lands without my express permission," she continued. "Understand?"

I nodded. Then, under her hard stare, added: "Yes, ma'am." I hated the word.

Mistress Alwina considered the four "sleeping" servants huddling in their individual bunks under thin wool blankets. A small fire heated the room, but because of its proximity to the hot kitchen, maintaining a constant blaze was not necessary. "We're short on night girls," she said finally. "We're still waiting for a carriage load to come in from the East. It would be useful if you picked up that slack. You will be paid a half-silver per night, assuming your work is good."

She wouldn't have had a shortage if the East hadn't driven all the Western servants and those loyal to my husband out of the castle. "Yes, Mother Alwina."

Looking disgusted, she narrowed her gaze. "You may address

me as ma'am, or mistress, or when in the presence of a noble, by my title and full name. I am not your mother."

Right, that was a Western custom. "My apologies."

"Don't apologize. Just get it done. Get some rest so you aren't so ragged for your night shift."

She thundered out of the room, and two of the servants rolled over, expelling a collective sigh of relief. I smiled in hello. They were too tired or frightened to engage me.

I sat down in my bunk, sinking down to the frame. Not the most terrible place to sleep—I'd slept on rocks and hay most of my life. Sliding a suspicious glance at the other quiet servants, I assessed my options. Sleeping was not one of them.

My first priority: doing a complete sweep of the castle and the grounds. Unfortunately, all the places I wasn't allowed to go were prime candidates to hide a frozen prince. Not that I was allowed in the castle in the first place. The gardens and the stables—I'd probably have to wait until night to sneak out there. As there were so many carriages coming and going, no doubt the stables were among the first structures to be repaired after the fire.

If there was Freetor magic at work, I would spot the faint light blue glow immediately. Even if I couldn't suss out Keegan's resting spot, I could assess how quickly the castle repairs were progressing, and perhaps find an easy way out—and in—for Monju, Bidelia, and my father.

One of the servant's soft, steady snores filled the room. Likely this place would be crawling with Eastern and Northern servants as the day drew to a close. I couldn't leave anything of value in here. I had a knife sheathed in my apron pocket, along with the cream. I'd have to reapply that soon. The only privacy afforded to the servants was the chamber pot, hidden behind a near-transparent curtain in the corner by the fire. That wouldn't do.

After waiting another five minutes in complete silence, I

slipped from the servant chamber and walked briskly past the kitchens, keeping my head down. If anyone asked, I was running a personal errand for Lady Linnaea.

There wasn't much I could do before sunset, but I could eliminate a couple of wings from the castle. I spent the next hour navigating the servant staircases, going from corridor to corridor, avoiding the Frostfire soldiers when I could, and scurrying by them when I couldn't. The servants I encountered largely ignored me, too engrossed in toting cleaning supplies, laundry, buckets of water, and trays of food. It reminded me that I needed to check on Laoise soon, to see if she was hungry, and to find out her evening plans.

I headed for the west wing when a cloud of blonde hair rounding a corner to my left caught my eye. Sylvia.

Trying not to seem too interested in the Daughter of the East, I picked up the pace and peeked around the corner. I frowned. Unless Sylvia had changed her attire—which she was wont to do—and her physical shape, this was not her. As the young woman turned her head to the side, peering at the closed doors to the many chambers in this corridor, I realized that no, this was not Lady Sylvia Frostfire. She looked remarkably familiar and not just because she shared an uncanny resemblance to Sylvia.

It was Lady Milda Seacream. We had met briefly months ago, during my stay in the castle as Dominique. Just as airy as Sylvia, if not more so, if I recalled correctly. Her hands neatly clasped in front of her, she walked with a quiet confidence down the corridor, towards the west wing: the noble quarters.

Sylvia had said she'd meet up with Milda today. I soundlessly pursued the Eastern lady, keeping a healthy distance. Milda glanced over her shoulder more than once, a concerned look painting her face. It wasn't unsafe to wander the castle alone as far as I knew, but much had changed in Marlenia City in the short weeks since I'd been gone.

Keeping my head down as a pair of guards walked by, I put a little more distance between me and Milda to ease her fear. We were in the west wing now. She walked right by Sylvia's quarters—or what had been Sylvia's quarters months ago. I counted seven open rooms as I passed by. Half appeared lived-in, while others had two servants within, cleaning and changing the bedsheets, readying the chamber for arriving Easterners. Once Milda stepped inside one of these rooms, it would be hard for me to continue following her without coming up with some kind of excuse. I could find an unoccupied chamber on ground level, sneak outside, and try my luck on the grounds? No, I had to see this through: I had to search the entire interior for Keegan, so I'd know for sure he wasn't here. I pressed on, further down the corridor. I would check every nook and cranny of the castle, destroyed or intact, for Keegan Tramore.

Yet that would take time. And I could only do so much before my presence became suspicious, or worse, before the cream ran out.

Finally, she stopped at the very end of the corridor, to a room on the western wall. Behind her was another corridor and a narrow servant staircase. I barely skirted behind the safety of a nearby corner as Lady Milda glanced up and down the corridors, and then produced a key from her bosom.

A key? Lady Milda was a guest in the castle, but there was something unusual and intimate about her possession of it. I didn't think I received a key when I was Lady Dominique. The Frostfires were truly paranoid about the Silver Spear curse spreading if they were now issuing keys to all noble guests.

She disappeared inside the room and shut the door. I was too far to hear voices. If I were to get closer...

Someone approached from behind me. I side-stepped and hugged the wall to encourage the other person to pass as I continued toward Milda's chamber. I dared not look over my shoulder. I was a servant, in a wing that hadn't been assigned to me. If anything, I needed to get out of here, pretend that I had an urgent message to deliver.

As I hardened my resolve and spun an elaborate tale about where and what I was supposed to be doing, the person clipped me hard on my left side. I spun around, my excuses at the ready, but my quick movement startled what turned out to be a young noblewoman. She dropped a load of tomes onto the hard floor, all save one that she had splayed open in her left hand.

"Oh no!" She shut the open tome and hugged it to her chest. "I'm sorry, I didn't mean to startle you."

"No, my lady, I am the clumsy one." I bent to pick up her books. Touching the binding of a blue tome, I remembered fondly when Keegan and I had explored the library, back when he had no idea who I was. When I had lived here, the library had been open to the public, to encourage peoples of all classes—besides the Freetors—to share knowledge. Things seemed simpler then, even though it was only two months ago. In many ways, the Freetors now were worse-off. Because of me.

I stacked three books. The top one was titled: *Local Legends of the Western Province: From 127 HOY to Now.*

"Studying up?" I asked, because I couldn't help myself.

She smiled. The young noblewoman was roughly my age, perhaps a year younger. She had the fair complexion of an Easterner, though her eyes were darker, like those in the North and West. Her attire also didn't portray her house colours. It was possible she was a minor relative of the Frostfires, but why would they bring her here during an occupation? Were they that desperate to fill the castle with Easterners?

"Studying helps the time go by. History is my favourite subject," she replied. "Sadly there is a shortage of Eastern tutors here, since the invasion. I heard they don't arrive until next week."

Invasion? My eyebrows shot up. Anyone caught calling it that would be marked as a Tramore sympathizer, or worse, a Freetor, and be thrown in the dungeon on the spot.

"Oh. I...I didn't mean to say invasion," she said quickly, waving her hands. She snatched the books and hugged them to her chest. "The liberation."

"You were here. In the castle. Before the Frostfires?" I asked. She wasn't someone I recognized—but then again, I only lived here for two fortnights before embarking on my quest for the Silver Spear, and I was far too busy trying to learn castle etiquette and improve my skills to learn the names of all the fostering families and permanent merchants living within the walls. Just another regret to add to the list.

"I've been living here for nearly a year," she said, nodding. She seemed less embarrassed, though her gaze darted around the hall in case Frostfire or Castillo ears hid within the stone.

I lowered my gaze. The cream my father had given me appeared to still be working. "I thought all those living in the castle before the liberation had been removed." Or killed.

"Oh. Many were. But I am Lady Elizabeth Schwinghamer. My family is Eastern. We are a small house, but old—not worthy of the Frostfire's concern, really—but because of my Eastern blood, I was allowed to remain fostering here. For now. It doesn't do much for my prospects, to be honest. Most of the other nobles unrelated to the East or North have been forced to leave. Not that I wouldn't be honoured to be married to the Frostfires or Castillos, of course." She added the last part as an afterthought, and then laughed nervously. "But I don't suppose you care much about that. Being a...servant?"

"That's right." I smiled weakly. Even with the cream, I had to be cautious. Servants were the eyes and ears in the castle, and I mustn't appear too suspicious or curious in front of the nobles—even if they suspected me a rat, Freetor or not. I couldn't trust anyone I didn't know in the castle. Just like old times.

"I shouldn't keep you from your studies, my lady. Please, excuse me."

"Of course. Thank you, for helping me." She waved the books.

I bowed, waiting for her to leave so I could resume my own illicit studies, when the door to Lady Milda's chambers reopened. Instead of the fair lady emerging, two Northern shadows dressed head to toe in black filed out of the room, carrying a long wooden crate. One hesitated—only for an instant—to readjust his grip on the heavy box. Long enough for me to catch the tiniest glint of blue glowing from between the wooden slats.

My heart pounded furiously.

A coffin. With a cursed body.

"What is that?" Lady Elizabeth asked.

Keegan.

I scampered down the hallway as the two shadows disappeared down the adjacent corridor. It didn't matter how or why Keegan had been hidden in there. All that mattered was stopping those two shadows and freeing my love from eternal sleep.

My feet warred with my mind as I turned the corner. They were already partway down the servant staircase with the coffin, their progress slowed by the sharp curve of the walls as it spiralled downward. Too engrossed in their task to notice me, I started down the staircase.

"Uh—servant girl! Wait!"

Lady Elizabeth's noble order couldn't be disobeyed, but I also couldn't wait. Keegan was so close. I crept down the stairs, my hands balled into fists, fingernails digging into my palms to keep me from running.

"Come back!"

Mid-step, I halted. Something in Lady Elizabeth's tone held

me in place, as frozen as my love. It was not just a command. It was a plea.

I had to go back and help.

Clenching my teeth, hating every second that passed as I did nothing, I turned around and took the steps two at a time, back to Lady Milda's chamber.

I had no way of knowing it was Keegan in the box. It was my heart telling me to fly down the staircase, hoping beyond hope that when I threw open the box, his frozen face would stare back into mine. I couldn't risk fighting two Northern shadows in the middle of the day to find out.

Tears rimmed my eyes, and keeping my head down, I marched back down the corridor. The Violet Fox didn't let her enemies get away forever. Tonight, I swore, I'd investigate.

Hopefully it wouldn't be too late.

The door to Lady Milda's chamber was wide open and Lady Elizabeth stood at the threshold. Seeing me return, she motioned me inside the room, and pointed.

The chamber was not unlike the one I'd lived in. A window overlooking the bailey and the city below was before us. To the right, a wardrobe, a mirror, and even a closet. A large bed to the left. Following Lady Elizabeth's finger and my keen sight, it was not hard to spot the obvious difference between this chamber and all the rest.

A frozen foot, wearing an equally frozen dainty slipper, poked out from the other side of the bed. Only moments ago had she walked into this room, with two Northern shadows lying in wait...

Immediately, I shut the door behind us. "Don't touch," I said, gripping the noblewoman by the arms, trying to keep the emotion from my voice. "And don't get too close."

Puzzled by my forthright behaviour, she said, "Do you know what happened here?"

"It's a sickness," I said quickly. "The head servant warned me about it this morning, and we've heard rumours. It's spread through touch alone. You touch her, you become like her. Frozen."

"We weren't warned about this," Lady Elizabeth replied. She wrenched herself gently from my grip, and cautiously crept toward the young woman on the floor. "I know her. This is Lady Milda Seacream."

As Lady Elizabeth knelt a respectful distance from the frozen noblewoman, I inspected the bed. A dip in the wrinkled blankets, the size of a person, made my heart sink into my stomach. I laid a hand on the sheets. They were cold and damp.

"He was here," I whispered.

"Who?" she asked, glancing at me.

I cleared my throat as my mind spun with the possibilities. Lady Milda may have come in here at the behest of Lady Sylvia. She'd had a key. What had Sylvia been thinking, keeping Keegan locked in here, so close to all the other nobles? Sylvia had never been that bright. She'd probably wanted him close to her, as close as could be managed in his state. A servant with access could have wandered in here of her own accord and put every castle resident in danger!

It wouldn't be long before Sylvia returned to the room, looking to visit her precious prince, only to find her best friend frozen instead.

Yet the Northern shadows, carting the coffin out of here—were they simply there to guard Keegan's body? It had been minutes between Lady Milda freezing and them making a swift exit.

My insides ran as cold as the curse. I didn't know how, or why, but Lady Milda's cursed, frozen state on the floor felt malevolently deliberate.

Sylvia wouldn't do this to her best friend. Dominique certainly would.

But why?

"I have to go find the head servant. And...possibly Lady Sylvia or Lady Dominique. We can't allow anyone to come into the room, lest they become like Lady Milda." I didn't want to face Sylvia or Dominique again—I couldn't risk the cream failing me—but I trusted Lady Elizabeth less to convey the message. The fact that she didn't know anything about the curse suggested the Frostfires and the Castillos were trying to keep Keegan's condition a secret. With the Frostfires' reputation for tyranny, I didn't want to think about what they'd do to a noble of a lesser house who had unearthed one of their secrets—especially one that had lived in the castle during the Tramore reign.

"My lady, I suggest you step outside the chamber and wait while I run for assistance. If a bannerman of your house comes by, tell him that he needs to find Lady Sylvia right away." No doubt the Frostfires would want to keep Lady Milda's cursed body a secret for as long as possible.

But Lady Elizabeth wasn't listening to me. "This appears to be Freetor magic," she said, almost to herself.

"I...wouldn't know," I said slowly. "Please, my lady, it isn't safe for you to stay in the room."

"The Freetors unleashing a terrible, magical pestilence upon the surface?" She set her books down and riffled through them. "I'm not sure if there's ever been an instance of this. Ever."

I strode across the room and gripped the doorknob tightly, unwilling to pull the door open and reveal Lady Milda's fate. "I'll fetch Lady Sylvia, or try to summon the first royal I find. Please, my lady, I strongly urge you to wait outside. If you were to accidentally touch her..."

More annoyed than touched by my concern for her safety, she heaved a heavy sigh and let the poor noblewoman be. "Fine. I'll stand watch."

"Thank you. I mean, good idea, my lady." I opened the door

just enough for Lady Elizabeth to slip through, and then closed it behind us. It was possible that Lady Milda still had the key clasped in her icy fingers, but I couldn't risk touching her and revealing my immunity.

Setting out with nervous purpose, I hesitated by the servant staircase. The shadows would be long gone by now. Even if I did track them, I'd be leaving Lady Elizabeth holding the bag with Lady Milda's body. I glanced back at her. She stared at me expectantly, equally as frightened.

I couldn't let anyone else fall to the curse. Not even a noble-woman supporting the enemy.

I did a lap of the square wing. Only other nobles chatting in twos and threes and a few servants who eyed me with suspicion and curiosity graced the corridors. The guards from earlier must have gone to another wing or floor. I'd have to do the same to find someone of use.

I was coming back around, several stone-throws from Lady Elizabeth leaning patiently against the wall when Lady Sylvia herself appeared from the adjoining corridor. Finally. I called her name, trying not to run and look desperate so as to scare her, and nearly fell to my knees before her.

"My lady," I said, bowing deeply, hair deliberately spilling over my face. "Forgive me, but—"

"You have a servant mistress to report to with your prob-lems, do you not? Out of my way, I have more—"

"Lady Sylvia," I said forcefully, blocking her path for the bedroom. "There is a noblewoman in there. Frozen."

Genuine surprise overcame Sylvia's face as she glanced at the door. "But...I told her..."

I lowered my voice. "It does appear to be Lady Milda, my lady."

"How do you know?" she demanded. "Why would you go in there? That is private quarters, occupied by an important noble—"

"It was unoccupied when I came upon it, my lady. The door was open and I thought perhaps...it needed a clean?"

It was a bold lie, one that Lady Elizabeth might not corroborate. Mentioning the shadows would only complicate things for us both.

Sylvia's face paled. She seemed unconcerned with my wobbly lie. "Unoccupied...?"

My stomach clenched. She didn't care about her frozen friend. She cared that Keegan was no longer in that room.

I gritted my teeth. Let Sylvia and Dominique have their squabbles—I only cared about Keegan and getting Laoise and I out of here in one piece. "The frozen noblewoman, my lady. She is of your blood. What are we to do with her?"

Rounding on me, she jabbed a finger in my face. "Besides you, nosy nit, does anyone else know about this?"

"I do, my lady."

Lady Elizabeth's calm manner surprised Sylvia; her cheeks flushed a bright pink. Clearing her throat, she turned to face the minor noblewoman with a false resolve. "And what were you doing in that room? Were you going to help this nosy servant girl clean?"

"No, my lady. The door was open. I didn't know that it was... restricted."

"And you make a habit of wandering..." She trailed off as she ducked into the room, resting a steadying hand on the paneling. "Oh, Mildie."

"Perhaps you should fetch someone to take her somewhere more comfortable," Lady Elizabeth suggested, moving to comfort Sylvia.

Sylvia rejected Lady Elizabeth's attempt at comfort and pulled the door firmly shut. Her gaze darted up and down the hallway. No Frostfire bannermen were in sight, but a group of nobles were coming our way, deep in conversation.

"Tell no one of this," Sylvia said, glancing from Lady Elizabeth to me as she pulled the door shut. She lingered on Lady Elizabeth. "If you do, you will be considered traitors to the Frostfire family and will be dealt with accordingly. I will take care of the particulars. But"—she pointed at me again as if I were a thing and not a person, then squinted—"you're Lady Linnaea's handmaid, are you not?"

"I am," I replied, unsure.

She nodded, somewhat relieved. "You'll both stand here until I return with bannermen. Let no one enter, not even another servant. And don't dare leave until I say. Understand?"

"Yes, my lady." I approached the door and squared my shoulders.

She started down the hallway, then thought better of it, turned, and headed in the other direction.

"My books are still in there," Lady Elizabeth whispered, her gaze following the angry Sylvia Frostfire down the corridor. Her feet tapped on the stone floor, itching to move.

"Don't go back in," I said hurriedly. Once the nobles had passed and Lady Sylvia was safely gone, I opened the door. "I'll get them for you."

Before she could protest, I dashed into the room and retrieved the tomes, taking one last long look at Lady Milda. She looked as though she'd been frozen mid-scream, her head turned to one side, looking over her shoulder at an assailant.

They were using my love as a weapon. No killing required.

I hurried out of the room, pulled the door shut, and returned the books to my new friend. Grateful, she smiled. "I think if we're going to share a tasty secret," Lady Elizabeth said, "you get to call me Liz."

* * *

It didn't take the castle long to consume that tasty secret.

"Did you hear about that noblewoman? Lady Milda Seacream? She was...frozen," said one of the servant girls as I re-entered the dorm.

"Frozen?" said another. "How?"

"Freetor magic." Three servants looked up at me as I stood in the doorway. The first, a fair-haired, dark-eyed girl about my age asked, "You found her, didn't you?"

I cleared my throat. There was no point in lying. "I did."

After Sylvia had returned with three Frostfire guards, Lady Elizabeth—or Lady Liz, as she'd insisted three times during our idle conversation—had tried to question Sylvia about the curse or pestilence as she'd taken to calling it. How many other cases were in the castle? The scholars were working with a few bodies in isolation. What can we do to prevent its spread? Touch nothing, avoid the cold, stop wandering the corridors alone. I'd stood quietly as Sylvia had answered her deep questions until she'd tired of the inquisition, and sent us both away. She hadn't bothered to reiterate our promise to silence. Apparently the news had already spread.

Now, as I took a seat in my bunk, the servant girls gathered around, more of them appearing from the woodwork, a captive audience as they began an inquisition of their own.

"Did you see the Freetor who did it? Was it one of the slaves?"

How I longed to ask about the well-being of my people. "She was just lying on the floor. The door was open, and I was passing by. I don't know what happened." It was hard to be dispassionate so I stared at the roughhewn boards on the floor, counting the knots in the wood.

"Lady Elizabeth Schwinghamer was there too. Do you think she could be a Freetor in disguise?"

My heart tightened. It took the suspicion off me to have them suspect her, but no one deserved to be falsely accused of a crime that meant imprisonment, enslavement, or if Dominique had her way, execution.

"She was here before we arrived..."

Mistress Alwina entered the room suddenly. The girls scattered like mice for their hiding holes, or in this case, their bunks. Pleased with her entrance, the mistress closed the heavy door behind her.

"Be careful of your wagging tongue, Emmine Potts," Mistress Alwina sneered. "Lady Elizabeth is of a small house, yes, but her great-uncle was a Frostfire. The emperor remembers the families who are loyal to him. Despite her curious behaviour."

Some of the Eastern servants failed to hold back their snickers as they stared at Emmine. She'd been the first one talking when I'd entered, and the one asking most of the questions. With a last name like Potts, now I knew why. That was a Western name, common to the poorer merchants and craftsmen in Marlenia City. Which meant she was not to be trusted.

"Rorda went into an unoccupied room scheduled to be cleaned, by herself." Mistress Alwina glared at me, as if this was yet another rule I was expected to already know. "The Freetor attack is tragic, yes. But we must remain vigilant. The rules protect us. All of you were selected to be here because of your loyalty to the Frostfire family. And the Castillos." Mistress Alwina nodded respectfully to the group of Northern servants, quiet as statues in the corner. "Tonight I will do the pairings. I don't want to hear any more complaints. Or talk of this Freetor attack."

"But Mistress—"

"Half rations for you tomorrow, Emmine!" the mistress snapped, advancing on her. Although the head servant did not touch her, Emmine recoiled as if she had been slapped. "The more you talk of them, the more they appear. Their magic is insidious: be vigilant. Come directly to me directly if you spot any suspicious Freetor activity, and speak to no one else of it.

They have eyes and ears in the very stones of the castle."

"That's probably why they're taking so long to rebuild," said one of the girls, with hair so blonde it was nearly white, in the bunk to my left.

Her comment earned a long, ugly scowl from the mistress. "That is not for you to speculate on, Kuni Sun."

Another Eastern surname, certainly of the common, low-class variety, given its length. If anything, Kuni's comment should have earned her half-rations, too. Yet the name was Eastern and had therefore saved her.

After another lecture on the safety of traveling in numbers within the castle, Mistress Alwina randomly paired the servants. Young women my age, tittering in the corner about the nobles they'd seen today, had their smiles wiped from existence as they were paired with others they didn't even know. I supposed this was to prevent strong attachments or friendships, though clearly some were on friendlier terms than others.

"Rorda," she said, after some time. "I did not get your family name?"

I noted how Alwina knew each girl's full name, and seemed to bestow a cold friendliness to the Eastern and Northern girls with better lineage. A common name from the East was better than a common name from the West, it seemed. And Freetor names, regardless of length, were lower than them all.

I'd given it some thought. "Cloth. I'm Rorda Cloth."

"Hmm. Your parents are clothiers?" she asked stiffly. "Were you born in Marlenia City?"

"No, mistress. I have lived in Baile Gareth my whole life, in Feenagh Forest."

"I see." This seemed to change things. "Emmine Potts, you will work with the girl who has never lived in the city. Show her how we treat the Westerners here in the castle."

Emmine Potts turned up her nose at me when the mistress

paired us for floor duty in the east wing. Her hands looked as though they'd seen many days of hard labour, though she crept through the halls as if today was her first day as well. She threw me many nervous glances as I carried two full buckets of water up the servant staircase, *splosh*ing it onto the stone, until she relieved one from me. How Laoise managed to do this for a fortnight in Baile Gareth, I didn't know, but I hoped she was soundly asleep and enjoying her castle bed now. She deserved it.

Emmine knelt and set to our task for the evening: scrubbing floors. Not a chore I ever had to do, as one could not scrub dirt. I mirrored Emmine's actions, throwing myself into the work as I devised a plan to get rid of my new servant friend.

I should have known that Sylvia would lobby to keep Keegan as close to her as she possible, no matter the consequences. For some reason, Dominique had sent Northern shadows to ensure Lady Milda fell prey to the curse. If I could follow the shadows' path down the servant staircase in the west wing, perhaps I could figure out where they had hidden the coffin. Surely it would have attracted attention. Then again, when one saw Northern shadows, one tended to look the other way, lest they wanted to end up blind. Wherever they had taken Keegan, he was probably guarded and covered, to prevent accidental exposure. Many chambers posted guards for extra security—trying to get inside each one would take days. Time I didn't have.

That left the meeting room and the cellar—assuming that hadn't completely collapsed—as well as the hedge maze or the stable, if he was kept away from the horses and the stable hands.

I had to start somewhere.

"What are you doing? You're going to wear the cloth out!"

"Oh. Sorry." I was so deep in thought that I'd been furiously scrubbing the same spot repeatedly. I'd torn a small hole in the fabric.

Giving me an odd look, she grabbed the torn fabric in my hand and unfurled it like a banner for inspection. "Now look what you've done. You'll have to sew that on your own time. Don't you use laidir cloth in Baile Garrett? Your parents are clothiers, they should have taught you. It's strong, but if you go too hard on it..."

"It's Baile Gareth," I said, swiping the worn, dirty cloth from her. "And no. I don't wash floors there. I am Lady Linnaea's personal handmaid."

"Lucky you, Your Highness."

I wrung out the dirty water in the bucket. "I didn't mean to be condescending. I just hate this."

"No one likes washing floors. It's just something that has to be done."

As I eyed the bucket, Emmine's words struck me with an idea. I gripped the top of the bucket of dirty water and leaned into it. The brown liquid spilled onto the floor, erasing the hour we'd spent hunched over, scrubbing.

"Oops! Oh no..." I said.

Although twice my size, Emmine leapt nimbly to her feet. She leaned against the wall, then thought better of it and reached for me instead. "Careful. Don't slip. A friend of mine hurt her back so bad that the Frostfires sent her away. Permanently."

Yet another story of terrible Frostfire misdeeds. Did all of their servants serve out of fear? "You stay there," I told her, rising slowly. "I'll replace the bucket with a full one."

"You can't go to the stables alone!" she hissed. The dirty water coalesced and spread ever closer to her slippers like a pack of beatag, closing in for the kill. "Please, don't leave me here alone!"

"I won't be long, I promise."

"What if the mistress comes by? What if she slips on the water? My family...!"

"Hey." I reached for her hand. To my surprise, she gripped it, hard. "It's going to be all right. I won't be more than five minutes. The water buckets are by the stables, right?"

Emmine nodded. "Hopefully there are some left. It'll take you more than five minutes to go out there and back. The mistress could come. She checks on all the girls. I'm coming with you."

"And if she finds out we spilled dirty water on the floor? Won't we be punished for that? What if she comes by and sees you just standing here, terrified? What then?"

Determined, Emmine's gaze darted around the dark corridor. "Fine. I'll soak up what I can with the cloths. Try to spread the water out more thinly. It doesn't look...too bad. It'll dry. I hope."

"Okay. I'll be right back."

I grabbed the bucket and took care as I hurried down the corridor. I certainly didn't want to end up with a broken back, not now, not when I was so close. Not when my best friend was putting her life on the line.

I'd bought five minutes. Maybe ten, since I had to lug the water back. Enough time for a cursory snoop in the stables. Emmine, Mistress Alwina, and the rest of the castle would be none the wiser.

After evading two patrols of Frostfire guards, I was nearly at the postern when I felt someone's eyes on me. A curious sensation, knowing you're being watched. It was a sense I'd come to trust above all others. I gripped the bucket and slowed my pace. I was just a servant going to get water. I didn't want any questions or trouble. The sinister presence wasn't an experienced predator. His uneven gait and loud breathing was a dead giveaway: he was not used to lying in wait in the shadows.

"I see you there, girl," he said, stumbling from behind a corner.

Leon Frostfire smelled of bluesberry wine and beer—a ghastly combination. The man was a walking brew house. I wondered if Linnaea knew of her future husband's inclinations. I would have run, too.

I spun to face him. I'd already run from this man, I reminded myself as he silently sized me up. I could run from him again.

"Where might a servant girl be wandering off to this time of night?" he asked in a sing-song voice, his smile cruel and animalistic.

"Doesn't the son of the emperor have better things to do than to bother servant girls as they work?" I demanded. I held the empty bucket in front of me like a shield. Emmine might have more than a broken back to worry about when Mistress Alwina found her alone.

Leon seemed displeased by my response. He stepped into a stream of lantern light. The liquid in his near-empty bottle sloshed as he shook it.

"Servant girls like you don't go gallivanting around the castle alone," he said, grinning in a way that made me sick. "Unless you're sneaking to places you're not supposed to be. Like outside the castle grounds. Planning to steal a horse and meet up with a friend, were you?"

So he wasn't completely stupid. He knew we were close to the stables, at least.

"I'm fetching water." I spun and hoped to lose him up the servant staircase ahead. I'd show him just how well this woman knew the castle.

"Where you going now?" he asked. His drunken voice echoed in the corridor, and part of me wanted to smother him with the nearest convenient pillow for being so loud and disorderly in a place of quiet and shadows.

I didn't respond. Just twenty more paces, maybe twenty-five...

He lumbered after me, and I took off into a run, but the

soldier was surprisingly fast as he caught up with me and grabbed my right wrist. He abandoned the bottle with a sickening crash on the stone.

Happy for the excuse, I drew my hidden knife and pointed at him. "Let go of me."

To my surprise, he did. As he eyed the blade, a new respect bloomed in his eyes. "Servants don't—"

"You better fly back to bed, little lord," I replied. "Unless you want to explain tomorrow why your face bears the red patchwork of freshly baked pie."

Leon smirked. "I could have you arrested for talking to the prince in such a manner."

You are not the prince! Instead: "That's assuming you can get out of this situation with your vocal chords intact."

Careful, said the voice of inner calm. I was talking like a Freetor, not a Marlenian servant. They would be afraid of such threats. I remembered Emmine's fear when I'd spilled the water: the fear of losing her livelihood. I gritted my teeth, hating to back down.

"Apologies, my lord."

Leon cocked his head. "Now that's no way for a commoner to address a nobleman."

"No, you're right, it's—"

"You're no servant," he said.

I said nothing, as I had been trained. Sweat pooled in my palm; I gripped the knife tighter.

"You're Lady Linnaea, aren't you. The real Lady Linnaea."

The flicker of surprise on my face could not be hidden. Leon caught it, smiling wide, as if he had just found a rare, precious gem.

"I knew that girl was far too common. Rejecting my advances, like no proper lady would."

I wasn't sure what that had to do with anything, but I lowered my knife, ever so slightly. This was a dangerous situation. And an opportunity. "And if that were true, what of it?"

"Well..." Leon advanced towards me. "I would first commend your cleverness. Switching places with your handmaid to fool my sister and the Daughter of the North. She is not easily tricked."

"If you like Lady Dominique so much," I replied, "Why don't you marry her?"

"I would," he said, in a more serious tone than I thought possible from him. "However, she's been promised to my brother."

"Would you prefer to marry her?" I asked.

Leon laughed. "You noblewomen. Does it matter? Your father has a small but dedicated force who knows Feenagh Forest well. You can help us root out the remaining Freetors in this province, and once your father falls in line behind us, the other houses will follow. We can't hold this province alone. Your father's contribution will serve us well."

My insides ran cold. The real Linnaea was probably sleeping on the floor of Feenagh Forest now in the company and protection of the Freetors. If they found her before we did...

"The Gareth family is happy to help," I said finally.

He leaned in closer. I stiffened as his boozy breath warmed my ear. "My dear sister and the Lady Dominique are going to extend an invitation to Lady Linnaea tomorrow for a private dinner. I don't suppose you'll continue the ruse until then?"

"We have to ensure that your family intends to honour the match," I replied, digging my thumbnail into my palm.

"And what exactly would convince you of my...honour?"

"Your honour needs no justification," I said dryly, wishing I had a hole to crawl into that didn't smell of bluesberry wine. "It's your father's. My family has endured much over the years and staying hidden in the forest has helped us. Not to mention, the Tramore family and those loyal to them—may be angry that my father is making a deal with the...shall we say...occupying force?" I smiled sweetly. "It is best I remain undercover, hidden, until the wedding ceremony, so my enemies may target my handmaid instead. That is how I will honour our match."

"If that is the truth," Leon said, eying me up and down with a narrowed gaze, "then I will honour it by keeping your secret... my lady."

"Thank you." I lowered the knife to my side. "If you will now excuse me..."

I wasn't sure if he was going to allow me to leave without a fight. As I sidestepped, he grabbed my chin and brought my face to his, his blue-stained lips puckered.

Instinct took over. I kneed him in the chest, hard. Stumbling, he fell backwards to the ground, groaning loudly in the otherwise quiet castle.

"You...tricksy..."

As he struggled to get up, I pointed the knife at him again. "Careful. There are things we should save for after the wedding. Don't you think?"

A slow smile spread across his face, though I could see the anger bubbling beneath. "I...think—"

"Also," I added, backing away slowly, "if Lady Sylvia and Lady Dominique hear of our conversation tonight, I'll know who is to blame. Am I making myself clear?"

"You're not a killer," he sputtered, holding his chest.

"Who says that I will need to kill you? If you know anything about the forest I'm from, then you know there are many beasts there all too willing to feast upon the flesh of a lost man." I smiled. "Good night, Leon Frostfire."

I turned from him then, and hurried down the corridor in my soundless flats. I heard him groaning and stumbling, but he didn't follow. Likely he was nursing his wounded pride. I blew out a relieved sigh. I had saved Laoise from discovery—barely. My late night wanderings had nearly cost us.

Hugging the bucket, I hurried to the postern, keeping my eyes peeled.

Seven

"You're not pulling it tight enough."

"Sorry. I haven't done this before."

"I know. Just listen to me. I'll guide you through it."

Laoise gripped the bedpost, wearing one of Linnaea's nicer gowns. I stood behind her, holding the corset strings, trying to help my best friend prepare for the day ahead.

Emmine, grateful and surprised I had returned with water, had spilled her fears of discovery on me, like I was the floor that needed washing. I'd barely had two hours of sleep, my back hurt from scrubbing and re-scrubbing the entire east wing, and my soul felt weary from listening to the servant girls express their fear and hatred of Mistress Alwina as well as speculate on who was a Freetor pretending to be a Marlenian within the castle.

Meanwhile, my mind led me in circles: where had they hidden Keegan? Why was I lying in bed when I could be out there, trying to find him? I felt like a walking corpse.

And now, just when I thought I'd have a quiet day to explore more of the castle grounds, Leszek had called a gathering in the throne room. It was the first since they'd taken the castle. The servants buzzed like hungry flies, preparing the hall for the lords and ladies in residence, as well as the public. Emmine and the servant girls sweeping the floors speculated that the emperor wished to resume the Holy One's tradition of hearing and addressing public concerns. No doubt he'd have to, after force-fully taking the city and putting all disloyal citizens to death. Rumours of the Freetor magic ravaging the castle simmered beneath the surface as well. To the common Westerner and the frightened noble, he had a lot to answer for.

"Kiera? Did you hear me?"

I snapped out of my daze, shivering. "Sorry?"

She looked over her shoulder at me, concerned. "You haven't slept, have you." It wasn't a question.

"Not after what happened with Leon." I'd told Laoise about my encounter with him as soon as I'd escaped my castle duties to help her dress for the gathering.

"I can't believe he thinks you're Linnaea. What if he tells his father? We can't afford to make this more complicated. Mother always told me, when you're pretending to be someone else, you have to keep your story simple."

"I know. I don't think he will. I think he enjoyed the prospect of 'romancing' me secretly." I pulled the laces taut. They felt as fragile as a strand of hair. "Are you sure this won't break? What happens if it frays in the middle of the court?"

"Well, as my only maid servant, you will have to deal with that situation if it arises. And you need to ensure that doesn't happen by pulling tighter."

"I've worn these. I don't want to collapse your lungs."

"You lived through it. So will I."

I tried to think like Bidelia and consider every aspect of Laoise's appearance. I was rubbish at doing hair, but Laoise's was short enough that placing one of Linnaea's golden combs within her thick tresses was appropriate. I recalled Sylvia's fondness for powdered faces and rouge, and made Laoise dab slightly too much on her fair, freckled face. She coughed as bits of white powder fell from the chubby brush and coated the dresser like snow.

"You're sure you don't want any of this?" she asked, holding up the brush and wrinkling her nose.

"No thanks. I think I have enough on my clothes now." I brushed off the errant powder and glanced at the door. "I should get you out there, so the Frostfires can see you."

I followed Laoise, head down, as we navigated the corridors and stepped into the bustling, cavernous hall. The entire throne room seemed something out of a tale spun by a hyperbolic bard. Alternating blue and red banners—the Frostfire colours—hung from the ceiling all the way to the floor. The air was heavy with the scent of lavender, yet my acute Freetor nose could detect the old smoke from the liberation fire. Why rebuild the most important room in the castle when you could dress it up and pretend everything was fine?

The entire complement of the castle's resident nobles and merchants had to be in attendance. Many of them recognized Laoise as Leon Frostfire's intended and neatly parted the way for us as we settled near the eastern side of the room, off to the right of the platform of thrones, housing three large, ornate chairs. Not the same thrones, as those had been eaten in the fire—but they were similar enough.

Laoise was thinking the same thing I was. "I wonder if they'll make me sit up there?"

When Keegan's father, Eamon Tramore, was alive, he'd sit in one of the twin thrones, and Keegan in the other. Ivor Ferguson was also allowed on the platform. That was how they heard the concerns of the people, and presided over the realm. When the Holy One was bedridden, I earned a seat in one of the thrones.

"Leszek will probably take the middle throne," I whispered. "Maybe Boris, he's next in line. I'm not sure if Sylvia's mother is here. She may have remained in the East." We had little intelligence on her, though I could only speculate on why Leszek wouldn't bring his wife to rule with him in the West. "Since

Dominique is his intended, she may take the third seat. Leon may want you to stand next to him on the platform."

"I hope not," she replied. "I don't want to get up there."

"You're doing fine," I said.

Frostfire men appeared at all three visible exits to the room. Behind the throne, the curtains jostled. There was a room behind there, where the rulers usually entered from. The gathering was about to begin.

"This could be your only chance," she whispered. "You don't have to stay here. You should use this time to snoop around. Check the hedge maze and the stables."

Frostfire men and a few Northern shadows lined the walls at seemingly random points along the walls, in addition to the exits. I doubted they would stop me from leaving, though the show of force troubled me deeply. Were they expecting something to go wrong?

The more soldiers that were here, the fewer there were outside.

Leszek Frostfire, High King in the Eastern Province, and usurper of the Western throne, emerged from behind the thick curtain. This was the first time I'd seen him in person. His hair and thin beard were as white as a noblewoman's freshly washed shift. His outfit showed off his famed wealth: a red velvet cape lay heavy on his shoulders, a bold choice for his equally brilliant navy tunic. He surveyed the crowd, hand gently resting on the throne as if it had always been his, the other just as casually brushing his cape back to reveal the scabbard at his hip.

His gaze washed over me. I tensed.

He took a seat in the middle chair.

Boris parted the curtains next. His attire was far simpler. No cape, but he wore Keegan's circlet today, and many of his rings. His blue vest complemented his father's, and he flashed a charming smile on his plain, square face, though his dark red pants reminded me that no smile could hide the bloodshed his family had caused.

To my surprise, Dominique was not next. As Dominique was betrothed to Boris, it would have been a show of respect and a sign of a strong alliance to have her on the dais with the Frostfires. Yet from behind Boris came Leon, looking far worse than me. He squinted at the crowd, his gaze devouring them reluctantly. He did not look like he wanted to be there. Perhaps this was a kind of punishment for his unsettling behaviour.

I searched for Sylvia: she should be here. Leszek seemed unconcerned that his only daughter was not in attendance.

Maybe she was with Keegan.

Laoise was right. Staying here was a waste of time. I didn't like sitting through the gatherings when I was up on the platform: I would not enjoy them now. She would fill me in on any important developments, and as a servant, I would not be missed.

I squeezed Laoise's arm. She nodded, understanding me immediately.

"Thank you all for coming," Leszek said. His voice was gravelly, but loud. "I promise I'll keep this brief. I'm sure we all have more important things to do today."

Polite laughter, but none of the adoration Keegan had received when he had been on that same platform, less than a month ago. Leszek spoke with the authority of a tired clerk. The East was known for its efficient mannerisms: talking to a crowd that had not been warmed or welcomed did not seem to concern him. I weaved quickly through the lesser lords and merchants, heading toward the easternmost exit.

"First, bring in the slaves."

Just as I'd cleared the crowd, two guards charged in the entrance before me, leading the march with at least two dozen branded Freetor slaves in tow. I turned, falling in line with the observing crowd so the slaves would not recognize my face, but it wouldn't have mattered. Nearly all of them looked exhausted from manual labour, their faces and hands grimy. Their wrists and ankles were shackled and their chains rattled as they were paraded to the centre of the room. Many of the nobles held a gloved hand to their nose in protest, while the merchants appraised each slave with interest.

This wasn't just a regular gathering. This was an auction.

I hurried back through the crowd, towards Laoise.

"Normally I wouldn't let these creatures step foot in here," Leszek began, "but I would not offend your sensibilities by showing you where we stable them. These twenty-eight slaves are too weak or too young for the rough manual labour required to rebuild the castle, but would make a good addition to a gentle household of good breeding, or with some training, they could handle menial tasks in any fine establishment. The first order of business today is the sale. Sold as a lot: the crown won't hear individual offers. Let's keep it simple and start the bidding at... twenty pieces of silver."

Merchants shouted numbers across the room. Some of the nobles joined in. I remembered the Freetor slave I'd saved when I was pretending to be Dominique. I'd had power and influence then. Now, I had no silver to buy their freedom. No important title to my name, not one that would carry weight with the Frostfires. If those who shared my blood, who knew the sorrow of growing up without rights, continued to be branded and punished, how could I in good consequence choose to leave and do nothing?

I shook my head. I couldn't leave. My love would have to wait in his frozen prison a while longer.

"Kiera?" Laoise looked at me questioningly as I appeared at her side once more.

"We have to save them," I hissed.

"What?" she replied, gripping my arm tightly. "I can't go out there demanding to buy all those people. You did that last time and it nearly blew your cover!" She set her mouth grimly. "We have to stick to the mission. If we stray...Keegan will be lost. So will all the other innocent Marlenians falling to the curse."

My gut hurt, knowing Laoise was right.

Leszek was no longer leading the auction. Boris had taken over, standing above the crowd, managing the interested buyers. "One hundred twenty pieces of silver. A bargain for twenty-eight slaves. Going once...going twice..."

I patted my pockets. I had two pieces of silver and magic cream.

"Sold!" Boris said, pointing at a greedy looking man in the front. They exchanged a few private words as they worked out the details. Then, louder: "Excellent. You can inspect them when the gathering is over. We'll have them carted and ready for delivery by the end of the day."

Satisfied by these terms, Boris motioned to the Frostfire guards, and the Freetor slaves were paraded out the way them came in. The nobles seemed to breathe easier once they were gone.

They were gone and I had done nothing.

"Maybe your father will have some ideas about the slave crisis when you see him," she whispered. "He'll know what's happening. Maybe Mother and Monju will have some ideas, too. Maybe the Freetors have already planned something."

It was a lot of maybes. She was just trying to make me feel better. I peered over the crowd in front of me. As the merchant produced a felt bag filled with silver and dropped it in Boris's hands, another darker thought crossed my mind. One hundred twenty pieces of silver was a tidy sum. Occupying the city, feeding all of the soldiers, keeping the nobles in a lifestyle they were accustomed to—the costs added up. Perhaps the Frostfire coffers were not as full as we'd assumed.

Once the transaction was complete, Boris returned to his throne and whispered in his elderly father's ear. After a moment, Leszek cleared his throat. "Second order of business is the people's forum. We have a long list and we'll try to get through as many as we can today—"

A brief uproar from the wealthier merchants was quelled as two of the armed Frostfire guards stepped away from the wall, towards the crowd. They didn't draw their weapons or actively threaten, but the merchants, remembering the deeds these men had done in the name of their house, fell silent.

"As I said," Leszek said, his tone suddenly cold and sinister. "We have much to do. I'd like to get this over with. Wouldn't you?"

Murmurs of agreement rippled through the crowd.

"Very good. First name on the agenda is Cass Kades. From the merchant district. Step forward. I assume you're here?"

A well-dressed man with a long beard stepped forward and bowed deeply. "Thank you for hearing me today, Your Highness."

"What is your grievance for the court, Mr. Kades?"

"Well, ever since the arrival of the East and the North, my business has been—"

The large doors to our left burst open with a loud bang, startling many of the lesser nobles and merchants at the back of the room. As the crowd parted, the surprise spread throughout the room. Surrounded by four Frostfire men and two Northern shadows dressed in dark colours was my father. His expression bore no clue as to why he was here.

This wasn't part of the plan.

My throat tightened. He wouldn't be here, unless he'd found out something important about Keegan. Or something terrible had happened to the Freetors.

"Ferguson," Leszek said, rising to his feet. From the malice in his tone, he had met my father before, and this was not a pleasant reunion.

"What have you done?" I muttered.

"High King Leszek. Or *emperor*, now, as I'm told." My father bowed grandly. "Thank you for agreeing to an audience with me."

"I did no such thing," the Frostfire patriarch said bitterly. "You knew we were having a gathering. You always know the perfect time to...interrupt."

I glanced at Laoise. Her knuckles were white from gripping her dress. I gently touched the inside of her wrist. I couldn't have her appear afraid. Not when things were about to turn against us.

"In my time, gatherings were public affairs, not just for nobles and slave merchants," my father replied, adjusting his shirt cuffs pompously. "Although it's my understanding that more than just the banner colours have changed around here."

Just as I was plotting how to best cut down five guards and take on two Northern shadows with one knife and Laoise in a bulky dress, Lady Elizabeth—Liz—squeezed in between me and another servant girl. She was late to the gathering, but everyone was too captivated by my father's entrance to notice the tardiness of one young noblewoman.

"Seems like I arrived at a good moment," she whispered to me. "This is going to be interesting."

"Why?" I whispered.

Her eyes gleamed. "You don't know the story?"

Leszek and my father were trading barbs laced with pleasantries, but Leszek was tiring quickly. "Why has he been brought here? I have other pressing matters. Take him to the meeting room—I will deal with him after the kingdom business is complete."

"I'm afraid I have some pressing kingdom business for you," my father said. "You are without an Advisor. In the West, that is custom. I am here to offer my services."

Leszek gripped his belt and descended the dais. He was done mincing words. "And why would I trust a two-faced, murderous lech? You should have been imprisoned years ago for your brutality."

The lords and ladies murmured in shock. One hand gripped the dagger hidden in my apron pocket. The other was ready to grab the hilt in my boot.

The former Advisor seemed unaffected by Leszek's insult, though he did take a step forward, as if accepting a silent challenge. "I can accept that my loyalties are in question. I served the Tramore house for almost a decade. But I have served the realm my entire life. As an Advisor, I can make difficult decisions when rulers cannot. Or...will not."

Leszek's red face matched his cape. He pointed at the guards. "I am emperor. The only advisors in my court will be those related to me by blood—or those who have served with me in battle." He gestured to the Northern shadow killers, careful to pay them the proper respect.

"I'm afraid I'm not so good with a sword," my father replied humbly.

"And what of spears?"

Lady Dominique's voice rang clear in the crowded throne room. I hadn't seen her enter, yet she stood off to Boris's right, almost in shadow. Blood rushed to my cheeks. She saw my father at Driscoll's End. Had she recognized him? Worse: did she realize my relation to him? She'd spent very little time at the castle so far—and had barely left the North prior to the Freetors capturing her. Still, I knew better not to underestimate her ability to navigate the royal world and get results.

My father seemed just as unnerved by the question, though

he recovered quickly. "I prefer to use my words. My humble background did not allow for early lessons in the finer points of combat."

"Humble background. Interesting choice of words," Leszek said dryly.

My father bowed his head, though his show of respect was undercut by his smug smile. "We cannot all have royal blood. It is because of my common origins that the former residents of this castle entrusted me with important tasks. The overseeing of the day-to-day common problems is best left to a commoner, is it not?"

"No," Leszek said, over the low rumble of wealthier merchants in attendance. "Lock him up."

Cold fear blanketed my body. I wouldn't let anything happen to my father.

I prepared to step forward, touching Laoise's arm for strength. But my best friend was already ahead of me. Before I could stop her, she pushed ahead, elbowing a few small lords and senior servants to clear the way. She fell to her knees before the Frostfires.

"Your Graces," she said in Linnaea's high-pitched plea voice, "I am Lady Linnaea Gareth, betrothed to Leon Frostfire. Please, I ask for mercy for this man."

"Mercy?" Leszek boomed. "Explain yourself, girl."

I held my breath.

"Advisor Ivor Ferguson has been serving my father for over a fortnight and a half, since he fled the fire during the liberation," Laoise began.

"You admit to harbouring this criminal within your baile?" Leszek demanded.

"I admit that my father has made a mistake," Laoise replied tactfully. "My father should have reported Advisor Ferguson's whereabouts to the crown as soon as he was made aware of the

Advisor's presence. However, Your Graces, if I may say, the Advisor has been of the utmost help to my family during his stay. When your son, Lord Leon Frostfire, expressed interest in a marriage between our two houses, my father wavered in his resolve. He was unsure if our two houses should join. After all, the Gareths have always been loyal to the Tramore family, and my father is a traditional man, slow to change. It was Advisor Ferguson who convinced him that my marriage to your son would not only be best for my family, but for the good of the realm."

As Leszek and Boris spoke in hushed tones and the rest of the court digested Laoise's words, I struggled to withhold my delight. If they didn't believe Laoise's claim, they ran the risk of disrespecting the Gareth family—the very family they were trying to win over.

She glanced up at Leszek. "Please, Your Grace. Consider my plea for mercy, for the sake of both our houses."

Leon was staring at me, his gaze a single question. *Is this true?*

I nodded.

Leaping dramatically to his feet, Leon gestured to Laoise, still on her knees. "Father. My betrothed speaks truth—can you not hear the innocence in her voice? If he was harmless in Baile Gareth, what could he do here, in the castle, surrounded by our brave bannermen?" He grinned at the soldiers guarding each entrance, as if expecting applause. "If we cannot trust the word of my betrothed, who can we trust?"

Leszek sneered at his son. "Sit down, boy. Gareth girl, get up. Let me see your face."

Leon obeyed and Laoise climbed daintily to her feet, lifting her gaze to the patriarch of the Frostfire family. His gaze narrowed and he inspected her as if she were merchandise in a shopkeeper's window.

"While I see your intentions are noble, my lady, I do not recognize Ivor Ferguson's title here," Leszek said finally, leaning back in the throne. "He is a criminal and his previous crimes must be weighed before I pass a final judgment."

"He cannot be trusted," Boris chimed in, eager to echo his father. "It was known even in the East that Ivor Ferguson coveted the throne, as much as he coveted Eamon Tramore's staff."

"A conduit for the Violet Fox's Freetor magic," Leszek said.

"Filthy half-breed," Leon muttered, crossing his legs lazily.

"I did not know it had that ability," my father said calmly, ignoring Leon's barb. "My interest in Eamon Tramore's staff, and the orb it cradled, was scholarly."

"That is yet to be seen." Leszek stood again, renewed with a sinister confidence of a lion who has baited a sheep into his den. "Ivor Ferguson will not be imprisoned. At least, not yet. It is a treacherous journey down to the dungeon. One of our bannermen died last week navigating the tunnels. The Violet Fox left her fiery mark on this castle before kidnapping the Tramore boy." He shook his head. "Appoint him chambers, and keep him under guard. I will convene my council to discuss the charges against you and make a decision by week's end."

"Charges? What charges?" my father asked. "I have a right to know what I am—"

"You know your crimes." Leszek momentarily lost his cool as his fingers tightened around the armrest of his throne. "They are many and will be compiled and read aloud during your trial at week's end." He gestured to the guards at my father's side. "Take him."

The guards swiftly dragged my father out the western exit. He didn't protest: instead, he levelled a bitter, smug glare at Leszek. It was a look I knew well, for I'd worn it myself. I wondered if my father was thinking up some magic curse to throw on the Frostfire patriarch—if he had the power to do so.

But then they'd know for sure he was a Freetor, and he'd be giving up the secret he'd fought hard to keep for ten years.

Lady Dominique was unreadable. Whatever her plan, she was keeping it close to the chest, which was bad for us. Ultimately, though, she knew Laoise was only telling half-truths, and that made everything worse. If she told the Frostfires about my father's presence at Driscoll's End, that he was colluding with the Violet Fox...

Beside me, Liz was slipping away into the crowd. I put my thoughts of Dominique aside for the moment to concentrate on a more pressing concern. I caught her by the shoulder. "My lady. What do you know about Ivor Ferguson and Emperor Leszek?"

She seemed surprised by my rough conduct, but didn't resist me. "Apparently the Advisor—former Advisor, I mean—killed one of Emperor Leszek's servants years ago. She'd been imprisoned during a Gathering, because someone accused her of being a Freetor. You'd think that would be enough, but no. He killed her, in cold blood, under no one's authority but his own. I suppose that was the way. Is the way? All the Freetors I know here have been enslaved."

"Yes," I said, trying to keep my voice even. "Still, you'd think the former Advisor would have been admonished for taking such...initiative?"

"He was never proven guilty, but he was found standing in her blood, supposedly," she replied, shrugging. "Having the ear of the late Eamon Tramore had its advantages."

Evidently. "I didn't know that the former Advisor and the emperor had that history," I said tightly. "Thank you for telling me."

"Sure." She glanced at the Frostfires warily. "I shouldn't be seen talking with a servant. Have a nice afternoon."

"I understand. You too."

I didn't want to believe that my father would murder a fellow Freetor in cold blood. Yet he had sent many people to their deaths as the Advisor. He was the most hated man among our people for a reason. Everything he had done, he'd done to keep his position, hoping that he'd someday be able to make contact...

But he didn't make contact. Not even when Rordan was burning in the Grand Square.

Laoise quietly slipped to my side, dropping her voice. "Escort me back to my quarters. Quick. Before Leon Frostfire or someone else corners me."

I did a quick sweep of the dais. Dominique had disappeared, yet Boris, Leon, and Leszek remained. Leszek seemed to be deep in conversation with his two sons, but Leon kept glancing our way, eager to escape.

I gestured for Laoise to walk in front of me, and together we hurried for the eastern exit.

* * *

I crouched on the windowsill in Laoise's chambers, my heart deeply unsure of this plan, but eager for the adventure.

"I wish you had better shoes," Laoise said as she kept a safe distance from the sill. It was several storeys to the ground. A sharp breeze whipped around the castle.

The Frostfires had posted a guard outside of Laoise's chambers five minutes after we'd returned. It was unlikely he'd try to restrict her movements—she was still an honoured guest and the betrothed to Leon Frostfire—but even though I had free roam of the castle as a servant, I couldn't risk being followed. Not where I was going.

"I've done this before. I won't have to go far." I hoped, anyway. Just far enough down the hall where the posted guard wouldn't see me, and far enough to quickly search the rooms along this wing. Assuming I didn't tumble to my death in the process. And assuming none of the guards, servants, or slaves restoring the lower levels noticed a young woman traversing the exterior heights of the castle in the mid-afternoon. "I'm more worried about Leon visiting you."

"I can handle Leon. He already thinks you're Linnaea. He won't bother me here, unless it's to find you."

"Exactly what I'm afraid of. And Dominique?"

"She wouldn't dare harm me. Go. Get to your father. I can handle myself, you know."

I smiled. "I know. Your mother's not here, so someone has to express concern for you."

"I...appreciate it."

"All right. I'm going." I gripped the stone. I only had to go over a couple of windows to find an empty chamber. Laoise had helped me tie my skirt around my legs: it would be easier to quickly untie the twine than to explain why a handmaid was wearing trousers around the castle.

A rickety wooden ledge half the size of my foot was all I had to stand on: balance was one thing, but I'd have to wedge my fingers between the stones and ease myself along the exterior. If I failed—well, it was a long way down.

Laoise watched me go, steadying me for the first few uncertain steps. When she let go of my hand, my heart lurched, but I didn't fall. Breathe. I reached the next window, my fingers glad for the steady grip. I had to move quickly, in case the occupant noticed. Two more rooms to go and I'd be free.

As I made my slow journey, I couldn't help but think the worst. Perhaps the real Linnaea Gareth had died and now Laoise had to pretend to be her for good. Or maybe the Frostfire and Castillo forces were so strong that there was no hope for a successful slave rebellion.

I gripped the next stone. It wiggled, raining tiny pebbles into the bailey below. I gasped.

There were two guards patrolling beneath me.

Don't look up, don't look up. Some Freetor magic would really do me some good now.

I chose a sturdier stone to grip. I couldn't keep doing this. It was a stupid idea. The structural damage was too far gone. I'd have to climb inside the next room and take my chances in the corridors, like a regular servant.

The window to the next room was close. I could make it.

One stone. Steady.

Two stones. Wobbly—but it held.

Third stone—the window was right there. My fingers, black with dirt and white from exertion, slipped between the stones.

The stone gave way. I reached up and grabbed onto the window ledge. The falling stone hit my foot on its way down: I screamed.

"Who is...?"

I was really in trouble now.

Shakily, with great effort, I grabbed the ledge with my other hand and pulled myself up. A set of arms reached through the window to help me.

A lie flowed from my lips. "Uh...I'm just testing the structural integrity of the exterior for the captain of the guard, to see which parts need to—"

I looked up and into familiar eyes.

"Kiera," he said.

"You're here," I said, with disbelief.

I fell through the window, but my father was there to catch me. He wrapped his arms around me, drawing me deeper into the room and setting me on the floor. Being with him again, I felt a small measure of relief. He was alive. For now.

Which only made what I had to do next all the harder.

"Listen. I have a message from—"

"Did you murder a Freetor woman?" I blurted out.

Taken aback, his hands fell from me as he shifted his weight and stood. Confusion only clouded him momentarily: he was a clever man. He knew exactly what I was talking about.

"I suppose you deserve to know," he said quietly. "The servant's name was Sarysa. I did not murder her. I loved her."

My throat tightened. "What—what? You...?" I could barely associate the word love with him.

"You find that surprising." He smirked. His fingers stiffened into a fist. "Five, nearly six years ago, the Frostfires came here for Keegan's name-day celebration. Leszek and his wife, Florinda, made the journey with Lady Sylvia. Because of this, they brought along an assortment of servants, including Sarysa. Leszek was in love with her. Even with his wife around, he made bold moves of affection. Sarysa tolerated his advances, not wishing to bite the hand that fed her and her family.

"Even though I had lived as Ivor Ferguson for years, I feared my heritage would be discovered. I'd encountered her many times, knew that there was a connection between us—but I didn't want to take the risk. If she found out who I was, even by accident, Sarysa would be punished for sympathizing with a Freetor. Or accused of being a Freetor herself."

"You mean she wasn't a Freetor at all?"

"No," he replied. "I tried to resist my feelings for her, at first. She was much younger than I was. Yet as it turned out, she felt as I did. Over the course of a fortnight, we trysted several times."

I remembered what Mistress Alwina had said when I'd arrived at the castle—how Leszek suffered no servant girl trysting in secret. "Why does everyone believe you murdered her?"

"Eventually, through the web of whispering servants, our affair came to Leszek's attention. His rage simmered, and yet he could do nothing: he was a married man. My trysts with Sarysa were an ill-kept secret at best, certainly not a crime. Leszek threatened her, in private, to release her from his service and punish her family. As her family lived in the East, it would have been hard for me to protect them. She feared that once they were back on Eastern soil, he would kill or imprison her."

"Then why not marry her to keep her here?" I asked, unable to keep the disdain from my tone.

"You know why," he replied. "A speedy courtship, a hurried ceremony—I felt like I was losing control. I'd only known her a short time. If I'd married her, and she found out the truth about me? Western sympathy for Freetors was far more common. Easterners are far harsher. I couldn't trust her. Not completely. It tore me apart. But you know about that."

I'd gotten lucky with Keegan. "So what happened?"

"Two days before they were supposed to leave, Florinda found out about Leszek's illicit affections and the threats he had made against Sarysa. The Eastern High Queen imprisoned Sarysa. However, the girl had done nothing wrong: she couldn't justifiably keep her locked up without raising suspicion, certainly not in a province in which she was a visitor. Nor could she imprison or denounce her husband without losing her own status. That's why she spread the rumour that Sarysa was a Freetor in disguise. This justified Sarysa's imprisonment and made Leszek look like a dirty fool. No one questioned the High Queen. It is hard to prove you aren't a Freetor."

"So just like you did nothing to save Rordan, you left her to die in the dungeon."

"I did everything to save her!" he exclaimed. "I went to Eamon Tramore to plead for her. Yet the Holy One did not dare release her and defy the East's claims. The lie had taken hold. She would have been left to rot or executed, depending on Eamon Tramore's mood.

"That evening, when I went to her cell to free her, it was too late. Leszek stood over her body. He'd dismissed the guards, so it was my word against his. As Sarysa was a servant, and

Leszek a king, the matter was dropped," he said. He delivered the words dispassionately, as if he'd recited them thousands of times. "The incident bolstered my anti-Freetor image. This, in turn, secured my position as a surface-born Marlenian."

I shivered. I didn't know what to say. "There must be some way to make Leszek pay for his crimes."

"There will be time for that later," my father said, a dark expression momentarily overtaking him. "But if I don't deliver the message from Bidelia now, our whole mission is in jeopardy. Getting Keegan back is the priority. Not a five-year-old tragedy."

Why did my father have to do this to me? I could never just be a daughter with him. He wouldn't meet my gaze; perhaps he regretted being so open with me. I knew so little of his time on the surface that I wanted to collect every scrap, no matter how morbid—especially if it proved him to be the good man I saw inside. "What's the message?"

"No need to be bitter. It's good news. Of a sort. Bidelia has made contact with the remaining Freetors and the fledgling apprentices. It was not easy."

I sensed a but coming on. "What happened?"

He crossed the room to the bed. "They don't believe you're alive. They require proof. Your presence should suffice."

"Let me guess. Without seeing my face, they won't help us. I suppose that's easily done." I ran a hand through my tangled hair. "That's the message? That's what you risked your life coming here for?"

"Once you're in the Undercity, you are to work with Bidelia to formulate a plan of attack to retake the castle."

"Retake the castle? What about finding Keegan? I thought he was the priority!"

"Calm yourself. Of course he's the priority. But since we're arguing, I suspect you haven't sussed out his location yet."

"I've only been here a day."

"And the Violet Fox would have found him in twelve hours if she really put her mind to it."

I was starting to see red. "I'm just one girl, sneaking around the castle, wearing another person's face and name, trying not to get murdered by fanatics and Northern shadow killers!"

"I know. But the city is far worse than I had imagined. Food shortages. Civil unrest. Half the businesses in the merchant district have closed, but they aren't allowed to leave. They've shut the gates. No one is leaving the city, Kiera, unless it's via the underground."

My stomach turned. "You're saying the people might rebel?"

"If we don't remove Leszek from the throne, they will."

"We have to help them. You should have seen the slaves—"

"Kiera," he said, cutting me off. "You're right that we have to help them. We help them by removing Leszek quietly and quickly. If a mob tries to storm the castle..."

He didn't have to finish his thought. The mountain castle was a fortress. "The Frostfires will not hesitate to kill them all."

Relieved, my father nodded. "Bidelia knows the particulars, but we believe a small team could infiltrate the castle and take care of Leszek and the other Frostfires. Capture them, preferably—but it doesn't matter. Once they're gone, there will be a power vacuum. One that you can fill."

My head spun. "You're talking about installing me as queen."

"Yes. Then we don't have to search every corner of the castle by night. We can find Keegan, find the Emerald Cloth, far more quickly. But, to do that, you need to get out of the castle before the cream I gave you wears off and get to Bidelia. She'll be waiting for you on Selby Street to take you to the Undercity before dawn. Be there."

I paced the room, trying to poke holes in my father's plan. The part of me that yearned for adventure wanted to lead the rebels now and save the day—save my people. I stopped short.

"What about Linnaea? Were you able to track her down?"

"Once we have the castle, we can deal with the Gareth family."

"What if it doesn't work? A small team is nothing compared to the Northern shadows. The more time we waste retaking the castle, the more likely more people will fall under the frozen curse. It's already being used as a weapon." I quickly told him about my encounter with Lady Milda.

My father paled. "Then it's as I feared and we have to act quickly. If we control the castle, we can control the people."

"It's all about the power with you, isn't it?"

"No, Kiera, I want to—"

The sound of a woman's voice and the shifting of the guard armour outside the door sent us both into a flurry of action—in different directions. I rushed for the two-door wardrobe, just as he pointed beneath the bed, light blue magic dancing between his fingers.

As I drew the wardrobe doors closed, the chamber door flew open, banging against the wall like the crack of a whip. Loud boots scuffed on the gritty floor as they walked with purpose into the room. I pulled my knees up to my chin, and even though it was dark, I closed my eyes, as if it would shroud me in even more darkness.

"Lady Dominique Castillo," my father said in his most charming voice. "I don't believe we've been formally introduced. I heard you were replaced by the infamous Violet Fox. My condolences—"

"I have no y'use pour pleasantries, esnake," she said thickly. "J'ou y'are not sorry, just as truly as j'ou wield vile magics."

Eight

It was hopeless to think she'd forgotten—or would fail to recognize—the Advisor at Driscoll's End.

"J'ou y'are a Freetor," she said. "And on dat false Freetor queen's side. Which means j'ou deserve to have j'our tongue ripped out."

"And yet, here I am, tongue intact. You recognized me in the throne room, and you said nothing, which means you want me alive."

"Do not mistake me. I have no use pour j'our games. I y'am givin' j'ou dis one chance only, now, to tell me what plans j'ou have set in motion."

"I am only here to offer my services to your future father-in-law."

"D'emperor has no y'use pour de Freetor magics. J'ou saved her, didn't j'ou. Y'and she y'is here."

My father was silent. I held my breath.

"Y'it was my mistake, not to stay until death took her."

She ventured closer to the wardrobe. I bit hard into my lip. She was going to find me.

"Freetor magic is powerful," my father said quietly. "And yet, it wasn't enough."

No, it wasn't. I reached for my dagger, removing it from its place in my boot. When she opened the door, Dominique would be in for a sharp, nasty surprise.

"Liar." Dominique gripped the handle of the wardrobe. A sliver of light invaded my space.

I prepared to lunge.

"And she y'is—"

The wardrobe opened just enough, but a loud explosion tore away Dominique's attention. I nearly dropped the knife. She released the wardrobe door in shock and it stayed open long enough for me to see the fireball engulf the bed before the doors fell shut with a bang.

"If you think you're the only one who can order this castle up in flames, you are mistaken," he said coldly.

"Guards!" Dominique shouted.

I pressed as far as I could against the back of the wardrobe as the soldiers burst into the room. I feared what I couldn't hear—a Northern shadow—for surely Dominique would not trust only regular men, no matter whose banner they wore, to guard the elusive Ivor Ferguson.

The crackling of the burning bed punctuated Dominique's accusation: "Lock up dis traitor. He has vile magics!"

"Come close," my father warned, "and I will do to you what I have done to this bed."

"Refuse, and the Fox, wherever she y'is, will die."

I could hear my father's smile. "You'll have to find her first. Maybe you should start at Driscoll's End, where I buried her."

"Strange dat a man as powerful as j'ou would stop to bury a Freetor rat."

"If you think that strange, then love must remain an elusive mystery to you as well."

The sounds of battle erupted with my heart. I gripped the dagger tightly. It was all I had wanted, to hear him say that he cared. If I jumped out of the wardrobe, I could join the fray and help my father. My false face was still intact; I still had several hours before I'd have to reapply the cream. Yet somehow I knew she'd know me if I lunged for her—she'd know from the anger in my eyes that I was the Violet Fox, and that I'd do anything to prevent my father from leaving me again.

The struggling seized as the smoke grew thicker. I covered my mouth, and in my mind, I was back on that balcony, watching my brother die as the flames engulfed him. How could my father do this?

Dominique coughed. "Take him to de dungeons."

I heard multiple men drag my father across the room towards the door.

"Tell Leszek he should come visit me in my cell," he quipped.

"I will tell not'in'," she replied. Her voice drifted towards the door, briefly muffled. "Only I carry de key to j'our cell, and de guards, dey are mine, shadows dat obey only me. J'our execution will be early mornin'. J'our plan, whatever it is, will fail. And j'our magics, dey will die wit' j'ou."

I couldn't let her take him away from me. Not now.

My father's voice, like magic, stopped me from revealing myself. "I'm not the only one who possesses magic."

The heavy pause from Dominique made her displeasure palatable, even in the dark. Then: "Keep his hands tied behind him. Watch him. Put out dis fire before y'it spreads," Dominique ordered. "And den search de castle. De Violet Fox is here. I know it."

A chorus of guards replied urgently with "Yes, my lady" as they set about their assigned tasks. I heard them take my father from the room, my heartbeat pounding in time with their heavy footfalls.

A sharp breeze combatted the smoke. The window was still open. My escape.

I undid the twine binding my dress and pulled the fabric up to cover my face. I had a minute, maybe less, before I'd be forced from the wardrobe. Less than that before my coughing would reveal my position.

Keegan, cursed. My father, captured. Laoise, in danger.

If I waited to contact Bidelia and the Freetors to help, it would be too late.

I had to warn Laoise.

***

I seized the opportunity to leave through the window, and shimmied my way across to the nearest window, escaping down the corridors and heading back to Laoise's chamber.

The guard was no longer posted at her door. A small victory. Without bothering to knock or announce myself, I threw open the door and burst in. "We have a problem, La—"

Two surprised faces met mine: Laoise's, and Dominique's. I averted my gaze downwards as Dominique erupted into anger. "How dare j'ou show disrespect to j'our lady by charging in—?"

Laoise tried to calm her. "It's all right, my lady. My handmaid becomes overexcited in times of crisis."

"Crisis." Dominique hissed the word, like it was her enemy. Her gaze narrowed and her nostrils flared as she advanced towards me. "J'ou smell like smoke."

"I heard there was a fire, my lady. I rushed to the commotion, fearful for the Lady Linnaea's life!" I looked desperately to Laoise. "I'd heard stories of the previous fire. How it destroyed so much...it's only a few chambers down. I hope the smoke doesn't ruin your nice clothes."

"Thank you, Rorda. Your...concern is appreciated but unwarranted," Laoise said, nodding in Linnaea's nervous way. "Lady Dominique informed me that her men have created a contained, controlled fire, to test the durability of a new Northern fabric."

"Oh. I see." I bowed my head. What a rubbish excuse. I conjured the memory of Dominique nearly discovering me in the wardrobe to redden my cheeks. The flightier I appeared the better. "Please accept my sincerest apologies, my ladies."

"Of course," Laoise said.

Dominique shook her head, disgusted. "J'our kindness is a front." Then, suddenly, she gripped my chin, forcing me to look at her. "Cross my path again and j'ou will regret it."

I glanced up at her; it had been a long time since I'd been this close. I noted the cord around her neck, which disappeared beneath the collar of her dress; the intensity of her gaze as it bore into mine. She was searching for something in it. Probably for me. I wondered how I looked to her: if she saw a similar face staring back. The face of a murderer, a liar, a thief.

I had to stop her from killing my father.

Satisfied she had thoroughly intimidated me, she headed for the door and didn't look back. "I'll see j'ou tonight, Lady Linnaea."

Laoise and I stood in terse silence for a long moment, holding each other's terrified gazes long after Dominique's footfalls fell silent.

"My father set the fire," I said, my voice a whisper. "I hid. Dominique saw everything. She has him. She's going to kill him at dawn."

My best friend's face paled further, though she took the news in stride. "She came to me just moments ago. I was terrified—I thought she was here to arrest me. I think she was here to see if I was you."

"She'll tear the castle apart until she finds me."

Laoise blew out a controlled, slow sigh. "That's only one of our problems. I keep worrying the real Lady Linnaea will show up."

Dominique had burst into the cathedral during Keegan's marriage ceremony to proclaim that I was an imposter. "I doubt the real Lady Linnaea would show her face in Marlenia City after running off with the Extremists. She's made her choice—true love."

In spite of herself, she smiled. "It's a nice choice to have."

"You'll have it too," I said, thinking of Monju. When could I tell her about his kiss? The stakes were too high now.

The moment passed and Laoise cleared her throat, regaining her composure. "Did you find out why your father risked his life to come here?"

Details of our parents' sketched-out plan and my conversation with him tumbled out of me as I sat down on the bed. "Retaking the castle...it seems like an insurmountable task. I feel like Keegan is so close. I only have enough cream to last to tomorrow morning. What if this plan to infiltrate the castle takes me too long and more people are frozen?"

Her cool, calm exterior melted away. "I agree with you about this plan. I'm sure Mother has it figured out with the remaining Freetors, but it's still incredibly risky. How are we supposed to hold the castle once we take it? We are making inroads here. Keegan is here. We have to focus our efforts!"

"I know!" I paced, biting down hard on my lip. "If I'm exposed, you can't let on."

"If something happens—which it won't," Laoise said, "I'm not going to let you rot in some cell."

"That's exactly what you have to do. If I die, you have to continue on the mission. Just like old times. It's what I did for Rordan. And I ask you to do it for me."

Laoise took my hand. "I know you feel guilty that you couldn't save him."

I took a deep breath. "If I'm captured, or killed, you have to find a way to rescue Keegan and depose the East. You won't be alone. You'll have Monju and your mother and the Freetors. If it helps to take up the mantle of the Violet Fox...do it. Do whatever is necessary to make sure our people are safe."

"I will, Kiera. You can trust me."

I nodded as my throat tightened. I wasn't very good at expressing my emotions. Besides anger, that one was easy. I'd been so angry for so long: angry at my father for leaving, angry at the Marlenians for what they did to my people, angry at myself for never doing enough. She returned my smile, her red-rimmed eyes mirroring mine. That was the nice thing about our friendship. We didn't have to say anything at all. With everything we'd been through, we were sisters. I would protect Laoise for as long as I drew breath, and she would do the same for me—for our people.

"There's something else," I said finally against my tightening throat. "My father told me that he was...in love with...a servant falsely accused of being a Freetor, and Leszek killed her."

This disquieted Laoise. "Both of them have sent many Freetors to their deaths."

"Yes. But this was personal." I swallowed the lump in my throat. If he'd managed to free her, how would things be different? Would my brother still be alive? "I don't know what to think about him."

Laoise sat beside me on the bed, not saying anything for a long time. "I'm going to suggest something. Don't get mad. But...but what if we...didn't save him tonight."

I heard the words. They settled on my heart like the snow in the mountains at Driscoll's End, but they weren't cold. They tasted sweet. The guilt of eating something decadent settled in.

"I can't unhear his exchange with Dominique. He could have blasted through them all with his fire. Instead, he used it to save me. To say that he loved me." My fingers curled around the bedspread. "I've waited a long time for that."

"I know." She folded her hands on her lap without judgement. "It's not my decision. He's not my father, but I've spent enough time around him these past few weeks. I know he cares for you. Maybe Keegan, too, from what you've told me. I just don't want him to hurt you."

I wiped away a silent tear. "I wish he hadn't hurt anyone, never mind me."

She exhaled slowly. "This means you're going to sacrifice your last night in the castle saving him instead of locating Keegan, doesn't it?"

"At least Keegan is asleep. If the Frostfires haven't disposed of him now—and if what I saw last night is true, they haven't—we can rest assured he's safe." Safe as a pawn in a scheme to eliminate political enemies. I hated putting my search for Keegan on hold just to rescue my father. I hated trying to sort out my feelings for him even more. "And if I don't save my father, then what kind of person does that make me?"

"A good person," Laoise said, half-smiling. "The Violet Fox does what is right for the people."

I wasn't sure if saving my father was in the best interests of the Marlenian people, but he was the one person who had knowledge on how to save Keegan and the others from the sleeping curse. If not because I was his daughter, I could save him for that reason alone.

"We only have a few hours before I have to go to dinner," Laoise continued, standing up.

"And until morning before Dominique executes my father." Unless her anger spurred her to make good on her threat before then. Not enough time to tell the Freetors to strike before that— not that they would, without evidence that I was still alive. "I don't want to go against Dominique and lose."

"I know. Can you think of anything she might have said to your father that we could use?"

I told her everything I could remember about their conversation. "She's keeping him in the dungeon. Guarded by shadows. Who knows how many. Even with Monju on our side, it would take a good many more Freetors to defeat them. Last time I fought shadows, I almost lost my arm." Keegan and I had barely escaped with our lives.

"There must be a way that doesn't involve fighting. If only Lady Linnaea were more influential. If only Dominique was more receptive, I could befriend her."

"There's not enough time." An idea struck me then. "The key. Dominique said that only she would hold the key to my father's cell, to ensure his continued imprisonment until morning. What if we could steal it?"

"She was wearing a cord around her neck," Laoise said, her eyes glimmering with the beginnings of a scheme. "But it disappeared under her shift. How could we possibly hope to steal it right out from under her nose?"

"You're the one going to dinner with her. Maybe you could spill something on her, and then she'd have to go change...."

"Ladies don't often get dressed without servants to help them. I've seen a handmaid come and go from her chambers."

"So you will spill a drink on her, and I'll be ready near her chambers to help her change."

Laoise wasn't convinced. "She's no ordinary noblewoman. She's tough. She already suspects you're alive. She might not allow a foreign servant to help her."

"Right. If that doesn't work, we could always try to steal it during the night. When she's sleeping." I grinned at the thought of her trying to fight me off in only a nightdress.

"It's a start. Any opening, I'll take the opportunity."

"As long as it doesn't compromise your position as Lady Linnaea." I crossed my arms, regarding Laoise's long dress, and then my ratty rags. "I'll try to volunteer for the dinner as a servant and help any way I can."

"It's a plan." She held out her hand, and I took it. "Just like old times."

* * *

Going to Mistress Alwina and asking permission to serve drinks at a private dinner for the nobles seemed the best way to draw her ire and suspicion, so instead of returning to my bunk in the servant dorm, I headed directly for the castle kitchens, clutching my skirts and fearing the worst.

At least thirty men rushed about in five different areas of the kitchen, chopping vegetables, kneading dough, boiling broth, tending fires, and off in another room, two men roasted meat on a spit, and in another still, two men handled pastries.

Despite the busy chaos, the head chef, a burly Eastern man, picked me out right away as I stood in the entrance, observing the activity I had rarely witnessed during my stay in the castle. He was directing the creation of some salads from carrots, leafy greens, and some purple vegetables I didn't recognize. He waved me over. My stomach pained, but I kept my thieving hands to myself.

"My name is Rorda," I said. "I am Lady Linnaea's handmaid."

"I'm aware of who you are. What does your lady require? We're in the middle of preparations. Not to mention the ration decree."

I blinked and couldn't help but eye the gallons of vegetables, meat, and pastries throughout the kitchen. "The...ration decree?"

A few of the men exchanged looks with the chef. "Yeah," the chef said, narrowing his gaze. "The Mistress didn't mention it this afternoon? She said she would. The whole no-snacks-for-royals, that?"

"Oh. That. Right. No, that's not what I'm here about." My heart and my father's words pounded in my ears. "I'm here because my lady has asked me to assist in the kitchen, in preparation for the private dinner tonight in her honour."

He scoffed, and the men chopping vegetables stifled their laughter. "She asked you to assist us, did she? What are you, her liege?"

"She—" I realized my error immediately as I turned beet red. "She told me that I should assist, yes."

"Well then," he said, looking me over as the snickering in the background died down. "You look strong enough. We need more water. Fetch some from the stables. Keep filling the copper. We're making soup for the main supper, but your lady and the other young nobles get to enjoy the hunter's spoils."

Fetching water? Again? This wasn't what I wanted. But at least I was in. Most or all of these servants were loyal to the Frostfires or the Castillos—and I wasn't familiar with the serving customs of the North or the East.

"Oh, and don't think this earns Lady Linnaea of the Forest extra greens on her plate or extra silver for your pocket," the chef said. "Now find a bucket, and start hauling."

The amount of food in the kitchen was truly mind-boggling. The East must have been squeezing their coffers for silver just to import all this food into Marlenia City. Especially with what was on the menu for the private dinner: desert boar—a delicacy enjoyed by Eastern nobles—fresh fish imported from the South, and an array of deargrotberry pies—a special berry that grew in the harsh climate of the North.

Food was a sign of wealth, and despite the frozen plague terrorizing the Marlenian people, the Frostfires wanted to assure themselves and their noble friends that everything was fine—now that they were in control.

I spent hours going to and from the well with three other female servants who preferred to do their work and make little conversation. As the kitchen was on the ground level and had its own entrance via the meat room, I couldn't wander off and retrace the steps the Northerners took with the coffin. I did, however, eye each crate and box as I strolled through the multiple rooms of the kitchen. None of them were big enough to fit a person—at least, not one lying perfectly flat.

I caught snippets of conversation during my rounds, confirming my father's words:

The chef: "Say goodbye to goat's milk, unless my friend Josef on the city wall can get his hands on some or they open up the gates again."

From a fellow servant carrying water: "I heard they're rounding up poor families in the merchant district and searching homes for Freetor sympathizers. That Violet Fox girl has the Daughter of the North in a frenzy."

The sun had begun its descent and my arms burned from the labour, but when I noticed two male servants bringing bottles of wine from the cellar, I saw my chance. The chef didn't object when he called for volunteers to serve the wine, and neither did the rest of the staff, for each were too consumed with their particular duties to cross the handmaid of their lord's future wife. Serving wine ensured I'd have a steady job throughout the evening. I wasn't about to leave Laoise alone, not longer than I had to. I took the cart stacked with bottles of whiteberry wine and wheeled it to the servant staircase.

"Oh, let me help with that," said a familiar voice as Emmine appeared at my side.

I couldn't hide my surprise. "I didn't know you had kitchen duty tonight."

"I didn't. But once the Mistress found out you were serving down here, she said she enjoyed the idea of us Westerners serving the East and now I'm here." She lowered her voice further as we struggled to carry and navigate the cart up the stairs. "Where were you this afternoon?"

"With my lady," I replied, trying to concentrate on angling

the cart so it wouldn't get stuck in the curve of the spiralling stairs. "She had me running errands for her all morning."

"Lucky," she replied. "Do you think she'd take me on? I don't have any experience being the handmaid of a noble...but I'm a fast learner."

"I'll...mention it to her." I thought of Lady Elizabeth and wondered if she had handmaids.

"You know, the mistress was steaming that you weren't in the dorm this afternoon. Not that we can know when she'll come. She burst in, told us all about this new ration decree, and then stripped us of an entire meal."

"I'm sorry," I said.

She made a face. "Why?"

"Because—" Because I'm leaving the castle tonight, and soon these terrible people are going to pay for what they have done. "Because it's not right."

"It's war," Emmine said, though we both knew those were the mistress's words, not our own.

"It's not war," I said quietly, bringing the cart to level ground. "It's a slaughter."

Emmine averted her gaze and didn't argue the point. "I'll get the wine."

The dinner was on the balcony, overlooking the hedge maze, the stable, and the great plains beyond where I had made my journey over a fortnight ago. As Emmine and I escorted the wine cart onto the stone, a gentle, cool breeze whipped our hair. The last time I'd stepped foot here, I'd told Keegan about my desire to find the Silver Spear. It seemed so long ago—had that person really been me?

Candelabras surrounded the railings as not only servants, but slaves, prepared the balcony for the private feast. I tried not to stare at the garish branding on their faces. Slaves were not allowed to touch the food, nor were they allowed to handle silverware, but they did set up the tables and chairs on the balcony: one large table for dining with a pristine, white tablecloth and several smaller, similarly dressed tables a few stone-throws away to set wine, water jugs, and other dishes upon.

"Did you hear what I said?" Emmine asked.

I cleared my throat. "No, sorry."

"Chef said the nobles will be arriving soon. He's already sent runners. Probably sent one to Lady Linnaea as well, but if you wanted to go see her, in case..."

I frowned, suddenly noticing the multiple place-settings. My stomach sank as I realized it was not as private of an affair as I'd first thought. At least two more people would be joining Laoise, besides Sylvia and Dominique.

Would Leon be here too? I couldn't let him see us together. Not with all this wine here. If his tongue became too loose...

I turned to agree with Emmine and was about to make a hurried exit when Sylvia, Dominique, and Laoise, all dressed in their finest, walked onto the balcony. I side-stepped beneath the awning, bowing my head in shadow, yet the three of them chatted away. Laoise looked nervous, but laughed amicably with Sylvia, their arms linked. Good. She'd managed to get dressed and earn Sylvia's friendship. Dominique looked well for once: her hair had been tamed into an updo and threaded with a fresh gelschon, a flower that grew in the Eastern deserts. Although she walked alongside Laoise and Sylvia, she seemed to be barely tolerating their display of friendship.

The cord holding my father's fate rested around her neck, ripe for plucking.

As the three ladies made their way to their seats, the slaves scattered and left the balcony. The remaining servants, save Emmine and I, also left to retrieve the first course. Dominique and Sylvia sat next to each other, and Laoise across from Sylvia. My nerves danced.

Emmine regarded me suspiciously and lowered her voice. "Why are you hiding?"

I looked at her sharply. "I'm not."

"You practically ducked out of the way when they came in." She glanced at the table. "Is Lady Linnaea mad at you for what happened yesterday?"

Yesterday. It seemed so long ago. "You mean with Lady Elizabeth? No."

She looked like she didn't believe me. "C'mon," she said, gesturing to me. "We have to start. With the wine."

"Oh. Right."

We rolled the cart to one of the small tables and began uncorking. Emmine, far more confident than either of us felt, approached Sylvia and asked for her preference, and served her a glass of white at the table. Even with Laoise's attention, Sylvia seemed distracted. She said little, allowing Laoise to carry the conversation, taking occasional sips from her wine glass, and staring out into the darkness over the balcony.

Here was my opening. As Emmine served Laoise, I gripped the fresh bluesberry wine and steadied my voice as I approached her left side. "Blue wine for you, my lady?" I asked Dominique.

Dominique sat to Sylvia's right. I'd spill just enough to get it on Dominique, and only Dominique. Just as I tipped the bottle and reached for her glass, Dominique waved me away. "No, tank j'ou."

I righted the bottle immediately, surprised by her refusal. "White, then, my lady?"

Her brows knitted together. She was getting annoyed. "I said no. Serve de y'others."

I glanced at Laoise, but she was concocting a story for Sylvia about Linnaea's childhood, possibly a lie. "Of course, my lady." I'd have to find another way to spill wine on Dominique.

As two Eastern servants arrived with the first course—soup—the two Frostfire brothers appeared. I hoped beyond hope that Leon would not notice me as I huddled next to Emmine, yet of course, as soon as he saw the wine cart, his face lit up. He probably saw it as some kind of sign. Emmine promptly poured Boris a glass of white, giving Leon a wide berth and me a look that said, you can deal with him.

Boris settled at the head of the table. He wore Keegan's silver crown and a ring on each finger. There was no one at the other end of the table: this was him holding court, a reminder that he was the eldest, and the heir to the throne of the world. To his left sat Dominique. Boris attempted to start a conversation with her, but her responses were curt and simple: this was not where she wanted to be.

As I prepared water for both of them, Leon leisurely took his seat next to Laoise. He gave her a warm smile and a wink, and then wasted no time revealing the bottle of bluesberry wine he'd brought from his private stash. He plunked it down between him and Linnaea like a trophy.

"We have wine here," Dominique said, raising a disapproving brow.

"Yes, and where's the fun in that?" Leon said, ignoring her sour tone. "Some of us have more refined palettes."

"A little too refined at times," Boris said, smiling good-naturedly.

Leon missed the jape entirely. "It's a gift for my bride-to-be that we can all share." He nodded at Laoise. He had the face of a man who could not keep a secret.

"That's very generous, I'd love to try some," Laoise said, and then to me: "Could we all get an extra glass?"

"None for me," Dominique said.

"Are you sure?" Laoise pressed. She made a show of looking at the label while Emmine and I distributed extra glasses. "Sarysa Vintage. Bottle four of twenty-two. Three years old? I don't know much about wine, but—"

"Oh, you'll learn," Leon said, looking at me instead of Laoise.

My ears burned at the name. Sarysa. The servant my father and Leszek had loved.

Sylvia paled, her gaze enraptured by the label. "I didn't realize Father had a batch with that name."

"Sure, why not? It's a good name," Leon replied, oblivious.

"It's just familiar, is all." Sylvia curled her hands neatly on her lap as if to prevent fidgeting.

A cold shiver overtook me. Did Sylvia know about her father's murderous past? Or was she simply perturbed at the idea of her father naming a wine after one of her former servants?

Boris shot his sister a warning look. She acquiesced to whatever silent order he communicated, averting her gaze to the extra wine glass before her. Then, to Dominique, Boris said: "Wine for you?"

"I will not indulge tonight," Dominique insisted, her voice laced with a warning as she gripped her empty wine glass by the stem and set it pointedly aside. "I have more to do wit' my evenin' dan just sit and drink de night away."

More to do? Did that mean Dominique planned to carry out my father's execution tonight, rather than in the morning?

Laoise and I shared a hopeless look as I finished placing the glasses. I canted my head slightly towards Leon's wine. One of us could spill it, as it was already on the table. She innocently leaned towards Leon to inspect his gift once more, brushing the gold and silver lettering with a delicate hand. I steadied myself on the wine cart, yet my quivering hand only made the bottles rattle.

"You," Leon said, thrusting a commanding finger in my direction. "Pour this for us."

I smiled, which Leon mistook as a signal of our shared secret. I picked up the corkscrew from the cart, brandishing it like a weapon between my fingers as I rounded the table. If Dominique did not plan on making this dinner last, then Laoise and I had less time than we thought to retrieve the key.

Despite my best efforts to set the past aside, my mind continued to ruminate on the five-year-old crime as I stood between Leon and Laoise and uncorked the wine. My grip felt slick on the bottle. The only remnant of the young woman's existence, a kind of trophy Leszek could flaunt and consume whenever he chose.

I cast a desperate look at Leon. How many other vintages did Leszek have hidden away in his wine cellar? How many others had my father loved and failed to save?

As I poured Sarysa into Leon's bottomless glass, he gripped the hem of my skirts. He dared not touch me directly—that would be a breach of protocol—but he could show me that he knew who his wife was truly going to be, regardless that my hems were filthy from a day's hard work.

Laoise stiffened. The rest of the table might not have noticed Leon's boldness, but the two of us did.

"Relax," I whispered as I poured wine into her glass.

Her brief, fleeting gaze replied: *I can't.*

I wrenched my skirts from Leon's grip and threw him a threatening look. He looked more than pleased with my reaction.

I went around the table with Leon's wine. Boris had a dribble and Sylvia consented to half a glass, though she seemed to regret it. I glanced at Dominique. She was focussed on Leon, who was making a show of explaining the vintage to Laoise, but glancing at me every three seconds to see if I was listening too.

"Yes, only twenty-two bottles of this particular wine were ever made. My father was extremely particular about that. I've helped myself to a few. It's the finest we've ever produced. I could swipe another, if you find it to your liking."

The idiot was going to get us all killed.

Standing between Sylvia and Dominique, I rested the wine bottle on the lip of the glass and poured. When it was half-full, I pulled the bottle away too fast, destabilizing the glass, spilling Sylvia's wine. In mock shock, I recoiled, ensuring that I angled the direction of the bottle towards Dominique. The blue wine splattered on the white tablecloth—and splashed onto Dominique's chest.

Dominique leapt to her feet. "J'ou clumsy—"

"I'm so sorry," I said hastily, drawing back further from the table and holding the bottle as a shield.

Leon stood as well and anger flooded his face. "My wine! Father will be furious if he knows I—"

Her hands balled into fists, Dominique was about to dole Northern justice upon me when Boris caught her by the underarm. "It was an accident. Let's not let it ruin the evening."

Her off-white dress absorbed the blue and created an ugly stain on the front. Yet she seemed unconcerned. Her gaze narrowed at me, as it had earlier in Laoise's chambers, as if she was trying to place me.

The cream. It was going to wear off soon. I didn't have enough for another coat.

"I can fetch a new tablecloth, my lady," Emmine piped up, suddenly at my side. She wrenched the bottle from my hands with a curious look.

"J'es," Dominique said, slowly turning back to the table.

As Emmine disappeared to carry out the task, Laoise and Sylvia used their napkins to dab at the stains on the table. I grabbed more napkins to help. "Would you feel more comfortable if you went and changed?" Laoise asked Dominique hesitantly.

"Would dat make j'ou feel more comfortable?" Dominique retorted. More wine dripped from the soaked tablecloth onto her dress as she returned to her seat, yet she took no notice. She levelled Laoise with a stare that made even me uncomfortable.

"Of course not, I only suggested it because...because I know it would embarrass me, if I were you." Laoise's face reddened as she looked to Leon and Sylvia for support.

"I do not get embarrassed by such trivial matters. I y'am fine," Dominique said. She grabbed her half-soaked napkin and laid it across her lap. "I y'am goin' nowhere. But dat servant"— she looked over her shoulder at me—"will not be allowed to serve me or Sylvia pour de duration of dis meal."

I averted my gaze to the stone as I took away the soaked napkins to one of the side tables. "Yes, my lady."

Emmine returned a few minutes later with fresh linens and together we quickly reset the table. As Laoise and the nobles finished their soup, Emmine pulled me aside to the balcony railing as we folded the soiled table cloth to place beneath the wine cart for later laundering.

"What were you thinking?" she hissed.

"It was an accident," I replied, glancing at Laoise. She appeared to be enjoying the soup. I hoped she ate plenty—it might be the last stable meal she'd have in a while.

"It was sloppy. Mistress Alwina will hear about this. We'll both get in trouble."

I hadn't thought of that. "I'm sorry."

"Don't make this worse for me." Emmine looked grim. "I'm trying to make a good impression on them. I need their good graces if I'm going to survive this Eastern climate."

Nodding, I bit back any further excuses. I'd have to wait for another opening to take Dominique's key—because if she was to be believed, we might not get a chance to take it while she slept.

While the men prepared the food in the kitchen, the women served it to the nobles. Emmine poured wine and I kept the waters refreshed for Boris, Leon, and Laoise. Two Eastern servants brought bowls of fresh beans and corn while two

Northern girls together carried the main course: boar meat cut and arranged neatly around the head of the beast. With its snout positioned upright to the sky, the slain animal was a fierce reminder of the power the Frostfires wielded at the table. One of the Marlenian servants served the meat on a plate, pre-cut in the kitchen: it seemed the Frostfires didn't even trust their servers with knives this close to the nobles.

With the main event served, Boris raised his wine glass. "To my soon-to-be sister, the esteemed Lady Linnaea of Baile Gareth. May our relationship be a prosperous one."

"Oh. That's very kind, Lord Boris," Laoise said, blushing. She raised her glass. "Thank you."

Sylvia and Leon raised their glasses, beaming, while Dominique raised her water tumbler. As the nobles clinked their glasses and expressed their pleasantries towards "Linnaea," Leon gave me a small smile and tipped me his glass.

I looked away. This night couldn't end fast enough.

After taking a generous sip, Boris set his glass down. "If you are to be my sister, Linnaea, we needn't waste time with formalities. Boris is fine. We are equals, you know."

"Oh. Of course. Boris." She smiled, blushing again as Linnaea would.

Sylvia grinned, her prior melancholy surrounding Sarysa forgotten. For the first time since she'd began aggressively chasing Keegan two months ago, she appeared truly happy. Even Boris seemed in good spirits now, and not just because of the elaborate display of food and wine. They were pleased with Laoise. Pleased that they were getting their hands on valuable Western land. Leon, now on his third glass of wine, even seemed to be taking a shine to Laoise, showering her with compliments at every opportunity.

"Forgive me, I'm not used to supping with such esteemed company," Laoise continued.

"There's nothing to forgive. You're among family now," Sylvia said warmly. "You'll become accustomed to our ways soon enough."

Laoise bowed her head in thanks and took another sip of water. I wiped down the wine bottles on the cart, preparing to fill Boris's near empty glass. This was not just an ordinary welcoming feast for Linnaea, I realized. This was just as much a test of Laoise's loyalties as Dominique's questions were when we arrived. I trusted Laoise with my life, but she needed to appear relaxed with her new family: if she remained tense, they'd suspect something was amiss, and our plan to rescue my father—to rescue Keegan—would fail.

Now that the food was placed, I made another round with the whiteberry wine for Boris and Laoise. Dominique watched me like a bird of prey, waiting for any excuse to cut out my tongue if I came any closer. I'd pour an entire bottle over her head just to spite her, but every drop of bluesberry wine since the spillage had found its way into Leon's mouth.

"This is an impressive display," Laoise said of the food as she tasted the boar. "Not even the kitchens at Gareth Manor could top this."

Sylvia beamed. "We employ the finest chefs from the finest families. We brought them all with us here, of course."

"They'll not all stay, though. I'm taking Chef Leben back with me to Cogold, after our nuptials." Leon stole a glance at me and then winked.

The nerve. No more wine for him, I decided. Surely Boris and Sylvia would back me up on that one.

Laoise smiled politely and sipped at her wine. It dawned on me then that neither of us had considered Leon leaving Marlenia City after the wedding. Perhaps Leon, being the second son, would take up residence in the Frostfire castle in the East, in Cogold: then Boris and Dominique would remain here, as heirs to the Western throne.

Before I could leave the table, Leon hooked my arm. "You're not going to pour for me, servant?"

I tensed. "I thought since you were enjoying the Sarysa—"

"You thought wrong! Pour!"

His theatrics annoyed me to the bone. This wasn't the deal. The more attention he drove to me, the more he was going to put Laoise in danger. I poured whiteberry wine into his second glass, counting the seconds until it was full. The entire time, he kept a firm grip on me, the woman he thought was going to be his future wife.

"Haven't you had enough?" Sylvia said. "You'll barely be able to taste the food, your senses will be so dulled."

The glass filled, I drew away, wiping the bottleneck clean before pouring Laoise's wine. Leon couldn't keep his gaze from me; it was fiery hot. Finally noticing his glass was full, he released me before turning his attentions to his sister.

"I remember a time when you indulged a little too much. Oh, every feast since your fifteenth name-day?"

Sylvia pressed her lips into a firm line, her solemn mood returning. "I've grown up since then."

"Really." Leon took another long sip.

"I've had to," Sylvia replied, glaring at Dominique. "Especially now that my best friend and dearest cousin has been cursed by Freetor magic."

Dominique wasn't the least bit intimidated. "Perhaps she would not have fallen prey to de curse y'if j'ou had agreed to go to nort' and spend time wit' my brother."

So Lady Milda's infection was deliberate. Marin, Dominique's young brother, wasn't even in Marlenia City, or so I had gathered. High King Matís Castillo was keeping a firm hold on the nine-year-old boy, especially with his rumoured failing health. At least the Frostfires didn't control everything. He was Sylvia's betrothed, although they would not marry officially until Marin was of age.

Emmine threw me a shocked look, unable to contain her surprise. I stood very still by the wine cart, hoping that Sylvia wouldn't remember my involvement in the discovery of Lady Milda's body.

Sylvia's grip on her fork tightened. "You are the most deceitful person I have ever met."

"I would rather dat then estupid," Dominique replied, cutting off another piece of meat and plopping it in her mouth.

"Ladies," Boris said, once again bored that he had to mediate their arguments. "Must we discuss the Freetor curse going around the city? We are having a lovely dinner in Linnaea's honour."

"Going around the...city?" Laoise said timidly, choosing her words with care. "Forgive me. News is often slow to reach Baile Gareth. I thought the sleeping curse had only affected a few nobles. A targeted act by a select group of Freetors."

Leon grinned, showing off his blue teeth. "Oh, my darling"—he stole a too-obvious sidelong glance at me—"I'm afraid you've fallen prey to the rumours we've put in the minds of the commoners. It's far from select. It's spreading as far as Sallingaire, last I heard." He hiccupped, now past the point of manners.

Sallingaire! I covered my surprise with my hand. The town bordering the West and the East, nestled between mountains and a near-impassable valley. It sat on the only survivable, practical route between the two provinces. I'd hoped the Western Army would retain the important holding, yet the East had reared their head there not long after they'd captured Marlenia City. The West simply didn't have the manpower to retake it and Marlenia City. At least, not without aid.

Laoise tried to ignore Leon's proximity to her face. "But how could it have possibly travelled so far in such a short period of time?"

Sylvia looked appalled and furious. "Yes, I would also like to know how it could have spread that far." Her gaze narrowed at Dominique. "I thought we had it under control."

"One concerned loved one is all it takes," Boris replied. "They touch a frozen infected person and it is transmitted instantly. Bodies can pile up fast."

"And not many places to put them, out of harm's way," Sylvia muttered. I wondered if she felt guilty for her part in spreading the curse. She glanced at Laoise. "I heard that even when we put Mildie in the cellar—a most ghastly place for a noblewoman, even in her condition—a kitchen hand found her and the others down there, became curious, and...well. I couldn't stand that a mere servant, even a frozen one, had collapsed on top of her like that. So I asked one of the stronger men to handle it, and then he accidentally brushed him..." Sylvia downed the rest of her wine and I went to refill it, but she shook her head. It seemed Leon was a deterrent.

The nobles fell silent, seemingly unsurprised at Sylvia's story. How many people had she inadvertently cursed?

"It's a shame something so terrible could spread so quickly," Laoise said to break the awkward silence. "Tell me, Boris, are your family's scholars close to a cure?"

Boris, surprised that he was addressed directly, gave her serious consideration. "Father has devoted resources to finding a cure, certainly. Though Dominique has taken more of an interest than me. I have been advised"—he glanced at Dominique—"that the curse will be contained."

I gritted my teeth. Contained wasn't the same as cured. Leszek would have no interest in waking up Keegan or finding a cure, not unless one of his heirs were affected. Even then, at the rate Leon was embarrassing himself, I highly doubted Leszek would care if Leon fell prey.

"I y'am workin' hard to rid us of Freetor magics," Dominique said. "Before de y'end of de y'evenin', dere will be no more magics on the castle grounds. And by de y'end of de week, dere will be no Freetor magics in dis city."

End of the evening? We had far less time than we thought to rescue my father.

"What do you mean, end of the week?" Sylvia asked.

"We cannot allow bodies to continue piling up. In de plague durin' Whilton Hightower's reign, two hundred twenty years ago. Do j'ou remember what dey did?"

The Frostfire siblings exchanged blank looks, but Laoise nearly choked on her corn.

"They...they burnt the infected. The dead bodies and those who entered the second stage of the plague," she said. "It was the only way to ensure that others didn't get sick."

"J'es. Dat's right. Dis is not just a curse. Y'it is a plague. Any people infected must be treated de same way. I y'am arrangin' transport pour d'infected outside de city. We will pile dem, provide de proper ceremonies for de sentimental hearts, and den light de fires."

Outside the city? Where?

Sylvia's silverware clattered loudly on her plate. "You mean all this time, you haven't been working on counter-measures to the Freetor magic? You've been plotting to...to murder good nobles and innocents who serve them? And Prince Keegan?"

"We cannot fight Freetor magics if we do not wield it ourselves. I will not estoop to dose levels. Prince Keegan will suffer de same fate as d'others."

No. I couldn't let him burn. I couldn't watch another person I loved burn to death.

"We could persuade Ivor Ferguson to tell us what he knows," Leon said, smirking. "I heard he—"

"He y'is a danger and should esuffer de same fate as all Freetors," Dominique interrupted.

"Ivor Ferguson isn't to be trusted," Boris agreed calmly. "I'm sure Father will devise a way to deal with that snake."

Dominique sipped her water and said nothing.

"Perhaps," Sylvia hedged sombrely, "the Emerald Cloth is the answer."

Laoise's gaze widened, her lips attached to the rim of her cup.

"One of Dashiell's four artefacts?" Boris said.

"That old thing," Leon said dismissively. "Locked away in Sallingaire, or Xii, or in some deep cavern underground—depending on which priest or travelling bard is in favour."

Boris let out a snort, and looked to Dominique to see if she shared his sense of humour. She did not.

"Y'it has Freetor magics. I will not touch it."

"I'm not afraid of a silly piece of cloth," Sylvia replied. "We don't even know if they're really dead. They could be awake beneath the frozen sheen, hearing and seeing everything. I'm more afraid of watching my best friend and my...my prince, my Keegan, burn to death."

Her Keegan?

Even Dominique's patience was wearing thin. "He y'isn't j'our prince. Keegan Tramore was a traitor who decided to marry a disgustin' animal. He deserves to die. Publicly. Y'it is d'only way to ensure support pour Eastern and Nort'ern Marlenia."

"How dare you speak such evil about Keegan!" Sylvia exclaimed, rising to her feet. "I was taking care of him, reading to him every night, until you stole him from under my nose, plotting and scheming with my father about Dashiell-knows-what. But guess what. I found him again. You think I don't know my way through that maze?" She thrust a finger over the balcony.

The wine bottle tumbled from my fingers and fell to the floor. It shattered and wine filled the uneven crevices of the stone.

Keegan was in the hedge maze, maybe at the centre. A strong gust of wind whipped my unruly hair over my face as I followed her finger. Keegan was here. Close enough that I could reach out and touch him. I'd only ever walked around the maze to get to the stables—never through.

I bet my father knew the quickest route.

My clumsiness—real this time—did not go unnoticed. Leon leapt to his feet. "Stupid girl!"

He reached for me but I sidestepped him. The two noblewomen were too entrenched in their personal war to notice what I'd done. I couldn't stop staring at Sylvia: her elegant gown, eating food cooked and served by slaves and servants in a castle that wasn't hers. Taking care of a husband that didn't belong to her.

They held everyone I cared for in their cruel grasp. And Sylvia believed that she deserved this.

"J'ou have been esneakin' around pour too long," Dominique said to Sylvia, rising from her chair.

"I won't let you take him from me," Sylvia whispered.

"J'ou will do y'as j'ou promised," Dominique replied, "and marry my brot'er."

"Ladies, sit down. Your quarrel is embarrassing Linnaea," Boris said, as if this happened every day.

"Clean this up!" Leon shouted at me, grinning. He was enjoying his power too much. "Do it, or—"

"Don't you dare—" The words were out of my mouth. All of this was wrong. This wasn't their home. They were conquerors.

But I'd spoken too loudly and out of turn. Sylvia, Dominique, and Boris finally noticed me, and the broken wine bottle, the remnants of bluesberry wine running along the stone like a sad, trickling river.

A fiery flame like what destroyed this castle and my brother lit within Dominique's eyes. She pushed her chair out of the way, walking around Sylvia and the table, heading straight for me. "J'ou..."

"Yes. Me," I said. It had only been a matter of time before she'd recognized me. The cream was due to wear off. "I—"

She cut me off. "J'ou have been clumsy pour de last time. And j'ou tink I haven't noticed j'ou drawin' Leon's eyes?" She glared at Leon and then turned back to me. "Do j'ou know what we do to de servants and eslaves in de Nort' who disobey?"

I hesitated. They didn't have to disobey to pay the price of silence—forever. "Yes."

"Not so estupid, perhaps," she said, smiling cruelly at Leon, and then at me. "On j'our knees, servant."

The glass beneath me didn't matter. I would have to kneel.

Leon was no longer smiling. "Dominique, she's not—"

"Quiet. Kneel, servant."

Slowly, I descended to my knees. My thick skirts shielded my skin from most of the glass, though it crumbled beneath my weight. Tiny shards embedded in the fabric and the hardness of the stone pressed them against my skin.

Emmine cowered by the wine cart, uncertain. Laoise rose to her feet. "Dominique. She's my servant. This is the West. Your Northern punishments, they aren't necessary here. I can punish her accordingly."

I pleaded with her silently, with a look. *Don't stick your neck out for me. You have to do as I did with Rordan. The mission is more important.*

Dominique seemed to consider Laoise's request. "Dis may be de West. But soon, I will be High Queen. And when I y'am High Queen, tings, dey are goin' to change."

"Then you'll forgive her? She's been my handmaid since we were children, I—"

"Estop talkin'," she said coldly, holding up a hand.

"Linnaea is right. We don't have to listen to you," Sylvia said.

"You might be High Queen, but my brother will be the High King. The emperor."

"And I'm telling all of you to sit back down so we can begin our dessert," Boris said.

Dominique stayed her hand. Like her white tiger I'd fought at Driscoll's End, her eyes gleamed with opportunity as she ignored Boris and stared at Sylvia. "J'ou dare place Frostfire interests above Castillo? We y'are y'equals. Wit'out de Nort'ern shadows, j'ou would not hold dis castle."

"We would have done—"

Sylvia began to make a dangerous argument before Boris gripped her arm, saving her from diplomatic incident—and Dominique's wrath. "We are grateful for our alliance with your family. Make no mistake of that," Boris said.

Dominique bent over to retrieve a large shard of the wine bottle. The key slipped from beneath her dress and hung loose in full sight.

I focussed on it and closed my fist around several small pieces of glass. They dug into my palms, but when she got close enough—Dominique would get a face-full. And then I'd have the key, and I could free both my father and my husband from this cruel place.

Laoise climbed out of her seat and tip-toed towards Leon. "What are you doing, Dominique?"

"I told j'ou to estop talkin'," Dominique said, turning from me to face the nobles at various points around the table. "I y'am teaching de Frostfires a lesson. Boris, j'ou will not order me around like a servant. Sylvia, a frozen corpse does not make y'a husband. At de y'end of de week, j'ou will travel to de Nort', where j'ou will stay until Marin is of age. And Leon." She paused, levelling him with an especially nasty glare. "J'our bride-to-be sits next to j'ou, and yet j'ou cannot estop with j'our lustful gaze to dis servant girl."

"Dominique, please listen to me," Leon began, but to my surprise, Laoise threw her arms around him. It distracted him and threw me off as well.

When I looked back to Dominique, she peered down at me. The glass shard shone in the candlelight. She was going to do what she failed to do at Driscoll's End—cut out my tongue.

"You're the disgusting animal, Dominique," Sylvia spat, advancing on her.

"Don't come any closer!" Dominique shouted.

As Sylvia charged Dominique, I took the opportunity and threw the bits of glass in her face. She shielded her face and swung her makeshift weapon at me and Sylvia.

"Hey!" I yelled at Dominique, leaping to my feet. Finally. I was going to fight her—and win.

Snarling, Dominique came at me with the glass shard, aiming for my throat.

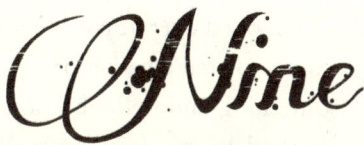

Nine

I SIDE-STEPPED AS the glass nicked my neck. I hit the balcony floor hard. Leon gripped his sister and spoke in a low tone with her, backing her away from the raging Northern woman. Sylvia screamed horrible things at her through her tears, drowning out whatever soothing words Leon spoke.

As Dominique forgot about me and charged Sylvia, Boris went to grab Dominique, but Laoise was faster, coming at Dominique head-on with a pacifistic embrace. She struggled fiercely but Laoise refused to let go. Confused, she backed into Boris, who grabbed her arms and steadied her.

Meanwhile, Emmine watched from a distance, horrified.

I sat up, glass digging into my palms, yet suddenly Dominique stood over me. Calm—but barely. She held the glass shard close to my mouth.

"Let dis serve y'as a reminder not to cross de Castillo family again," Dominique said coldly. Then, to Laoise: "Y'if I see dis servant again, I will end her life."

"I...I will release her from my service immediately," Laoise replied.

Dominique walked around the table and headed for the exit. "She can go...y'after she cleans up dis mess."

I watched her leave. She was going to execute my father. Kill Keegan and everyone else who had suffered because of me. I couldn't let that happen.

"I believe dessert is now out of the question," Boris said, throwing up his hands in defeat.

"Yeah," Leon said. He looked over at me, a curious expression passing his face as he contemplated whether or not to help me.

Sylvia muttered something unintelligible and stormed out after Dominique. I climbed to my feet, unsteady, wanting to follow her and stop whatever schemes they'd cooked up, but upon looking at Emmine's fearful expression, I had to stay.

Boris grabbed another piece of meat and chewed it on his way off the balcony. With only Leon left, Laoise touched his arm and said goodnight. On her way past, she glanced at me, and to my confusion and surprise, grinned.

No. She didn't.

Somehow, during the fight, she'd managed to get the key.

Nodding, she jerked her head, towards the hedge maze below.

I could barely believe it. I wished I could follow her, help her release my father. It would only be a matter of time before Dominique realized her key was missing. But I couldn't leave now—not with Leon hanging around near the door, and Emmine clearing away the dishes, watching me with equal suspicion. As long as Laoise was in the castle, pretending to be Linnaea, I had to act the part of Rorda Cloth, the now-disgraced servant.

I just had to act quickly.

I swept the shards into a dustpan and placed them on the wine cart. Emmine and I would take it down to the kitchen—and from there, I'd try to escape to the hedge maze.

Except that wouldn't be so easy. Leon remained on the balcony by the door, his arms crossed, leaning against castle wall. Waiting for me. Emmine scraped the leftover food onto a large plate and stacked the dishes. I pulled away the chairs and gathered them together for other servants or slaves to remove.

Emmine kept glancing at Leon and then back at me. "You know the rules."

I lowered my voice. "It's most definitely not what you think."

"Isn't it? Clearly you have some kind of...connection." She looked conflicted. "I wish I had the love of a prince."

"Believe me, it doesn't solve your problems. It only creates new ones." I took her hand. "Just forget about this. I...I hope that things get better. I'm going to try and make things better. I promise."

"What do you mean?" she asked. She looked down at our hands, and that's when she noticed the violet fabric on my forefinger. "Wait. You're...?"

I snatched my hand away. I'd nearly forgotten about my ring. I would never remove it, but I shouldn't have been so careless. "Again. Not what you think."

"You married Leon Frostfire?" The look of surprise and concern in her eyes was so severe I thought they'd fall from her head as she stared at Leon.

Believing this to be an invitation, Leon pushed off the wall and joined us, smirking. "Yes, it's true. She really is—"

"No, no, no, no!" I pulled him towards the exit. "Goodbye, Emmine." I thought about telling her to keep quiet, but if all went well, after tonight Laoise and I would be gone from the castle, and only Leon would have to answer for any dalliances he'd had with Rorda Cloth, aka Linnaea Gareth, aka the Violet Fox, aka Kiera Driscoll.

Further away, down the corridor, I glanced around to ensure there were no guards, and then slammed Leon against the wall. "Wipe that smirk off your face. Do you realize that you almost told that servant who I was?"

"She seemed to be your friend," he said, searching my face. He looked like a man who enjoyed the game he thought we were playing. "What did she ask? Did she figure out our... relationship?"

Disgusted, I drew back, releasing him. "We don't have a

relationship." Emboldened by Laoise's success, I glanced back the way we came. In less than an hour, I'd have Keegan back. There was no need to keep up this charade with Leon. He'd been an annoyance long enough. "And because of your appalling behaviour, I'm withdrawing my betrothal. Say goodbye to my father's land and his arms."

All amusement drained from Leon's face. "Don't say things like that."

"Why? You really think anyone would want to marry you, with the way you've been acting?"

"You don't know what it's been like for me. You're a naive noble girl, having a bit of fun pretending to be a servant before she's forced to marry a stranger." His throat tightened. "You don't know what I've done."

"I know exactly what you've done, Leon Frostfire." I dared to take a step closer. "You marched around the Western countryside, selling favours in exchange for human lives. How many Freetors did you kill in your family's name?"

His eyes blazed. I'd hit a nerve. "I never took you for a sympathizer. But that's no surprise, living as you did in those woods. And yes. I marched from here to Iar Bunsula, flying my family's colours, routing out Freetor nests. Have you ever killed someone, Linnaea? Ever looked into a person's eyes as they died?"

Blood rushed to my cheeks. I'd only ever killed once. It was not something I'd enjoyed, and I'd hoped I'd never have to do it again.

He continued. "I thought it might be easy. Freetors aren't people. They're rats, scurrying around underfoot. Annoying, but they have their place. Until Father said, go west, prove yourself a man. So I took my men and we marched. We went to every single village, town, and manor west of Marlenia City, paying for any information that led to the capture of Freetors. You'd be surprised how willing people were to betray their neighbours for enough silver to buy a loaf of bread.

"Then we got to Iar Bunsula. I fought the Violet Fox and Prince Keegan before they ran off to the Forever Sea. Next day, we got up. Couldn't go any further west, so we headed back. We reached Baile Jerrold. Suddenly people were more reluctant to help us. I told them, the Violet Fox isn't even a real Freetor, she's just half Marlenian, and she'd wormed her way into the castle. Even that didn't matter to them anymore. Somehow, with her magic, she'd convinced them all that cooperating with the crown was bad. We knew the Freetors were out there, hiding in their nest, repopulating, plotting against my family and the North.

"The men got restless. We moved on to the next town. Finally, someone came forward. Said there was a whole bunch of Freetors hiding in her friend's cellar. They'd dug tunnels in, but she'd seen them emerge at night from the house, with lanterns.

"We paid her friend a visit that evening. Burst in, demanded a confession. They denied everything, of course. My men searched the house. Found a hidden trapdoor. Opened it. Sure enough, a dug-out cellar. We climbed down, there were about five of us.

"The place was full of crates, boxes, other junk. Who knows what they were really doing there. But in the centre of it all: women. Children. A couple of men. All starved, thin, and weak like twigs. They were just sitting there in a circle, encouraging the kids to eat bread and apples. They saw us and they huddled together, but they didn't run. Maybe they had nowhere else to go."

Leon became quiet as he lost himself in the memory. "I drew my sword, gave some kind of speech about how they were now the property of the crown. My men started to round them up. But one of the male Freetors, he got angry, attacked one of my men. A fight broke out. The children scattered. The women fought. I fought. I wanted to protect my own. I swung at a child..." He frowned, looking down at his right hand. "He fell.

I didn't think I hit him that hard. I just couldn't stop staring at him, the blood, his hair. He looked up at me as he died. I didn't hit him hard enough—he was dying slowly.

"I thought I was under the influence of Freetor magic. My men were fighting around me and I couldn't summon the strength to swing my sword, not even to end his misery. Later, my men taunted me. They thought I couldn't handle killing a child rat. Hadn't I killed before, they asked? This was different. My men said he was barely real. I've said things like that before. Now...his blood was...it was real. His eyes...they were like a green fire."

He touched the hilt of his hunting knife, sheathed at his belt. "I was weak for one second—now I'm weak forever. My reputation, ruined. Because I didn't have the strength to fight."

"It took the death of one person for you to realize that Freetors are people too," I said, "but what about the thousands who died here, in the capital?"

"What?"

"The people executed, when your father was calling for the death of the Violet Fox and Prince Keegan. Every day they didn't return, he executed more."

"What about them?"

"That didn't move you?"

He became defensive. "I wasn't here for that. Weren't you listening? I was in the West. Routing out Freetors. I killed them because I thought they were animals. But then, that one child—"

"I heard you." I was done here.

"So why do you think I'm down there, trying to drink it out of me?" He smashed his fist against the wall. "I keep thinking, maybe this will be the last bottle. Maybe this will be the one that makes me forget it all. But no. Freetor magic's the only power strong enough to do that, and tough luck getting them to help me now.

"So yes. You're right. I'm not suitable for marriage. Not right now. But"—he reached for my hand—"with your help, I can get better. I don't know how to solve the Freetor problem. Let Boris and Dominique and Sylvia handle it. Let them handle it all. I just need...I just need your help."

My fingers curled as I stared at his outstretched palm. His guilt didn't erase his crimes. It didn't make me forgive him. It only made it harder to hate him in the same way.

"I don't know if I know how to help you, Leon," I said quietly. "Maybe someday I will. But not tonight."

"No, I'm not letting you go now." His knees buckled. He looked ready to beg. "I've scared you off, haven't I?"

"I just want to be alone."

"I can't allow that. I have to make you understand."

"I understand perfectly."

"I don't think you do." He grabbed my arm.

"Let go!" I tried to wrench myself from his grip to no avail, then tried for my knife, but this time, he caught my wrist. He'd learned.

"I thought tonight would be the night that we could connect. Somehow you look...different. Prettier."

The face cream. It had finally worn off. Yet, he still didn't know who I was. Would he still act this way if he did? I spat in his face and kneed him in the stomach. He doubled over, loosening his grip as he went for his own knife.

It was time to get out of here.

Summoning my courage and strength in the form of a loud war-cry, I pushed him back as hard as I could and kicked him in the chest. He collapsed to the stone floor, seething with hatred. "You are supposed to support me."

My hand hovered over my knife, but I thought better of it. "No, I'm not."

A low growl, the one of a wounded animal, escaped his throat as he struggled to get to his feet. "Help!" he cried. "Frostfire men, to me!"

There was no one there to answer the call—but I ran anyway, down the servant staircase. Heavy footsteps followed, men shouted to one another, but I was faster and quieter. I hurried into the kitchen and slipped between the busy servants washing dishes, tending fires, and eating the remains of the boar.

"Rorda," the chef called. "You get something to eat? You're allowed—"

His voice faded as I entered the meat room, ran down the narrow corridor, and out the door. I dashed into the cool breeze, pressing myself against the stone walls of the castle. I glanced back at the kitchen. No doubt Leon's men, if he managed to convince them I was a real threat in his state, could come after me.

Approximately ten stone-throws lay between me and the hedge maze. I crept along the wall, keeping to the shadows. I recalled just a month ago that I'd received sword lessons here in this very courtyard by Captain Murdock—the man who used to chase me through the streets less than two months before that. He'd sacrificed his life so Keegan and I could escape the castle during the fire. So many people had died just because I wasn't here to protect them. Because we weren't here.

That would change once Keegan was awake. If the small lords of the surrounding bailes knew Keegan was alive and not a victim of Freetor magic or torture, they'd surely throw support behind their rightful monarch, and with the help of the Freetors, perhaps we could drive the East and the North back to where they belonged.

Then, my people could finally get the land—and the freedom—they sorely deserved.

Before me lay the backside of the bailey, and at a distance, the hedge maze. A patrol was some distance away, but they'd come around soon enough. I steeled myself. I could make it before they came, if I sprinted.

Gritting my teeth, I crouched, and...

...a heavy hand caught my shoulder.

Whirling around, I drew my knife and threw my attacker against the wall. My blade pressed against tender flesh before I realized he was hissing my name. His hands glowed a faint blue. "Kiera. It's me. Stop that."

I recoiled, shocked. "You got here so fast. Where's Laoise? Is she all right?"

"Yes, she's fine for the moment. Dominique knows her key went missing and the list of suspects is thin." My father held up a hand at my protest. "She's safest if she remains as Lady Linnaea Gareth, in her quarters. Even if she realizes that Laoise took the key, she has no evidence to prove that Laoise isn't who she claims to be, and seeing that Dominique imprisoned me without the emperor's knowledge, she cannot outright harm his future daughter-in-law. She should survive the night, though we might not need that long. As for what I'm doing here, I came to help you locate and rescue Keegan. Assuming what you overheard at dinner was true."

Frustration welled inside me. "I don't think Sylvia would lie under duress about Keegan."

"Anyone can lie about anything. It's not terribly hard."

"You'd know, wouldn't—?"

Approaching footsteps cut me short. The patrol! My father and I disappeared into the shadows as a two-guard patrol wearing Frostfire colours walked by, chatting in hushed tones about the particulars of their rounds. My gaze roamed the small courtyard: the Frostfire guards might not be the only ones out and about. The shadow guards loyal to the Castillo family concerned me more. My vision in darkness was exceptional, but their ability to hide troubled me more, especially since I doubted my father's vision was as good after living on the surface for nearly two decades.

"If you're here," I whispered through gritted teeth, once the Frostfire guards had passed, "then you can help. Did Laoise tell you where they were keeping Keegan?"

"There was no time," he replied. "Outside the castle?"

I pointed in the direction of the maze. "In there."

A small smile crawled across his face, as though he were lost in a pleasant memory. "Ah. Fortunate I came with you. I know my way through."

"I think he's in the centre."

"Even better. Perhaps you don't need me, then."

"Wait." I grabbed his arm out of fear, though he'd made no move to leave. "First you offer to help, and then you're quick to abandon me?" Again. "I mean...I can find my way...just fine. It can't be that hard. But if you know the most direct route..."

"I do. Likely the Frostfires do as well, to a degree. They've had control of the castle for nearly a month now. That might have given them enough time to practice. Not to mention, if Lady Sylvia found her way through, no doubt there are others."

I checked the bailey again. Only the wind whipped by the castle walls and around the mountain. There was another patrol, about a minute away. My father took my arm and together we slipped through the shadows towards, and across the back courtyard, to the entrance of the maze.

"It's the perfect place for him if they want to limit his contact with everyone else," I whispered. "Sylvia should have put him in here in the first place."

"No one said she was the sharpest sword in the armory."

The maze stood at least thirty hands tall, possibly more. The rightmost perimeter of the maze led directly to the stables, and from there, the open plains and western forests, where Keegan, Monju, and I had journeyed to Driscoll's End. The left was a steep ride down the mountain, to the road that twisted around to the city below. Upon entering, I continued straight; my father didn't protest as he fell into line behind me.

"So," my father said, glancing up at the night sky. "Have you a plan for the guards at the centre?"

I blushed, feeling fortunate that my father couldn't see my face. "I was going to deal with that when we got there."

He grabbed me and spun me around to face him. "What do you mean? You have no plan?"

I wrenched myself from his grip. "You said yourself they'd be limiting contact with Keegan. I don't expect there to be that many. If you're not prepared to fight—"

"I am prepared. But you're not thinking clearly. If we don't manage to escape tonight, Laoise will have to go another day as Linnaea. If you maim or kill the guards at the centre? Someone is going to find out. And then suspicion will fall on your friend. Or you. It's bad enough that you sent her to rescue me in the dungeon, when you should have let me rot—Dominique will watch her closely. If her cover is blown, and word makes it to Lord Ansel that his daughter is missing—he will assume we are responsible. We have a small window of opportunity here and it's closing fast. Now. What is your plan to remove Keegan from the maze? Drag him?"

I swallowed. "Now that you're here, you can use magic on him to wake him up."

"We've been over this. I'm not powerful enough."

"Not powerful enough to escape Dominique's clutches on your own, either."

"If I'd have done that, she would have assumed I was guilty."

"Aren't you?" I searched his face for the father I desperately wanted—and the good man I'd heard while hiding in the wardrobe.

"I was biding my time," he explained patiently. "I assumed

Leszek would come for me eventually and discover I wasn't in my assigned quarters. If he hadn't by morning, before my scheduled end, well, then I would have taken more drastic action."

A risky plan. I let it go and turned around. "You must be able to conceal Keegan's appearance. Or run fast. You hinted at those abilities when we were in Baile Gareth."

"Some of those things are possible. They take an inordinate amount of energy. To conceal myself is one matter. To conceal three—four if you count Laoise—for an extended period is another. The preparation for such a feat would take me days."

"What about concealing two? You—and Keegan?"

"Might be possible. And what will you do?"

"I'm not abandoning Laoise. I was going to return to the castle and help her escape before the sun rose." I continued down the maze. When I didn't hear my father's footfalls behind me, I stopped. "Fine. So there are some things I didn't think through. I just...I need to at least see that he's...here. Even if... even if I can't remove him tonight."

"I know you're worried about him."

"I don't know what I'll do if I can't get him back." I dug my fingernail into my palm as the cool breeze whipped around my warm face.

"Let's see if he's there, first." He was right behind me now; I hadn't heard him approach. He laid a firm hand on my shoulder. "Then we can formulate a plan from there."

I nodded. My father's face, bathed in the pale moon, betrayed his age and experience. I had to trust him. Even if certain fibres in my being still associated that face with death and destruction.

We walked side by side through the maze, turning left, and then right again.

"I haven't been able to ascertain Linnaea's location. Some merchants reported some unusual bandit activity in Feenagh

Forest last week. Painted faces, black outfits. They said they were heading for the South."

"And every day we spend here, the further away they get." Talking about the Extremists made me think of my brother, and his horrible, public execution. "What would be in the South for them?"

"Escape. Sympathy. Land. Opportunity for terrorism."

Another beat. I steeled myself for a harsher answer. "If he had survived the fire, would you tell me?"

"He's dead, Kiera," he said softly. "So are many other Extremists. Many made martyrs of themselves during the executions weeks ago. Yet, they persist, stronger than ever. It is unlikely they'd help us. They are blind with anger. We have nothing to offer them." He pointed at the next juncture. "We're close to the centre."

That was code for, we should shut up now.

The centre of the maze was an enclosed dome. A round patch of sky shone through at the top, just enough for the moon to peek through and shine upon a rectangular bier in the centre, draped in a white cloth stained with dark splotches. Not blood. Some kind of liquid.

I searched the dark recesses. There were two ways in and out of the centre: the way we came in, and another path directly across from us. No guards. No Northern shadows lying in wait. Only the soft wind whistling above us and the insulated dullness that muffled the night sounds outside of the dome.

I trudged to the bier and touched the white cloth. It was only as cold as the night, and no colder. No telltale blue light of Freetor magic.

Yet we were not alone. On the other side of the bier, half hidden beneath the draped cloth, was the frozen body of a Northern shadow. His arm shielded his face while the other was outstretched.

Sylvia had been right. Keegan was here.

And now he was gone.

"We...we were so close," I whispered, covering the man with the stained cloth.

"We mustn't give up," my father said quietly. "This is why we need the..."

He trailed off at the sounds of rustling behind us. I spun around as Sylvia furiously pulled back a dark green hood. "You. I should have known you'd try to steal him away."

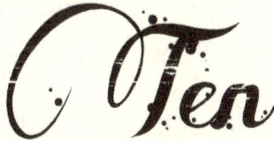

Ten

I HADN'T HEARD her behind us. My father, however, didn't seem surprised. "So good of you to join us, Lady Sylvia."

I pointed at the Daughter of the East. "You let her follow us here?"

"I thought she'd get lost eventually," he replied. "Apparently, though, Lady Sylvia has memorized her way through the maze."

Sylvia snorted defensively. "You think I'm vapid? What have you done with my future husband?"

"Your future..." I touched the violet cloth around my forefinger. "Funny, because I was going to ask you the same question."

"Where have you taken him?" Her face red, Sylvia bunched her skirts and trod through the wet grass in a huff towards us. She had no army, no weapons, but her desperation made her the kind of dangerous that I couldn't ignore. "Dominique said you were in the castle, somewhere. She's always right about those kinds of things. Tell me what dank cave you've hidden Prince Keegan in, and maybe I won't call the guards."

I raised my eyebrows. "That's a generous offer, but I didn't move him. Maybe you should ask Dominique where she plans to execute him. I thought he was here, but..." I glanced at the bier.

My father cleared his throat. "Lady Sylvia. It is not a crime to walk through the hedge maze. Perhaps I could escort Lady Kiera off the grounds for you, and the two of us could forget this bit of unpleasantness."

"Lady Kiera, is it now? I don't recognize that title." She gave him the once over, her eyes narrowing. "And, if I'm not mistaken, my father confined you to your quarters under heavy guard."

"He did. But a man must have his fresh air."

"Must he?" she asked coldly. "I'm sure my father would be very interested in your midnight walks in the maze with the young and charming *Lady* Kiera."

He looked pained and suddenly eager to leave. "Kiera—"

"I'm not done my midnight walk. C'mon."

I spun around to return the way we came, but not quick enough to see the flash of fear on Sylvia's face. "No. Wait. I forbid—"

"You have no power over me," I muttered. "You won't keep me from him."

Sylvia shook with rage. I'd touched a nerve. "You're not special, you know. You and Dominique, you're both the same, as much as you would hate to admit it."

Rage as powerful as a rolling storm welled up within me, my tongue lightning, waiting to strike. "I am not like her."

"You are both murderers, liars, and thieves."

"My people have suffered for two hundred years—"

"Enough." My father's words were clean and cold. "Lady Sylvia. Clearly Dominique is a step ahead of you, no? She knows your affections for the young prince and has moved his body in the hopes that you will forget about him and concentrate on fostering a relationship with Marin. Kiera." He heaved a sigh, as if not quite sure what to say. "Keegan isn't here. There aren't many places he could be at his point on the castle grounds, especially if Dominique is planning to execute him publicly, as you said."

Sylvia trembled as she fixed me with an intensely angry stare; I could see right through her, down to her core. She was afraid.

Heartbroken. She turned away from us. "She...she did this..."

"Where could Dominique have moved him so quickly? And how?" I asked my father and my rival.

Sylvia touched the bier longingly. "This isn't the first time. She must have my father's help. He must have realized how much time I was spending at Keegan's side...when I'm supposed to be getting to know Marin."

"Sylvia, this is important." I moved to her side cautiously. "Do you have any idea where—?"

"Even if I did, why should I help you? You...you traitorous...!"

I attempted to grab her, to silence her and her screeching, but she pulled away. Tears streamed down her face, glowing in the high moonlight.

"Sylvia. We..." I thought quickly. "The longer Keegan remains frozen, the more likely people are going to touch him and spread the frozen curse."

Her gaze narrowed. "You want to...help him?"

"Of course I do. And I know you do, too. Please, if you care for him, help us." I glanced at my father, and a hint of pride rushed through me at his encouraging smile. "As much as you hate me, as much as it seems like I'm your enemy, we can both agree that Keegan doesn't deserve this sleeping, frozen fate."

"I..." Sylvia wrung her hands, unsure. "If I...if you..."

The far-off calls of men and their footfalls on grass urged my hands and feet into a fury. I drew my dagger. My father heard it too. He raised his hands, possibly readying some unknown magic. Sylvia, at first afraid we were going to attack her, ducked, and then, hearing her approaching men, rose uncertainly and backed up against the grassy walls.

I cursed. "Guards. Probably Frostfires." It was far less likely we'd hear the Northern shadows until they were upon us.

"She's going to know we were here," Sylvia whimpered. "That I tried to visit again..."

My father took me by the shoulders. "Take Lady Sylvia and lead her out of the maze. I will handle the guards."

"No. You're already in too much trouble. They'll know... they'll suspect..."

"I still have cards I haven't played yet," he said with a quick smile.

"Do you really think we can trust her?" I whispered, quiet enough so Sylvia couldn't hear.

"I trust you can figure that out for yourself."

Frantic boots on the grass several stone-throws from us, and more hurried yells urged me to flee, yet a terrible dread planted me where I stood. A fear I hadn't felt since I was six-years-old.

What if I never see you again?

His fingers combed through my hair lightly, the barest of touches, a surprise to me, and maybe to him, too. "Come now, Kiera," he said softly. "You know I can handle myself. Trust me, as you trust yourself."

Sylvia gave me the strangest look, but I didn't have time—or the desire—to explain.

"I'll protect you, for now," I said to her. "Only because he wants me to."

She looked over my shoulder at my father. He raced out of sight, into the labyrinth. I barely remembered the last time he'd left. Flashes of cave walls. The magic book I'd used as a journal for years, before sacrificing it at the God Tears.

Now, he was sacrificing himself to ensure we had a chance.

"This way," I said, heading for the exit on the other side of the maze.

"It's a dead end that way," she hissed.

"If we have to, we can cut through the hedges."

Blue light lit the sky. The sounds of men thumping on the grass.

Could he be dead? Would the Frostfires kill him on sight after seeing that the Advisor had Freetor magic?

Sylvia looked uncertainly towards the fighting. "Maybe I could call off the guards."

"Too suspicious." I couldn't let my father's sacrifice go to waste. I grabbed her hand and dragged her along. "Let's go."

"Go where?" she asked as we disappeared into the maze.

I turned left and right, no longer certain of the path. We reached a dead end immediately. I doubled back, feeling the trimmed hedge leaves in the darkness. The sounds of the fight were still behind us, but they were nearing. I stuck my knife into the hedge and hit branches. I sawed quickly. Bits of leaves and twigs fell away, creating a small opening at eye level. Peering through, I saw only more darkness, more hedge.

"This is a waste of time!" she said anxiously.

"I'd appreciate help!" I replied. I sawed through more of the branches, this time at knee-level, and then began tearing at them with my hands to increase the size of the opening.

To my surprise, she gripped the brush and tore at it. I worked on the bottom while she cleaned up my efforts. The sounds of the fight grew loud as a man let out a piercing scream, and then fell silent.

"That's going to have to do." I sheathed the knife, and pushed Sylvia forward. "After you."

She grimaced, muttered a complaint about her dress beneath her breath, and knelt to crawl through. I glanced behind me, towards the domed centre. Sylvia knew her way through the maze. I could go back, help my father...

"Are you coming?" Sylvia asked. Her voice trembled.

Holding in my fear, I crawled through the hole. Branches tore at my clothes and my skin. I tried not to think of my father lying cold and alone on the grass. I tried not to think of the Frostfire guards dragging him off to a dark, dank dungeon. As my palms touched the soft dirt and I climbed to my feet, I tried not to think at all.

"I...I don't know if we can get out this way," Sylvia said.

"We can." I took her hand and led her down the path with more confidence than I felt. As long as she couldn't see my face, I would make it through.

"How do you know?" she demanded.

"Stay quiet." I didn't know what I'd do if she didn't: threatening her wouldn't do us much good right now. I didn't think I had the heart to seriously harm Lady Sylvia, if it came to it. She was just a foolish girl who desperately wanted Keegan for herself. Maybe we were more alike than I thought.

"Oh! You're going so fast! Your hand hurts!" she whispered loudly.

Or perhaps we were nothing alike. "Do you want to be caught?"

"I'm not the one going to be caught."

"Dominique might disagree with that, especially if she believed we were collaborating."

"Collaborating!" She twisted her face as if the word had left a bitter taste. "I—"

"You can talk about how much you hate me later, when we're both safer," I said.

Huffing indignantly, Sylvia resigned to an impatient silence. The fight in the distance had ended, but the sounds of men talking echoed across the maze as together, my rival and I navigated back to the castle in the dark.

* * *

We re-entered the castle through the postern and climbed the servant staircase to the west wing. Only a few servants were performing their duties in pairs, as Mistress Alwina had instructed. I wondered how much trouble I was in for not reporting for my night shift, if Emmine had relayed my crimes to the mistress, and if

Sylvia would excuse my presence if we were caught.

"How long have you been in the castle?" she asked suddenly as we neared her quarters.

"A few days."

"How did you manage that?"

"Magic," I replied. "You never recognized my face, did you?"

Giving me the once over, realization dawned on her face and she scowled. "How did I not...? Never mind. Keep your head down and keep quiet. We're going to my chambers. Hopefully Dominique has had enough of me today and won't pay a visit."

Yes, hopefully she was too busy dealing with my father's escape—and sacrifice—to bother us.

Sylvia's quarters were much like any other in the castle, although hers appeared far more lived in. With the amount of drapery over the windows, the extra canopy, and the light pink silk covering the charred stone, as well as the piles of dresses draped over her dresser chair, the open closet bursting with clothing—it was as if she'd been living in the castle for over a year instead of nearly two months.

Once she'd shut the door, I whirled on her. "Where has Dominique moved Keegan?" I demanded.

She seemed taken aback by my bluntness. "Shh. Not so loud! You're always so loud."

"Don't test my patience," I muttered. "Did she give any indication...?"

"No. And I don't think Dominique was acting alone. Father... he...he didn't approve of keeping him here, either." She moved to her bed and plopped herself down and scuffed her shiny shoes against the rug, as if trying to remove any errant dirt from our whirlwind trip through the maze. Then, as if remembering I was there: "So. You and Ivor Ferguson want to find Keegan. Why?"

"He's the rightful ruler of the kingdom." *And my husband,* I wanted to add, but my father's presence pressed down on my shoulder, although he was not in the room, urging me to be tactful.

"You don't need him to rule," Sylvia said. "As Father says."

"Your father invaded this city. Destroyed the castle. Killed hundreds, thousands of people."

She leapt to her feet defensively. "They wouldn't have died if you had just surrendered!"

"Your family has blood on their hands. You don't get to blame their deaths on me. Or Keegan."

"I would never blame Keegan," she said. "He is innocent. Unlike you."

Her affection for him fuelled her every response and nauseated me to the core. "I don't know if you're aware of this. Our encounter at Driscoll's End was...eventful. But Keegan and I married in the old tradition, at the God Tears."

Her nervous gaze darted to the closet, then the dresser, and back to me. "Is that so?"

"Yes."

"Well," she said, squaring her shoulders. "I highly doubt anyone will recognize that marriage. With no witnesses or an audience? Done outside a church? Without a priest?" A guffaw of a laugh escaped her. "Who would believe the word of a fugitive Freetor?"

"Anyone who believes and trusts the word of the rightful ruler."

Her amusement faded. "I want Keegan," she said firmly. "That's my price for being your ally."

"That's not going to happen. Witnesses or not, he's still my husband."

"Maybe he won't want you when he wakes up," she replied, clutching her skirts. "Especially since you're the one who put him to sleep. Especially since..." She faltered momentarily and then tried a different approach. "I'm the one who has been taking care of him. Tending his frozen body. Placing pleasing aromas around him, singing to him late at night. He is alone, trapped in his body, with no one."

A harsh reply rushed to my tongue but I bit it back. Guilt surged through me. "I am...grateful...for everything you've done. Dominique would have killed him outright."

Her smug mask dropped for the barest of moments. "I would do anything for Keegan."

"Even if he wasn't a prince or in line for the throne of the entire realm?"

She looked hurt. "Why do you think I'm risking everything to find him? To be with him?"

"If you're willing to risk everything, you have to be willing to be uncomfortable. To sacrifice all that you have. That includes this life of leisure and all that comes with it. I may have even sacrificed my relationship with him just to bring hope back to my people"—I squeezed my eyes shut; I couldn't think about that now—"so tell me, are you truly willing to stick your neck out to see Keegan back on the throne?"

Sylvia Frostfire stared at me for a long moment, as serious as I'd ever seen her. "Yes."

I took a deep breath and nodded. "The important thing is that he's alive. We need to find a way to stop this frozen magic from spreading."

"What do you think I've been trying to do? Ever since Keegan arrived, I've been trying to reverse the curse you put on him."

I ignored the jape because I deserved it. "You haven't had any luck, I take it."

Sylvia, frustrated, began pacing the room. "No. Every healer I hired or ordered to treat him either became frozen or too afraid of the Freetor magic. My father told me that loving him was a mistake. That chasing you to the end of the world was a mistake. That trying to honour the marriage that his family made with mine before he got tangled up with you was a mistake. Well, I was tired of always making mistakes." She stopped, and whirled on me. "So I went to the cathedral to pray."

"I didn't take you for a religious person."

"Is anyone truly religious nowadays? No. But the Church comforts the common. Surely it must do the same or better for the noble-blooded."

"Let me guess. You went there, and some priest told you the story of the Emerald Cloth."

She looked stunned. Then angry. "No! I prayed and prayed until my knees were sore and I ran out of things to say. Then I flipped through some of the old texts, until the priests told me I shouldn't touch them or the parchment would crumple. Hmph! How dare they speak to me that way! I am the Daughter of the East! So when they left me alone once more, I stole into their secret archive. The Church has all kinds of secrets, you know. Most of them not very interesting or useful. After a whole night of digging, though, I discovered references to the legend of the Emerald Cloth." She considered me for a moment. "How do you know about the healing properties of the Cloth? Did you sneak in there too?"

It was hard to imagine Sylvia sneaking everywhere, considering the dresses she always wore, but I didn't dare underestimate her drive to save Keegan. "Does it matter?"

"No. I presented the idea to my father: find the Emerald Cloth so we could save Keegan and the other cursed people. He didn't dismiss it outright, but he assigned some scholars to research the possibilities. They were taking too long. After a week, I figured out that my father was just humouring me. So I went back into the archives myself. Turns out, there is a collection of Cloths."

"Cloths. Plural?" I sat down on the bed. "Where?"

"Yes, of course plural. In—" She fell silent. "Hold on. I'm not just going to trade all this information for free, you know. Why should I help you? I could have you imprisoned right now!"

I took a deep breath. "Because right now, you and I have a common enemy. Lady Dominique Castillo, and your father. I have no love for the East"—I stopped myself from bringing up the massacres—"but right now, Dominique and your father stand in the way of retrieving Keegan. You can't do this on your own. Even though I've only been in the castle a few days, I know you're just as much a prisoner as the slaves I want to save. We both have resources the other doesn't. If we work together, we can pool those resources and we can each get what we want: Keegan and our people, uncursed and free. When he wakes up, he can decide who he wants to be with." An easy choice, but no need for her to know that.

"After that...well, that's up to you. You can either agree to marry Dominique's younger brother when he comes of age and kiss all hope of ruling goodbye. Or, you can help us overthrow your father's reign of terror. I'm sure that if Keegan were here, he'd want his throne back, and his people safe, no matter whether they were born on the surface or underground."

Guilt crossed her porcelain face as she contemplated her next move. She took a deep breath. "I could argue with you for days and it would only waste time."

"Finally, something we both agree on," I replied, allowing myself a small smile. A short silence fell between us. I couldn't allow the progress we'd made to stagnate. "You were saying about the multiple Emerald Cloths?"

Sylvia nodded and continued her story. "Several hundred years ago, common thieves and peddlers came forward, claiming to have discovered the Emerald Cloth. Every day, it seemed like there was a new Emerald Cloth. Some of them were clearly rags sold by good liars, but the Church had trouble verifying or dismissing other, older pieces. So they collected the most likely specimens and put them on display. As an attraction. They collected a lot of silver for it too. Those ledgers were so boring to read. Did you know the Church used to have more silver than the entire Frostfire and Tramore fortunes combined?"

The Church had been in decline for hundreds of years. "So the potential fakes are here, in the cathedral?"

"No, I wish. I checked. They're in the cathedral in Sallingaire."

The most defensible city in the realm. Of course they'd be there. My eyes widened. "Didn't Dominique mention that the curse had spread to Sallingaire already?"

Her expression matched mine. "Maybe that's where she moved him!"

"Would she have had time? What about the sealed gates? When did you last see Keegan?"

"She moved him back to the maze after she cursed my poor cousin Lady Milda. If she took him after that...if a carriage rode hard, it's possible he'd be there by now."

I shook my head. This was getting out of our control. If my father was here, he'd know exactly what to say. What to do. "If she moved him to Sallingaire, and she's planning to move others, she's taking a big risk. Why not burn him here?"

"I'm not sure. To prevent you and me from saving him, probably."

"And she doesn't know that the potential Emerald Cloths are in Sallingaire?"

"You heard her. She doesn't place much stock in the power of Dashiell's artefacts. I doubt she knows or cares. And Sallingaire isn't the easiest place to get to, especially now that my father has sealed the gates—she'll do anything to prevent me from going anywhere except North, to Marin." She shrugged. "I'm surprised she hasn't infected me. I don't know who her enemies are. Her mind is dark and twisted. She probably would curse all of Sallingaire if she thought one Freetor walked among them."

"Assuming that we're right, and Dominique moved Keegan to Sallingaire to further her schemes. Besides the problem of getting to Sallingaire, we'd have to access the Cloths and find out if they're real. Do you know anything about the collection?"

"As far as I could tell from the Church records, it was a public exhibit in Sallingaire. The Church gathered all the likely Cloth candidates together. I couldn't find any indication they'd been moved or destroyed. That was twenty years ago."

I had a feeling my father would have already tried to verify their authenticity as well during his time as Advisor. Yet he also hadn't mentioned the exhibit. Maybe he didn't know about it. "There's no guarantee any of those Cloths are real."

"Well we have to try them, don't we?"

I stood. "There is a way to know for sure, just by looking, if one is real."

"How? Freetor magic?"

"Yes."

Her eyes narrowed. "So you do practice it."

"A little," I lied. If I told her it was because of the Spear or the Orb, she'd be too frightened to cooperate. "Get me in a room with the Cloths, and if one is legitimate, we'll take it and use it to lift the curse and free Keegan. First, though: can you confirm that he's in Sallingaire and find us safe passage into the city?"

"I...might." She looked uncertain. "My father and her father have a very strict agreement surrounding possession of the city and the castle as well as traffic in and out. My father owns the largest share, of course, given his contribution to the liberation effort..." She trailed off. "I mean...I guess you'd call it the invasion. The occupation. In any case, I know Dominique has unquestioned use of many of the carriages in the stable. She sends out those sneaky Northern shadows and goodness knows how many other agents to do her awful bidding. Can't you arrange us passage? Don't you have tunnels?"

"Tunnels only go so far. Horses are faster. I could steal, but it's less risky for you to make legitimate arrangements. You're the daughter of the most powerful man in the world, after all."

She turned her nose up at me. "Fine. I'll see—"

A knock at the door startled us both.

"My lady?" a gruff voice came from the other side. "I hear voices in there, are you all right?"

Her eyes became as round as saucers. I assessed the room. Window—nope, not going out that way, not again. No wardrobe. Bed? My father's magic fire haunted me. I darted for the open closet and dove into the pile of dresses.

"I'm just talking to myself," Sylvia said as she hurried for the door. Almost an afterthought, she raced to the closet and shot me an untrustworthy glance. "Don't touch anything."

Instead of inviting the guard in, she left the room and shut the door. A muffled, heated argument ensued.

I parted the dresses and peered into the now-empty room. I would not have believed that I could cooperate with Lady Sylvia Frostfire, but for once, we both wanted the same thing. Keegan. Not that she could ever have him. We'd deal with that once Keegan was awake.

After a minute, Sylvia's light footfalls moved away from the door and the heavy steps of the guard with her. I frowned and slowly stepped from the closet into the open room once more.

Our alliance, whether Sylvia knew it or not, was temporary. Once she realized Keegan wasn't going to want to be with her, she might do something drastic. I doubted she would want to free the slaves who were rebuilding "her" castle. It had taken the death of a Freetor child for Leon to realize that Freetors were people, too—I didn't want to think about who needed to die to make Sylvia see reason.

The way she'd acted when she found out Keegan and I were married. Surely spending that much time with his body, she would have noticed the ring. Yet she'd been uncomfortably surprised when I'd brought it up.

I had to trust my Freetor instincts and put my skills to use.

I patted down the bed, checking quickly under the mattress, then the pillow cases, and under the bed itself. Nothing. I got down on my knees and felt around the wooden floor for a loose board. Everything appeared solid.

The dresser with a pristinely clean looking glass reflected my suspicious face. I brushed my hair from my eyes and ran a hand along the wood. A hairbrush, yesterday's jewellery, and various pins lay scattered on the surface of the dresser. An ornate jewellery box rested in the middle, locked only with a simple clasp. Unable to resist, I opened it, expecting rings, precious pearls, and gemstones.

I nearly recoiled at what was inside instead.

Was that...?

The finger, rotted black and blue, was non-descript. But the rich violet fabric wrapped around its core I'd recognize anywhere. The fabric Keegan and I tore from my cloak, at the Throat, when we made a promise to always be together.

She knew we were married all right: and she'd tried to rectify that.

Rustling of skirts outside the door.

She would pay for this.

I hastily shut the lid and turned as Sylvia re-entered the room. I clasped my hands behind my back, and then rethought that—a guilty Freetor always hid their hands—and balled them into fists instead at my sides.

She chopped off his finger. More likely, she got someone else to do the dirty work for her, and then kept it as some kind of gross talisman and a way to erase my marriage to him. So that no one would know the truth.

"What happened?" I asked.

"Oh, nothing," she said wearily. "I sent the guards who were coming on shift on a pointless, long errand. Well, perhaps not so pointless. Leon is in the wine cellar again. The palace will have no stores of bluesberry wine come winter, I'll say that much."

If I admitted that I knew what she'd done, I'd lose Sylvia as an ally—our one chance to leave the city without crawling through tunnels and make quick passage to Sallingaire. How could I trust her to find Keegan now?

"So. Where were we in our plan?" she said.

I swallowed over the lump in my throat. My mouth felt dry. An awkward silence settled between us. I glanced at the dresser. The longer we were the quiet, the higher the chance I'd bring up the finger. "You were going to get us horses so we could ride east to Sallingaire."

She nodded and crossed her arms. Glancing at the jewellery box, she looked thoughtful—and suspicious. I held my breath.

"Advisor Ferguson said you came here as Linnaea's servant. Does that mean...?" Her eyebrows lifted expectantly, waiting to hear the truth.

That wasn't the question I was expecting. Sylvia and I had established a certain level of trust—a trust that only extended so far. The only person I trusted completely right now was Laoise and there was no way I would put her in jeopardy. I promised her mother I'd protect her. All it took was one slip of the tongue—something Sylvia was notorious for—and suddenly Lord Ansel would know that the young woman in the castle with Linnaea's name was not, in fact, his daughter.

The mission had to continue—and that meant Laoise had to remain for another day and do her duty, just as I had to do mine.

"The noblewoman I arrived with is the real Linnaea Gareth," I said steadily. "I was at Baile Gareth. I infiltrated their staff and became a servant. Eventually I earned Linnaea's trust enough to convince her that I wanted to go to the castle, to serve her."

"You and Ivor Ferguson were at Baile Gareth—together."

"That's right."

Sylvia's eyes widened. "Linnaea is innocent, then. If she ever found out about you..."

"I wish I didn't have to lie to her."

"We could tell her who you really were. Convince her to help us! If she didn't marry my brother, then my father wouldn't have access to Baile Gareth, and we could use their resources to help us find Keegan!" She grinned, waving her hands excitedly. "Oh, this is fun!"

"No, we can't involve her. She's innocent and deserves to stay that way." My gaze darted around the room. I needed a distraction. If Sylvia got any more ideas and acted independently, our mission would go even more off-track.

A wall shelf beside the window provided ample fuel for my fire. Three books lay flat, brand new and freshly bound. I grabbed the topmost book and tore out the first page.

Sylvia was outraged. "What are you—?"

"Do you have a quill?"

Screwing up her bottom lip, she pointed to the dresser, at the quill and the ink. "You're destroying my property, Freetor."

"For good reason, I promise. I'm writing a note to Lady Linnaea. To tell her that I'm sorry for what happened tonight at dinner and that I'm leaving her service. It's not the most graceful goodbye, but...hopefully she'll understand." Sitting down at the vanity, I unscrewed the ink cap and dabbed the quill. A blotchy spot soaked the parchment. I nearly used a Freetor symbol before remembering that the real Lady Linnaea wouldn't know how to read it. My Marlenian hand was shaky at best. Laoise barely knew how to read and write—I'd been teaching her—but surely she would find someone to decipher it for her, and she'd know I was all right, that she should stay put, and the mission was back on track.

With a slight alteration. I folded the parchment and handed it to Sylvia. "Please give this to Lady Linnaea."

"You trust me to deliver it?" Her fingers were poised, ready to open it.

"You can read it if you want. There's no secret message in it."

She peeked at what I had written and then closed it again. "Your handwriting needs some work, but I suppose it's pass-able...for a servant."

"As long as it's readable." I crept toward the door. It would be tough to leave the castle grounds, but the cover of dark-ness would help me get down the mountain and make my meet-ing with Bidelia. The brisk night air blew in from the window, reminding me of how little sleep I'd gotten in the past few days.

I turned, and Sylvia was watching me with a curious expression.

"Where are you going now?" she said finally, looking down at the note and curling her fist around it.

"I have to confer with the Freetors. I have to...retrieve the magic that will allow us to find the real Emerald Cloth. Can you find out what carriages have left the castle within the past day under Lady Dominique's control and meet me on Selby Street tomorrow, late morning? It should be crowded enough in the market that we won't attract attention if we keep our faces hidden."

"Leave the castle?" She looked uncertain. "My father would never allow....oh. You want me to sneak out, I suppose."

"Do whatever is the least suspicious. If they find out we're working together...you will be thrown in the dungeon."

"I'll find a way out. It won't be easy."

I nodded and reached for the door. "Oh, right. You should also know. Your brother Leon? I may have led him to believe that I was secretly Linnaea. To protect Lady Linnaea from his rude behaviour."

Sylvia gasped. "So that's why, at dinner..."

"Yes. Just keep that in mind."

She folded the note in her hand and looked at the jewellery box once more. "I will."

* * *

It was close, but I managed to leave the castle. It took me nearly an hour. I evaded ten separate patrols as I navigated down to the kitchen. I grabbed a nearby water bucket as an excuse to wander outside, then abandoned it as I crept around the bailey, pressing myself into the shadows.

Going down the mountain road was the trickiest, as there was no cover, but the patrols were mostly concentrated near the top of the mountain. The Frostfires didn't seem to care if the peasants wanted to climb the mountain road—they only cared if you wanted to get into the castle proper.

The streets were quiet. Darting from alleyway to alleyway, I felt like a new person in an old body. I'd been to the end of the world and seen what many Freetors believed to be a hoax. I'd found not one, but two artefacts of the man-god long gone. And I'd found love, only to lose it to my enemy.

Selby Street was like any other merchant street, with two-storey buildings, each housing a shop and the family living above. The wooden signs advertising their wares seemed drabber than I remembered; the windows, less pristine. Even a shop or two looked abandoned, yet upon closer inspection, I saw multiple families huddled in the darkness, trying to keep warm.

I ducked into a nearby alleyway to wait for Bidelia. She may have left, thinking I wouldn't come. Although the wall surrounding the city blocked my view of the horizon, the faint glimmer of dawn painted the edge of sky that dipped below the wall.

Footsteps approached from behind me. Light, practiced, and delicate. Not Bidelia. My hand went to my knife as I spun to face the potential threat.

"Monju!" I blurted, surprising myself. I pressed against the gritty stone wall of the building, glancing about for hidden threats. "Where's Bidelia?"

Monju remained in the middle of the alleyway. The assassin was unafraid and exuded calm in the dark, yet his presence here made me uneasy. This was not part of the plan. His hair was dishevelled, and my good Freetor eyes could pick out the bits of dirt clinging to his brown vest and black trousers. "Bidelia is in the Undercity. The Freetors, they do not trust Monju so much. Preferred that Bidelia stay with them. She has an authoritative presence."

After what Monju did to the apprentices, I couldn't blame them. "You have the code words for tonight?"

"Yes. How is Laoise?" he asked. "Why did she not come?"

"She has to continue being Linnaea. At least a little while longer." We still needed to figure out a way to get her out of there before Dominique raked her across the coals. One problem at a time.

Monju shook his head, muttering a Southern curse. "Knew it was going to be dangerous. Should have—"

Three shadows darkened the alleyway, silhouettes of two Frostfire bannermen and a shorter, less armoured person: a Northern shadow killer. "Who goes in there? Come out!"

Monju and I held our breaths. We had two choices. Run. Or fight.

One of the Frostfire men stepped forward, his hand on the hilt of his sword. Monju and I drew back instinctively. "Show yourselves, in the name of Emperor Leszek."

Eleven

WHILE MONJU AND I could run from the guards and lose them in the maze of city streets and alleyways, the Northern shadow killer would be harder to shake. Still, we had to try. Better that we weren't—

One of the guards raised his torch into the alley. "Is that the Violet—?"

—recognized.

"Yep." What gave me away? Dominique had probably sent them out here, searching for me or anyone loyal to me. I drew and swung my knife in a wide berth. "Don't come any closer."

"She has magic," one of the Frostfire men whispered to the other. "I wouldn't—"

Northern shadows obeyed no authority. He rushed me. I saw the glint of the hidden dagger in his sleeve too late. Monju was faster. He shoved me hard against the wall as his steel met the shadow's.

No time to thank him. The two guards, emboldened by the shadow, jumped into the fray. The shadow slashing at Monju beside me paid me no mind—likely he had already noticed Monju's deadly skills and his deft footwork and preferred to focus on that challenge. The alleyway was narrow: the long-swords of the Frostfire bannermen banged against the brick and stone as they both attempted to attack. I ducked beneath their weapons and slashed at their shins. The fabric of their trousers tore, infuriating them further.

Frustrated, the lead bannerman yelled to the shadow, "Kill the Violet Fox, leave the prancer!"

In that split second where the shadow turned his head to locate me, Monju grabbed his opportunity. He nicked the shadow in the upper arm. Undeterred by a simple wound, the shadow advanced. Before me, the Frostfires redoubled their efforts and charged.

The shadow stumbled and fell. Shadows didn't stumble. They were far too nimble. As he fell, Monju used the shadow killer's back as a jumping-off point. I went low; Monju went high. Slashing wide, I carved a thin, long line in the vulnerable point in the guard's armour between their chestplates and their greaves. Monju, with his long, curved blade, made two quick cuts: one for each man, on his exposed cheek.

Their necks were exposed—barely. It would have been the easier target. Yet Monju always chose the non-lethal path when he could.

I crawled between the two men, escaping the alley. I found my feet and doubled back, preparing for the men to follow and to initiate another attack with Monju now flanking them— except that was entirely unnecessary.

Like the shadow, the men collapsed in a heap. They convulsed briefly, then stilled. Afraid, I stepped gingerly towards them, expecting them to pop up at any second and deliver a surprising, final blow. Their breathing was hoarse, but even.

"Poison blade," Monju explained. "Not fatal. Painful, though, once they wake up."

"Clever," I muttered. At least one sleeping curse had a remedy in this city. "We'd better get underground before their friends find them."

As we moved the unconscious men deeper into the darkness of the alley and then took off for the designated safe entrance to the Undercity, I explained what had happened at the dinner, my father's capture, escape, and recapture, and our new alliance with Sylvia Frostfire. He seemed less than thrilled with the latter, but he was in no position to comment on our allegiances, having worked for the other side.

"Monju will protect Laoise." He pronounced her name tenderly; preciously.

"She's my best friend," I said. "If something happens to her...I'll never forgive you."

"Strong words from the Lady."

"Then don't mess it up." I drew a deep breath. Nervous energy bounded within me; I felt like I could run a lap around the castle grounds and still not be rid of it. I needed to put this to use finding Keegan, but the thought of Laoise trapped in the depths of the dungeons, as I had been, filled with me unspeakable rage.

"They would not have an opportunity to hurt Laoise. Monju promises, on his father's life. On Monju's life, as much as this is worth to Lady Kiera. He owes her this."

I leaned against the walls. "Your life is worth something to me, Monju. I appreciate that you care for her." I stared into his patient, dark gaze. "But your feelings come awfully quick."

He nodded, his face a mask of stone and stoic thought. "It is said the feelings of a Southern man are like the stormy winds that roll in from the sea. Sudden, swift, and all-encompassing."

"Well, my feelings are just as strong—in that if you betray her, or me, you might just drown."

His hand lay across his breast as he contemplated. "Monju's feelings for the Lady are that of an artist, and his muse. The Lady is...she is a song in mid-sing."

"I'm also a human being with feelings. Just like Laoise."

"Monju understands this. Monju...I..." He faltered: the Southerners only referred to themselves in the first person in private, intimate conversations. "I only wish to serve along-side the Lady. And her prince. And Laoise. To be a...trusted companion."

"I want that too," I said quietly. "I'm just slow to forgive."

"Monju does not expect the Lady to forgive him, but hopes he can make it up to her, by proving his loyalty in each action he takes, forthwith."

I took a deep breath and nodded. I wanted deeply to forgive. To trust. I'd lived my whole life relying only on my brother, and the other Freetors who fought with me on the surface. It was hard for me to forgive transgressions, even though Monju had had a forgivable reason for acting in the enemy's interests.

We continued in terse silence for a while as we quietly nav-igated the streets toward the secret entrance. "Laoise can take care of herself," I said finally. "If you lose her within the castle, it's probably because she doesn't want to be seen. She's...really good at that. She knows those walls just as well as I do—prob-ably even better."

The corners of his lips turned upward. "This, Monju did not know."

"Well...hopefully we live long enough that we can all get to know each other a little better."

"This, Monju hopes too." He looked up at the wall sur-rounding the city, then to the west, and back north. "Is not far now. Down this street and around the alley."

Back when the city was controlled by Keegan's family, but before I'd truly met him and things were still bad, a Freetor could enter and exit the Undercity through specific guarded trapdoors and hidden underground passages. While the guards knew the location of some of the entrances to the underground, anyone without the proper code in the proper location would be met with an unpleasant jab to the eyeball should they dare pull up the hatch or step into the wrong passageway. Monju said the code and I repeated it above the trapdoor hidden beneath a heavy barrel. After a moment, a series of knocks on the door confirmed receipt, and Monju and I pushed the barrel aside. A Fighter threw open the hatch, regarded us both briefly, and then disappeared into the darkness.

I knelt before the entrance and found the rope ladder. As I turned, preparing to climb down, I noticed he kept a respectful distance.

"You're not coming down?"

The bard assassin smiled awkwardly, his silver canine tooth a glint in the dark. "The one who killed the apprentices, stepping into the Undercity? No. Monju will be here, and then, in the castle, where Laoise can call upon him if necessary."

"All right. Be careful."

"Always," he replied, and then, he was gone.

I climbed down the frayed ladder, a sense of calm and familiarity enveloping me as the scents of the earth filled my nose. A Fighter stood guard at the foot of the rope and after a cursory glance, gave me a respectful nod.

Ahead was a junction: one tunnel led left, the other right, and there stood Bidelia, arms crossed, impatiently waiting for me. I grinned. She launched herself urgently from the dirty cave walls. In one hand, she held an oblong, wrapped object that could only be the Spear. With the other, she grasped my shoulder, her bony fingers digging into my skin with equal parts relief and desperation. "Conal got you the message."

My heart dropped into my stomach upon hearing my father's real name. "Y-yeah. I'm here."

"So you are. How is Laoise?"

I bit my lip. "She's fine."

She didn't believe me. "What happened?"

"Later." I glanced at the Spear, bundled in raggedy cloth. The cursed item that I wished I'd never set eyes on. "Laoise is safe, for now. Tell me about this plan my father risked his life for."

Letting out a slow breath, Bidelia became more concerned, but she didn't ask after him. I followed her as we trod down the low passageway. "I've gathered everyone I could find in the Great Cavern."

As my eyes adjusted to the dim lighting offered by the faint glow of the cave moss and the occasional magical lamp mounted to the walls, I caught Bidelia looking back at me as she led the way. "I can't lie to you, Kiera. Things are grim. We need a victory. To see you alive...it is what the Freetors need right now."

"Anything I can do to help." After my inability to save the slaves in the castle, I was desperate to be of use to my flesh and blood in the Undercity. The plan to infiltrate the castle with a small team and capture Leszek Frostfire sounded better and better by the minute. "What do you mean... everyone you could find?"

"After the death of the apprentices, and the slaughtering in the streets, the Undercity was not the same. The structure of our society dissipated like smoke. The remaining apprentices tried to hold order, but when everyone heard that the Violet Fox, the young Freetor woman who was set to rule the land, had died..." Her sigh was laced with regret. "Many Freetors scattered deeper into the caves, fearing for their lives. Many had loved ones who died at Frostfire hands during the invasion. Others lost hope that they could ever be free. In many ways, it is worse than before."

She stopped then, turning fully to face me. "Kiera, it's not just the Frostfires or the Castillos or the surface-born that are the enemy now. If we do not figure out a way to reunite the Freetor people, to give them some kind of hope or better future to look forward to, we will lose the Freetor people. For good."

"Do you want me to go in there with a violet cape and a mask and tell them not to give up?"

"No," she replied. "I want you to go in there as you are, hold up the Spear, and rally them to your cause."

"My cause is to free Keegan and the rest of my people from the sleeping curse. You mean for me to rally them to infiltrate the castle."

"No. It's beyond a small-team infiltration now, Kiera. I need you to enlist them in a siege."

"We can't siege..." Our voices echoed in the caves. It was hard to have a private conversation here—or anywhere—in the Undercity. "I won't march them up the mountain and down into their graves."

"If you don't, they'll starve down here. Slowly. Would you prefer that?"

I would prefer if no one had to die. But that wasn't an answer. There had to be another way. I held out my hands, and Bidelia passed me the Silver Spear. I turned it around, cradling it with disdain. I had to inspire my people to live.

How I was going to do that, I had no idea.

"We need a big demonstration to show everyone, surface-born and Freetor, that our voices will be heard in the face of oppression," Bidelia continued. "We could arrange for a small group to capture one or more of the Frostfires. But what good would it do? You squash one bug, and another rises in its place. If Leszek Frostfire falls, who is to say that his son Boris would be any better?"

The thought of Boris becoming emperor—with Dominique as High Queen at his side, whispering commands in his ear—made me sick. "How do you think this siege will play out, Bidelia? The moment the Frostfires suspect any kind of rebellion, they'll kill everyone. With the food shortage and the closed gates, the fewer hungry mouths to feed, the better, in their eyes."

"Perhaps siege is not the right word," she admitted. The ghost of a smile settled on her face, all the more eerie in the faint glowing light of the moss. "Tomorrow, Leszek Frostfire is going to announce a celebration ball in the castle. It will be the first of its kind since they stormed the city."

My eyes widened. "I didn't know about this."

"We only found out a few hours ago after one of our runners intercepted their night riders, carrying the message to some of the small lords outside the city. We had hoped to hold off our attack for at least a week until we'd heard back from our friends in Feenagh Forest, but we can't waste this opportunity."

"So what, a bunch of us disguise ourselves in gowns and masks, we go in there...?"

"No. Too risky. They'll be expecting that. The celebration is for nobles and the wealthiest of merchants only, by invitation. This is where you'll come in. They know you as a servant now—"

"Yes, but I have no more face cream. And I've been...sort of...asked to leave. Officially."

Bidelia's expression darkened. "What happened?"

We neared the Great Cavern. "I'll tell you after. I might be able to get back in. Tell me the plan."

"You'll have to get us in. Before the fire, there were tunnels in the cellar. The same ones you used to escape the fire before they collapsed. On our end, tunnels stretch beneath parts of the city and Feenagh Forest—including a few that go under the castle. Most of them had been collapsed over a hundred years ago, yet every now and then, an enterprising Freetor would attempt to clear them. Now we have our strongest people working on clearing the most stable tunnel, but it's exhausting work."

"You don't know where the tunnel leads?"

"We're nearly certain it leads into the cellar. We were hoping you could find a way to dispense with the guards or anyone in the lower levels of the castle, so we have a clear passage in."

"I...suppose," I said slowly. Other than Leon's frequent visits to the wine cellar, I didn't know much of what was going on down there. Yet another mission for the Violet Fox.

"I'm sure you can come up with something," she said quickly. We stopped just before the entrance to the Great Cavern. "Once there, we will surround the Great Hall and keep the nobles contained. Smaller territory, easier to defend. We will make our demands at first, though I expect they will not want to listen to reason. It will be a tough fight."

I caught her arm. "Bidelia, there are Northern shadow killers there. And trained, armoured Frostfire men. What kind of people will we have on our side?"

Bidelia was rarely amused, but tonight, she looked truly smug. "An alliance the Freetors have never seen." She handed me the Spear and gestured the Great Cavern.

The thin stream of sunlight beaming in at the centre of the cavern like a long rod punctured the darkness: the only place in the Undercity where sun permeated our dark space. I'd heard the voices in the corridor, yet now as I stepped into the large domed gathering place of smoothened rock and stone, the number of people gathered together to fight the Frostfires hit me, hard. I'd been fighting alone, or with my few allies, surrounded by enemies for so long that I'd forgotten the feeling of being part of a more powerful whole, united with one goal—one cause.

Yet it wasn't the pale faces of my Freetor brothers and sisters that caught my immediate attention. There were surface-born here, and not just any common peasants. At least a hundred Roamers—so identified by their colourful rags, their instruments, and general jolly disposition—cheered as I entered, mixing their voices with the crowd of Freetors lining the cavern walls.

"The Violet Fox is alive!"

"She has brought us the Spear! We are saved!"

I weaved through the people as they crowded around me,

heading for the Roamers. Bidelia followed in my wake.

"How...?" I asked her.

"This is courtesy of Monju," she said dryly. "And apparently, you and Keegan."

Pascal Antony, the large man who had welcomed us into the Roamer camp and then tortured Keegan, lumbered forward, favouring his left leg, grinning despite his physical condition. We had parted on strange terms. The former general had fought as a mercenary for Leszek Frostfire in the trade war with the North in his younger days, but when he didn't receive adequate payment, joined the Roamers and lived the traveller's life ever since. He had seemed eager to fight any authority figure—Leszek especially—for a price.

I kept my distance from the man, standing before the ray of sunlight. He respected this, preferring to remain out of the artefact's generous reach. This was my territory—and as we exchanged polite nods, our unspoken agreement was clear: we had endured punishment in his camp for breaking Roamer laws, and if he dared to disrespect our customs, he would face a similar fate.

"So, you're not dead," he said simply. His voice was boisterous and friendly, and hard not to like.

I stuck the butt of the Spear in the ray of sun, allowing the artefact to bask in the one strip of hope my people had left. "I'm hard to kill."

"Evidently your prince is not. Heard he's in Leszek Frostfire's clutches."

"He's not dead yet either. Neither are the rest of my people who have been cursed. But..." I paused, eager to get to the matter at hand. "What brings you here? Dangerous to be travelling when the Frostfires have closed the gates to the capital."

Antony grinned. Roamers enjoyed telling tales—in fact, it was their main currency.

"We've had an adventure or two since we last spoke. We headed east, for Baile Gareth, to find Ivor Ferguson, as Prince Keegan had suggested. You were right: the Frostfires on the throne are a menace to society—and an opportunity for us to fight once again." Some of the Roamers exchanged inside jokes and jostled each other. "But imagine our surprise when Lord Ansel denied the presence of the traitorous and former Advisor! Once his allegiances—and his empty pockets—were made clear, we quickly left the dark forests." He shivered dramatically, earning scattered chuckles in the crowd. "Fortunately Monju Farin always knows how to find us, doesn't he? Spun us a real good tale about how the Violet Fox and her prince on Mountain High would appreciate our help. Escorted us all here."

I nodded. My voice sounded more confident than I felt. "Yes. We—"

Antony held up his large hand. "Your—mother? Aid?" He gestured to Bidelia respectfully. "She informed me of the plan. We have our own demands."

My breath caught. I hoped Monju hadn't made promises to the Roamers that we couldn't keep. Couldn't they just help for a good cause? "Like I told you before. Leszek Frostfire and his family won't stop until the Freetors and anyone who opposes his ideal way of life are eradicated. What you see is what we have." I dug the Spear into the dirt to emphasize my point.

Antony's gaze fell upon the Spear with a fearful curiosity. "You might have married a prince, Violet Fox, but that don't make you our queen. You're a convenient figurehead. And last I saw, you aren't in a position to turn down our demands, either. So, for the final time: do you want to hear our demands, or should we offer our services to other interested parties?"

"Tell me your demands." I gritted my teeth. Despite his insults, he was right about one thing—we weren't in a position to turn him down. Collecting and composing myself, I imagined how my father had endured years of negotiating with lords large and small, merchants rich and poor, and rulers with egos larger than their heads. He'd survived—so could I.

"We have three major demands," Antony began. "First—we would like a plot of land. Roamers travel by nature, but we'd like a permanent residence where we can rest without fear of persecution."

"The Freetors want that too. I can't—" I bit back my argument. I could argue both sides all night. It was hard to bestow and re-distribute land without taking it away from someone else, regardless of who it belonged to hundreds of years ago. Inevitably, someone would end up losing. "What are your other demands?"

He looked suspicious at my initial reluctance, but continued. "Second, of course, is silver. Enough to compensate the hundred people standing here today, plus extra to start them on a new life under your benevolent rulership."

"And how much silver is that?" I asked.

Antony grinned with his rotten teeth. "I suspect whatever is in Leszek Frostfire's personal vault—as well as some of his highest value items—will be sufficient."

Nerves tumbled inside me. Leszek Frostfire was not as wealthy as he had been, yet that did not stop the nausea I felt at the thought of Pascal Antony and the other Roamers raiding the castle for valuables. "You can have whatever silver or treasure the Frostfires deem valuable. All of it is coated in the blood of Freetor slaves. Even the silver."

This unsettled Antony. "All silver, all things, are forged in blood, Violet Fox. Even that Spear you prize so highly."

I glanced at it warily and tightened my grip around the staff, wishing I could bury it in the earth. "And the third demand?"

"Ah." Some of the Roamers looked uncomfortable and drew away from their unofficial leader. Antony himself looked suddenly humble before me. "This demand is not uniform across us hundred here, but among some of us, it is the ultimate prize. An...insurance, we'll say...that we won't be harmed by anyone, ever again."

I had a sinking feeling. I knew exactly what he was going to say. It wasn't mine to give. "Can't my word be insurance enough?"

"Your word is valuable, Violet Fox. The actions of your prince have guaranteed his word, too. Though not among all of us. And what are words against the pure force of Freetor magic?"

Bidelia's eyes widened. "Magic cannot be given. It is born, moulded! The Elders are dead, the apprentices scared and scattered—"

"I'm aware," Antony said, waving his large hands again. "Give us an apprentice to live among us, then, to protect us from those who would do us wrong. Perhaps they could attempt to teach us their ways."

"I'm not the keeper of Freetor magic. I won't order one of my own to serve you," I said firmly. "Magic is unpredictable enough."

"Surely one magical item, one not so dangerous, would be enough to ensure our safety?" Antony asked.

I hesitated. One magical item wouldn't go amiss. Just for them to use to scare off their enemies. I held the Silver Spear with both hands, considering it. A magical item could be anything that glowed blue—anything inherently imbued with magic from Elders or apprentices that came before me. Something small for the price of the safety of the West, of all those who lived in fear in this moment, fear of being murdered because of their sympathies or allegiances. The one hundred Roamers before me could tip the scales in our favour in this clandestine invasion. Yet the faces of the twisted apprentices, the face of Elder Erskina in her blind rage, and even Keegan's face as he froze in place before me at the end of the world—all it took was one artefact in the wrong person's hands to spread terror and evil.

"I can't give you magic, under any circumstances," I said.

Surprised by my words, Antony looked to his concerned comrades. "That so. It is three demands or nothing, Violet Fox. Otherwise, we leave by tunnel."

"Goodbye, then." I turned away. The words burned; I couldn't take them back.

"Kiera, what are you—?" Bidelia hissed.

"Wait!" Antony's booming voice echoed in a deafening way in the cavern. "I admire your resolve, Violet Fox. But are you willing to sacrifice the survival of your people just to let go of your control of a single magical item?"

I turned around slowly, looking to the Spear. "Even if you fought me now for this Spear and won, I would destroy it before you could touch it." Despite what Antony had done to Keegan, I didn't wish him an eternally frozen fate. "We are all afraid. The lives of my people—all of my people—are not worth assuaging your fear. The silver you can have. The land, you deserve as much as any of us here. But the only magic anyone is getting from me is the power to heal those with the sleeping curse."

"We have heard tales of it," Antony said slowly. "That you kissed your sweet prince Keegan and he fell deep into an icy sleep. Easy for the Frostfires to slip away with him."

"More like he was kissed by the Silver Spear," I said, holding it up, "and because of the magic curse made by Alastar the Hero, all surface-born who touch it fall prey. Do you want that kind of responsibility, General? Possessing a magical artefact, knowing that you can't control that which you covet?"

The murmuring among the Roamers erupted into full-blown discourse, which settled as Antony raised his hand again, the amusement draining from his face. "I see your point. We...

accept your terms. The hundred Roamers standing here will aid the Violet Fox and her followers in her scheme to retake the castle from Leszek Frostfire and his Northern allies."

I blew out a strong breath I didn't know I was holding in. "Good. The tunnels will be ready tomorrow evening."

The Freetors crept from the walls in shy reverence of the Spear. They had always been there, of course, quiet as nothingness as they had been taught.

Bidelia raised her eyebrows.

Right.

I inhaled deeply. "I know it's hard. We're hungry. We're tired. Our leaders have been beaten. It seems like they're winning. In some ways—they are.

"They only win when there's nothing of us left. When there's no one to don the Violet Fox mask and remind them of our presence. You thought I was dead. I almost was. I'm sorry. I'm sorry they're punishing you for a curse you didn't create. That's why I went to the castle, to try and stop it." A few protests bubbled up from the crowd, but I shook my head. "The curse only affects the surface-born, it's true. Yet if we stand by and allow the innocent to be frozen and then crushed, how does that make us different from the evil we have fought our entire lives?

"I snuck into the castle under their noses. I knelt on my knees before the Daughter of the North, and she stared into my eyes— yet here I am. Alive. We have operatives in the castle, eating away the foundation of the North-East alliance. Now, tomorrow, with the help of our Roamer allies, we will take the castle and remove the Frostfire and the Castillo families—and those who support a regime of oppression and tyranny."

"And what then, Violet Fox?" Antony asked softly. "Will you take up the mantle for yourself? Install your Prince Keegan Tramore, whose family has a long history of oppressing your flesh and blood?"

The words stung, but they rang true. "My priority is ridding my people of the sleeping curse." I hesitated, as my marriage to Keegan wasn't public knowledge, or a real reason in Freetor eyes to claim the throne. "I will do what the people have asked of me. As I always have."

"We will follow you," said a Freetor voice, deep within the crowd.

"The Violet Fox is our High Queen. Our empress!" added another.

A chant began and rippled through the crowd. With each voice that joined and echoed in the cavern, the safer I felt—my people were acting as one, with one voice, as they never had before. Cradled by their words, the weight of them settled on me like a boulder. They wanted me to rule them. They didn't care about Keegan, or the curse, or whose hands held the magic— they cared that I held the Spear and that I had promised to protect them from further oppression and death.

I bowed my head, feeling like the lowliest peasant under the strain of an invisible Crown than ever before.

* * *

Later, when the Freetors and the Roamers in the Great Cavern had filtered out to find rest and food, Bidelia escorted me down one of the tunnels. I followed without thinking—my body desperately craved sleep, and I hoped that's where she was leading me.

"I'm proud of you," she said, after we had walked in silence for some time. "They asked for the one dangerous thing we could not give and you remained strong."

I almost did, I thought, feeling guilty. How much was too much to sacrifice for my people's happiness and safety? "Thank you."

Bidelia nodded. "Now, tell me everything that's happened. Tell me about Laoise."

I relayed everything: how well Laoise had fooled the nobles, my encounter with Leon Frostfire, the slavery in the castle, the new servant dynamics, the curse spreading in the castle, and the disastrous, near-fatal dinner on the balcony. Whether he died in the hedge maze or he was locked deep in the dungeons, they knew he had magic now, and Leszek would not allow him to live now. My father was lost to me, and I told her that too. I nearly didn't tell her about Laoise's involvement with my father's escape and our subsequent encounter with Sylvia in the hedge maze, but I could hide nothing from Bidelia. Not now.

"You put her at great risk," she said after I'd finished. "I don't know if it was worth it. Conal has been recaptured."

"I would have spent precious time wandering the maze if he hadn't been there. The guards would have caught me and then we'd be in the dungeon together." I also might not have thought to bargain so openly with Sylvia, either, but I didn't mention that. "Now that we know for certain that the Frostfires are going to exploit the Silver Spear sleeping curse, we can't ignore the Emerald Cloth any longer. Sylvia thinks she has a lead. In Sallingaire."

"You can't leave now," Bidelia hissed. "Or have you not learned your lesson? The last time you left to chase down an artefact, the castle burned and hundreds—thousands—died."

"And if I don't find the Emerald Cloth, like my father suggested, many more will die at the hands of the Frostfire family. I can't stand by and watch them pick and choose who will live and who won't. I have to think of all of my people—regardless of whether they're surface-born or not."

"You certainly didn't think of Laoise," Bidelia said bitterly. "You should have been the one to let Conal out of his cage. Or you should have left him there. Now her cover is at risk."

"We made a decision together. I stand by it, as she would, if she were here. Monju is up there. He'll keep an eye out."

Bidelia snorted indignantly, folding her arms. "I'm sure."

"He will," I said, more serious this time. A memory returned to me strongly: Rordan, receiving carefully penned letters from admirers broaching the subject of marriage. If Monju were a Freetor, no doubt Laoise and Bidelia would already be composing such a letter. Perhaps I would have helped her write it. I shook away the past. "It is only until late morning, early afternoon at the latest."

"Yes, after your meeting with Sylvia." Bidelia didn't like that part of the plan either. "All this backdoor dealing. The secret collusion with the enemy. I don't like it." She fixed me with an intense stare, equal parts frustrated and afraid. "You have too much of your father in you."

"And why is that a bad thing?"

Her eyes widened, and in that moment, I knew why. As much as I resented him for what he did to the Freetors—for what he did to me and Rordan, leaving us to fend for ourselves, I wanted to like him. I wanted him to be part of my life, as chaotic and impossible as it was right now.

"I will tell you this about Conal Driscoll," she said finally, leaning against the wall. "I've known him nearly my entire life. We would run in these caves together, him, me, your mother, and Mahon." It wasn't often she mentioned Laoise's father. "Conal was an ambitious boy. He had big dreams. Like you. He taught himself to read and his dreams became as big as the words in the books he stole. Even when he was rejected—twice, mind you— as an apprentice, he didn't give up. He believed that we would be free to not only live on the surface with the Marlenians, but that all knowledge would be free as well. He soaked up every scrap of gossip, memorized every shipping route, counted every patrol and learned their names. Hoarded information like it was food. He was a good thief, but he didn't have to steal. He tricked the Marlenians into giving him what he wanted."

A knot twisted inside me. I had no idea my father wanted to be an apprentice. In fact, I didn't know much about his childhood. I'd been too young to ask. "It sounds like you admired him."

"When I was your age, I did," she said bluntly. "But when I discovered he hadn't died that day, that he was keeping his belly full while you and Rordan and my Laoise stole and risked your lives each day for the well-being of your neighbours...well. I realized then that while he'd changed his name and his situation, his ambition was stronger than ever."

"Why are you telling me this now?" I asked.

"Kiera. You truly believe it was a coincidence that he saved Keegan that day on the streets?"

My father had saved Keegan's life, thus earning the Holy One's trust—and a position of power. I leapt to my feet. "No. Stop."

"I'm sorry. I don't mean to dishonour his memory. He did a very noble thing for you tonight. But noble deeds can come from all kinds of men, including deceitful ones."

I turned away. "I want to remember him in the best way possible. Like...like I remember Rordan."

"I know you do." She launched from the wall and placed firm hands on my shoulders. "I'm sorry he's gone. I'm sorry that everyone will remember him as Advisor Ferguson, and not as Conal Driscoll. It is for the best that we keep his Freetor connection quiet. We'll think of a way to honour him once our fight has been won."

Bidelia's words settled on me like heavy rain. "The fight never ends, does it? The war ended two hundred years ago and we're still fighting."

"Endings are subjective. Each day is a fight for many of us.

One day, we will live in the sun again, without the tyranny of the surface suffocating us." She hesitated. The Bidelia I knew was practical and direct. Even though she was like my surrogate mother in many ways, I had never had a deep conversation like this before.

"You don't need Keegan to retake the castle," she said finally, after many minutes of silence. "The people will follow you. They want you to rule."

"Yes, but I don't want to march into the mountain with a handful of peasants, mercenaries, and frightened Freetors, only to be slaughtered." The tip of the Spear seemed even sharper in that moment as I handed her the artefact for safekeeping. "I won't rule over a realm of sleeping, cursed people. And I won't rule over it without Keegan. I want him at my side. Forever." I glanced up at her, feeling sick to my stomach. "Do you think that's selfish?"

"As Freetors, we use what we're given. We fight for what we need. Which, most of the time, is very little, on both counts." She clasped her hands neatly around the staff. In that moment I wished I remembered what my mother looked like, wondering if she would be as strong as Bidelia. "Always remember, Kiera. The people are first. But do not neglect your heart, either. It will tell you what is right. You follow it and we will follow you."

* * *

In the adjoining cave that used to be my sleeping chamber, someone snored softly. Three people huddled together in the corner under one large blanket. I tip-toed passed them towards the far cave-room. Rordan's private chamber. A ratted blanket was rolled up on the rock-bed, but whoever currently occupied the space wasn't sleeping here tonight.

I hugged the blanket to my chest and lay on the hard stone,

staring up into the darkness. When I closed my eyes, Rordan appeared before me, arms crossed, leaning against the stone wall, somewhat amused that I chose this cave, this room to commune with him.

"I wish you were really here," I whispered.

He smiled, and then shrugged. He was exactly as I remembered him.

"I wish you didn't die hating our father."

Crouching before me, he spoke in an echoing voice that lulled me to sleep. "I didn't."

Twelve

"AM I DRESSED appropriately now?" Sylvia asked sarcastically, gripping the dirty brown robes in disgust as we emerged from the alleyway. "I don't want to be recognized, but I also don't want to be regarded as a monk who forgot to wash." She gave my somewhat cleaner black robes and hood the once-over as she tugged her own hood down over her face. "Tell me why you get to wear the clean robes."

In the underground, there was only darkness, which had made waking up on time difficult. When I'd opened my eyes and remembered where I was, hearing the rustling of the other Freetors in the adjoining caves as they went about their day, I'd raced to the rope ladder. There, to my surprise, Bidelia had been waiting for me with two sets of robes. She'd correctly assumed that Sylvia wouldn't think to disguise herself.

"You could have brought clean robes yourself, had you thought to traipse around the city as someone other than Sylvia Frostfire. Surely someone must have recognized you!"

"People are too scared to look me in the eye. That's what Gabian is for."

As we entered the bustling market streets of Marlenia City, she gestured over her shoulder. I risked a quick glance: sure enough, in the far distance, a single fair-haired man, unarmoured but sporting a pin with the Frostfire crest, kept a stern eye on the two of us.

My eyes widened. "I told you to come alone."

"You really think that I, Lady Sylvia Frostfire, would dare to walk the streets of Marlenia City alone?"

"At midday? Yes."

"What better time for thieves to dive into my cloak for silver?"

I bit back a clever reply. While it would bolster my ego to win an argument against her, Keegan remained frozen in the clutches of our enemies. I took a deep breath. "Have you found out anything useful about Keegan? Where Dominique or your father might have sent him?"

"I've confirmed with my stablemen. Three carriages with Northern banners left the castle grounds late yesterday and last night. Two with supplies for the North. And one with supplies and a rather strange, large box, accompanied by three shadows." She looked troubled. "Dominique has, without a doubt, sent him to Sallingaire!" Sylvia exclaimed, so loudly that a couple of passing merchants turned their heads. She pulled her hood down further. "Ugh, this cloak is itchy. And it smells like it hasn't been washed in months."

It probably hadn't been. I tried not to let my amusement show. "What do you know about the city? All I know is it's a highly defensible position, from both sides."

"I've passed through it, of course. You have to, if you're travelling in an entourage. Otherwise the horses and everyone will starve. If she thinks I wouldn't follow him there, she's insane. She probably is insane, you know."

I didn't argue that point. "So you are planning to follow him there?"

She looked surprised. "Of course I am. Aren't you?"

"I am. I'm going with you."

She turned up her lip. "I say I'm going to do something, and you attach yourself to me like a tick to a dog."

"It's in both our interests to go together."

"I don't see how. You'd only slow me down. Try and steal away my true love—"

I was starting to get sick of Sylvia's voice. "If you leave the capital and you aren't going to the North, Dominique will have her shadows on you so fast you won't know what hit you. You're going to need my protection if you want to make it out of the city alive."

"I could always take the Northern road and double back through the mountains."

"You really want to spend more time outdoors, while Keegan sleeps, frozen, spreading the curse to our people? Do I have to remind you that without my Freetor magic, you're not going to be able to find the real Emerald Cloth?"

Sylvia, tight-lipped and annoyed, turned away and pressed deeper into the crowd. I sped up to keep up with her. "I haven't forgotten. It's the most annoying thing on my mind." She sighed. "Fine. We'll travel by carriage. Leaving from the stables is the only way to leave the city without passing through any check-points, but we will have to travel through Silent Thief's Pass."

Silent Thief's Pass was the tunnel through the mountains that allowed travellers going east-west to bypass Marlenia City—but at a steep cost. In the Holy One's time, because of the high number of bandit, Roamer, and Extremist activity, it was guard-ed by a platoon of tough soldiers. They were just as effective at extorting peasant travellers as they were getting rid of the "scum" that plagued the area.

"How do you think we're going to get through there without being noticed?" I asked.

"My charms, of course," Sylvia said, flashing a smile. "And my name carries weight, you know."

She really had no idea what she was getting into. "Perfect...I'll think of something else, though. Just in case."

I glanced around. The sun was high in the sky. Just nine, maybe ten more hours until the Roamers and the Freetors would be waiting in the tunnels for me to see them through safely into the castle—and the siege would begin. But Sylvia didn't know that. Hopefully, once I'd helped the Roamers secure the ball room and capture Leszek Frostfire, Sylvia and I could escape in a carriage to Sallingaire. I hoped that Laoise and Monju would accompany us—the thought of having to mind Sylvia the entire way frustrated me beyond compare.

"One more thing," Sylvia said, suddenly cheery. "My father is throwing a ball tonight. He's calling it the Liberation Celebration. It's very last minute, but all of the noble families within the city and in the bailes surrounding are invited."

I raised an eyebrow, pretending to be surprised. "Does he usually throw lavish parties at the last minute?"

"No, but with so many people wanting his head, he can't be too careful." She turned her nose up at a merchant trying to get her attention with a basket of fresh bread. "I'm not telling you because you're invited. I'm telling you because we can't leave until after the party."

My throat tightened. "And when is that? Midnight?" I could only hope.

"No, of course not! Dawn. Even in the East, noble parties last until dawn. Of course, many of us will have already taken a room at that point, but to truly show your respect, you stay until the first light of the sun!"

"Wherever Keegan's gone, they've got a day's head-start—"

"If I'm not at this party, my father will assume I have been kidnapped and flood the city with soldiers. At the very least, I need to make an appearance. Have a few drinks. Then we can leave, when my father's men are too busy making merry to realize we've made off with a carriage."

It wasn't a bad plan, but it made me nervous all the same. I felt like a Roamer juggler, trying to keep six balls in the air. "All right. But I'm not going to allow you to have too much fun. I'm going to this party, too."

"What? No, you can't!" she hissed, gripping my arm so tight that her sharp nails punctured my skin. "Dominique will recognize you. She's still convinced you're somewhere in the castle. She won't stop talking about it, going on and on about what's she's going to do to you when she finally has you locked away. Not to mention, what will Linnaea think if you suddenly reappear in her service? Your note will have been for naught!"

"I'm not going to go in there dressed like...like a princess!" I retorted. "All I'm going to do is ensure you don't forget the mission. And"—I met her gaze reluctantly—"now that you're helping me, I need to ensure you're not harmed. By anyone. Consider me a personal guard."

She didn't look too pleased. "A Freetor, protecting me, the Daughter of the East? If only my father could see me now."

Hopefully, he would remain oblivious to his daughter's sneaking around. Thinking of him brought to mind another wash of emotions. Perhaps there was no point in asking. I had to know, however. "About...the Advisor. Do you know if he survived the fight with your father's men?"

The same look from last night marred her features, a kind of perverse confusion. "Why do you care about that weasel?"

"Because he's..." How could I explain it to her? She cut off Keegan's finger. I couldn't trust her. Not with that secret. If he survived, he needed to keep his cover. And if not...then I had to let Advisor Ferguson rest in peace. "He helped me."

"Hmph." She was quiet for a minute. "I saw my men remove a body about his size from the dungeon this morning. My father seemed pleased: he was down there too. He never liked the Advisor."

My heart sank. I shouldn't have asked. I'd prepared myself

for the possibility that he might be dead. I swallowed my sadness. I couldn't process this now. I had to ensure Laoise was safe and clear those tunnels. "Never mind, then. Can you sneak me back into the castle?"

* * *

Sneaking back into the castle proved awkward. Sylvia had taken a carriage down the mountain with Gabian, her personal guard. He took one look at me with his narrowed gaze, and immediately suspected I was not who I appeared. Sylvia and I sat next to each other in the carriage, across from his constant, suspicious gaze.

"I was in the market alone," she told him sternly, noticing his gaze. "This is my associate from the North. A shadow killer trainee, you might call her."

He sat up straighter.

As we wound up the mountain, she gave further instructions. "I'll get off at the front doors, of course. You'll ride with Gabian to the stables. From there, you're on your own. We'll see each other at the masquerade."

I nodded, like a shadow killer from the North would do.

"My lady," Gabian said hesitantly, "does this mean you no longer require my services?"

"Gabian, you are my favourite guard, and I would never dream of dismissing you. This is extra security, a secret from my father and that dreadful Dominique, just in case something terrible happens. This shadow killer knows the North inside and out—it helps me to anticipate Dominique's moves. We might be allies but she cannot be trusted. Do you understand?"

"A wise tactical move, my lady. I understand completely." His cheeks coloured as he bowed his head. Now he could wither under my gaze. I smiled. Perhaps Sylvia was getting the hang of this after all.

* * *

Bypassing the maze, tempted to run through it to find evidence of my father's downfall, I felt the weight of everything bearing down on me. Keegan depended on me to find him. Laoise depended on me to rescue her from her position as Linnaea. Sylvia depended on me to locate the Emerald Cloth. My people depended on me to lead them in a rebellion—one that might fail—tonight.

I kept my head down as I rushed in the kitchen entrance, weaved through the servants preparing for tonight's feast, and made my way up to the west wing. Once I got to Laoise's chamber, everything would be fine. I could decompress for a few hours, find out the best way to clear the lower levels so—

"Where have you been?"

The harsh voice of Mistress Alwina seized me mid-step in the long corridor. I stood as frozen as a victim of the Spear's curse.

"Face me, girl."

Terrified, I turned. She looked as if she'd chased me all the way up the mountain, dishevelled and red with rage. For a brief moment, doubt clouded her judgement. I looked different without the face cream—but not different enough. I was still the same height, I had the same complexion, and I'd responded to her demand with the fear of a servant. To claim I was someone else would mark me as an intruder. I hung my head. Either way, I was in trouble.

What puzzled me more was why Mistress Alwina didn't know that Rorda Cloth had been removed from Linnaea's service. Why hadn't Emmine said anything? "I was on a special assignment for Lady Linnaea."

"More special than your duties here in the castle?" Her looming figure closed in on me, pressing me against the gritty stone wall. "That is not an excuse. You have girls that depend on you. If even one girl shirks her duties, do you know what happens?"

I glanced down the hallway. I couldn't leave Laoise hanging—she might even think me dead. I'd promised to get her out of this castle. "Um, the west wing floor doesn't get scrubbed?"

The mistress was not amused. In a calculated move worthy of the Northern shadow killer, she pinched the tip of my ear and dragged me down the servant staircase, down the corridor, and all the way into the servant quarters. I struggled; she yanked harder. She was difficult to keep up with, and by the time we burst into the crowded quarters, I was just as red and dishevelled as she was.

"Girls," she said. "Look who I found, wandering the corridors like a Freetor rat."

Emmine, Kuni, and a dozen other servant girls from the East and the North gathered in the centre of the room. Half of them looked ashamed for me and averted their gaze, but Emmine had the look I'd seen in Freetors many a time: Stand up to her. Show her who you really are.

Mistress Alwina finally released my ear and threw me a disgusted look. "Rorda Cloth has shirked her duties."

"I have not," I replied, straightening. "I was—"

"Stop lying. Do you know what the Castillo family would do if they caught you spinning your deceit?"

"Yes, I do," I said bitterly. I couldn't believe Emmine hadn't reported my misconduct to the mistress. I was stuck. I couldn't admit that Dominique had forcibly dismissed me from Laoise's service—then I'd be punished for sneaking around the castle where I clearly didn't belong—and I couldn't have that happen, not before tonight at least. "I... apologize for brushing off my castle chores. But if you just spoke to Lady Linnaea, she'd tell you—"

"You think I'd bother a noblewoman for the truancy of one

servant?" Mistress Alwina said, aghast. "A punishment for one is a punishment for all. All of you are on half rations until further notice."

A chorus of complaints rippled through the room. I whirled on the mistress. "No! Give them their meals. Punish me."

"You think that your one self-sacrifice is enough?" The mistress made her large hands into fists, staring each of us down as if we were misbehaving children. "We all have to make sacrifices for our provinces, our realm. It isn't glamorous. We are at war. This masquerade, however, is important. We have to civilize these Western lords. You'll be able to gorge yourselves like noblewomen later. Until then, half rations and quiet gratitude. Yes?"

A quiet, disgruntled chorus of "Yes, mistress" rippled across the room.

"Good. Now stop lazing about. Didn't I assign you all tasks for this afternoon? The ballroom must be perfect for tonight's guests. Rooms must be readied. Those without tasks should be looking for messes to clean around the castle. We don't want these Westerners to think we can't keep an orderly estate." She cast another hard stare in my direction. "Except you. If I see you wandering around the castle again, I'll throw you off the second storey and no one will ask questions."

A shiver ran down my spine. As her threat settled upon the other girls, the mistress turned and left the room, slamming the door behind her.

I almost couldn't face the other servant girls. When I did, the righteous anger on their faces filled me with an anxious shame. I had done this to them. These girls worked day and night for single pieces of silver, just to keep their families' bellies full.

"I'm sorry I caused this," I said sincerely, looking each of them in the eye. "You're angry. I know what that feels like." My stomach grumbled. I hadn't eaten yet today. I'd manage. I had before. "I'll see what I can do about getting you extra food. Or you can split my portion."

"Extra food?" Kuni said, crossing her arms in disgust. "What are you going to do, steal it?"

"I saw all the food in the kitchen this morning, when we went for water," Emmine said, looking up from the floor. "They probably wouldn't miss a few loaves of bread."

"You're talking like a Freetor rat!" said Kuni, pointing an accusing finger.

"Hey!" I said, rising to the challenge. "No one is talking like anything. Emmine's right. There's no reason any of you—us—have to suffer for the noble class. You—we—have more power than we think. Without us, their precious castle wouldn't be clean, their meals wouldn't be delivered, and they'd have to dress themselves."

Murmurs of agreement passed between the girls, but Emmine's gaze narrowed as she saw me in a new light. "Where were you, anyway? I thought you'd deserted or been killed."

"I heard that Lady Dominique threw you from the castle for breaking her wine glass and stealing at a private dinner the other night," said Kuni.

"I did break a glass," I admitted. "But I didn't steal anything. I was...punished. Now I'm back." My gaze swept over the servants. All of them, young women my age, some younger. Their faces were gaunt like the Freetor slaves. With the way things were going, it wouldn't be long before they were treated like slaves, too. "I'm...I'm back to help you all."

"Help? Don't you mean rebel? That's what you're trying to do here, right? Start some kind of...servant rebellion?" Kuni said. Some of the other Eastern girls spoke up in agreement:

"Someone has to serve!"

"We can't rebel. We are in the middle of a war!"

"I have to earn silver for my mother somehow!"

I spoke over them. "Of course someone has to serve. But you don't have to be packed in here, treated inhumanely as...slaves. You deserve to be paid for your time and treated with respect."

"If we don't work, the Frostfires and the Castillos will have our heads! Not to mention the mistress will kill us!"

"We are easy to replace," Emmine said sadly.

"No," I said. "Maybe to them you are. But not to your families. You have to stay alive to support them. To support yourselves."

"Easy for you to say," Emmine muttered, glancing at my hand.

A few of the other servant girls sneered and shook their heads.

I frowned. "What did you tell them?"

Emmine stood and folded her arms. "Some of the girls had already noticed, but didn't say anything. I didn't say who, though."

My cloth ring. I held it up so everyone could see. "Yes. I'm married. But not to whom you think. That's why I'm here. That's why we have to stand up to the mistress. And those who believe that mistreating the less fortunate and selling people as property is..."

I trailed off. I had gone too far. The Eastern and the Northern girls looked confused, even a little afraid, but the colour in Emmine's face drained away. Maybe she'd suspected already, but now she knew for certain. My face was not well known in the East or the North. Only my street name, the name that frustrated the soldiers and the nobles, and inspired hope in the Freetor-born.

"What exactly are you planning?" Emmine asked.

I held her gaze. She was in. If I kept my composure, I could convince the others as well.

"I have a job for all of you," I said.

"A job," Kuni sneered. "We already have jobs. We should

be doing them." She went to leave, but some of the other girls caught her by the arm. They were intrigued.

"If you do this job well," I said, "then all of us could be free. Not in a few years when you've saved up enough silver, or when your family marries you off. Tonight. On your own terms."

* * *

Laoise wrapped her arms around me, forcing the air from my lungs. "You're alive! I wasn't sure...I'd hoped..."

I returned the embrace fiercely then pulled back. Laoise looked like she hadn't slept for days, even though it had been only twelve hours. "I went underground. I saw your mother. She's fine. So is Monju."

Her gaze flitted to the entrance of her chambers. Emmine had escorted me here with an Eastern servant as they went to sweep the floors in the throne room. A small smile crept across her face. "When I woke, there was a rose outside my door."

My face heated as I stared at the floor. The more this relationship progressed, the harder it would be to tell her about Monju's previous affections for me.

She lightly touched my shoulder. "And your father?"

Her kindness only made it worse. I turned away. "I think he's gone. Dead, for real this time. He helped Sylvia and I escape the maze—"

"Sylvia?"

"Yeah. She's...going to help us. For now." I filled her in on the details of our encounter at the centre of the hedge maze, our plan to find the Emerald Cloth, and how I'd found Keegan's finger in her jewellery box. I sat down on the bed. "I know it's a risk to trust her. But she has connections we don't. And she's also been searching for the Emerald Cloth, independently of us. If we work together, at least...maybe we have a chance."

Laoise looked grim. "The moment Keegan opens his eyes, she will betray you."

"After that, it won't matter. Keegan will be awake, and we'll have the Cloth to stop the curse from spreading. She might be able to wake him up, but she can't control his feelings." I arched my back, stretching. It had been a while since I'd slept on nothing but rock and hay. "Have you heard about this ball tonight?"

"Yes, I received this." Laoise lifted a long scroll from her dresser. "Last minute, isn't it?"

"It's as good a time as any to steal away to Sallingaire." I told her of my time in the underground and my dealings with the Roamers.

"It's risky. How are you going to ensure that the cellar and the path to the throne room is clear? No doubt the castle will be brimming with guards and shadow killers."

"I already have that covered," I said, smiling.

Laoise looked less than convinced, but trusted me regardless. "As for me...I want to go with you to Sallingaire. I'll pack some of Linnaea's things for us, clothes, anything we can pawn for silver. I hope I can get away." Her brow furrowed as her gaze roamed the scroll. "This goes until well after midnight, but if I'm reading this correctly, Linnaea's name has been deliberately scrolled at the top. I doubt Leszek or Dominique will allow me out of their sights." She allowed the scroll to roll up and tossed it on the dresser. "And what about Leon? What if, after too much wine, he tells his father that I'm not really Linnaea? What then?"

I touched my feet to the rug. "Leave Leon to me. I'll distract him. Ensure he leaves you alone." Somehow. "You'll have to appear at the ball, yes. So does Sylvia. But we just have to make it until midnight. That's when Sylvia promised she'd have the carriage ready for us. Then Linnaea can run off with a charming young bard into the forest."

"If Dominique sees you, either as Rorda Cloth or as the Violet Fox, she's going to kill you."

"I'll be too busy sneaking around, helping the Roamers get into the castle. She'll stick to the ball room."

"Maybe." She moved towards her trunk and lifted it, revealing a piled mess of Linnaea's dresses. Pinching her fingers, she lifted an emerald green dress from the silk mountain, holding it up to herself. "I was thinking of wearing this tonight. Light, breathable. Stylish, but I can run in it."

"It's...green," I said, because that was all I could think to say about it.

"That's it? It probably costs two years of a servant's wages." She looked and sounded like her mother, which made me smile.

"I'm sure you'll look nice. I think I'll just wear this," I said, fanning out the filthy servant skirt in a mock curtsey. "It's not that light, but it's breathable and stylish in the servant circles."

"Funny." She folded the dress neatly and placed it on the bed. Gesturing, she drew my attention to a large, full-face mask with black feathers extending around the top from ear to ear. Tiny diamonds shimmered around the eyelids. "This arrived for me. A present. From Leon." She held up a folded piece of parchment. "I'm supposed to wear it tonight. Or perhaps, you. He says he's sorry for the way he acted towards you and begs forgiveness."

A pang of shame and disgust rippled through me. "I'm fine if you want to wear it. I don't think it goes with my dress."

Laoise tossed the note on the floor. "I'm nervous, Kiera. This ball...there's going to be small lords throughout the West coming. What if one of them sees me, and knows I'm not Linnaea?"

"You just have to survive for two hours," I told her. "The ball starts at ten. The Roamers are striking just before midnight, assuming we can get them in position. The attendance won't be as large as the Gathering ball. Only so many noble families will be able to make it on less than a day's notice. Then...after that...

the Freetors will have control of the castle. We'll beat Leszek and the rest of the Frostfires. Then we can head for Sallingaire, and beat Dominique at her game and free Keegan."

Her grim smile didn't reach her eyes. "I hope this works."

I took a deep breath. "We'll make it work."

Thirteen

THE HOURS LEADING up to the masquerade were a blur of sneaking around in crowded corridors to ensure the servant girls were in position and helping Laoise in her chambers prepare for the daunting evening ahead.

Laoise donned the rich green dress over a pristine chemise. Linnaea didn't have much jewellery, but we found a string of white pearls and a matching hair pin. The face mask was the centrepiece: it obscured her entire face, except her eyes. I wondered if Leon had delighted in picking it out—if he hoped that he'd have the chance to remove it, only to find my face instead of Laoise's.

Most annoyingly, Sylvia tried not once but three times to assist Laoise with her preparations. Because Sylvia still thought Laoise was the real Linnaea and that I had been dishonourably discharged from her service, I had to hide every time Sylvia deigned to burst into Laoise's chambers to "help" her prepare for the masquerade. First, I'd barely made it under the bed. Second and third time, Sylvia knocked, and I rushed for the wardrobe. She spent at least ten minutes lecturing Laoise on the latest Eastern styles and criticized her dress choice and the mask, even offering to lend her one of her own large garments. Laoise was tactful but firm.

Fifteen minutes after the masquerade had officially begun, the gentle knock on the door fired explosive nerves within my stomach. I took my position at the wardrobe.

"Who is it?" Laoise called.

"Uh...a servant, my lady. Wondering if I can enter."

Laoise and I exchanged glances. Swiftly, I answered the door, finding Emmine, reflecting my fear back at me.

"I can't stay," she said. I let her into the room.

Laoise noticed Emmine's presence and merely nodded, keeping up appearances. Emmine gave Laoise a suspicious look. "I can...come back...?"

"Are the girls in position?" I asked her.

She nodded, still averting her gaze to Laoise. "Is she really Linnaea Gareth?"

"It's best you don't ask too many questions, just in case this goes bad."

"Right." She cast her gaze downward, at her hands. "If I'm caught...if this plan of yours fails...escaping to the underground won't help feed my family," she said. "My mother, my little brother..."

"I can't promise it will go well. But I'll do what I can to help you."

Smiling thinly, she nodded. "The work is almost done. Most of it was cleaned already—I don't think the Frostfires realized how extensive the underground tunnel network is. We removed the stones we could from our end. The tunnel otherwise is relatively clear. I met with a young Southern man—"

Laoise tensed.

"—and he said the tiger's name at Driscoll's End was Salavajee. That's supposed to prove to you that he's...with you, I guess. I am to return to him with a piece of similar information, as confirmation of the message."

I nodded. While we had thought the white tiger guarded the cave of the Silver Spear, it had been Dominique's pet—a sign that she had been waiting for us. "You can tell the young Southern man that Laoise got the rose."

In the mirror, Laoise smiled and blushed.

"Something else," Emmine said. She produced a thin, black piece of fabric with eye holes and held it for my inspection. "The mistress handed these out. The servants are to wear them over their eyes while they serve at the masquerade tonight. If the nobles aren't showing their faces, neither can the servants."

It wouldn't make me unrecognizable, though it would be handy if I had to navigate the masquerade before the Roamers and the Freetors attacked. "Thank you."

"I should be getting to the ball. Mistress Alwina assigned me to serving duty." She inspected her hems: brown dirt had stained the blue-white fabric.

"No one will be looking at your dress," I tried to assure her.

"I hope you're right...Violet Fox." Emmine nodded respectfully to me. "Good luck."

"Thanks...you too."

With a wan smile, Emmine excused herself from the chambers, shutting the door carefully.

"You should go down there," Laoise suggested. "If anything goes wrong...if a guard sees..."

"I will." I had to retrieve something from Bidelia before we left. "You should be getting to the ball."

"Yeah." She turned from the mirror, worried. "Do I look all right?"

"Of course you do," I said, smiling. "You can do this. Make some small talk, try to avoid Dominique, ensure Sylvia isn't having too much fun, and be out of the ball room before midnight. Meet me at the stables."

"I wish I could take part in the action," she said wistfully, waving her fan.

"This is its own kind of action."

With a curt nod, she confidently strode into the corridor. I shut the door and made my own preparations.

I tied the black mask around my eyes. It was no match for my Violet Fox mask—this black fabric was cheaper and far thinner—but it would do. I pinned my hair back, attempting to master it so no noble could complain of long, black curly hairs in their drinks or food. Then, using a bit of Linnaea's rouge, I brushed my cheeks, attempting to subtly change my facial shape. I had no idea what I was doing, and it wasn't a substitute for my father's cream, but I looked less like myself than before.

Between my skirt and my corset, I hid my sheathed knife, and tied a second one around my ankle. The Roamer attack on the castle would create massive chaos and confusion, and while I intended to fight, I also intended to use the situation to my advantage. While they re-took the castle and dethroned the Frostfires, we'd follow Sylvia's lead to Sallingaire, hopefully ending the Silver Spear curse once and for all. I wished I could stay and oversee my people through this terrible turmoil— nobles rising and falling, playing with their lives like puppeteers—yet retrieving the third famed artefact of Dashiell was a far better use of the Violet Fox's talents. Once Keegan was awake, we could return to Marlenia City and deal with the particulars of the throne. Hopefully it would be safe in the hands of the Roamers and the Freetors.

I halted before the door. Bidelia had said I had too much of my father in me. The Emerald Cloth would save countless lives. That was why I sought it. Not for the thrill of it.

Why couldn't it be both?

I scurried into the hallway, keeping my head down, trying to focus on the task at hand. No one stopped me as I weaved between the nobles gathering in the hallway outside the throne room. I peeked inside as I hurried by: I thought I saw Sylvia's mess of curls, but that was a common Eastern trait. Rats. If she stayed in the throne room for too long, she'd get caught up in the brewing rebellion, and I couldn't let my ticket out of here be captured or killed by Antony and his men.

As I hurried towards the cellar, the faint touch of fresh air found my arms. Gooseflesh rippled. The tunnel had been cleared. Excited, I bounded for the entrance to the cellar.

Strong arms immobilized me as blunt steel pressed against my throat.

"Who—oh." Immediately I was released, and Bidelia spun me around, half with surprise and relief. "Kiera. What are you doing down here? Aren't you keeping an eye on Sylvia?"

"Laoise can do that. I came to check on things down here."

"They're halfway in. How did you manage to get those girls to help you?"

"It took some convincing," I admitted.

Bidelia reached into her shoulder bag and retrieved a ragged cloth wrapped around a spherical object. Even through the thick fabric, the glow of Freetor magic was unmistakeable. I took the round orb in my hands, hugging it to my chest.

"Conal managed to piece it back together," Bidelia said. "I...I didn't know if I should give it to you. But the Spear is too dangerous to wield in the open."

I nodded. I needed one of the artefacts to help identify the Emerald Cloth. When in close proximity, they would glow brightly. The Spear would be safer in Bidelia's hands—she was one of the few I trusted with its power.

"Bidelia..."

She cut me off, wagging her finger. "None of that. You have to take Laoise out of the castle. To Sallingaire. We will handle the Frostfires and hold the throne for you."

For me. "You make it sound so easy."

"Well, it won't be. But the power of the Spear is on our side. If anyone dares oppose—"

"No," I interrupted her. "Please, I don't want anyone else

falling prey to its power. If we abuse it, we're no better than Dominique and Leszek."

Bidelia grimaced. "I can't make any promises, Kiera. We may have to freeze Leszek and the other Frostfires to subdue them. They won't die—as far as we understand the magic. Once you have the Emerald Cloth, you can choose to use it on them, or keep them frozen. They've killed our people—enslaved us like animals. There must be some justice."

I didn't like it. Ruling through fear—it wasn't right. Yet in my Freetor heart, Bidelia's words fed my anger. The Frostfires had stormed into Marlenia City and rounded up Freetors and sympathizers and executed them for their birthright and their beliefs.

"I know," Bidelia said, resting a warm hand on my shoulder. "There's no easy way to dole out justice. That is part of being a ruler. Even part of being a parent. Making hard decisions that will benefit your child. All of your children."

"I will find the Emerald Cloth to free those who have been already cursed," I promised her. "Promise me you'll only use the Spear as a last resort."

She sighed. "Fine."

"I trust only you with it, Bidelia. I...I know you'll do what's right."

A rare, genuine smile interrupted her stern features. "Take care of my daughter."

"I always do." I glanced down the corridor. No one. I frowned. "You haven't seen Sylvia come through here, have you?"

"No."

It had to be nearing the eleventh hour. "I suppose I should check on Laoise and Sylvia."

"Do that. I'll ensure everyone is in position before midnight. I don't want to see you in the throne room when we attack."

"But—"

"No, Kiera. When we're going in, you should be already at the stables. You can't be caught in the crossfire. If you're killed, the Roamers will be freed from their agreement with us. They'd probably take the castle for themselves and Keegan and the other cursed will be forgotten. I don't believe Pascal Antony is as fair or just as you or I. He cares about silver just as much as Leszek Frostfire."

I hadn't considered that. A deep, real fear penetrated my body. Whatever happened to loyalty for loyalty's sake? "We'll be gone."

With a long look, I departed from Bidelia's company. Each step I put between us just made me more miserable. Was leaving the castle really the right thing to do? Laoise could go—as a Freetor, she could see the light blue glow of Freetor magic just as well as I could. She could find the Emerald Cloth using the Orb of Dashiell—and return my prince here. I could stay with Bidelia and manage the realm, keep all of my people safe, and dole out justice as it was deserved.

I shook my head, eying an approaching male servant who appeared nervous and focussed on heading to the kitchen with his empty tray. No, it had to be me—if only so I could tell Keegan I loved him when the power of the artefact woke him. Bidelia would keep the realm safe.

As the male servant drew closer, I fumbled out an excuse that the chef needed him in the kitchen, and swiped his tray. He appeared relieved; as I entered the fray of the throne room, I saw why.

This was no small gathering of Western nobles. At least two hundred lords and ladies filled the lantern-lit room, the surroundings coloured with Eastern blues and reds. My eyes hurt as I struggled to take in the spectacle. The couples waltzing in the middle of the room, picturesque and synchronized like I had never seen. Musicians played a jaunty Eastern melody in the far southeastern corner. Up on the dais with the three thrones sat Boris, deep in conversation with Dominique. She held a glass of whiteberry wine and took occasional sips, uncharacteristically interested in her intended's long-winded story.

Keeping my head down, I skirted the edge of the room towards the closed double-doored entrance. Although servants carried hors d'oeuvres and goblets of white and blue wine on silver platters, a long row of tables donned with sweets and desserts to my right: many Eastern and Northern favourites, I guessed, for I didn't recognize more than half of them. Nobles gathered along the sidelines of the dancers, deep in conversation, and pressed against the walls were Frostfire soldiers. No doubt shadow killers hid among the crowd, just out of sight.

The Easterners normally had no stomach for overindulgence—that was a Southern stereotype—yet even in the face of famine, the Easterners put their richest, most decadent foot forward. A celebration of liberation, indeed.

The orb, safe in my apron pocket, felt heavier than ever.

It wasn't hard to find Sylvia. Her dress was a fierce red, swelling from her frame like a wilting rose. She held two glasses of wine as she stood, awkwardly, on the fringes of a group conversation between three Eastern nobles I didn't recognize. She would occasionally make a loud remark that was followed by not-so-covert glances between the men before they'd resume conversation.

Remembering that the tray was not a shield, I held it horizontal with both hands and darted lightly between the nobles, keeping my head down as I approached Sylvia.

"My lady," I said in a low voice, so as not to disturb or attract the attention of the nobles. "I can take your glasses if you are finished."

"I'm not, thank—" Her gaze met mine and she faltered, suddenly snarling. She spoke up. "Why yes, I do want more—"

Turning away from the nobles and their disgusted looks, Sylvia led me closer to the western end of the room, near to the buffet tables. I took up a post at the end of the table, hoping the nobles would see me as more of a statue where they could place their empty drinks, while Sylvia picked at the dessert offerings in a nonchalant, bored way.

She placed one of her glasses on the buffet table. It was empty. Annoyed, I swiped the half-full glass of wine and wrenched it deftly from her grasp.

"What are you doing?" I demanded. "Drinking, when we're about to make a big move?"

"I'm just—" She reached for it clumsily; I held it behind my back. Glancing about to see if anyone was watching, she leaned in closer. "I'm trying to enjoy myself. This might be the last time I'm ever going to see my father. Or live like...this." She gestured wildly about the room.

I averted my gaze, tightening my grip on the glass. "Wine impairs the senses. I need you sharp. If you fall asleep before midnight..." I didn't want to think about it. If the Roamers and the Freetors attacked and she was in the throne room, it would be hard to remove her without compromising our entire mission to escape the castle.

"I won't!" she insisted. "Give me back my—"

"Don't have any more." I returned her the glass.

"I'm not my brother. Have you seen him?" She looked suddenly wistful. "I should say...goodbye."

I hadn't. His absence from the ball filled me with swirling dread. What if he was in the cellar, disrupting the Roamers and the servants? They could probably take care of him if he became a nuisance, but his absence would raise suspicion. "Half-past eleven, get out of this room and start heading down to the stables. Promise?"

"Fine." She drifted away from me, back to the buffet table.

We'd already been together for too long. Worrying at her lip, she threw me a disdainful look. "I don't even know why you're going to all this trouble."

I frowned. "Why would you say that?"

"Because you don't really love Keegan!" she hissed.

I blinked. "Of course I do. I wouldn't be here, risking my life, the lives of my friends, if I didn't love him."

Her resolve strong, her bright gaze searched mine for the truth, and only saw herself. "I don't know what your game is. Your real game, I mean. I lay awake trying to figure it out. It makes me dizzy. But I know you're in love with..."

"Who?"

"You know exactly—"

A large figure and a loud, distinctive voice caught my sensitive hearing. A few stone-throws away, Mistress Alwina let out a great belly laugh at the new Eastern captain of the guard's joke.

What was she doing in the throne room? I hadn't thought she'd show herself so brazenly among the noble class, yet there she was, wearing a modest black gown, her short hair fixed with a stark white feather, and her large, ringed hand clasping a mug of dark, shiny liquid.

If she saw me in here, even with the strip of black across my eyes, she'd have my head.

While Sylvia droned on about something-or-other, I set down the tray and in one fell swoop, I ducked under the buffet table. The long tablecloth hid me, but I couldn't stay here forever. Shadowy long legs and large skirts darkened the white sheet. I could stay here for as long as I liked, but emerging at an inopportune moment would be embarrassing at best.

"What...?" Lifting the cloth, Sylvia stared at me as if I were mad. "If you think I'm going in there with you, think again."

"Why would I want that? Put down the tablecloth before someone sees!"

Immediately she obeyed, yet she remained in front of the buffet table, slightly crouched so as to facilitate conversation.

"See the servant mistress behind you, several stone-throws—"

"What's a stone-throw?" she asked, way too loudly.

"Shh!" Sylvia was useless, especially after a glass of wine. "I have to stay here until the mistress is further away. If she sees me, my cover will be blown."

"Your cover. Ha. Flimsy as it is."

"You're not helping. Go away." Then, as an afterthought: "Wait. No—Sylvia, tell me where the mistress is now."

"Still where she was two seconds ago."

"Distract her."

"No! I've done enough for you." I heard her stuff some tarts in her cheeks as she mumbled some other choice words.

"Then can you at least—?" No, I couldn't tell her to get Laoise—to Sylvia, "Linnaea" thought I had left the castle. Perhaps I could crawl out and leave without the mistress seeing. "Be at the stables before midnight, Sylvia."

"And to think you were going to be queen. I was supposed to be queen," Sylvia muttered as she whirled around, her gown brushing the white tablecloth as she left.

"Ugh, Sylvia, wait..." It was no use: she was gone. Careful not to disturb the fragile artefact in my pocket, I crawled beneath the row of tables. They ended near the western-most side exit. Close to the dais, unfortunately. Perhaps I could slip out before the mistress—or anyone else—noticed my recognizable face.

About halfway down the row, one of the white tablecloths fell a pinch shorter than the rest, and I recognized the deep forest green of Linnaea's dress. Laoise!

Hurrying as fast as I could on all fours with precious cargo hanging in the balance, I tried to get her attention as covertly as possible. "Psst. My lady."

No answer.

Of course—the music was too loud. I reached delicately from beneath the tablecloth and tugged at the hem of her dress.

Startled, she jumped back, and revealed her worn flats. Definitely Laoise. No proper lady would wear such plain shoes with her gown.

I stuck out my left hand, revealing my cloth ring. "It's me."

"What...?"

"Stay upright, don't kneel down. I'm hiding."

"Shouldn't you be down in the—"

"I was, and I saw your—"

"Shh!" She nearly kicked me in the face; I recoiled as a figure in a long dark skirt approached the table. "Ah. Dominique. Nice to see you here tonight."

"Of course," Dominique replied, almost polite. "I y'am not much pour dese occasions. Too many people."

I leaned against the wall, my knees pressed against my chin.

"Crowds also make me nervous," Laoise admitted. She no longer had to fake Linnaea's anxiety.

"I y'am not nervous in crowds. Our castle in de Nort' was filled with many nobles and merchants. Wine?"

"Thank you." Laoise paused and I heard her take a glass. "I've been struggling with drinking all night, with this mask."

"Can j'ou—?"

"Oh, it's all right. I'll just loosen...there. I can lift it when I need to."

"How do j'ou feel about de ball itself?" Dominique continued.

I frowned. Was Dominique actually making small talk?

"I feel...like I've never been anywhere so lavish in my life," Laoise said, equally as surprised. "My father would throw gatherings for the local small lords, of course. But this spread of food...and all of the women dressed so beautifully..."

"J'ou y'and I grew up in esimilar environs. Despite my title, conditions are harsh in de Nort'. I agree dat dis is extravagant."

I heard Laoise shift her mask to take a big gulp as if to buy more time to think of a clever response. After a moment, she said, "I don't think I've tasted whiteberry white like this before. What is it?"

"Y'it is a Nort'ern vintage," Dominique replied. "J'ou do not like it?"

"It's quite tangy," Laoise admitted.

"I prefer it over dat drivel Leon served d'other night." She hesitated, possibly downing the rest of her glass. "I y'am not one to apologize pour my behaviour. But per'aps I acted out of turn dat night."

"Oh. No. My servant was the one who acted out of turn. I ensured she was expelled from the castle."

"Good. If j'ou like, I can recommend a young woman pour your personal service."

"If—if you like." Another pause. "Thank you, Dominique. I appreciate your kindness, if you don't mind me saying."

"Not at all. We are to be sisters in dis house of men. A trustwort'y ally is hard to find, no?"

"You're right. It has been hard." I heard her set her wine on the table as she turned her body to retrieve another sweet.

"Come by my quarters later," Dominique said. "When j'ou are tired of dis show of force."

"Thank you. If I don't fall asleep before then, I will."

Dominique lingered for another moment before her shadowy figure slipped away. I blew out a long breath against my knees, waiting half a minute before daring to speak.

"Are you all right?" I asked Laoise, lifting the tablecloth.

"That was strange," Laoise whispered. She peered into the wine and beneath the mask I heard her smack her lips in distaste.

"Very," I agreed. "Can you look around and see if Mistress Alwina is still over there?"

She did. "I don't see her."

Finally. I crawled out, brushing myself off and earning a few odd stares myself. I curtsied before Laoise for effect, keeping my head bowed.

"I should go down to the cellar now. See how that's progressing," I said.

Laoise nodded. She looked pensive. "I've been in here for about five minutes—do you think that's a long enough appearance for Linnaea Gareth?"

"It'll have to be. I'll go, and then—"

A deafening blast from a horn sliced through all conversation and music, clearing the air for the orator near the double-doored entrance to the hall. "Now entering, Lord Ansel Gareth of Baile Gareth. Father of Linnaea Gareth, intended of Leon Frostfire, second son of our illustrious emperor."

Laoise and I exchanged a look so desperate, we clung to it like a lifeline.

"Get out of here," I said to her. "Hurry."

As Laoise turned tail and dashed as quickly as a polite noblewoman could for the nearest side-door exit, Lord Ansel entered through the large, main doors. He was flanked by two Gareth men—thankfully, neither of them I recognized.

Boris suddenly materialized, surprised and as delighted as his statuesque face could be, as he eagerly greeted the Western lord. Lord Ansel bowed respectfully, yet he seemed to be in no mood to observe pleasantries. He minced no words: even his attire was not as pressed, his air askew. Something was wrong.

I snuck closer, standing behind a few of the gathering lords and ladies waiting to great Lord Ansel Gareth.

"—arrived as quickly as I could. I'd like to speak with my daughter," Lord Ansel said gruffly.

What if he knows...?

"She is in the room," Boris said, gesturing about. "It is a masquerade. I believe hers is a large mask with black—"

"Fine. And your father?"

"Not on the floor yet. Just before midnight, he should make his entrance."

"It's urgent. I must have an audience with him." He lowered his voice then and whatever he said to Boris made his face pale.

Boris cleared his throat. "That is not an affair I am involved in, my lord. But if you..."

He knew. I whirled and darted through the crowd, startling many a noble, and out the same exit Laoise had used.

The hallway, while not as crowded as the throne room, was populated with lords and ladies having intimate conversations, tucked away like lovers against the walls. Because of this, I almost didn't see Laoise—she steadied herself on the wall with one hand, her head bowed, the other hand clutching her chest. To my surprise, Monju stood protectively by her, alternately whispering comforting words and dismissing passing nobles who took interest. A noblewoman frowned at him.

My heart raced as I approached them. Reluctantly, Monju took a few steps back, staying just within arm's reach of Laoise. "What happened?"

Her mask was still on, so she was not immediately identifiable, but beads of sweat poured down her neck. "I...I don't..."

"Poison," Monju said, just below his breath.

I leaned against the wall, feeling the cold hands of death at my own throat. Dominique. The wine. Cursing, I gripped Laoise's hand and led her further down the corridor, away from the activity of the ball. Monju followed.

"How bad?" I asked him.

"Hard to determine. She must remove the mask."

I glanced behind us. If Lord Ansel were desperate enough, he'd roam these corridors. He'd probably gotten the description of Laoise's dress by now.

I pushed all scenarios aside, trying to focus on my ailing best friend sweating beside me. Stopping, I rested her against the wall once more and positioned myself between her and the ball entrance.

"I'm taking off the mask," I said to Laoise.

"No...I think I'm..." Her pleas were laced with desperation and fear.

Monju gripped her arm. "Lady Laoise must not die."

She sobbed, hanging her head in defeat. Then, looking up at me, she nodded.

I rapidly untied the ribbon securing the mask and plied it away from her face. Red and slick with tears and sweat, Laoise tried to hide herself in her hands.

"No, please," Monju said, gently taking her hands in his, removing them from her sickly complexion.

"She did this to me," Laoise said, breathless. "I feel like I'm... dying..."

"Is possible," Monju said calmly. He squeezed her hands. "But can't tell unless Laoise trusts Monju."

"I trust you," she replied immediately, meeting his helpful, imploring gaze.

Embarrassed, I looked down at the mask, wishing I could put it on.

Monju cleared his throat. "Lady Laoise, this is strange, but breathe out."

She frowned as her cheeks flushed even more. "Breathe out...?"

"Monju means..." He glanced at me, worried. "I must smell your breath. That is how I can tell if the poison runs in your veins."

With the use of his first-person pronouns, Laoise's eyes widened. She nodded hurriedly and closed the short distance between them. Monju leaned in as Laoise exhaled gingerly, averting her gaze to the floor as her hands trembled.

I gripped Laoise's hand to steady it. We both had to be strong if we were going to escape the castle in one piece.

Monju's grave look said it all. "Certainly poisoned."

"How long do I have?" Laoise asked soberly. She squeezed my hand so hard I thought it would fall off.

"Can't say for sure. How much did Laoise ingest?"

"A mouthful," she said. "I thought it tasted strange..."

"Is possible Laoise could live a day. Lady Dominique has potent poisons, but many require complete ingestion to be quick. Likely there will be...much pain."

"Do you have any antidotes? What about the liquid you gave me at Driscoll's End?" I asked, desperate.

He shook his head sadly. "No more of that left. But Monju may be able to construct a temporary antidote. Slow the poison."

I glanced over my shoulder. The ball was well into its second hour. People were already making merry, dancing, and stuffing their bellies. Leszek still hadn't shown himself and Leon Frostfire had been uncharacteristically absent. Hopefully Lady Linnaea would not be missed from the proceedings. "Tell me what I must do."

Laoise gripped her stomach, bending suddenly as if about to vomit. Monju caught her before she could fall. "Lady Kiera must fetch ingredients. Monju has some. In his pack." He pressed a free hand to the pouch on his belt. "Others, more common, may be found in the kitchens. Could go down there—"

"It's less suspicious if I go," I said. While my face was somewhat known, at least to the nobles, we'd have more trouble if a Frostfire guard found a Southern Roamer-looking man snooping about in the kitchens. "Tell me what I need to get. Take Laoise to her chambers. I'll meet you there with the ingredients."

Monju nodded swiftly and rattled off a description of three spices. "Monju has a canteen and some oils. Will mix with the spices. Will alleviate some pain, keep Laoise safe."

Laoise nodded, trying to look strong. "Hurry, Kiera."

I turned and bolted down the hallway. Didn't matter if the nobles in the hall saw my face now—Laoise's life was on the line. Save Laoise, grab our things, and get to the stables before Antony led my people into rebellion.

As I darted through the halls, I concocted a cover story for my presence in the kitchen, yet when I stepped across the threshold, I found the kitchen strangely quiet. Perhaps the chef and his staff had been given a night off, after spending inordinate amounts of time preparing for the feast. Disturbed by the silence, I beelined through the various areas of the kitchen, trying to remember where the dried spices were kept.

I heard the lumbering footsteps behind me. Hoping it was a guard, I hurried deeper into the room. But a strong grip caught me by the shoulder and I spun into the arms of Leon Frostfire.

"Why, hello, my future wife," he said, his voice as sickly sweet as honey.

I pushed him away. "You're not supposed to be in here."

"Neither are you. In fact, I would much rather see you on the dance floor, in proper noblewoman attire, wearing the mask I gave you, and yet, you continue to dress as a servant while your servant pretends to be you."

"Go away. I'm on a secret mission."

"That sounds exciting." I scooted away, though he wasn't leaving much distance between us. "What sort of mission?"

"One that doesn't involve you. Now go, before I call upon my handmaids to throw you out."

Leon was on my tail. "That is no way to speak to me. I thought we had a discussion about that."

I whirled on him, tired of his face, his voice, and his games. "And I thought I told you that our marriage is off."

To my surprise, he burst out laughing. "You really think the word of a noblewoman can erase the written, binding contract between the most powerful man in the realm and your father?"

"Yes," I said firmly.

He scoffed as he advanced on me. I drew back. "There's nowhere for you to run now," he said slyly. "I know why you're in here."

"I highly doubt that."

"You need to give me more credit. You'll learn that, when you're my wife." He held out his hand. "Come now. No more games. Father may be displeased when he learns you have deceived us, but he will understand after a time. And after midnight, it won't matter."

Something in his tone begged for me to ask, but I'd hit a wall of spices. Three chubby mason jars crashed to the floor, spilling red and green substances onto my flats and between the stone crevices.

Leon screwed up his face. "Ugh. What did you spill, that smell is disgusting!"

"Good. Now leave me be." I turned and grabbed the dried disciple daisies, the leighroot, and the izlech pepper, shoving them into my apron pockets.

"And what, pray tell, are you going to do with those?"

"Maybe I'm making a cake," I said dryly. I whizzed past him, staring him down in a silent challenge, but he didn't grab for me—not this time. He just smiled smugly as I headed for the exit.

"That's right, back to the ball you go. Just thirty more minutes, and then...well." He grinned. "You know."

Disgusted, I turned tail and ran as fast as I could from him. I most certainly did not care for whatever he was implying. Fifteen minutes, and Laoise, Monju, Sylvia and I would be riding free in the mountain air towards Sallingaire, and my true love.

Or, Laoise would be dead, and then we'd all be in trouble.

My feet were a blur as I hurried back to the west wing, avoiding the throne room as if I were susceptible to the Silver Spear curse itself. I heard no light footsteps of scheming Roamers, no telltale pale faces in the rare servant that crossed my path. The Roamers should be in position right now. Had the Roamers already taken care of the patrols? Perhaps the guards were indulging themselves at the celebration. I saw increasingly tipsy nobles heading for the throne room. I hoped one of those tipsy nobles was Sylvia, on her way out to the stables. After I delivered these spices, I'd have to go down the lower levels and speed things along. Hopefully, the servant girls hadn't run into any trouble.

I dashed inside Laoise's chambers. Monju nearly threw his knives at me in surprise. He breathed a sigh of relief as I produced the three jars of spices. Laoise, now paler than a newborn Freetor, lay on the bed in her small clothes. Her skin glistened with sweat. Her emerald dress draped across the chaise near the window, drying. I hurried to her side and took her slick hand as Monju mixed the spices on the dresser.

"Kiera," Laoise said, her voice hoarse. "My mother. Is she...?"

"She's here," I promised. "Not in the room. She's—"

Tears lined her eyes. "Could you...would you...?"

My heart tore in two. I looked up at Monju. "How long?"

He turned around, holding a dirty teacup from this afternoon's tea. "This concoction will hold off the poison for a day. Can administer it every day, twice a day. But it only works for so long. She will need a real antidote."

"Can't you...I don't know...sneak into Dominique's room? Surely she has some kind of antidote...?"

Monju approached the bed, cupping the mixture tentatively. "Hard to come by. Especially here, now. This poison is similar to the one she used on Lady Kiera at Driscoll's End.

Highly potent. Very effective. But slower. Doubtful Dominique would keep the antidote so easily reachable. Monju believes Dominique wanted Laoise to suffer."

"Because she thought you were me," I said, clasping my other hand on Laoise. "I'm so sorry."

With great effort, she shook her head. "This is the mission."

"Here," Monju said. The two of us helped Laoise tilt her head so she could drink Monju's concoction. She grimaced, nearly gagging, but she gulped it down.

Laoise wiped her mouth. "I want to say I've had worse... but...ugh."

"The Roamers should be in place by now," Monju said. "Does the Lady wish to lead them in the siege?"

I looked down at my best friend, hating to leave her. "Yes, but if the servant mistress finds me there, she'll out me. And Lord Ansel knows my face. He'll demand to see Linnaea." We were supposed to protect her—and we'd failed. Lord Ansel would take his wrath out on me and the Frostfires once he knew he'd been deceived.

"Put on the dress," Laoise said, lifting a heavy hand to point. "The mask...is over there."

My eyes widened. "If Lord Ansel wants to see my face..."

"He won't," Laoise said. "You know how...to...to avoid him."

I hated to disguise myself as another noble, but it was the only way to move through the crowds. I hurried to the garment, sizing it up against my body. Laoise and I were about the same size, though she was slightly taller. It would fit.

The emerald silk between my fingers gave me an idea. "Come with me to Sallingaire. Both of you."

"Is not wise to travel in her condition," Monju said.

"And what are you going to do for her here? The last time you went searching for an antidote for a dying loved one, it took you years, and he died in the process." I buried my face in my hands; my hateful words had startled the three of us. "I didn't mean it like that. What I'm trying to say is, if you come to Sallingaire, there's a chance that the Emerald Cloth might be there."

Monju perked up. "The Lady has found it."

"Maybe. I don't know yet. It's a flimsy lead, but it's all we have."

Forgetting my remark about his search for the cure to his father's addiction, he knelt before Laoise. "Is that all right?" he asked her.

Laoise nodded at me.

"It might not be. We have to prepare ourselves for that, too," I said over the lump in my throat.

"Anywhere...better than here," Laoise said.

I took a deep, steadying breath. "Then it's time for us to switch clothes."

Monju respectfully turned his back as I stripped off the dirty servant clothes I'd been wearing for days and wiggled into Linnaea's deep green gown. Baggy in the hips and tight in the arms, I struggled to adjust the fabric to my liking, mindful of the ticking clock. I tied a leather sheath around my thigh, containing my knife. Hard to access, but better to have than not. Monju helped me clasp the white beads Laoise had donned.

"The hair is completely different," I muttered. My black curls and Laoise's short blond hair were inexcusable. "So are our eyes. Someone will notice."

Handing me the mask, Monju gave me a thin smile. "No one will notice."

"Yes, hopefully they'll be too busy dealing with the Roamers and the Freetors." I tied the full-face mask around my head and Monju pinned it in place. It was heavy and hot; the narrow eyeholes didn't leave much room and tiny nostril holes barely gave relief.

"Sylvia should be down at the stables now. I hope. She's prepared a carriage for us. Don't let her leave without me." My
voice sounded muffled beneath the mask. I retrieved the bag
Laoise and I had packed with clothes and some food I'd taken
from the kitchen and added the Orb of Dashiell. If I couldn't
make it out in time, they could use it to continue the mission.
Or at the very least, Laoise could use it as a weapon if Monju
became incapacitated. I handed the bag to Monju.

"Monju will wait with Laoise," he promised.

Smoothing back my unruly curls behind the full-face
mask, I headed confidently into the corridor. I needed to
get to the lower levels to ensure all the Roamers and the
Freetors had made it into the castle and guarantee the servant girls were safe.

I turned a corner and saw dozens of nobles in various
colours and masks hurrying into the throne room. Good. I
slipped between them. Down the corridor, I thought I saw a
Freetor holding a sharpened wooden spear duck back around
the corner.

They were coming.

"Lady Linnaea?"

I pretended not to hear and weaved between the nobles fil-
tering into the throne room. Making it past most of the crowd,
I continued down the hallway, towards where I saw the Freetor
in hiding.

"Um...hello? Did you hear me?"

I balled my hands into fists and turned around, coming face-
to-face with Liz. Or rather, part of her face: her black-and-white
lace mask covered the left side. She smiled warmly at me. She
thought I was the real Linnaea.

"Oh," I said, feigning Linnaea's high-pitched voice at once.
"Lady Elizabeth. I don't know if we've had the pleasure of—"

"Only briefly," she replied. "Did you do something different with your hair?" she asked, trying to peer around.

"Yes, just a different look for the masquerade. Why only change my face when I can change my hair, too?" I let out a nervous laugh. Get me out of here. "Well, it was nice to chat with you, but I must—"

"Yes, you have to get into the throne room to be beside your father. And your intended. Come with me, I'll help you through." She took my hand and practically pulled me down the hallway.

"Uh..." I was going the wrong way! I did not want to be in the middle of the chaos when my people attacked! "I don't think..."

"You do know that Emperor Leszek is about to make an announcement, right?" she asked, searching my masked face.

"I hadn't heard. I wasn't feeling well."

"Too many glasses of wine?"

"No, it's difficult to drink in the mask."

We joined the river of nobles flowing into the throne room. At least a hundred Western nobles, a few rich merchants, and the Eastern and Northern nobles occupying the castle gathered close to the throne dais. Leszek loomed over them, dressed in his finest, with Boris to his left and Dominique to his right. No sign of Sylvia. Thank goodness.

I sidestepped close to the buffet table and backed up against the wall, clasping my left hand to cover my cloth ring. "I'll just stand here," I said to Liz.

"Are you sure?" she whispered, joining me. "Your father is—"

She pointed across the room. Lord Ansel and his men had gathered like restless dogs on the left side of the dais. He surveyed the crowd closely. Evidently, he had not yet found his daughter. Or anyone claiming to be his daughter.

"Oh, I don't want to disturb him now. Later, after the emperor's speech."

Frowning, Liz settled beside me against the wall. "Suit yourself."

The flow of nobles into the room trickled off. Leon entered from the opposite side of the room, close to Lord Ansel. I slid down the wall, trying to make myself shorter and invisible.

Attack, I thought, pressing my hands hard against the gritty stone. Attack so we can fight. Attack so I can get away and save the people I love.

I glanced at Lady Elizabeth. She appeared almost as nervous as I felt. She was innocent in all this. She didn't deserve to be held hostage. Her family might be Eastern, but that didn't make her an invader.

I cleared my throat. "Um, Liz, maybe we could..."

Her gaze darted immediately to mine. Before she could reply, Leszek's booming voice overtook the room.

"Ladies, gentlemen, good people of the court," Leszek began. "I want to express my gratitude for your presence on this special occasion tonight. As you know, I am not one for grand speeches"—a few of the noblewomen laughed politely—"so I will be brief. Yes, tonight we celebrate the liberation of our capital. Yet we have one other important reason to celebrate." He clasped Boris's shoulder. "My son, Lord Boris Frostfire, is engaged to be married to Lady Dominique Castillo, Daughter of the North. My second son, Lord Leon Frostfire—where are you, boy?"

Leon, grinning, darted past Lord Ansel, leapt onto the dais, and stood next to his brother. "Here, Father."

Leszek gave him the once over, and judging him to be of suitable appearance and character, nodded gruffly. "Yes. My second son, Lord Leon Frostfire..."

Oh no.

"...is engaged to be married to Lady Linnaea Gareth." He glanced over at Dominique. "Where is the girl?"

Lord Ansel's hand gripped his scabbard, on high alert.

How desperately I wanted the earth to open up and swallow me whole.

Liz nudged my shoulder. "Go."

"I can't," I whispered.

She nearly pushed me. "No, I mean, get out of the room."

"How did you—?"

The nobles exchanged glances. Leon had the most disgusting grin I'd ever seen as he leaned over, saw me, and gestured. Others picked up the cue and all eyes turned to me. My mask was unmistakable.

"Don't be shy, girl, come up," Leszek said.

Keeping my hands clasped, I stepped forward. Lord Ansel's face lit up at the sight of me. He was in for a rude, terrible surprise. I felt sick. I had let his daughter go into the woods—why had I done that?

For love. Like with everything else, I did it for love.

I concentrated on putting one foot in front of the other as I climbed up onto the dais. I didn't dare move my head much, in fear of more people seeing my wrong-coloured hair. Dominique's small smile was one of camaraderie, but in the depths of her dark eyes, I saw victory.

Laoise isn't dead yet. There's still time. Perform for the nobles, then run.

Liz pressed herself against the wall as she slid towards the exit. She couldn't mask the fear painted on half her face. She'd recognized me as the servant she'd befriended. If she told, I'd be dead.

Why weren't the Roamers and the Freetors attacking?

Keeping my gaze downcast, I stood up straight on the platform, beside my worst enemies.

"Now that we're all here, a special announcement," Leszek said. "I hope you've all partaken in the food. The music. The dancing. Because this is not just a celebration of liberation. It's a celebration of unity. For the union of my two sons to our new allies will not take place in the spring, as previously announced."

Shock rippled through the crowd.

"It will take place tonight," Leszek continued. "Immediately."

Fourteen

Run. That was all I could think.

Yet I couldn't. I was trapped in the gaze of a hundred nobles.

"Stand before each other," Leszek commanded.

Dominique, Boris, and Leon turned side-on. I angled myself in a similar fashion, trying and failing to hide my curly, dark hair. I hoped everyone was more interested in Boris and Dominique than unimportant Linnaea Gareth.

"Your masks. Remove them, so you may stand before each other with no secrets."

I could barely contain my gasp.

Perhaps none of this is real, I thought, as Dominique undid her ribbons and slipped the mask from her face.

I should have just kept walking. I'd be with my people by now. Leading the attack.

Boris removed his simple mask, holding it steady in his left hand.

Silence from the corridors. No one was coming to rescue me.

Leon's mask was fabric; he pulled it up onto his head, his goofy smile persisting like an ugly stain. He canted his head to me, lifting his eyebrows in expectation.

My hands shook as they gripped the hard mould. Lord Ansel was waiting, staring at me as if the sun rising tomorrow depended on me lifting the mask and showing my face.

Leszek, however, was not paying attention. He had already

begun Dominique and Boris's marriage rites. "As emperor of the realm of Marlenia, I am blessed to oversee this union between houses and provinces: the East, and the North. Divided by war a generation ago, these two provinces can finally find peace in this holy, royal union. Boris, do you agree to uphold the law and protect your intended with your sword, wits, and fortune?"

At the word fortune, Boris's stone mask of a face faltered. He glanced at his father, then back to Dominique. "I do, yes."

"Dominique, do you take this man...?"

I felt sick. I took a step back, and then another, wishing I could sink into the floor and escape into the Undercity. Or the dungeon. I'd even take the dungeon over this.

"...to protect him and honour him, and treasure your place within the holy role of wife to the future emperor..."

An irritated sigh escaped Dominique. "J'es, j'es. I do."

Leszek seemed surprised that Dominique wanted to rush the ceremony. Nevertheless, despite my silent, terrified and unseeable objection, he obliged. "Your lives are now one. As emperor of Marlenia, I pronounce you husband and wife. You may share a kiss."

Dominique looked over her shoulder at me and smiled.

She knew.

Boris and Dominique shared a chaste kiss that Dominique pulled away from as quickly as possible. She clasped Boris's hand as the two of them turned to the audience and received a round of enthusiastic applause, mostly from the Easterners and the Northerners.

"Leon and Linnaea. Step forward," Leszek said as the applause died.

Attack or no attack, husband or no husband, I couldn't allow this sham of a wedding to go forward. Especially since both Linnaea pretenders were about to embark on a dangerous adventure.

Leon took his brother's place in front of Leszek as Boris and Dominique stepped aside. Clasping his hands respectfully, Leon actually looked at peace, as if he'd waited his whole life for this moment. He probably had.

"Linnaea?" he prompted. "My love, remove your mask, show yourself to our people."

I gulped. The exit behind me was close. If I threw myself off the dais and scrambled for it...

Dominique looked smug. "Per'aps she y'is not well."

Oh, I'm healthier than you think. I said nothing.

"Well? Get on with it girl, we don't have all night," Leszek said.

"You're not having second thoughts, are you?" Leon said loudly.

Lord Ansel vibrated with concern. He knew something was wrong.

Every second I stalled was time bought for the Roamers and the Freetors—yet they didn't seem eager to cash in. I'd have to keep everyone in the room in a different, far more dangerous way. Sylvia, Laoise, and Monju could make it to Sallingaire without me. If this was what the fight for equality demanded of me, then I would not shy away from my duty.

Closing my eyes, I said a silent goodbye to Keegan. Laoise will wake you. Somehow. Then you can rule, like you always wanted.

In one swift movement, I pulled off the mask and threw it upon the dais. The pins slipped free and my curls tumbled around my shoulders, revealing my true self to the throne room.

The crowd rumbled lowly. Nearly all of them knew I wasn't Linnaea. Yet only a few of them—those who had lived their lives in the west—recognized my true face. To them, I'd risen from the dead, and they recoiled appropriately.

"Linnaea. My intended!" Leon said, his knees buckling with joy. "You have revealed—"

From the middle of the audience, a red-faced Mistress Alwina pushed her way to the front. "That girl is servant filth!"

"You idiots," Ansel Gareth said, approaching the dais with his weapon drawn. "That's not my daughter. That's—"

"The Violet Fox," Dominique hissed, drawing her knife.

I'd already drawn mine. "I am Kiera Driscoll. The Violet Fox and rightful High Queen of the realm."

"J'ou are not a queen," she spat. "Queen of de rats, maybe."

Before Dominique could pounce, Lord Ansel Garth parted the crowd, gripping the edge of the dais like a feral animal, snarling. "Where's my daughter?"

"With someone she truly loves," I said, nearly choking on the words.

"You were going to marry me. For the crown," Leon said, taken aback.

I held up my left hand. "Sorry Leon. As foolproof a plan that would be, I'm already married, in the old tradition, to the true prince of the realm, who has been imprisoned by these invaders!"

"We do not recognize those traditions," Leszek said gravely. The Frostfire men converged on the dais, ready to strike on command. "And we did this city a favour by liberating it from your influence."

As arguments broke out in the audience, Lord Ansel slammed his fist upon the wooden floor of the dais. "Tell me where you put my daughter," he said in a low, threatening voice. "Or I'll—"

"No one invited you here, Gareth," Leszek interrupted. He gestured to his Frostfire men. "Escort this errant lord from the premises. Immediately."

My eyes widened. What?

"No," Dominique shouted.

At her silent command, three Northern shadow killers launched themselves from the wall and surrounded the Frostfire men. They didn't even have to draw their weapons. Their presence—even while outnumbered—was enough.

"I invited him here," Dominique said simply. "Someting was not right wit' dis girl. I knew she could not be Linnaea Gareth. A fat'er should be y'at his daughter's weddin', no?"

Leszek grabbed her and spun her round to face him, his voice a low growl. "Stupid girl. I don't care if she's a Freetor spy in Linnaea's clothing. The marriage is what counts."

Of course. If Laoise as Linnaea had stood before them and married Leon, then Leszek would have gained control over the Gareth land. Now that Dominique had invited Lord Ansel here, and he knew that his daughter was missing, the marriage, and thus their agreement, could not go forward.

"If my daughter is not found, Emperor Leszek," Ansel said with disdain, "consider my support formally withdrawn."

"Do that," Leszek replied, "and you will be executed for treason. As we did to your son Joel this morning."

Ansel paled. "I saw him last night. He rode on ahead, eager to get to the capital—"

"Too eager. We picked him up just outside the wall. We needed insurance, in case of trouble with the marriage."

"Do you always execute your insurance, Leszek?" I asked loudly.

As intended, the crowd stirred, and many of them demanded justice of their own. The Western nobles in the audience became restless. Lord Ansel might not have much in the way of fortune or retinues compared to the rest of them, but he was of an old house, and Leszek's admission put him in dangerous territory.

"It was...an unfortunate accident," Leszek said to Ansel, and the people. Then to me: "It wouldn't have happened if your precious Advisor had cooperated."

Dominique, seeing that they were losing the crowd, became frustrated. "J'our daughter—j'our real daughter—y'is here. She is probably in her chambers. Go to her, before she dies."

"Dies? What have you done?"

"Poison," I said to Ansel. "She thought she was poisoning me."

Alarm marred Leszek's features. "Dominique..."

"I tought she was an imposter! And she was!"

"You have crossed me for the final time," he hissed.

I took advantage of the deadlock between the two families and drew my second knife, sticking both points against the exposed flesh of Dominique and Leszek's necks.

"Don't move," I said.

Leszek made a small affirmative gesture to his sons and the guards. They remained still, but ready.

"Ivor Ferguson," I said, unable to keep the emotion from my voice. "Is he dead?"

His gaze lifted to mine. He hadn't expected that question. "He was found in the hedge maze last night, badly wounded after his escape. His injuries were too far gone. He is dead."

I squeezed my eyes shut, trying to maintain my composure. Opening them again, I let the tears flow freely down my cheeks. "I see."

I searched his face. A kind of stoic malice lived there, the kind moulded from years of hatred. He had no reason to lie about my father's death. He had waited patiently for the day.

"You could kill me, Violet Fox," Leszek said, equally as patient, "yet you would still have my army to contend with."

"Maybe I can magic them away," I replied.

Despite the weapon at his throat, he smirked—it was the same as Leon's. He gestured to his men. "Go ahead, then."

I regretted putting the orb in Laoise's bag. As my confidence wavered, so did the pressure on both knifepoints. "Well—"

"You see? She is just a Freetor. Like the rest of them." He nodded at Dominique, eager and waiting. "Kill her."

"Tank j'ou," she said roughly.

The war cry stabbed the air as Dominique turned to face me, yet the cry was not hers. It was the sound of a hundred Roamers and countless Freetors who had tunnelled up from beneath to speak in the only language the East and the North could understand.

Invasion.

The sudden noise shocked and distracted everyone. At once, the throne room flooded with Roamer and Freetor men and women. Pascal Antony led the charge, his longsword a beacon of light.

I jumped from the dais into the flood, narrowly missing Dominique as she made an attack of opportunity on my mid-section. I passed Pascal Antony, touching his arm in solidarity as we went separate ways. Him, into the fray. Me, away from it.

"You're late," I yelled to him.

"The fight begins when I arrive," he replied, and sliced through a Frostfire bannerman with one powerful swing.

"Follow her!" Dominique cried. Four dual-wielding Roamers leapt onto the dais and surrounded her, drowning the order.

Antony's one hundred men overwhelmed all exits from the throne room. Recognizing me, but partially because they were thirsty for the battle itself, they allowed me to squeeze through. Time to get out of this cursed castle.

Behind me, however, as the last of the attacking force hurried into the throne room, one masked man made it through. He'd taken up Linnaea's full-face mask and as he was barely armed, not a visible, immediate threat to the Roamers. He was probably grinning under there as he took off at a run after me.

"I'm not about to let you get away for the second time," Leon Frostfire called after me.

"Yes, you are," I said, and ran faster.

Last time I'd run as the Violet Fox away from Leon Frostfire, I'd been on horseback, outside, heading for the edge of the world. This time, I darted down straight, narrow hallways. My feet carried me swiftly, yet Leon in his rage ran equally as fast.

I slowed to make a corner: my mistake. He caught my skirts and tore, hard. The fabric held, barely, yet it threw my balance. Together we spun into a heap into the wall. I scrambled to find purchase. Suddenly, Leon was on top of me, holding my shoulders square with the stone floor, the mask now gone, face red and tortured.

He'd borne his soul to me and for that, in his mind, I had to suffer.

"I'm going to take you to my father," he growled. "Or Dominique. One of them will execute you. Then they'll have to respect me. Then they'll have to give me the real Linnaea."

His strange reasoning earned him a punch in the face. As Leon tumbled off me, I looked up. Monju stood over me as he pointed his curved sword at Leon.

"That is for disrespecting Lady Kiera," he said sternly. "Next blow will be for breaking Monju's guitar."

I scrambled to my feet as Leon, fazed, used the wall for support. "What guitar? Oh... you're that prancer from Iar Bunsula..."

"Came back in case Lady Kiera needed assistance. Ready to go," he said under his breath, advancing on Leon.

I added my knife to Monju's blade. "I think I've got this one under control now, thanks."

"You have nothing," Leon said. Despite the blades, he launched himself from the wall at me. My knife caught his cheek and Monju sidestepped him gracefully, allowing Leon to stumble forward.

"Should knock him—?"

The question barely left Monju's lips. Leon climbed to his feet and reached for Monju as Lady Elizabeth Schwinghamer rounded the corner without her mask, holding a large tome. He didn't see her coming. I grabbed Leon by his collar and pushed him at Liz, and she raised her tome, smashing him over the head hard.

He fell to the stone floor, unconscious.

The three of us shared a surprised look.

"He was a pompous, smug bastard, wasn't he?" she said.

"Where did you even get that book?" I asked.

"I always keep one nearby. For these sorts of occasions." She hugged it to her chest, side-stepping Leon's body, and bowed. "At your service, Violet Fox."

"You knew who I was this whole time?" I said.

"Not the whole time. But tonight, you called me Liz," she said. "I only told the servant known as Rorda Cloth to call me Liz. And"—she smiled—"after our encounter with Lady Sylvia and Lady Milda, I had a sneaking suspicion it might be you."

I smiled, but was distracted by quick, flighty footfalls. Rounding a corner, Bidelia looked left, then right, and lifted her dark eyebrows when she spotted us.

"What are you still doing here?" Bidelia demanded. Her worried expression danced between me and Monju. "Where's Laoise?"

"Bidelia," I said breathlessly. "She's fine. In the carriage. Monju just came back—"

"—to ensure you escaped? That's the only answer that matters. Get out of the castle, before someone has your head." Suddenly noticing Liz's presence, she paled. "Who are you?"

"Lady Elizabeth Schwinghamer," she said, curtsying quickly.

"You're an Easterner," Bidelia said, but her gaze asked me, Can we trust her?

"She's on our side," I replied. "Look after her, Bidelia."

Unsure of her new charge, Bidelia knew we didn't have time to argue. "Can you handle a weapon?"

"I had a few lessons."

"Get ready to move to the top of the class." Bidelia shoved a knife into Liz's hands, and to her credit, Liz got over the shock of being thrust into action rather quickly.

I was about to leave when a nearly forgotten promise sprung to mind. "Liz. Many of the servant girls who helped us tonight will now be criminals or considered enemies of the Frostfire and Castillo families. Some of those girls are Easterners and Northerners."

She understood my question before I could ask it. "I can arrange their safe passage to my family's land and find them appropriate work within our baile."

I nodded, relieved. "Thank you."

"Good luck, Violet Fox," she said, inclining her head. "With everything."

* * *

Monju and I raced outside through the kitchen exit and ran around the side of the hedge maze to the stables. No one seemed to be around. A light rain descended upon us, hissing against the line of torches stuck in the ground a safe distance from the rebuilt stables and the hedge maze.

I followed my bard assassin friend into the open plains, and just where the ground began its slow, steady decline into the untamed west and the hunting grounds, there sat our ride. Not the enclosed carriage Laoise, Monju, and I had arrived in, but a two-horse wooden hay wagon filled to the brim with straw.

Sylvia spun to meet us, infuriated. "Finally! I thought you'd died!"

I looked uncertainly at the wagon. "This is what you got us?"

Monju looked ready to give a quick answer but of course, Sylvia was louder. "I told them I didn't want this one! The stupid stable hand stupidly prepared—"

"Don't care. We have no choice." Laoise already lay on the hay within. I climbed up beside her, begrudgingly helping Sylvia in her giant gown.

"Monju will drive." He leapt onto the seat. "Hold on."

The wagon lurched to life, knocking Sylvia into the hay. I barely kept my balance. Laoise groaned and woke suddenly.

"S'all right," I said to her as the hedge maze and the stable shrank behind us. "We're en route."

"Monju...?" Laoise asked, her gaze wandering lazily.

"I didn't know you were working with him," Sylvia said, attempting to brush the hay from her gown.

A couple of stable hands yelled and started after us. One of them carried a bow and a quiver, and the faint glow of fire briefly lit his face. Apparently not all of the stable hands were on our side.

"They're going to tell the Frostfires where we went!" I said.

A flaming arrow flew towards us and struck the grass, narrowly missing our aft wheel. The arrow petered out in the sprinkling rain.

"Monju thinks they'll follow regardless!" he called from the front.

He was right. As we hurried down the long incline and turned east, meeting the dirt road that bordered the forest hunting ground and the neighbouring mountains, I made out distant riders saddling up, preparing for a chase.

"Can we lose them?" Sylvia demanded.

"I don't know," I answered honestly. We were a two-horse hay wagon. They were riding the fastest and the finest. "How long until Silent Thief's Pass?"

"Minutes," she said. "We might have to pay a toll. What

will the guards say? They'll think I've been abducted! I didn't bring—"

"No time for tolls," I interrupted. "This is going to be a rough ride."

Silent Thief's Pass loomed before us, lit by two lanterns affixed to the entrance to the massive tunnel. It curved through solid rock for less than a league. It was the only way through. The cliffsides were too steep for horses and too dark to safely scale—especially in Laoise's condition and Sylvia's disposition.

Movement caught my eye. Two—no, three men, stirred from their posts at the tunnel entrance, and I saw the glint of steel as we raced towards them. They swung their massive swords as we left them in our dust. One nicked the siding of the wagon, shaving off some splinters that blew back in his face.

The dark night abruptly turned cold as we entered the tunnel. Men shouted after us only to have their words thrown back at them from the massive surrounding rock. We twist-ed and made at least two turns—the wagon scraped against shale. One moment it seemed like the walls were about to crush us. Another, we had several stone-throws of room. I couldn't even see my hands in front of me. My Freetor eyes were of no use. With no lanterns or torches to light our way, we drove blind.

The horses whinnied. One of them nearly reared. We halted, dead in the road.

"What—?"

"Too dark too quick!" Monju called.

I heard the Frostfires behind us, twisting and turning as we had, and then they came into view. Ten men on horseback. Some of them carried lights. They were on our heels.

Unsteady in the hay, and afraid I'd be thrown from the wagon if we jerked into action, I stood and removed the Orb from our sack. It emitted a faint blue light only Laoise and I could see, nothing compared to a torch, especially since there were no other artefacts present.

I closed my eyes and concentrated. As Monju muttered soothingly to the horses, Laoise moaned in pain, and Sylvia shrieked with panic, I tried to think what my father would do. How did he call magic? Had it always been within him? How had I done it before, deep in the castle, and in the town square?

A feeling swirled in my stomach, more concentrated than nerves. The same voice that urged me when to run and fight spoke to me now, more real than instinct, yet elusive, just out of earshot.

We need to see.

The wagon lurched forward and I nearly lost my balance. Our horses spurred to life and took off faster than before, but it wasn't enough. Unless the tunnel narrowed suddenly, the riders would overtake us. Blue light flickered from the Orb, stronger than I'd ever seen it, painting the walls with the constantly changing, ever-approaching shadows of the enemy. It was as if the sun had risen within the tunnel. The enemy, awash in the cold light, were right on top of us.

One of the guards maneuvered his horse alongside us and drew his sword.

"Stay back!" I warned him, holding out the artefact. "I will use this."

Grinning, his teeth glowed in the blue light. He was undeterred. He looked instead to Sylvia and Laoise, huddling on the opposite side of the wagon.

"Can't go faster!" Monju shouted. I could barely hear him above the roar of the horses.

We were almost through. Just a little further now—though the bad steering, two-horse wagon would not survive without drastic action. Staring up at the rock above, a horrible plan twisted to mind.

Another rider flanked us, squeezing in as the tunnel gradually widened. He reached out and grabbed for Sylvia, narrowly missing.

"Do something!" Sylvia screamed at me.

I held the Orb above my head. "Don't let them get us!"

Lightning penetrated the rock above, hitting the glowing blue artefact, narrowly missing my fingers. Rocks tumbled as the tunnel gave way to sky, conveniently falling around, but not on our wagon. The horses flanking us shrieked and threw their riders as they succumbed to the onslaught. I could no longer see the other guards on horseback as the pass filled with boulders and debris. Thunder followed, drowned out by the collapse. I knelt with Laoise, grabbing Sylvia, shielding their bodies with mine as rocks large and small rained around us.

"Faster!" I cried to Monju.

The cold night was ahead. As we burst into it, the exit crumbled into rubble.

The only way out now was through—to Sallingaire.

Fifteen

SYLVIA SNORED AND muttered in her sleep as we rode over rough roads in the cold night. I offered to relieve Monju and he refused. He was just as determined to get to Sallingaire to save his beloved as I was to save mine.

Beside me, Laoise dipped in and out of sleep. I wouldn't leave her side. She had risked her life for me, and I had lied to her just to spare her pain. She was the only family I had left. If I lost her....

This wasn't the right time. All the opportunities to reflect had collapsed behind us, like that tunnel, or had burned away, like my brother, or had been ripped away, like my father.

"I need to tell you something," I said to her.

Her eyes fluttered heavily open. "What?"

"About Monju. He...he kissed me. A while ago. When we were in the Roamers camp."

Eyebrows knitting together, Laoise parted her dry lips. "Oh..."

"I don't like him in that way," I continued quickly. "I don't think he likes me in that way. I think he just got caught up in—"

"S'all right," she said, a small smile spreading across her pale face.

I was still unsure. "I should have told you earlier. It's all right if you're mad at me."

"No," she replied. She gazed up at the early morning sky. "I figured something had happened. From the way you kept acting when I would bring him up."

I felt uncomfortable. "I didn't know how to tell you. I didn't want to break your heart. You were—are—so happy when he's here. I didn't want to take that away from you. Not after…" Not after Rordan.

"You can't take that kind of thing away." She put her hand over mine and we stayed like that for a while, quiet in each other's company as the wagon lulled us into a dreamless, light sleep.

Minutes, maybe an hour later, Laoise spoke again. "Did he die?"

My father. "Yes. Leszek said he had him executed." I wanted the words to be hollow and empty, yet they were heavy with regret.

"He made a sacrifice for us. We won't forget that."

"You made a sacrifice for him. If you hadn't let him escape in the first place, Dominique wouldn't have poisoned you."

"Maybe. We can't change what's been done. We did what we could with what we had."

She was truly Bidelia's daughter. "I promise I'll find a way to heal you with the Cloth."

Slowly shutting her eyes, she smiled again. "I know."

* * *

Three days of solid riding put Sallingaire in our sights. Green plains and tall, foreboding forests gave way to sand, dirt, and grass so yellow it looked like the hay in the wagon. I chewed on a piece and felt sick. Our only rations were stale biscuits Laoise had nicked from her mid-afternoon tea the day of the masquerade and the dwindling supplies Monju needed to keep Laoise from the brink of death. Even those were in short supply. Although I'd taken all three full jars of spices, the oils required for the temporary antidote ran danger-ously low.

"How bad?" Laoise asked, on the first full day on the road.

"Might be able to last until Sallingaire," Monju said grimly. "After that, will have to find herbal shop. Or, preferably, the Emerald Cloth."

On the first night, we stopped only for four hours to rest the horses. We dared make a fire with some of the hay. The four of us lay down solemnly: Monju, lost deep in sleep; Sylvia, tossing and turning, sleeping perhaps for the first time without luxuries and filled instead with fear for tomorrow; Laoise, restless and in pain; then me, my mind racing with scenarios of what awaited us in Sallingaire and dreams of my father and brother, finally reunited and at peace.

It rained the second day, putting us all in a foul mood. With no roof over the wagon, the hay became sodden and so did we. Laoise became worse, shivering uncontrollably. I sidled up to her, trying to give her what little body heat I had. The Orb of Dashiell was an uncomfortable lump between us, wrapped in an apron that I refused to have anywhere but in my grasp.

"Get over here," I said to Sylvia.

She slumped in the middle of the wagon, unwilling to go near Laoise "in case she was contagious" and refused to sit up front—even where she'd be more comfortable—with Monju, who continued to push the horses hard.

"N-n-n-no," Sylvia shivered through the rain. She ducked her head between her knees.

"You can be cold over there," I shouted at her, "or you can be warm over here with us. Up to you."

Groaning loudly, Sylvia crawled through the hay like a beast and settled on Laoise's other side, arms folded. "I hate this."

"No one likes this," I said.

Later that evening, the rain trickled to a drizzle and we

dared to stop at a road-side pond. As everything was wet, we couldn't make a fire, but Monju had left his canteen open and it had filled during our tumultuous ride. The horses took what little respite we could give them before we pressed on, me in the driver's seat. To my surprise, Sylvia opted to sit with me in the front.

"I swore I'd never turn my back to that dreadful man again," she said, squeezing out rainwater from her now-heavy dress, "but I'd rather sit here than beside him...and her."

The wrapped-up Orb sat on my lap, a heavy reminder of our mission. But Monju's songs distracted us from our worries, keeping me awake while Sylvia nodded in and out of sleep. A few times I grabbed her arm to prevent her from falling out altogether. Grimacing each time, I received no word of thanks but her fearful face, her gaze knowing that her life was in my hands.

By noon on the third day, Sallingaire was before us. Unlike the walled-off edifice of Marlenia City, Sallingaire crept up on you. At first, farms and pastures. Then, huts and houses. Harvesters plucking ripe red fruits from rows upon rows of trees. Our mouths watered. We stopped and Monju worked his charms, earning us four ripe apples.

We resumed slowly along the farmland road as before, dread filling me as large houses approached, and other roads intersected with ours.

"What can we expect when we're entering Sallingaire?" I asked Monju and Sylvia.

"Inspection," Sylvia said with disgust.

My eyes widened. "Why didn't you say that earlier?" I urged the horses to stop and turned around to face the now-rebellious Daughter of the East.

Sylvia looked incredulous. "I got us the wagon. I told you where to go. I fulfilled my end of the bargain."

"Yes, but if we can't find a plausible way into Sallingaire,

Keegan and the rest of the cursed will die." Not to mention, if the Frostfires got ahold of the Orb of Dashiell, our mission as it was would be finished.

She tried to steel her nerves, yet I saw the worry deep within her gaze. "I know that. I just thought you knew as well."

I'd been so caught up in escaping the castle and taking down the Frostfire family that I hadn't thought this far ahead. I could hear my father now, scolding me for not considering every angle. The Frostfires now had control of Sallingaire. It sat on the West-East border—of course the Frostfires would fortify and defend it in any way they could. A deep pain, a sorrow I hadn't felt since Rordan's death, soured my belly.

"Is all right," Monju said calmly. "Monju will drive into Sallingaire. Ladies will sit in the wagon, unspeaking. Monju will sing for the guards, and the Ladies as well, if necessary."

"As charming as we are, I don't think that'll be enough," I said, not unkindly.

Sylvia crossed her arms. "They might recognize my face. They might let me through."

I shook my head. "We can't take that risk. We'll have to hide your face. Your family may have sent word that you've betrayed them."

The word struck a sore nerve. "*Betrayal* is a—"

"Strong word. Yeah. And that's what you did."

"I did it for a good reason," she muttered. "In any case, none of us have papers proving our identities, so we might be denied outright no matter what. My father has men posted there. No doubt at the city limits as well. They might know me. But after your little stunt, taking Dominique's name, all the major noble families are terrified that you or someone like you will try to do the same. They are no longer taking chances."

Right. "So an inspection is inevitable."

"An idea," Monju said suddenly. "Monju will take the wagon

into town with Laoise. Guards may let her through as she is truly unwell and just looking for a healer. You two sneak around..." He paused, gazing up at the mountains. They had always been there, but now they seemed like they were about to fall on top of us. "On second thought, hard to sneak through the mountains."

"I'm not sneaking," Sylvia said, crossing her arms defiantly.

"Difficult, in the Lady's current attire," Monju muttered.

Difficult to sneak in any circumstances. Twin mountains cradled the town of Sallingaire, yet the countryside itself sloped from fertile ground to rocky terrain with very little coverage. Squinting against the sun, I swore I saw a man high in the peaks, surveying us.

"Patrols in the mountains, anyway," I said. "The only way in is through whatever checkpoints the Frostfires have in place."

"Unfortunate," Monju said. He began muttering the problem under his breath, sweeping his finger to and fro in time to a melody only he could hear.

I crawled over to Laoise. The four of us had spent days in the hay. Sylvia's golden locks had adopted many of the thin stalks, yet her dress, as garish and out of place as it was, had repelled the hay, like boots to the rain. Without her dress, Sylvia was little more than a peasant, just like the rest of us.

"I have an idea," I said. I looked to Sylvia, grinning. "No sneaking, but you're going to have to take off that dress."

* * *

The valley air was fresh but cold on my bare skin. I drew my knees up to my chin. The thin, sleeveless chemise provided little coverage, yet in a moment, none of that would matter. As Laoise and Sylvia shifted into position near the back of the wagon, Monju drew me aside.

"No more oils for concoction," Monju said quietly. "Ran out this morning."

"How long?" I didn't want to know.

"Hours."

I nodded, my head heavy. "Sylvia says the Cloth—or the potential Cloths—are in the cathedral, on display."

"Hope she is right," he said darkly.

"Me too," I muttered.

"I need help," Sylvia said.

Monju looked away respectfully, taking up the driver's seat as I crawled on my exposed knees to the back of the wagon. The dresses Laoise had packed—two light gowns in blue and red, as well as a servant's skirt, chemise, and apron—had been folded and stacked on the hay behind Monju. The emerald green dress, wrinkled and worn but eye-catching, along with Sylvia's dress, folded and pressed as flat as the fabric would allow, were directly behind Monju at the front of the wagon.

I pried the Orb from Laoise's sleepy grasp and rested it between my legs. It wasn't the most comfortable solution, as the Orb was unwieldy enough for one hand alone, but I trusted it nowhere else. My prized knife, safely strapped around my forearm, was my only protection for what was to come.

"What if they shove pitchforks in the wagon bed?" Sylvia asked. She finished covering Laoise with hay. I could barely see her. Sylvia lay against the other side of the wagon, scooping up piles of the stuff and spreading it over her light red, long-sleeved chemise.

"Then I'll jump out and attack." My other knife rested in Laoise's slippery grasp. I feared she may be gripped with uncontrollable shakes: if so, she'd have to reveal herself and stab any nearby interloper, which would provide ample time for me to jump up and make my own attack.

If it came to that. I helped cover Sylvia. The hay was plentiful, yet Sylvia was twice my size at least.

"I can see your ribs," she said, frowning. The chemise's thin fabric hid nothing of my scrawny frame.

"Yes," I replied, feeling suddenly self-conscious. I'd shed any excess fat during my journey to the end of the world, and living with the Gareths hadn't lent itself to decadent eating.

She straightened her head, peering up at the sky as she readjusted some of the hay over her stomach. Colour flushed her cheeks. "If my father's guards find me like this, they'll suspect I've gone mad."

"Well, they'll find us, too, so we'll all be mad together. Close your eyes." Without further warning, I dropped hay over her face. "Sylvia, stay still—"

It took fifteen minutes and Monju's help to cover both me and Sylvia. She didn't complain further, though she wouldn't stop twitching. The hay itched all over.

"Try to think of something else," I told her, accidentally eating a stalk of hay as I dared to speak.

"Mmmphaphaha," came Sylvia, which I interpreted as, "I can't, you stupid Freetor, but thank you for the words of encouragement and solidarity."

After a minute, the wagon shook as Monju jumped up onto the driver's seat. "Looks good. Time to go."

We were off. The three of us lay beneath the hay in our small clothes shoulder-to-shoulder, praying we wouldn't be discovered. My eyes closed, I concentrated on taking deep breaths.

To my left, Laoise twitched. I felt her sweat through the hay. To my right, Sylvia struggled to inhale and exhale quietly.

After an eternity, the wagon rolled to a stop. Far in the distance, deep voices barked orders.

"Why aren't we moving?" Sylvia whispered.

"Probably a line," I replied.

Sure enough, the wheels crackled on the gravel as we lurched forward.

"Hello," Monju said loudly as he gently brought us to a stop. Shuffling of many footsteps on the ground ensued, and beside me, Sylvia whimpered.

"What is your cargo?" a gruff voice asked.

Monju was quick. "Ladies' dresses."

"A large wagon for a couple of dresses."

"Ran into Freetors and bandits. A chase ensued. Had to dump most of the cargo or die."

Faint sounds of scribbling and footsteps around the wagon. I held my breath and Laoise's hand tightened around mine. A presence halted beside my head.

"Are you ill?" the man asked Monju after a minute of inspection.

Monju hesitated for a fraction of a second. "No, sir."

"Do you have papers from a healer certifying your good health?"

I bit down on my finger. The curse was here.

"Monju does not. But can visit a healer upon entry and return with certification, if this pleases the man?"

More mumbling between the men. Sylvia stiffened beside me. Then: "You came right from Xii?"

"Yes, sir."

"You didn't pass through Marlenia City?"

"No. Bypassed."

Silence.

Then: "Unusual for a prancer to avoid the colour and opportunity that the capital usually brings."

Prancer was a derogatory term for a Southerner. Monju ignored it. "Heard from fellow traders that business has declined. Gates have shut. No way out after going in."

"Hmm." More conferring between the men. "All right. You're doing a return run to Xii?"

"Once Monju finds suitable trade to return with, yes."

"Find it quickly. You have two days. I want to see papers from a healer when you come back through. Get on that now. The healing houses and beds are near capacity."

"Yes. Monju thanks the man sincerely. Will do as suggested."

"Three silver, then, for the entry."

I stiffened. We didn't have silver. We're going to be—

The light clinking of coin and the dull thud of it landing on a palm.

"You can proceed."

After more yelling and muttering, one of them banged on the wagon—eliciting a loud gasp from Sylvia—yet not loud enough to be heard over the sudden lurching of the wagon as Monju spurred the horses into the city proper.

"I didn't know he had silver," I whispered.

"I think my mother gave him some," Laoise replied.

"We could have stayed in an inn," Sylvia lamented.

Sylvia seemed ready to spring from the hay, but I slowly slid a hand over and laid it on her arm, staying her movements. She did not shy from my offer of comfort.

The wagon jolted over uneven cobblestone, rattling my teeth and displacing some of the hay from our bodies. I wondered if the sides of the wagon were high enough to hide us—otherwise, I hoped any passersby believed Monju carted bodies, in which case, he might be left alone.

Briefly, the Orb warmed my legs, and my muscles tightened around it to keep from rolling all over the wagon. The closer we came to an artefact of power, the hotter it would become, and the more fiercely it would glow.

After a time, the gentle heat died. The ride continued. We rolled into a colder spot of the city and Monju brought the wagon to a standstill.

"Is all right," he said. "No one around."

Sylvia and I sprung from the hay, gasping for air. I removed some of the hay from Laoise; she was asleep. Monju had pulled into a quiet, wide alley. Around us were tightly packed houses, many hands tall, each adorned with white-shuttered windows, disciple daisies, and painted doors.

"Quickly, dress," he said, tossing us our clothes. "Lady Sylvia, she must wear the garb of a commoner, like Lady Laoise and Lady Kiera."

She grimaced, peering out onto the cobblestone street. "You have silver—which you didn't tell us before. We could buy new clothes and rid ourselves of these rags!"

"Monju is accustomed to hiding silver from nobles," he said, smiling, flashing his silver tooth.

"Then you do have more—!"

"Stop it. Laoise is dying," I interrupted with a low hiss. "This isn't the time to argue about clothes." I grabbed the nearest skirt and crawled over to Laoise, shoving her legs in. She woke, groaning and shivering, looking far worse.

"Sallingaire?" she croaked.

"Yes. We're here. Just getting you dressed."

Monju moved to help Sylvia do up her corset, but Sylvia slapped him away. "Do you really think—?"

"Apologies, my lady," Monju said, stepping back. "Only trying to speed this along."

"Laoise, can Monju help you with your clothes?" I asked her.

She nodded and Monju and I switched places.

"Really," Sylvia scoffed, glancing disapprovingly at Monju. "It's not proper for a man to dress a woman. In any circumstance. How he knows how to tie and untie corsets—well, that's a whole other matter." Then, in a lower voice: "How can you trust him? He was Dominique's pawn."

I pulled Sylvia's corset laces taught. "He was trying to save his father."

Neither of us succeeded in that, I realized. Grief washed over me anew. I hid my feelings in the corset laces, ensuring it bound Sylvia's waist tightly, as if it could bind her tongue as well.

"Besides," I continued, after I'd swallowed my sadness, "you're letting me help you. How is that different?"

"It just is," she replied.

Unwilling to press the subject further, I peered into the streets. "It's unlikely our faces are known here—except maybe Sylvia's. You should put your hair in a wrap."

In parts of the East and the North, unmarried commoner women would pin up their hair, wrap it in colourful cloth, and roll the cloth in a spiralling bun. Not only did it keep the hair fresh for longer, but the quality of the cloth sometimes denoted a family's economic status, and thus made the woman a more desirable marriage option.

We didn't have proper hair wraps. I grabbed Sylvia's dress and tore off some of the red fabric. She whined briefly, but as the dress had been dirtied by days of travel, she didn't put up too much of a fight. With the corset and the quality fabric of her hair wrap, she looked like a wealthy merchant's daughter.

"You know I do believe I have a cousin here," Sylvia said indignantly as she fluffed out her blonde curls. "We could call upon him. He would have no choice but to show us hospitality."

"Yes and then when your father and his army shows up, you don't think he'll call upon the same cousin and find you drinking tea and eating biscuits?"

"Hmph. I could go for tea and biscuits."

After I'd prepared Sylvia, I quickly dressed myself. As my chemise had no sleeves, and thus was not appropriate to wear in public on its own, I pulled on the emerald dress and tied the apron around my waist. In the apron pocket, the Orb remained hidden and safe, along with one of my knives. The second I had sheathed and tied around my thigh.

Now dressed appropriately, the four of us ventured through

the quiet, narrow residential lanes into the large, bustling streets of Sallingaire. Laoise and I walked arm in arm. Her steps, slow and calculated, attempted to hide her exhaustion.

Unlike Marlenia City, the carriages here roamed fast and free, taking advantage of the wide cobblestone streets. Walking citizens paid little mind: they stuck close to the buildings or, when there was an opening, they strode brazenly in the middle of the streets. Frostfire men on horses rode lazily along—the four of us tried not to look guilty as we passed. No open markets stalls lined our way—all businesses had inside storefronts, even the farmers and the artisans. I followed Monju and Sylvia's lead, trying to ignore the carriages and wagons whipping by as well as the horse dung.

"The cathedral is in the middle of the town," Sylvia explained as she diligently avoided a large pile of horse excrement. "We'll have to find the exhibit, but it shouldn't be too hard."

As desperately as I wanted to believe that, I knew that nothing was truly easy.

The street widened into the town square. Here carriages and wagons waded through the pedestrians, the street performers juggling fire, and the unusually high number of guards. Laoise's grip on me tightened. No one else seemed concerned, however. The people of Sallingaire visited their shops, enjoyed the performers, and rode their carriages as if the Frostfires had always occupied their town with a large show of force.

Mountains overtook much of the sky as they cradled the town, simultaneously unsettling and awe-inspiring. In Marlenia City, the mountains had been a physical manifestation of the crown's power, standing tall in solidarity with the castle. Here, they cradled every building. Despite the armed men patrolling the streets, there was something comforting about the mountains' presence. The Frostfires could run us through, yet they could not destroy what nature had placed here—no one could.

The cathedral cast a long shadow in the square. As tall as the castle in Marlenia City, the structure sat like a ruler upon its throne of one hundred steep stone steps. Three guards patrolled the steps, urging resting citizens to move along and stopping everyone who wanted entry into the historic building.

"It looks like they're turning people away," Laoise said as we approached.

"We have to try." My grip on her tightened. She stumbled; Monju caught her other arm. Together, with Sylvia at our heels, we hurried for the cathedral steps.

The guard at the base immediately spotted us. "Hold on there. High Priest Phillipman is in the middle of a service."

Laoise coughed, unable to keep her sickness under wraps. It drew the ire of the guard immediately.

"What's wrong with her?" he asked. "The cathedral isn't taking any more potential plague victims. Not after what happened yesterday."

"What happened yesterday?" I asked, dreading the answer.

The man considered us for a moment. "A group of priests fell prey to the Freetor threat. Completely fine in the morning. Frozen by the afternoon."

"Here, in this cathedral?" Sylvia asked.

"Yes. We have men investigating, but we can't explain it. Can't move the bodies, not easily—spread by touch, as we found out. So the catacombs are off limits until further notice."

Sylvia's pleasantries faded away to impatience. "The catacombs are where the Church's holiest treasures are kept. They are open to the public."

"Not anymore, as I said, ma'am."

Bristling at the improper address, Sylvia looked ready to unwrap her hair and assert her true authority. "But we wanted to see about—"

"Please," I said evenly. I stepped closer to the guard and held onto Sylvia, silently urging her to shut up. "My sister and her husband and"—I glanced sideways at Sylvia—"our cousin, we only want to kneel in the cathedral and pray. All the healers in town seem to be full. Her illness isn't...she's pregnant, you see. And she's having a rough go at it. We only want to pray to Dashiell for the safe carriage of her child in the months to come. Maybe obtain a blessing from the priest. We don't mean any trouble and we don't know anything about this awful Freetor plague."

The guard looked uncomfortable. "I understand. My apologies for holding you up. It's full in there, though. I can't guarantee the priest will see you."

"Thank you, thank you!" I grinned in false gratitude, hurrying Laoise up the stairs with Monju's help. Sylvia was slower, seemingly stupefied. "Come along, cousin," I said to her, gesturing.

She gave me a withering look and yet I didn't stop grinning as we ascended the many steps. The guard at the top opened the heavy door for us.

"Pregnant?" Laoise whispered to me.

"I figured he wouldn't ask any further questions that way," I replied.

"Monju has a few questions," he said dryly.

Sylvia leaned in close to me. "You should have let me ask about—"

Our loud whispers earned harsh stares from the people gathered behind the crowded pews. Even the aisles were littered with eager families with flushed cheeks, necks craned to the high priest conducting his service.

Yet it wasn't any kind of ceremony I'd seen before. Not that I'd seen many myself. Four bodies lay in a row before the congregation on top of four sealed golden coffins. The attendees in the pews prayed as if their lives depended on it: eyes shut, hands clasped, heads raised to the stained glass window within the apse behind the priest depicting Dashiell giving one of the Loyal Four the Orb. As we navigated around to the left side of the church to get a better vantage point, the priest—garbed in light blue robes, holding a silver sceptre—waved his arms dramatically over the four bodies. Keegan was not among them.

"Dashiell hears us! He knows our plight—this Freetor plague sweeping the land must end!"

Turning his back to his flock, he raised his hands to the stained glass. "Now, together as a congregation, we ask you to heal our loved ones, as you were healed."

As he spun around dramatically, his once-free hand held a ratty piece of green fabric.

The Orb burned in my apron pocket and glowed a brilliant blue.

The Cloth. That was it! Sylvia nudged me encouragingly. Even Laoise, sweat pouring down her face from exhaustion and poisoning, looked up, colour returning to her pale cheeks.

The priest waved the Cloth over each body as if saying goodbye to a friend. Then, muttering parts of some ancient Marlenian text, he gently placed the fabric on one of the sleeping victim's forehead.

Everyone held their breath. Even Laoise was mesmerized, her hand suddenly intertwined with Monju's.

By the disappointment in the priest's face, I saw his faith in the man-god weaken. Setting his lips in a hard line, he repeated the task with the other three sleeping people, taking great care not to touch them with his bare hands.

"I am sorry, my children," he said, his arms outstretched. "It appears Dashiell wishes to keep his chosen in slumber for one more day."

Frustrated murmurs gripped the congregation, but the priest continued. "We must not lose our resolve. We must trust in the man-god's plan. You must be strong, not only for those who are stilled by this cursed ice, but for those who are not."

As the high priest continued with the service and the congregation prayed feverishly, I turned to my friends. "I don't understand," I whispered. "It's definitely Freetor magic of some kind. Yet I've seen tomes glow more brightly than that piece of fabric."

"Maybe it is imbued with Freetor magic, but it's not the Cloth?" Laoise suggested.

"Maybe." The Orb felt like an Extremist explosive, ready to blow. "It's here in the cathedral. Sylvia, you mentioned the catacombs?"

"Yes, that's where all relics are," she replied shortly. Her gaze remained fixed on the four sleeping people on top of the coffins and the priest. Behind him, there were several steps up to the altar, and twin doors leading to what I assumed were the sacristies. "I don't know how big it is. It will take forever to search. How are we going to explain ourselves? We're already fugitives."

"We have a half-day at most on your family," I whispered. "After that, the city will be truly looking for us. I—"

As the crowd milled behind us to find a better spot, I noticed an unguarded set of stairs leading down. A single red rope had been strung on the railing to discourage visitors from entering. Sylvia, Monju, and Laoise followed my gaze, and as one, we navigated the masses towards the stairs.

With the crowd enraptured by the priest, the four of us snuck under the rope and down the spiralling stairs. Torches lit the way. The Orb burned so hot against my leg through my clothes, I removed it from the pocket and cradled it with both arms. I glanced over my shoulder: no one followed.

Getting Laoise down the stairs quietly and managing the Orb was tricky. Laoise's sense of balance, even with one hand on the wall, was failing. The bottom was in sight. Monju grabbed a torch from the wall, handing Laoise off to Sylvia, who begrudgingly led my best friend the rest of the way down the stairs.

The familiar comforting smells of earth and natural decay surrounded me, twisted suddenly by the skulls embedded in the hard sandstone walls.

"The faithful," Monju said. "Watching in death."

Sylvia snorted. "Watching who? Other dead people?" She pointed to rows of wooden coffins embedded in the walls surrounding us.

"Is possible," he replied. "Many of the old defenders of the faith were buried with weapons, jewels, and other valuables."

"Seems like an easy target." Dust covered the coffins, undisturbed and ripe for plundering.

"Ah," Monju said with a smile. "Bad luck for thieves to steal from the Church."

"Since when has that stopped anyone?" I asked.

Halting suddenly, he pressed the torch as close as he dared to one of the sarcophaguses. The lid had been pushed slightly ajar, barely wide enough for a child's hand. Thick, dried mucus ran down the wood and stone.

"Sealed with special poison," Monju explained. "Deadly, like Dominique."

"I've heard enough about...about poisons," Laoise said.

Down the narrow walkway we trudged. Eventually, the ceilings sloped upwards, giving relief to my neck as we filtered into a circular room with one wooden door before us. Two ornate coffins, worn by neglect and dust, had been shelved in the stone walls at waist-level. All around us on display stands, in carved out crevices, and in boxes, were relics of the Church of Dashiell, packed away because the public no longer cared, or to protect them from the Eastern invaders.

Sylvia appeared reverent. "This is it. The room of reliquaries."

The Orb glowed more brightly than before. "The Cloth is definitely in here."

Laoise slumped against the wall while the three of us

searched the room. Starting on the left and working my way counterclockwise, I held the Orb out like a lantern, allowing it to guide me.

"Hmm," Monju said pensively, considering a plaque on the wall near the corridor. "This room is not just for old relics. Two dead saints here, too." He gestured to the coffins. "High Priests, from the treatment of the bodies."

"Heath and Aveline. They were lovers," Sylvia said matter-of-factly, noting the names on the silver inscription on the coffins. She peered at a gold cage reliquary holding a rotted toe. "But they couldn't be together. The faith forbade it. They disobeyed their vows and ran off to a remote part of the world and built a community. Only hundreds of years later did the Church relent and put them in the catacombs. Caving to popular opinion."

Don't think about Keegan's finger, I told myself. We have to find the Cloth, then we can free him.

As I passed the coffin, the blue glow illuminated a curiosity. I'd assumed the coffin had fit snug in its stone shelf above the ground—to prevent worms and other creatures from eating through the wood—yet another, smaller box had been wedged between the end of the coffin and the stone. The Orb pulsated brilliantly.

With one hand, I managed to pull out the box. Upon closer inspection, it was no ordinary box: it was shaped like a wooden house, large enough that it was awkward to carry with one hand. Setting the Orb down gently, I picked up the reliquary house and turned it around. Dusty, thick glass made up the back, a window showing a single square piece of dark green fabric. Even through the dirty pane, the faint glow haloing the cloth was unmistakeable. A golden plague read: 652 HOY. The roof was hinged and clasped shut with a lock. It required a key.

"In here," I said.

Sylvia rushed for me, her arms outstretched. She squinted. "That's...it?"

I handed her the box and knelt to retrieve the Orb when I noticed it had rolled towards a crate filled with wooden display signs, naming the various saints and holy men within the catacombs. The brilliant glow had not faded: in fact, it nearly blinded me.

Rummaging through the crate, I found beneath the signs five more identical reliquaries. I removed them from the crate one by one. Each contained a piece of fabric varying in shades of green, as well as a golden plague detailing where the piece had been found. The locations made my jaw drop: Iar Bunsula. Sallingaire. East of Xii. Toram Lake. Sanarplesh.

"More," Monju said. He retrieved three others hiding behind a group of rusted jewellery boxes.

"Sylvia, how many fakes are there supposed to be?" I asked.

"I-I think at least ten," she said. She arranged them in rows on the floor, giving them all equal consideration. "But maybe more."

"I think I see one," Laoise said hoarsely. She pointed in the far-right corner of the room, on top of a shelf.

I swept the rest of the room with the Orb and we found two others, totalling twelve potential Cloths in identical wooden reliquaries. The three of us towered over them, and Laoise contemplated her fate sleepily from afar.

"One of them is the real one. It's just hard to get a clear reading from the orb. We need to remove them from the boxes, then I'll stand on the other side of the room, and we'll test them one by one."

"Or we just take all of them. Figure it out somewhere else." Sylvia's gaze darted down the open hallway. Anyone could come down the stairs and see us burglarizing the relics.

"Impossible to smuggle this much out at once," Monju said. "And to where?"

"We could remove all of the pieces first and then smuggle them," Sylvia insisted.

She had a point. Laoise could barely keep her eyes open. She didn't have much time. "Let's remove them first. I have an idea."

"But how, each requires a—"

Fortunately, Monju and I were on the same page. In one swift motion, he knelt and punched the roof on one of the boxes, hard. The wood, being stored in the damp underground and neglected for over a decade, gave way easily. Still, he shook his wrist and winced before pulling out a forest-green, fraying piece of cloth.

"Test half on Laoise," I told him. "And I'll test some on the Orb."

Monju and I punched through four of the boxes. He tested two on Laoise with no luck. Our hands were sore and bloodied. Sylvia winced as splinters shot into the air and landed all around her as she tried to pry apart one of the reliquaries without resorting to what she termed "extreme measures." I trembled as I held a near-white piece no larger than my thumb to the Orb. The Orb lit up, its glow so sudden and powerful I nearly dropped the priceless artefact.

"This one."

Eagerly, Monju snatched it from my grip and pressed it to Laoise's forehead.

We waited five long seconds for a miracle.

Laoise winced.

Nothing.

I tried another. "This one also gets a reaction."

Monju tore off the previous piece and threw it to the side, trying the new specimen. Still nothing.

"Maybe the magic doesn't work anymore," Sylvia said, slumping into the dirt. She wiped her brow. "It's too old."

"All of Dashiell's artefacts are supposedly the same age. Even this Orb, after it smashed and my father put it back together, it still—" I inhaled sharply. "They're all the Cloth."

Laoise's eyes widened in surprise as Sylvia uttered an expletive. "All of them? How is that possible? I thought there was only one."

"Because," I said, grinning, "they are one. Dashiell's wife tore part of her dress to dry his sweat and blood, according to my father's version of the story. Over the years, people probably tried to tear the Emerald Cloth, either as an attempt to spread the healing around or to prevent it from falling into enemy hands."

"Of course," Monju muttered, retrieving the piece he'd carelessly thrown.

"That's why they all have a faint blue glow to Freetor eyes," Laoise said. "And why they all respond to the Orb."

"And why one piece doesn't work on its own." I looked to Sylvia. "Help me punch through the rest of these. We're taking all the pieces."

Grimacing, Sylvia considered the box she'd been fiddling with, and scrunching up her face, drove her fist deep into the ancient wooden reliquary. "Ow!"

We added each piece to Laoise's skin. She held two to her forehead, Monju placed several on her legs, and I put some over the ugly wound she'd sustained during our fight with the Extremists. As we removed the last of the pieces from their prisons, Monju retrieved a needle and thread from his pack and began sewing his pieces together. I noted how, despite centuries of wear and tear, some pieces seemed to naturally belong with another. It was not immediately obvious to the naked eye, but rather a sense of knowing. Monju, even though he wasn't a Freetor, seemed to sense this as well, and wove his thread in and out, joining three pieces together in a row.

Quietly, Sylvia joined us, and placed the last one on Laoise's cheek. She murmured.

"C'mon, Laoise," I said. "We did it. We found all the pieces."

"Did we...?" she asked, a small smile lighting her flushed face.

Her whole body glowed and pulsated with the light blue effect of magic. Even the Orb, held captive by the force of the Cloth's power, wobbled and rolled in a tiny orbit on the floor. All twelve pieces ran hot, yet none of us, not even Sylvia, relinquished our grips. The blue glow spread from Laoise to each of us, dancing and swirling around our arms. The cuts on my knuckles disappeared. My hunger subsided. I felt...peaceful.

Eventually, the magic waned, withdrawing like liquid to the individual pieces of cloth. The blue glow on Laoise's skin gave way to a healthy pallor, and when she opened her eyes, they were greener than I remembered. She blinked: the hazel irises returned.

"It worked," I said quietly. I held the three pieces I'd touched in my hands, in near disbelief. Remembering my best friend, I threw my arms around her. "You're all right!"

"A little light-headed," she said as she drew away, rubbing her temples. Looking suddenly alarmed, her gaze danced around the room. "Where is this place? Are we in the underground? I...I had a dream we were in Sallingaire...?"

"That's where we are, in a cathedral. We found the Emerald Cloth. Er, the pieces of it, anyway." I held them up for her to see.

"Oh. Right." She leaned against the wall and yawned. "Everything is so fuzzy."

"She needs rest," Monju said.

Brightening at the sound of his voice, she cupped his face with her hand and grinned. "You're here."

He returned her smile as if there was no one else in the room and boldly kissed her. Laoise's eyes widened at first in surprise, then closed again as her innermost desire was realized.

Sylvia averted her gaze to the exits, wringing her hands in her dress.

Laoise's cheeks flushed as they drew apart. Monju didn't seem embarrassed by his display of affection for my best friend; his gaze found mine, ready to return to the task at hand. "Will take some time to locate Prince Keegan. And restore the pieces into a new whole."

We'd overstayed our welcome in the catacombs. Light footsteps above us startled me. It was only a matter of time before someone came down here—a guard, a member of the Church. We'd have to hide the broken reliquaries and leave soon before someone found us.

Monju began arranging the Cloth as I stacked the broken boxes quickly in one of the crates. I snatched the listless, rolling Orb from the floor and replaced it in my apron pocket. He managed to fit and hastily sew the pieces in three-by-four rows, yet a gap remained as large as my forefinger in the middle.

Sylvia looked pensive. "Twelve pieces. And twelve boxes."

"Then why are we missing one?" I asked.

"What about the high priest?" she said. "He had a piece, and you said it glowed."

"Twelve pieces were enough to heal me," Laoise said. Her head rested on Monju's shoulder.

"That doesn't mean it's enough to cure the curse," Sylvia pointed out. "We need to find the last piece to complete the artefact. In fact, I'm surprised the high priest hasn't come back down here and—"

Heavy footfalls descended the stairwell. "We might not have time," I said.

I only had to glance at Monju and Laoise to know we were thinking the same thing. We couldn't let the Emerald Cloth and the Orb of Dashiell fall into enemy hands, especially when our chance of escape was so little.

I tossed Laoise the Orb. As Monju snatched the Cloth and Laoise searched for an appropriate hiding spot for both artefacts, I grabbed a bewildered Sylvia and threw open the door, pulling her into another long hallway of sarcophagi and the skulls of the long-deceased devout. The footfalls of our enemies intensified, and within a moment, Monju and Laoise followed, slamming the door shut. To our right was a set of narrow steps, leading up. I climbed them two at a time.

"Where are you going?" Sylvia hissed, wrenching her arm from my tight grasp.

"Trying to find a way out!" I retorted.

"I don't—"

"Go!" Laoise shouted.

The guards threw open the door in the corridor we'd just left; Sylvia didn't argue. The three of them followed me up the steps to the closed, unlocked wooden door. We entered a musty room, painted white and scattered with wardrobes, pedestals with old tomes, and shelves containing high priest vestments, some of which had been moth-eaten. This was the sacristy, where the priests prepared for their ceremonies.

As Monju and Laoise shoved pedestals and other heavy objects to block the approaching guards, I headed for another wooden door with a square peep-window. On the other side was the apse: the semi-circular main theatre of the church that housed the altar. The priest from earlier was nowhere in sight; the service was over.

"This way," I said, throwing open the door.

Sylvia, panicking, ran after me. The heavy wardrobe and pedestal wouldn't hold the other door much longer.

The four of us raced out of the sacristy onto the apse. Before us were several steps down to the golden coffins and the now-empty pews. The frozen bodies had been removed.

As the last of the guards descended the winding stairs to

the catacombs where the four of us had disappeared not too long ago, I left the apse and hurried down the wide steps into the rows of pews—until the twin front doors of the cathedral swung open with a bang. I halted mid-step, retreating back up to the apse, as the entire cathedral flooded with more guards—led by none other than Boris, his sword drawn triumphantly in the hunt, and just behind him, Leszek, trudging angrily down the red carpet between the pews, his silver crown skewed on his head.

"You are surrounded, Violet Fox!" Leszek said woodenly, his voice echoing in the empty, tall cathedral. "Surrender."

The sacristy door flew open to our right and four guards burst out, their weapons drawn. Laoise and Monju drew weapons, but we were woefully outnumbered. Sylvia raised her hands in surrender.

"Father!" she said, daring to step forward to the edge of the steps.

Leszek's expression betrayed no alarm. Boris led his men—there had to be two dozen, at least—down the red carpet and settled before the steps.

"Nowhere left for you to go," Leszek said to me. "Stop this embarrassing charade."

Sylvia, in her seemingly infinite well of nervousness and pride, ran her mouth. "I-I had to go with them, Father, they captured me and put me in this stinky old wagon, and made me cut up my favourite dress, and—"

Directly to my left, a second sacristy beckoned. I took one sidestep towards it. Behind me, I heard Laoise and Monju mimicking me. Boris's men followed my every movement, while trying to be respectful of Sylvia's rant.

But before I could make a run for it, that door, too, swung open. Out stepped Dominique, dressed in a black rough-hewn gown. Sylvia's whining trickled away. As the door shut behind Dominique, I saw the high priest cowering in a corner.

In one hand, she held a long, curved knife. In the other, between her bony fingers, the remaining piece of the Emerald Cloth shined limply. "So. J'ou y'are here."

LESZEK TRUDGED UP a few steps, his men ready to lay down their lives for their emperor.

"Set down your weapons," he barked at us.

Two dozen bannermen, Dominique, Leszek, and Boris— versus the Violet Fox, a newly healed Laoise, a skilled assassin with a moral code, and a useless princess.

I hated to admit when I was outnumbered. But no Roamers waited in the pews, or hid in the catacombs. It was just us against a sea of enemies.

Turning my head to the side, I nodded at Monju and Laoise. They lowered their weapons to the wooden floor. Sylvia's mouth burbled anxiously.

"I...I don't have any weapons!" she protested.

Leszek seemed suspicious of his daughter, but he held up a hand to stop Sylvia from prattling on further. "Fine."

Slowly, under the watchful gaze of over two dozen armed men, I withdrew the knife from my apron pocket and set it on the floor.

"Good." Leszek gestured to his men. "Guards, take—"

"She keeps at least two." Dominique's sharp tone cut through Leszek's command. His men faltered.

I glared at her. She'd probably made it her duty to know everything about me. After a tense moment, without breaking eye contact with Dominique, I hiked up my dress and unstrapped the sheath belt around my thigh and dumped it on the floor. Some of the men, uncomfortable, averted their gazes.

"Anything else you want me to remove?" I asked her.

"J'our tongue," she replied. "Once—"

"In time," Leszek interrupted, shooting her an impatient look as his men grabbed our weapons. "That's the artefact?"

Dominique examined it with disdain. "Supposedly."

I wondered if the high priest had told Dominique about its failure in his earlier service.

"Thought the Lady had half a day on them," Monju muttered behind me as six bannermen closed in on us, pointing their swords at our throats.

Honestly, I'd thought that between the disruption of Silent Thief's Pass and the coup at the castle, we'd bought ourselves more time than that. Apparently not.

Dominique strode towards Laoise and circled her with contempt. "J'ou seem in good health."

Laoise said nothing, as we were taught when faced with the enemy. Her hands shook.

Holding up the green piece of the Cloth, her gaze darted between the suddenly healthy Laoise and the potential artefact. "Dis y'is not d'only piece. Search dem."

Two of the men had to hold me down as another ran his hands through my apron pockets, squeezing the fabric of my dress, and feeling up my waist.

"Das enough," Dominique commanded of the men handling me. "I will search de women."

They fell away from me and Laoise at once. Sylvia had already batted away her bannermen, shouting threats and screaming insults. Leszek seemed annoyed with the whole affair. "Dominique..."

"Lift j'our arms," she told me.

I did. I had nothing to hide—not on my person, anyway.

"Dominique, this is a waste of time," Leszek said, his voice strained.

"De Violet Fox always has tricks. If we catch dese tricks, dey can no longer hurt us." Putting the Cloth piece between her teeth, she patted me down roughly and methodically from armpit to ankle. Unsatisfied, she sneered at me and moved on to Laoise, performing the same fruitless task.

I shot Monju a quick glance. The guard drew away from him after giving him a similar rough treatment, shrugging at Dominique.

Relief flooded me. Good. They'd successfully hidden the artefacts in the reliquary room.

"Sir," said one of the bannermen to Boris and Leszek. "Nothing."

"Fetch me y'a torch," Dominique said suddenly to one of the men.

"I've had enough of this charade," Leszek said.

But Dominique listened to no one. When none of the men obeyed, she went down the steps, grabbed a still-lit candelabrum next to the four golden coffins, and returned to the apse. She brandished it like a weapon, moving past Leszek, Boris, Sylvia, and the others as if they didn't exist. To her, they didn't. It was just her and me. As it always had been. As it always would be.

"What are you going to do? Burn my clothes off?" I taunted her. As long as I still had my tongue, I would use it against her, until my dying breath.

She smirked. "Not j'our clothes. Just dis."

From her fist, she produced the Cloth again, holding it dangerously close to the flames.

"No, don't!" I exclaimed.

"Why not?" Dominique asked, smiling. She tipped the fabric to the flames, and tossed it on the floor.

"No!" My knees gave out. The men beside me hooked my

arms, preventing me from interfering with the burning artefact. The fire consumed the fabric, turning it from a light green to an unpleasant, unholy black. As the fire petered out into embers, Dominique kicked it across the floor. The burnt cloth trailed a black, sooty stain as it skipped towards the altar behind me.

Now the artefact would never be complete. Keegan might never wake up. No one affected by the curse would ever have freedom under the sun.

"Find de rest of de y'artefact," she said to the men surrounding us. "If j'ou find nothin'—burn every piece of fabric j'ou find."

The men looked to Leszek for approval of this order. He trudged up the rest of the steps and pointed towards the sacristy we'd emerged from. "Do as she says—but burn nothing without bringing it to me first."

Dominique rounded on her father-in-law. "Dat is not—"

"I refuse to destroy the one thing that will cure this Freetor curse," he said with a hint of finality. "There are good people who I can't afford to lose."

"I y'am destroyin' all dose y'infected tonight," she said through her teeth. "I will not have dis curse hangin' over our heads. It only gives dat rat"—she pointed to me—"power."

"We will discuss it later," Leszek said. He gestured to Boris. "Go with her to the catacombs. Ensure she doesn't cause trouble."

"Yes, Father," Boris said with a deep bow.

Dominique sneered at him and threw open the sacristy door. She glanced back at me. "We will destroy j'our curse. And den, I will destroy j'ou."

She slammed the door behind her. Boris reopened it, frustrated, and half a dozen men followed him into the sacristy and down into the catacombs.

I shared an anxious look with Monju and Laoise. They hadn't had much time to hide the Cloth and the Orb. Though only Freetors could see the light blue glow of magic, an Orb was still an orb, and a collection of green patches might not be hard to miss.

Sylvia had been silent throughout this exchange, staring at her toes. With her brother and Dominique gone, she dared to speak again. "Father, please believe me. I didn't want to be here."

"Then you shouldn't have come," Leszek replied, without sympathy. He returned his focus to me. "You have cost me time and resources, Fox. Worse, you have endangered the very people you wanted to protect."

My heart sank. "You murdered my people. You attacked my city."

"Your city." He shook his head. "Freetors don't really have possessions, do they?"

That stung. I'd underestimated his knowledge of our customs. "We have few. Thanks to those who pushed us down, those who continue to—"

Leszek wasn't even listening. He muttered something to a guard at his side, and he rushed down the steps, down the red carpet, to the cathedral double doors. Then, to me, Leszek raised his eyebrows. "You were saying, Fox?"

My words meant nothing to him. I was a thorn in his side. A troublemaker that he should have killed when he had the chance. He wasn't frightened by speeches on moral right and wrong. He simply wanted to take what wasn't his.

"You're here and alive," he said finally, glancing over his shoulder at the doors, "for one reason alone. Bring him in."

The bannerman pulled open the double doors. In stepped two other guards carrying a third man in irons—a man I thought I'd never see again. His head drooped from exhaustion, yet at my gasp he lifted it to meet my gaze, his bruised and bloodied face alighting with joy.

I couldn't stop myself. "You're...here. Alive."

I ran down the steps towards him, arms outstretched, blinded by a painful longing. No one moved to stop me. He was in chains, but my father had come for me. Leszek had lied. Of course he'd survived the fight in the hedge maze. He had the magic of our people in his veins.

Yet he had the look of a man full of regret, which halted me in my tracks.

Of course Leszek hadn't executed him. Ivor Ferguson—Conal Driscoll—was far too valuable to kill. Especially after his demonstration of magic in the hedge maze.

"Kiera," he said, his voice soft. Mournful.

In that word, I knew what he had done. The price he had paid to stand before me now. How they'd made it from Marlenia City to Sallingaire with an entire army, just as quickly as we had travelled with four beaten-down people in a two-horse hay wagon.

"But why would you help them...?" I said, swallowing over the lump in my throat. I could barely finish my question. It made it too real.

My father's gaze never left mine as the guards released him, setting him down on his feet. "I couldn't let them hurt you."

Hurt me? We'd escaped. We had found the Cloth—we would have found Keegan, too, if they hadn't arrived as soon as they did. He was the one who'd hurt me. I drew away from him, confused and wounded.

"Take them," Leszek said, bored. "Find a place in the catacombs to store them until we have sorted the chaos here."

"Hold on," my father said, rattling his chains at the Frostfire patriarch. "That wasn't our deal."

Leszek smiled thinly. Although not as tall as my father, his position on the altar steps gave him the presence of a holy figure, and here in the cathedral his deep baritone voice carried to the heavens. "The Violet Fox and her band must stand trial for her crimes before you can have them. You think I'd let her walk away without facing the people's justice?"

"You said she would be freed! Your version of the people's justice is death or slavery!" Desperation stained my father's expression.

"Well," Leszek said, with a rare chuckle, "let us hope that justice does not call for death, and only for slavery, hmm? Then you may buy her for the appropriate market price. Which, I imagine for the Violet Fox, would be a handsome sum. Certainly triple her weight in silver. You'd have to compete with other bidders, of course. That would only be fair..." Leszek trailed off, as if thinking how full his vault would be after such an auction.

A dark cloud passed over my father. He had no silver. He barely had his false name.

My hands clenched into fists as two guards gripped me under my arms and started to pull me away. "You can fight him!" I shouted at my father. "If you won't, I will."

"That is ill-advised," Leszek said darkly.

A guard slid a cold blade under my throat. I stopped struggling.

"You use any of your vile Freetor magic," Leszek continued, gesturing to my father, "and I will kill her. There are those who will pay for her, alive or dead."

So he knew the truth about my father's heritage. I locked eyes with him, willing him to do what he must. Leszek was a tyrant. My father had a duty to his people to destroy him—no matter the cost. I was but one person in a vast sea of those in need.

Slowly, sadly, he shook his head at me, as if to say that killing him would make no difference. Instead he gestured behind me, to the two doors leading into the sacristies, to where the other guards had disappeared with Laoise, Monju, and Sylvia. "And what of your daughter? You wish to sell her too?"

"She will be dealt with separately, but she will spend some

time in the catacombs with the criminals. That will help her come to her senses." He nodded at the two guards holding me. The knife was removed, and together they lifted me up and carried me down the aisle and up the apse steps to the wooden door to the sacristy.

"It is as it was before," Leszek said solemnly, his voice echoing as he descended the steps to face my father.

"Don't let him win," I shouted at him. "He can't win while you still stand."

I wrestled with my captors, yet I struggled more with keeping my father's attention. He averted his gaze, staring only at his enemy. A deep hatred marred his features, and even though the chains held him back, it was then I saw Conal Driscoll, the Freetor.

"It's not like before," my father said to Leszek.

"I have eyes. She is exactly the same." He gestured to me, grinning. "The difference is I don't care about this one and you do, which is better."

This one. The guards dragged me further away.

"This is not the same," my father said again, more hurt this time, unable to look me in the eye as he pleaded with his enemy. "I am not in love with her."

"Aren't you?" Leszek punched my father in the gut, driving him to his knees. Satisfied with his cruelty, he glanced at me, grinned at my terror, and then stuck a fat finger into my father's sternum. "You lured Sarysa from me with your Freetor tricks. Now I will take your new lover from you. That is justice."

I felt as though Leszek had struck me down too. "I'm not—You're the one who murdered Sarysa," I shouted. Then, to my father: "Do something."

"Be quiet, Kiera," he replied, smiling grimly. "The lie is all he has."

One of my guards threw open the door and ushered me into

the sacristy, but not before Leszek knocked the wind from my father, driving his face to the floor. He did not resist.

Once again, decisions my father made long ago rippled to the present, catching me in the force of their current, robbing me of agency. He had abandoned me before. Now, by refusing to rise up, he was abandoning me again.

* * *

Back through the priest's ready room, down the narrow steps, and a swift right down the corridor—I fought them at first. I wouldn't be a Freetor if I didn't resist. Yet the dark holes of long-gone eyes regarding me with indifference was its own deterrent. I settled for dragging my feet in the end. My father had acted weak. He said he did this all for me. Yet it didn't make sense. Leszek could have me killed, yes. But my father could kill all of them—he was more powerful than anyone, possibly the last person with true knowledge of Freetor magic. Why would he subject himself to this humiliation and allow Leszek to have this control over him?

Maybe that's his plan. Maybe something else is going on.

I desperately wanted to believe that. His actions had caused so much suffering—so much death—for our people. Always, he said he did it for the remote chance that he'd see me and Rordan again. He never tried to find us.

I closed my eyes. It was time I faced the truth. My father was not the man I wanted him to be. I was tired of fighting for his approval, of justifying his goodness when he'd collaborate with the enemy for his own reasons, in the guise of saving me.

Mostly, I was just tired.

They led me down yet another long corridor of sarcophagi. At the end was another wooden door: it had already been busted in by the two other guards. Inside, doors lined the walls of dusty, abandoned prayer rooms. From the trail left in the dust by my friends, it seemed they'd dragged Laoise and Monju into one room. I didn't see any locks on the doors—this wasn't a proper dungeon—but as we were outnumbered and now without weapons, escape would be difficult. A guard sat with the satisfaction of a king in a chair at the end of the short hallway.

To my right, one of the men thrust open the door to the nearest room and out came Sylvia, her fists catching the man's chestplate.

"I demand you release me at once!" Sylvia said, pushing against him futilely.

The guard caught her, smiling. "Your father wants to teach you a lesson, my lady. When he decrees it, you will be free."

I stepped into the prayer room as Sylvia, indignant, pushed the guard away and crossed her arms. "When I am High Queen, you will be dismissed immediately from my service. That is a guarantee."

I coughed as the dust from the cellar blew into my nose. The guards shared a laugh as they shut and bolted the door.

"What happened?" Sylvia asked as she twirled around. Her dress blew up more dust from the floor.

My body ached. All I wanted to do was sleep. It would help me forget the pain. Of course I had to be put in the same room as the loudest person in the cathedral—maybe the loudest in whole realm.

"Your father and my—uh—the Advisor have a complicated history," I said, waving away the bits swirling in the air. I scrubbed my face with my hands. "Your father is taking his revenge, and enjoying himself very much, I think."

"My father always gets what he wants," Sylvia said quietly. "He always hated Ivor Ferguson, too."

"Well, now we're suffering for that hate. The Advisor always thinks that he can win, that he can outsmart the man in power. Maybe not this time."

Sylvia seemed to chew on my words for a while. "You never call him by his name."

"The Advisor?"

"Yes."

I clasped my hands and leaned back against the wall. He had already occupied too many of my thoughts. He didn't deserve it. "It's hard to know what to call him. He's been a lot of different things in his life."

"Or because you love him."

Like a small flickering candle within me, the answer flamed yes. My knees buckled. After all he'd done, how could that be the answer? Just because we shared the same blood, that didn't mean that I had a strong bond with him. He killed to advance his status. He let my brother—his son—die to keep his position a secret. To keep my position a secret. He betrayed us all, just now—because he thought it was the right course of action for whatever game he was truly playing.

Yet he'd saved my life at Driscoll's End. He didn't have to follow me there. He'd looked out for me. He could have left me for dead on that cliff and taken the Spear for himself and he didn't.

He had come for me when I thought I had no one.

Even when Rordan had been captured, he'd locked me in my chambers to try and distance me from the fallout—to protect me. He'd put his position in danger.

Without him, we would not have been safe at Gareth Manor.

He'd gotten himself captured by his most hated enemy just to deliver Bidelia's message.

He'd put himself on the line for me—when he had nothing to gain. Maybe he did care.

As my heart warred with itself, something in Sylvia's words

struck me oddly. A laugh bubbled up inside me and echoed in the small prayer room. I clasped my chest as I relished in the sound of freedom. The freedom to tell the truth. "You think I'm in love with...the Advisor."

"You're finally admitting it." Sylvia leaned against the stone wall, smirking. "Took you long enough. I knew you'd finally come to your senses. When we find Keegan, I have to be the one to—"

"Sylvia."

"Don't interrupt me! You're a liar and you've said enough. I wanted to give you a chance. Not every girl—woman—knows when she's in love with someone else. I wanted to give you the chance to figure it out. You had...time...with the prince. You went off into those horrible woods, and maybe, somehow, you convinced yourself that you could love him. Infatuations pass. True love...true love prevails."

I shared her smile. "In the songs. But—"

Now she climbed to her feet, and began pacing. "What did I say? If you love him, you have to go to him. I don't know what you see in him. He's far too old, in my opinion. Though it wouldn't be the most unusual match. He has been charmed by young women in the hedge maze in the past. The romance of it all! He risked his life, betrayed us to save you! But the sooner you tell him your true feelings, the sooner—"

"Sylvia, the Advisor is my father."

"—I can smooth this over with—" She caught her breath, and whirled in place, her tattered skirts fluttering. "He's...what did you just say?"

I took a deep breath, savouring the moment. "Advisor Ferguson...as you know him...he's my father."

"But..." Her eyes widened. "He let you into the castle. He set this up so that the Freetors—"

"Nope, it just—"

"This is a Freetor plot—"

"It would be a terrible plot if that were true."

"You...you half breed!"

"Not even." I stood and pressed a foot against the wall, crossing my arms. "Do you want to know the whole story, or do you want to keep guessing?"

She clutched her skirts, knuckles white, as she shifted her weight from foot to foot. "I suppose we have time." She blushed furiously and turned her cheek. "How dare you let me prattle on about romance! You enjoyed that."

"I did, yeah." I'd needed it.

She slumped back down to the stone floor, sitting on a pile of straw. "I am a stupid fool."

"You're maybe a little foolish." She shot me a resentful glare. "But I don't think you're completely stupid."

"Yes, you do. Just when I think I have it figured out, I am told I am wrong. That's how it's been, my whole life. It's why Father is marrying me off—to a child, no less. So I wouldn't be his problem, anymore."

"Sorry," I muttered.

"I don't want your pity." She brushed her hand against the dusty floor, and lowering her voice to a level she thought I couldn't hear, whispered, "Just when I thought I could have true love..."

I averted my gaze. She probably forgot that Freetor eyes and ears in the darkness were superior to those who had lived their whole lives on the surface. I had thwarted Sylvia's chance at happiness with Keegan multiple times now. She'd even sawed off Keegan's finger, as if that would invalidate my marriage—my feelings—towards him. Even though she couldn't understand that he didn't want to be with her, I wondered how many times her family had told her she had to marry a prince—or someone fitting of her station—to be happy.

"Dominique doesn't know the truth about my father," I said finally.

She sniffled. "She...doesn't?"

"I don't think so. Only you, Monju, my friends. Keegan."

"Half the world, then."

I clasped my fingers. "Not everyone knows the whole story, though."

She brightened. "Well?"

"All right." I took a deep, wobbling breath. My throat tightened. "It started the day he brought me home a journal, when I was barely six-years-old..."

Seventeen

I SLEPT LIGHTLY, lingering in a place between waking and dreaming, before a violent force shook me into action.

"What? What!" I flung my limbs everywhere, grabbing hold of Sylvia's blonde curls.

"Ow! Get off me!" Sylvia tumbled into a heap beside me, recoiling from my rough treatment as I came to my senses. She backed up against the opposing wall, indignant and offended.

"Why won't you let me sleep?" I asked.

"We've been here for nearly two hours and all you've done is talk and sleep! It's time for you to get us out of here. I hear men talking out there!"

Groggily, I pressed against the stone, feeling each rough edge dig into my back. It helped stimulate my senses, reminded me of the time I'd spent locked up in the dungeon in Marlenia City. My father hadn't rescued me then, either. Not right away.

I didn't need a rescue. I needed real sleep. My body had endured days of spotty rest, soaked in rain and grief for a man that was not only very much alive, but who I couldn't trust. Maybe I shouldn't have trusted him in the first place. He'd softened me with a tale of lost love and promises of magical aid. I rubbed my eyes. "I thought you were content to wait in here for your father to judge you innocent."

"It's been two hours. Didn't you hear me? He would never leave me here this long. He must truly believe I hate him. As for you and the other two, he'll likely execute you in the early morning if you don't get out of here." She pointed at the door. "Your friends are over there. I don't think they've made an attempt either. They're probably waiting on you."

That sobered me. I'd been wallowing in self-pity and agonizing over Conal Driscoll so much that I'd selfishly abandoned all thought of immediate escape. Of course the East would execute us without ceremony. I had done so many treasonous things. I figured Dominique would want to torture me for a bit—but in the end, death was certain, and not just for me.

"Right," I said. My voice was hoarse and my eyes, watery. "Suggestions?"

Momentarily forlorn, she drew her knees to her chin. "I...I have to show you something."

I blinked away some sleep. "Something?"

She lifted her skirts, revealing one of her bare legs. A brown strap wound tightly around her thigh. Quick as a shadow killer, she pulled out a knife—I recognized it as Laoise's—tightly wrapped in its leather sheath.

"Have you had this since we got in here?" I demanded, leaping to my feet.

"I believe a thank you is in order," she said haughtily. "And yes, of course I have. I hid it when my dear father burst into the cathedral."

"Why didn't you—?" I took a deep breath to contain my anger. "I'm impressed, all right?"

She preened. "I'll take that. Now, tell me what your plan is."

"My plan." The future seemed foggy and unimportant now, and I could no longer rely on my father's voice within, telling me to focus and make plans and don't fall asleep with the enemy.

I pressed an ear against the door. Sturdy and unlocked, the doors—and perhaps the entire room—had been designed to block out exterior sound. The guards, at least two of them, spoke at full volume not even a stone-throw away at the end of the prayer room hallway, muffled by the walls. Not only would we have to get past them, but any other posted guards alerted by the commotion in the catacomb hallways. Who knew how many men Leszek and Dominique had down here with us, ensuring we didn't escape.

"Is there a different way out of the catacombs?" I asked.

"I believe so. But my research didn't involve schematic sketches."

I sighed. "All right. You're going to pretend to faint, or feign a sickness, and then when the guard comes in, I'll stick him with the knife." I put out my hand expectantly.

Sylvia made a disgusted face. "Absolutely not! I am not giving you the knife."

"So you want to be the one to stab the guard?"

That appealed even less. "No! I don't want to kill any of them. They're my men!"

"Not anymore. You think they're going to forget that you turncoated your family? Isn't that social suicide for nobility?"

"You might be a murderer, but I'm not."

"Then why do you have a knife?"

"For...hurting!" She looked sheepish. "Or! You could dig with it."

"And dull the blade? This is stone. You know we're not getting out of here without a fight, right?" I flexed my fingers, putting out my hand again. "Trust me, Sylvia. I won't hurt you."

She threw me a glare. "You wouldn't dream of it."

"It's not in my interest, nor do I want to," I replied. "Look, I trusted you with my father's secret. I didn't do that lightly."

She considered the blade. "You're not killing my men."

"I can't make—"

Pressing the knife to her chest, she turned up her nose.

I raised my eyebrows. "Fine. I will make a concerted effort

not to kill anyone. But I will probably have to hurt them. Knock them unconscious, at the very least."

She handed me the blade hilt-first. "Very well. Only if necessary. They mishandled me—this will be their punishment."

If that was her justification, I could live with that. "I can't take on half a dozen guards myself. So as I take on these two, hop on into Monju and Laoise's cell. That will even the odds a bit."

"But they took their weapons!"

"Your men will be armed—once we take out a few, we'll take their blades. Then we'll see if we can find ours again, if that even matters to Monju and Laoise." I sounded more confident than I felt. So many things could go wrong. This was the oldest trick in the book. It was likely they wouldn't believe us. Sylvia had been right about one thing: we had to retrieve the Emerald Cloth and the Orb from the reliquary room and then get out of here. I desperately needed real sleep, but I didn't want to think about what Dominique and Leszek had planned for Laoise and Monju—and Keegan—when they returned.

I squeezed to the right of the entrance, knife unsheathed. "Go ahead."

Sylvia, looking somewhat embarrassed, knocked on the door. "Help! Please, I...I don't feel well!"

The men continued talking in their low rumble. I nodded at her encouragingly and added my voice to the affront and pounded on the wooden door. "Hey! Lady Sylvia is not well, please help!"

Voices faded away and Sylvia retreated from the door, getting down on her hands and knees. The door creaked ajar. "You stirring up trouble over here, my lady?"

"I don't feel well, you idiot!" Sylvia whined, gripping her stomach and gagging.

"Uh huh. You're fine." The door started to close.

"No wait!" she called, reaching desperately for him.

I grabbed the knob and yanked the door open to see my action mirrored in the door across from us. Laoise and I jumped the same man. The knife met flesh in his leg. He screamed. Laoise had leapt onto his back, going for his eyes. Laoise's cautious expression melted into a grin when she saw me.

"Good timing," I commended her.

"Maybe," she said, tightening her grip around the guard's neck as he tried to throw her off.

The other guard drew his knife and aimed for Laoise. I removed my blade from the first guard's leg—blood poured from his wound onto the stone floor—and advanced on the second guard. He narrowly avoided my attack. Laoise scrambled off the first guard as he tumbled to the floor. She tried to grab the longsword at this belt, but he fell at the wrong angle, making it impossible to grab.

A single, open door separated the catacombs and the prayer room hallway. I slammed it shut to buy us some time, yet even in doing so, I heard the rustling of clanging armour. Things were about to get dire.

Sylvia, hands on her ears, dashed into Laoise and Monju's cell. "What happened to you?" I heard her ask Monju.

Before I could check on him, the second guard drew his longsword. Laoise managed to unsheathe the other man's weapon as he hung on the verge of consciousness, bleeding out on the floor. She swung at the second guard, but the weapon was too heavy for her, and she lost her balance. The guard laughed.

"Get back in your cell, girls," he taunted. "Dead or alive, it doesn't matter—less of a mess for us all if you cooperate."

"No chance," I said.

I leapt forward, swinging, and he backed up against the wall. His reach was far longer. One long swoop, and he drove us towards the hallway door. Laoise used both hands on the longsword, fighting to keep it balanced in her grip.

Sylvia, seeing our struggle, appeared in the doorway of the prayer room, hands on her hips. "Stop! I order you to stop at once!"

The guard hesitated, hardening his resolve. "I can't do that, my lady. My orders come directly from—".

I took advantage of the distraction and rushed him. Laoise followed my lead. He blocked Laoise's attack, but I evaded him, grabbed his arm, and got him in the armpit.

Growling, he spun, wrenched his arm from my grip, and I fell to the floor, prone. Laoise stuck the longsword in his leg and he fell to his knees beside me. His dirty fingernails dug into my bare leg. I kicked him off multiple times, struggling for purchase as I righted myself, sunk my hands into his blond hair, and hit him hard on the stone, knocking him unconscious.

Outside, in the catacombs, I heard heavy footsteps and men shouting. We had to get out of here.

Laoise dragged the longswords into the prayer room with Monju. He didn't look well. Propped up against the wall, Monju grimaced and clutched his side, but when he saw me, he straightened and hid his pain.

"Monju tried to escape. They beat him," Laoise replied.

"Is fine," Monju said, climbing slowly to his feet. "Must find artefacts and the prince."

"Where is the Emerald Cloth?" I asked. "And the Orb?"

Monju glanced at Sylvia, uncertain if he should reveal the location in front of her. "Safe. Hidden, among the reliquaries."

"We'll retrieve them and get out of here," I said. "If we can survive the guards."

The longsword was heavy for Laoise, but she wielded it anyway and gathered two more knives from the Frostfire men's belts. Sylvia paled when I offered her the knife, coated in blood. "They wouldn't dare hurt me," she said.

"Take this one. Is clean," Monju said, offering one of the Frostfire knives.

Reluctantly, she wrapped her noble fingers around the hilt. We were as prepared as we were going to be.

Weapons readied, I threw open the door to the catacombs.

A middle-aged guard charged us.

Conal Driscoll materialized from the darkness behind the man, grabbed his neck, and snapped it.

The four of us drew back into the hallway, terrified.

Sylvia kicked the door shut. "What. Was. That?"

I blinked. I could still see the man reaching for us, and my father appearing from nowhere, killing him.

Laoise grabbed my knife hand to stop the shaking.

He was calling my name. "Kiera? Can I...come in?"

I shook my head no. "Yes."

Sylvia looked at me as if I were insane. "You saw what he—"

The door creaked ajar, revealing my father bit by bit, until it hit the opposing wall with a sickening bang. He held my stare. "You're in the middle of an escape, I see."

"Why are you so surprised?" I asked, my voice wavering.

Why did you just kill that man in front of us?

"My apologies," he said, wiping his unclean hands on his trousers. "Especially to you, Lady Sylvia. I hadn't meant to kill him. When I saw him here, before the four of you—I acted impulsively. Forgive me."

She fixed him with a terrified, blank stare, unable to unwitness the violent, senseless act.

"Why are you here?" I demanded. Of all the questions I had for him, that one found its way out first.

"Like you, I escaped," he replied simply.

"Seems unlikely." I couldn't stop trembling. "Where are the Frostfires now? Leszek? Dominique? Boris?"

"Dining, with a royal relative within the city," he replied.

Sylvia crossed her arms, jealous.

"And how did you escape?" I asked.

"Leszek hit me across the head, but not as hard as he thought. I pretended to be unconscious. Dominique returned and they argued about what to do with me--he envisioned an elaborate emotional and physical torture, she was ready to burn the cathedral down with you and me in it. He forbade that and some of his men escorted her out. The guards put me in a different wagon, intending to transport me to an underground prison within the mountains. We weren't out of the city before I crawled out and escaped."

"No one followed you here? They must know you're gone by now—"

"That's why we need to hurry. Where is the Emerald Cloth?"

Monju and Laoise exchanged glances. I didn't know whether to trust my father either.

"If we don't have the Emerald Cloth," my father pressed, "we can't wake up Keegan."

I balled my hands into fists. "Do you know where he is?"

"I do."

Sylvia brightened. "Take us to him at once."

"The artefact first. Or artefacts. I assume you brought the Orb to identify the Cloth."

I stared at the floor. To cooperate with him without knowing his true motives frightened me. All I knew is he would go to great lengths to keep me safe—or at least, what safe meant in his mind. "We'll retrieve the hidden artefacts," I said, gesturing to Monju and Laoise. "And Sylvia will wait here, with you."

He smiled. "No. You'll stay with me and they can retrieve the artefacts."

I stiffened. He knew Monju and Laoise wouldn't leave me, not without waking Keegan. I dreaded being alone with my father. Not now. But it was better than him snooping around among the reliquaries. It was also unlikely Sylvia would successfully steal the Emerald Cloth pieces under Monju and Laoise's noses. The further from Keegan she remained, the better, as our alliance drew to a close. "Fine."

Nodding, he headed down the hallway and gestured for me to follow. "We'll be in the cathedral proper. By the coffins."

Laoise shook her head slightly. I shrugged. I didn't want to trust him, either—but what choice did we have right now?

"Will hurry," Monju promised.

Sylvia leaned against the dirty stone wall. "I should go with you."

"I'm not going to steal Keegan," I said.

"I suppose not," she relented. "But he might."

My father had disappeared around a corner, hopefully out of earshot. "I won't let him take Keegan anywhere. And I won't let him out of my sight until Keegan is awake and we're out of the city."

Monju cleared his throat. "Would prefer not to harm the Advisor, but if the Lady asks...."

"I hope it doesn't come to that," I said.

"Be careful," Laoise said.

I smiled at my friends and followed my father's footsteps through the corridors, up the narrow staircase, through the sacristy, and into the massive cathedral once more. Eerily empty, the ancient stone, tall ceilings, and stained glass echoed my footsteps as I stepped into the apse. Down the steps, my father leaned against one of the four golden coffins, arms crossed, looking up at me as if he hadn't seen me for years.

Behind him, the Silver Spear lay on top of one of the coffins, glowing fiercely.

"Why do you have that?" I demanded. "I gave that to Bidelia for safekeeping."

No. The capital. They'd failed. The thought of Bidelia lying dead in the throne room struck me hard. I left to save Keegan instead of staying and fighting alongside my people.

My father nodded. "Do not worry, Kiera. Bidelia and your allies are safe. The castle is in their hands. I merely borrowed this. For insurance, in case Leszek broke his word en route. A gentleman's agreement is only as good as the gentleman."

An agreement he never should have made. "How did you hide it on your way? How did no one hold it by accident...?"

"Wrapped it, secured it, as we did before. I can shroud things, temporarily, as I told you. Kiera, you are focussing on the trivial."

"I don't want that thing anywhere near Keegan. Or anyone. You didn't use it on all the guards...did you?" My grip on the knife tightened.

"What does it matter? We have three of the four artefacts. Wake them if you want a fight. Otherwise, they're in for a long rest," he replied. "Your friends had best hurry, before reinforcements arrive. I did leave a nasty trail of frozen bodies behind me."

My body shook. I didn't know what to say. We had taken great pains to hide the Spear in Baile Gareth and in Marlenia City. Now, my father had brandished it across the province and used it to further his own crusade.

"I'm sorry, Kiera," he said softly. "You're angry with me. But if you—"

"Angry doesn't begin to describe it," I said, my voice wobbling. "You rescue me, then you chastise me for wanting to rescue Keegan, then you send me on a quest, then you leave me without telling me what you're doing, then you show up out of nowhere again and change the mission. And then you pretend to be dead because you're collaborating with the enemy!" I pointed at the Spear. "This is only more fuel for Dominique's fire that is going to kill innocent people!"

"If I had the capacity to send you a message, I would have. But it would have endangered you and Laoise further. The Spear helped me find you, Kiera."

"You should have killed Leszek when you had a chance," I spat. "Instead of transporting his army here."

"He deserves to rot. Painfully," he said patiently. "I played him as he played me. I am working on a larger scale than you—"

"Spare me. Once Keegan is awake, I don't want to see you again."

Taken aback, he straightened, looking concerned. "If that is your wish."

"It...it is." I averted my gaze. I wished to not have this conversation with him.

Our words faded into echoes as the heavy weight of silence descended upon us. The building creaked, and beneath the floors, I thought I heard the scurrying of my friends below.

"Do you really know where Keegan is?" I asked. "Or is that a lie, too, just to get me alone with you?"

"Oh, I do know. Dominique discussed it at length on our journey here."

"With you?"

"No, but my hearing is...exceptional."

"Then where is he?"

Again, his smile was condescending. "Here, in the cathedral. Dominique had him placed here days ago. She plans to use the cathedral as a large pyre for her mass cleansing of the frozen plague. Destroy the symbol of a dying religion, destroy the magical artefacts and the irony of magic-hating Marlenians coveting them—that sort of thing. When your friends return, I'll show you Keegan's location. Then you can decide what to do about the Daughter of the North."

He could never resist a captive audience. "If you care about him, you'll show me now. Or is he not the son you never had?"

His smile faltered. "He is. It gives me no joy to be this way with you. Yet I know you don't trust me now. And why would you? I haven't been honest. I've kept my cards close to my chest. I've had to, Kiera. For so long."

"You didn't have to." My voice felt small as I descended the steps towards him. "I want to trust you. Give me a reason."

He canted his head. "I will do anything for you."

My mind spun. I felt drawn like a moth to open flame, except this flame roared with the fury of a burning castle. "Why?"

A flicker of emotion passed his face, as it had before, when we spoke in the castle. The crack in his stony visage showed me who Conal Driscoll could be, and my heart lurched, desperate to grab hold of that man.

"You're the only one I have left," he said.

"You abandoned us," was all I could say. My mother died. He'd left us and had a whole other life on the surface...and had the nerve...? I shook my head. "You could have saved the young servant woman: Sarysa. And yet, you didn't."

"Had I the power I do now," he said, "it would have been easier. I would have snuck into her cell faster and freed her, before Leszek could spill her blood and let it pool around his boots. I would have returned to the underground and found you and your brother again. We would have been a family."

I crossed my arms. "How do I know any of that is true?"

"No more lies from me, Kiera," he said solemnly. He held out his hand. "I promise."

My fingers curled, tempted to reach out for him. I simply looked away.

Instead of pressing the issue, he glanced over my shoulder. "You saw me in the maze with Sarysa, Lady Sylvia, that night when I confessed my feelings for her. So you know I don't murder women in fits of rages, like your father."

Monju shut the door to the sacristy, joining Sylvia and Laoise before the altar at the top of the steps. I hadn't heard them come in. Laoise held the Orb, using her skirt as a glove to protect from the searing heat. Monju gripped the roughly sewn Emerald Cloth reverently.

"We have the artefacts," Sylvia said coldly, her face pale. "Give us Keegan."

Laoise and I exchanged glances. She could see the glowing Silver Spear just as well as I could.

"Very well," he said. He walked around the golden coffins, making a show of palming each one, breathing deeply, and muttering. As he performed his ritual, I grabbed the Spear. There was no way I'd let my father have it now. It felt welcome in my grip, as if it had always been mine.

He didn't seem to care that I'd taken it. After a moment, he finally gestured to the second coffin from the right. "He's in here."

I knelt and peered closely, and sure enough, three well-hidden hinges hit my fingers as I scrubbed the edges. They weren't just decorative, as I'd assumed. "Is this going to poison us if we force the lid?"

"He can open it," Sylvia said to my father. "Then we'll know."

Smugly, my father inclined his head at the rebel noblewoman. "As you wish, my lady. But unlike the catacombs, these coffins are mainly ceremonial. They are not meant for actual bodies, but rather, as representations of the four loyal servants of Dashiell, who carried the four artefacts in the four cardinal directions, to spread Dashiell's message of love and prosperity. If the Loyal Four really were entombed in them, they'd be silver. No, likely they're used for storage, most of the time."

I thought of the four bodies that had lain on the golden coffins, and the families that had wept for them, praying for them to wake. "Let's get on with this."

My father slid his thumbs along the thin edge of the lid and pulled. Nothing. He tried again, heaving with all his strength.

Being solid gold, or a golden alloy—supposedly—the lid obliged briefly before snapping shut.

"I'll need some help," he said, glancing at me.

"Could be poison," Monju warned.

"That's what the Cloth is for," I replied. I set my knife on top of the adjacent golden coffin. I positioned myself next to him, feeling suddenly like the thief I was, breaking into the cathedral to steal riches from the Church. I prayed the man I loved was really in here, that I had not been led astray by the false hope and promises of my father.

Struggling with one hand, I helped my father lift the gold lid to the shallow coffin. The dim light of the cathedral crossed him like a sunrise. Keegan. He was here. Whole. Mostly. Minus his left forefinger—but that didn't matter now. I'd found him. We had found him. Seeing his face as he slept peacefully, his lips slightly parted in question, I was overwhelmed emotionally. I couldn't tear my gaze from him.

"We did it," I said.

"Not yet." Sylvia peered into the coffin, scrunching up her face. "Why would she put him in here? Gold, yes, but surely a silver is more befitting—"

"What better for Dominique to begin her destructive trail of fire than in a holy place?" I said, interrupting my father, who had begun to quip something similar. His remark petered out, and he nodded at me, smiling. He was proud of me.

"The Emerald Cloth?" my father asked Monju, beckoning him near.

Hesitantly, Laoise and Monju came down the steps together. He looked far better than he had in the prayer room. Just carrying it seemed to return his smooth swagger and air of confidence. He held it daintily by the corners, revealing the hole in the centre, where the final piece would forever elude us.

To prove its validity, Laoise raised the glowing Orb higher, silently enduring the heat. The Spear pulsated in agreement, yet nowhere near as hot.

"That is it?" Although the Cloth glowed fiercely in response to the Orb and the Spear, my father couldn't keep the surprise from his voice.

"No guarantee this will work," Monju said warily, holding out the roughly sewn, fragmented cloth. "Not without missing piece."

My eyebrows knitted together as I climbed the apse steps to the altar. Where had Dominique kicked it?

"It worked on me," Laoise said. "I'm fine."

"Curing poison not the same as curing a magical curse," Monju pointed out.

I snooped around the altar on all fours until my fingers grazed it. The final piece of fabric, nuzzled between the gold-silver altar and the stone wall bracing the large stained glass window. I coaxed it free. Only the edges had blackened from Dominique's flame. The rest emitted a faint, pulsating blue glow, as the other pieces had when they touched Laoise's skin. Cuts and bruises I'd endured from imprisonment felt less urgent, and I climbed to my feet, grinning.

"I found it," I said.

Monju and Laoise turned in surprise and Sylvia looked equally stunned. "But Dominique—!"

"Earthly means cannot destroy an artefact," my father said, looking pensive as I gave the missing piece to Monju to sew into the mini tapestry. "Though, obviously, it can be broken into pieces. Likely that's how it eluded scholars and collectors all these years."

"Edges are uneven. Could be that there are more pieces than this," Monju mused. Once he'd affixed the centre piece, he offered the Cloth to me. "There. Now the Lady should wake the prince."

As I took the artefact, a low rumble filled the cathedral. The double doors buckled under a severe weight, as if under siege. Two guards, their weapons drawn, ran towards us from the transept bisecting the area with the pews and the double doors, immediately spotting us. There must have been another entrance to the cathedral down one of those corridors.

"I thought you'd gotten rid of all the guards," I said to my father.

"Patrols found us. I locked the doors, but...." White-blue lightning danced between his fingers, but it abruptly faded. Alarmed, he tried again. Nothing.

"Laoise, the Orb," he commanded, holding out his hand.

She recoiled.

"Unless you know how to use it, you'd best give it to me. Now."

The guards had doubled their numbers. They grinned as they neared. No doubt there was more on the way. Laoise and I shared a silent, reluctant look. My father had already abused the Silver Spear. I certainly wasn't going to follow in his footsteps. Yet this was an ambush, and we were outnumbered. We needed his magic.

I nodded and she passed my father the glowing, crackling Orb.

Confident again, he strolled towards the guards, as if inviting them to a gathering in this cathedral he owned. "Good of you to join us. I imagine you heard what happened to your comrades."

Shouting commands, the attackers ran down the red carpeted aisle. Monju ran into the fray after my father, drawing a sword as the four men charged.

Thwap! The white lightning shot from the Orb and hit the lead guard in the chest. Gasping, the man fell to his knees as the white sparks sank into his body, turning him from solider to rag doll in seconds.

Demoralized, the other three hesitated, and Monju met their blades eagerly.

Laoise readied her blade. "Take care of Keegan. And her." She gestured with her head to Sylvia.

I nodded, rolling the Cloth in my hand. The pounding on the double doors intensified. I saw no blue glow on the door: it wasn't enchanted. Whatever my father had done to lock it, it wasn't going to last much longer.

Keegan slept peacefully, blissfully unaware of the fight. This wasn't how I pictured waking him. Likely he wouldn't be strong enough to help us fend off Leszek's men.

This was what I'd come to do. As Laoise, Monju, and my father kept the enemy at bay, I folded the Emerald Cloth lengthwise and pressed it to Keegan's forehead, dabbing away the ice. Sylvia watched, but made no move to stop me—perhaps equally apprehensive of the Cloth's power and the fearsome Silver Spear I brandished.

"Please wake up, Keegan," I whispered. "I didn't get a chance to tell you before. I should have. But I...I love you."

A warm blue glow enveloped his body, as it had with Laoise. Yet the Cloth, stronger now as a whole, burned my hand. I cried out, gripping my cool skirts, which offered no relief. The ice beaded into water and slid up his body into the Cloth. The artefact drank hungrily, absorbing the curse of the Silver Spear, undoing the work of its sibling.

The sounds of battle seemed distant now. I leaned in close, caressing his damp face, running my thumb over his scarred lips and kissed him.

He blinked. His unfocussed, yellow-green gaze darted from me to the Cloth as it slipped, forgotten, from his forehead into the coffin bed. His gaze settled on me again as he inhaled sharply. My spirits lifted. I'd done it. Keegan was awake. Alive.

"Who are you?" he asked me.

Eighteen

MY MIND COULDN'T comprehend the question. I'd come so far, sacrificed too much to play this game with my husband. "Keegan, I'm Kiera. Your....your wife." I smiled despite the advancing guards. It felt good to say those words to him now that he was awake. Now that we were finally together again.

Monju and Laoise barked orders and my father responded as they rushed to deal with the onslaught of attacking Frostfires. Sylvia maintained a cautious distance, as if unsure which side she truly supported.

I waited for that spark of recognition to return in his gaze. Laoise's mind had been foggy at first, too.

"I'm Kiera Driscoll. The Violet Fox," I said again. I hesitated. "At first, when we met, we didn't like each other. Because we were on opposite sides. But then we fell in love." I took his three-fingered hand, remembering what Sylvia had done to his sleeping body, wishing I had physical proof of our private ceremony.

He slowly sat up, withdrawing his maimed hand, comparing it to his dominant hand, as if studying it for the first time. I quickly snatched the Emerald Cloth from the coffin and shoved it in my apron pocket. Lost, frightened, he looked to me for answers.

I was a stranger.

"Say my name, Keegan," I pleaded. "You promised, when we said our vows..."

In my frustration, I lifted my arms, revealing the Spear. His eyes widened in fear.

"Nightmares," he said, shaking his head. "That...thing..." He climbed awkwardly out of the golden coffin, falling to the ground with the balance of a newborn calf. Hurriedly, he righted himself as he rounded the coffin. "Stay back!"

The fear in his eyes was more than I could bear. It was a weapon against my heart. "I'm not who you think. This..." I held the Spear as far as I could from my body without releasing it. "This isn't me. You have to remember who I am."

He shook his head. All he could see was the staff. But I couldn't put it down, not with our enemies so close, not when I had to protect him.

Sylvia, like a sabre-tooth tiger lying in wait, finally found her opportunity. She approached Keegan as he hid between the golden coffins. I adopted a defensive stance. I should be helping Monju, Laoise, and my father. Yet another battle unfolded before me, one I could not leave, not until Keegan regained his senses.

Seeing her approach, Keegan braced himself as he rose to his feet. "Who are you? Stay back!"

"No. Keegan, listen to me." She was oddly calm, one hand extended as if to pacify a wild animal, and another, reaching for her skirts. "I'm your wife, Keegan."

"No you're not!" I exclaimed. "How many times do I—?"

"Behind!" Monju shouted at me.

I spun as a guard charged through the pews and smashed his staff against my spear. I dispatched him quickly, knocking him out against the pews. Turning my attention back to Sylvia, I saw she'd lifted her skirts and had untied something around her left thigh. Another weapon? My heart pounded, and despite the three approaching enemies, I charged for Sylvia. I wouldn't let her hurt him.

Instead of another knife, however, Sylvia pulled out a small leather drawstring pouch. Keegan, unsure, drew back against the golden coffin, glancing at me with equal suspicion and mistrust.

"Keegan," I began. "Whatever it is, don't—"

The plea fell short as Sylvia withdrew Keegan's rotten, cloth-ringed finger.

It took my prince only moments to make the connection between his purple, jagged three-fingered hand and the digit in Sylvia's grasp.

"What did you do to me?" he demanded. He shivered in disgust, recoiling further.

"I did it to prove you belong to me," she said, trying to close the growing gap between them. "She forced you to marry her, you see. Look at that ring on her finger! It is a lie! You had to marry her, you see, because she used magic on you. That was why I had to remove it! It was her foul magic that put you to sleep. I was the one who came all the way here, put my royal neck at risk, just to save you!"

Keegan shook his head compulsively. He nearly tripped as he backed against a massive pillar. "Stay away!"

"No! You must remember me, Keegan!" Sylvia whined.

"She cut off your finger," I said, trying to keep desperation from my voice. My credibility waned as I raised the Spear against the approaching guards. "If you don't want to be frozen like Lady Milda Seacream and the others, you'd best fight someone else."

Their faces paling, they turned tail and took the fight towards Monju, Laoise, and my father instead. They held their ground by the double doors. Monju and Laoise stood back to back while my father slung tendrils of white and blue lightning from the Orb and his fingers.

"Both of you...leave me alone. I...I don't even..." Keegan looked wildly around the cathedral, immense and menacing as it tossed around the confusing sounds of battle. "I can't do this."

He took off through the pews, around a pillar, and nearly tripped again as he threw aside the red rope and descended the staircase into the catacombs. My friends had bottlenecked the guards, driving them back to the double doors, yet they kept coming through the transept. It was only a matter of time before they found Keegan Tramore wandering around in the catacombs and recaptured him.

I ran between the pews after him. It was the most direct route. But the wooden seat banged against my shins, and holding the Spear slowed me down. Yet Sylvia was just as determined, and she dashed around the coffins and blocked my path at the end of the pew, her presence as large as the pillars supporting the cathedral, bunching her dress with fury. "You knew this would happen."

"Knew?! If I'd known this, I wouldn't have woken him up in the first place. More like you knew, and cut off his finger just to gain his sympathy."

"I cut it off because you don't deserve him!" she spat. Immediately, she blanched as a hint of regret marred her fair features. She shook it away, determined. "I will make him remember me. He will be mine. You'll see."

"Sylvia—"

She spun and headed after him. I held up the Spear. I considered using its long reach to jab her into frozen silence. But I'd be no better than my father if I did that. She was a blind, desperate fool—and she needed to be shown the error of her ways. I blinked and she darted down the catacomb stairs after Keegan.

About to follow, I whirled instead as I heard the clanking of armour. Another guard had made it past my father and my friends and clambered into the pew. I clashed my spear with his halberd and kicked him in the stomach, sending him backward into the aisle. His weapon clattered to the stone at my feet.

I needed a different weapon, one that wouldn't petrify anyone at the slightest touch. Tossing the Silver Spear into the pew beside me, I picked up the fallen attacker's halberd and knocked him over the head.

Another roar—this time, of victory. Not ours. The double doors buckled and opened halfway, enough for a wave of men to squeeze through, into the cathedral. We'd lost our bottle-neck. Monju, Laoise, and my father retreated from the entrance, forced down the narrowly carpeted aisle to my side. I left the pew, but unwilling to leave the Silver Spear unguarded, I adopt-ed a defensive stance.

"The priest's room," Monju said, somewhat winded, point-ing to the sacristy door up the stairs.

"Too indefensible. They can get into the catacombs over there—"

My father brushed by me and collapsed into the pew, next to the Silver Spear. It was within his reach, yet his grip faltered, his breathing hoarse. He was tiring. He hadn't lied about magic taking a toll. He looked like he'd aged ten years in the past ten minutes. He couldn't keep up this assault.

"Where's the Orb?" I demanded of him. Both the artefacts on my person glowed.

"I have it," my father gasped. "But Leszek is sending all patrols to converge here."

Beside me, Monju had put up a good front, and although the Emerald Cloth had mostly healed the beating he'd received earlier, it could not restore a good night's rest, which none of us had had in days. Sweat poured down Laoise's face and coated her dress. We couldn't keep this up.

There was a commotion at the double doors. A woman yell-ing—it sounded like Dominique. I had no desire to fight her or her shadow killers, if she'd brought any. An older man, shout-ing in return. Boris, or maybe Leszek. The guards had stopped their advance—they gathered and blocked at the entrance. Some shifted their weight anxiously, as if conflicted by competing orders. If we were going to escape, now was the time.

The problem would be getting my father out of here. I grabbed his arm, pulling him up in the pew, and withdrew the Emerald Cloth from my apron. The tips of his hair had whitened, like the peaks of the snowy mountains. I didn't know if he was absorbing magic from the artefacts to use against our enemies, or if his deep well of power was his alone, but I couldn't leave him dried up here in the pew for the Frostfires to find and abuse.

Laoise and Monju beside me were getting antsy. "We have to go," Laoise said.

"Find Keegan and get him out," I told them.

"Better that the Lady—"

"He doesn't know me," I interrupted Monju. "Sylvia's down there. Find them both. I'll deal with the Frostfires." Laoise began to protest but I cut her off. "We have three of the artefacts. Dominique is out there. I have to face her and put an end to this."

"I won't let you do that alone," Laoise said.

"She's not alone," my father rasped. His voice sounded stronger already.

"We'll get Keegan," she agreed, "but then we're coming back for you."

"No," I said, glancing at the Frostfire guards. The shouting match on the other side of the doors intensified, and the guards idled by the door, their weapons ready, but stilled by some unknown order. I handed her the Emerald Cloth. "One of us has to use this on the frozen. It will erase their memories, but it will break the curse."

My father considered the patchwork artefact in a new light as I passed Laoise the Emerald Cloth. She clasped it tightly, nodding reluctantly. The price of the cure was high, but it would save our people from eternal, frozen slumber. Questions swirling in her hazel eyes, Laoise grabbed Monju's hand. "Don't die."

"I'll try," I replied.

Monju nodded silently. There was nothing for him to say that I didn't already know.

Together Monju and Laoise ran hand-in-hand the rest of the way down the aisle, up the steps to the apse, and disappeared into the sacristy. The guards exchanged a brief conversation and ultimately allowed them to escape. Their gazes rested on me, as if waiting for me to give them an excuse to attack.

"You should have gone with them," my father said.

"I'm not leaving you here defenseless against the Frostfires."

Disbelief crossed his eyes, with a hint of amusement. "I thought you didn't want to see me again."

"I don't." I gritted my teeth, steeling myself against the regret that came with those words. Maybe he wasn't so defenseless. Maybe allowing him to die at the Frostfires' hands was the way to go.

There was no time to reconsider. The Frostfire guards scattered at the threat of a blazing torch Dominique carried as she squeezed through the partially open doors. She stormed down the aisle, her gaze burning with a singular purpose: kill the Violet Fox.

I raised the halberd. I would gladly fight her just to give my friends a chance to escape and break the curse of the Silver Spear.

"J'ou cannot escape fire," she said thickly. "I should have done dis earlier."

No one dared to stop her—except Leszek, who scrambled into the cathedral after her. He called her name, his voice nearly hoarse from arguing. Armoured and caped like the emperor he was, Leszek carried an immense broadsword. His focus shifted from Dominique to my father, prone and weak in the pew.

"There you are," Leszek growled. He readied his sword like an executioner. "You've outlived your usefulness, Ferguson. Or whatever your real name is."

"It's Driscoll," I spat.

His white eyebrows lifted, distracted by the truth, and Dominique swung her torch at me. I leapt back, nearly tripping backward over an unconscious guard. I wouldn't be caught off-guard again. I came at her hard with my halberd. She attempted to meet me with equal vigor but all she had was the torch. I knocked it from her hand and it rolled into the pews to my left. The flames licked and blackened the wooden seat. She stooped to retrieve it, but I drove her out of reach.

Now weaponless, she recoiled towards Leszek, who now seemed more fascinated with my rivalry with Dominique. My father's gaze remained on Leszek's broadsword as his hand neared the Silver Spear.

For a brief moment, none of us moved.

As much as I was happy to stall them both, I also wanted this to be over. I wanted my husband back. I wanted my people to live peaceful lives under the sun without fear of persecution.

My resolve renewed, I rushed Dominique. Leszek met me instead, crashing his broadsword against my halberd. My non-magic weapon snapped in two.

I evaded his swing, the blade narrowly missing my toes. I searched the floor for weapons. My knife—I'd set it on one of the coffins, but it was too far. Save the Silver Spear.

Leszek grinned.

My father swiped the Spear from the pew and Leszek heaved his broadsword at him. Nimbly, my father stepped out of the way and the broadsword struck the pew. The blade became stuck in the split wood.

I locked eyes with my father. I didn't have to ask. Rising to his feet with grace and elegance, he tossed me the cursed weapon and I brandished it at Leszek and Dominique.

The growing flames warmed my side and the smoke returned me to past tragedies, the last place I needed to be. I squeezed my eyes shut, tears gathering in my eyelids. No. I have to focus.

"Kill her," Dominique ordered her father-in-law.

The telltale plink of Leszek freeing his blade had me opening my eyes. He sneered at her, breathing in the smoke. "I am your sovereign."

Leszek lifted his sword high above his head and aimed for my father. He wasn't about to listen to Dominique. My father retreated a step, hand on the back of the pew in front of him, but seemingly unsteady on his feet.

The High King of the East swung.

Dominique clasped her hands tightly, grinning.

The guards at the door were statues, gazes fixed on their emperor.

"No!" Shifting my weight and screaming strength into my arm, I hurled the Silver Spear at Leszek Frostfire.

My aim was raw and true. As it was two hundred years ago in Marlenia City, so it was again in the cathedral in Sallingaire, when a rebel drove a magic spear through the chest of a nobleman. This time, it wasn't the tyrant's son who paid the ultimate price—but the tyrant himself.

The Spear slid through his chest, melting its path through his chestplate on impact. Shocked at his impalement, his mouth hung open, bobbing hoarse pleas. The frost spread outward from the puncture wound, and now desperate, he looked to me, his eyes wide and sober as his broadsword tumbled to the broken pew and then to the stone floor. "Reverse this foul magic," he said. "Reverse—"

He craned his neck to Dominique, but her smile reflected the flames, wild and unexpected.

Frost coated his neck and wound up his face. I didn't want

this! The man had to be awake to answer for the crimes he'd committed against my people. He deserved to be imprisoned in the darkest cell—not to endure eternal sleep, filled with blissful nothingness.

But I didn't have the Emerald Cloth. Laoise did. And she was hopefully far from here.

Dominique drew back from the cursed ice as I approached him and withdrew the Spear from his chest, hoping against hope it would stop the spread. It was too late. The ice completely enveloped him and his hand no longer had purchase; he toppled in the aisle. The force of the impact did him in. He shattered into millions of hard, icy shards, flying into the pews, the carpet, and even into the fire—unmelting and eternal.

I stumbled back. I hadn't meant for that to happen. If I had only caught him—

And then I saw Keegan at the top of the catacomb steps, holding on to the railing, horrified at what I had done.

Forgetting my father, Dominique, and the guards, I held out my hand to him. Had Laoise not found him? Why did she not remove him from this place? "He...he surprised me," I stammered. "If I hadn't..."

He shuddered. There was no excuse for murder. Not when he didn't know Leszek. Not when he didn't know me.

Keegan spun and ran for the entrance, noticed the guards staring at him like he was a ghost. He turned towards the transept, disappearing down the long, dark corridor of seemingly infinite archways. One of the guards looked from Keegan to Dominique, and decided he had a will of his own. He started off down the transept. I got ready to run too.

"Estop!" Dominique shouted at him, her voice so bellowing and powerful that it halted both of us. She smiled at me again, a truly terrifying sight. To the guards, she said: "Wait pour me y'outside. Go."

The guards exchanged glances. They wore Frostfire colours: their emperor was dead. One dared to speak. "My lady—"

"My husband is j'our new emperor," she said patiently. Her tone was laced with poison. "I y'am his voice. Obey."

A small smile portrayed my father's amusement, but he said nothing, and looked content to do the same. The guards conferred quietly and seemingly decided to listen to her--for now. Begrudgingly, they slipped through the partially open double doors a handful at a time, leaving Dominique to deal with me and my father.

She seemed unconcerned that she was now outnumbered. Perhaps she had always been that way.

"J'ou have given me a gift," Dominique said to me. She kicked the tiny crystal shards, ruffling the carpet beneath her boot.

She stood with the confidence of a shadow killer, yet she had no weapons. I raised the Silver Spear and I couldn't stop shaking. I was a murderer. I'd killed before. I'd killed recently. I'd crumbled Silent Thief's Pass, crushing nearly a dozen men.

So what was one more murder, if it meant my people could be free?

My thoughts had the same curse as the Spear, freezing me in place, and Dominique knew it. "I certainly didn't mean to."

"Per'aps he was right," she mused, staring at Leszek's remains. "It is better pour j'ou to remain alive. To feel dat pain of losing."

I swallowed over the lump in my throat. "I don't feel the same about you."

"Den try to kill me."

She waited. My throwing arm shook. The Spear remained trapped in my grip.

Grinning again, she turned. Without looking back, she walked down the aisle and squeezed through the double doors.

Something in me snapped, and it was only then that I hurled the Spear. It flew through the air and clattered to the floor a stone-throw from the entrance. She was already gone anyway.

It was just my father and me now and all I wanted was to be alone. I tore down the aisle.

"Where are you going now?" he asked finally.

What did it matter? I'd told him I didn't want to see him again. Let him remain in this sure-to-burn cathedral. I retrieved the Silver Spear and planted it like a flag in the stone and peered down the transept. "To find Keegan. Obviously."

"Leave him. You saw his fear. All he sees is a murderess."

Standing on the red carpet next to the flames as if it were a mere campfire, he surveyed the shards of the emperor covering the carpet and stone like a light icy snowfall and then pressed his boot into the floor. The crunch echoed in my ears.

"That's not who I am." My face was damp. I was weak. My father was right. I was a murderer. I'd unwillingly paved the way for Dominique to seize control of the East, which would only prolong my people's suffering.

"You have to give him time," he said, strolling towards me. "With Leszek dead and three of the four artefacts retrieved, we have bought ourselves a day, perhaps the night, before the Frostfires reorganize their troops and their priorities."

I held tight on the Spear, glowing as he approached. "We can't rest. Dominique won't. We have to calm Keegan down and get out of here before he runs right into her hands—she'll sell him into slavery!" I didn't know what Sylvia would do if she found him first—whatever had happened to her.

He looked grim. Perhaps it was the fight. He straightened his bloodied vest and dirtied, billowing coat. From his pocket, he pulled the Orb of Dashiell. I breathed a sigh of relief. He still had it. He inclined his head, his gaze fixated on the glowing sphere, responding greatly to the proximity of the Silver Spear.

Fine. Let him stew in his magic. I turned and started towards the transept.

"If you find him now, he will never truly love you again."

I nearly tripped on his words. Using the Spear for purchase, I turned, leaning on it as I regained my balance. "What does that mean?"

"He's running now, from everyone. He trusts no one. He has no name. No title. No lands that he can remember. I imagine he's found a way out of the cathedral and is huddling in an alleyway somewhere. It's raining now." He gestured to the stained glass all around us. "His features are gaunt from his time in the woods. Someone may recognize him, take him in for the night—but with his three-fingered hand, and his back flogged as it is, it is unlikely anyone would believe he is truly Prince Keegan Tramore. If no one finds him, then he has learned a valuable new skill. To run and hide and fight another day. Does that sound familiar?"

My breath was raspy. "He's alone out there. I can't let him think that he's alone, that he's always been alone."

"Not forever, of course. Think, Kiera. You have freed him from the burdens of the crown."

"He was never burdened. He wanted to rule." Unlike me.

"Then you are giving him a gift. The one thing you could never explain or share with him, not really. Now he will know how you lived, even if it is just for a brief while. Perhaps he will return on his own, his memory restored, with more love for you."

I stared down the dark, arcaded corridor. Although the flames slowly devoured the pews and the smoke surged to the high ceilings, I was reluctant to leave my father within the main area of the cathedral, alone. Something had changed between Conal Driscoll and I, more than just his hair, now shockingly more white than black.

He noted my hesitation and moved with me slowly towards the corridor, keeping a safe distance. "What do you plan to do with Keegan when you find him?"

"I'll tell him the truth. I'll wait for his memory to return. Then he can decide."

"His memories may not return. Ever." His voice lanced my deepest fear. "But I could help you with that."

My flats scraped against the floor as I slowed.

I'd spent all this time looking for Keegan and the Emerald Cloth—and at what cost? My people, enslaved and executed and frozen on the order of tyrants. I had followed my selfish whims instead of remaining in the castle, where I belonged, where I needed to be to help free those who had been wronged.

I faced him. "What would help Keegan?"

He lit up, glad I'd asked. "We cannot stop now, Kiera. Once we have freed those who deserve freedom and punished the wicked, we must continue our quest. We have three out of the four artefacts. The orb. The spear. The cloth...."

"The slab," I said numbly.

"The Granite Slab, the Midnight Tablet—it has many names. It is said to contain the first spark of magic," my father began. "It is said that anyone who possesses it can learn any and all secrets they desire. They could have anything they have lost. The last recorded location was four hundred years ago, in the Southern part of Xii..."

My thoughts drifted as I turned back to the cathedral. I had been so busy fighting I hadn't noticed there was more than one stained glass mural, placed high enough in each cardinal direction that only the devout craning their necks would see them. The one in the apse, with Dashiell handing his monk friend the Orb. Then, to the left: a monk holding a staff, facing the double doors. Above the double doors: a monk with his back to the congregation, looking over his shoulder suspiciously as he held a granite tablet at his side. Finally, to my right, a woman nursing a man in bed with a striking green cloth.

Each of them was so focussed on their artefact, so singular

was their purpose they couldn't bear to be in the same mural. They were too invested in their own mission: separate the powerful objects, so that no one person could possess all.

So no one person could become godly.

"Why is finding all the artefacts so important to you?" I asked, tearing my gaze from the murals.

I had interrupted his story. He became flustered. "The more important question is, why isn't it more important to you, Kiera? The Orb saved Keegan's life. The Spear cursed Keegan. The Cloth awakened him. Freed him. And now, the Slab—the Midnight Tablet—will restore him completely."

I could have Keegan back. For the price of finding one more artefact, of holding that much power.

"No," I said, backing away. "None of this would have happened if you hadn't put this idea of artefacts in my mind. I won't get stuck in this endless cycle of magic curing magic." My voice shook as I spoke the hideous truth, the truth I'd wanted to ignore, but could no longer. "Magic is the problem. Not the solution."

"Magic is in your blood. It defines you. The Freetor cause. All magic has done is serve you."

"No. Magic has served you." My palms stung with the pain of my nails, but I didn't care, it helped me focus. "Elder Erskina's thirst for power was her undoing. The apprentices, they were corrupted, too. Magic was so carefully controlled by the Elders because they knew it could destroy anyone who wanted to acquire more of it. It made the surface people fear us and it was why they drove us underground. Magic doesn't heal, it only kills, and drives people mad. We can never be at peace when there's someone out there wielding dangerous, powerful relics." I cradled the Spear and took a deep breath to strengthen my resolve as I approached him. "Magic must be destroyed."

"No, Kiera—"

"You've become an Elder. The very thing you hated. All it takes is one person to abuse their power, and countless could die."

"Think of the good we could do, Kiera. Marlenia City would be protected. No more invasions. No more threats. Once I have the artefacts, I can help you and Keegan unite our people. You could rule—we can rule without the East and the North breathing down our necks."

"And what happens when you've vanquished that threat? You'll look to the South, and you'll find an enemy there. You'll spend your life spinning in all cardinal directions, seeing your flaws reflected in others, and you'll destroy them all. You'll become just like all the others who craved power and died for it. Please, Father. Don't be like them. Don't leave me again."

I gripped the Spear fiercely with both hands to keep from trembling. He had to see reason. I could. Conal and I were the same, Bidelia had said.

He brushed my hair from my face and then moved past me, into the arcaded transept. "All I have done, was for you and Rordan."

Even mentioning his name broke down an old barrier, one I had placed there just to survive. I bowed my head, unwilling to face the man who did this to me, to us. Fortunately, he was just as unwilling to see me cry. His stride was confident. He didn't even look back. He thought he'd won.

I mustered my courage. "I'm glad Rordan isn't here. Nor my mother. They wouldn't recognize the man you've become."

He halted abruptly, frozen in mid-step.

"You didn't need a servant's love to return to us," I said, stumbling after him into the corridor. "We could have been enough for you. And yet...we weren't."

Turning, he had the most peculiar look on his face. The same expression he'd given Leszek Frostfire, right before they'd imprisoned me in the prayer room. The snarl of a deceiver who had been caught in his own web.

"I have been patient. You always speak in anger. I tried to teach you. And I was going to let that go," he said. "But I've changed my mind."

My body slammed against the wall, hard. Stunned, the Spear fell from my grasp and clattered to the floor. Groaning, I braced a foot on the wall, willing to fight him if I had to, yet my limbs became tangled in thorned vines emerging from the stone. The more I struggled, the tighter they wound around my ankles, my wrists, my torso, and finally my neck.

Conal Driscoll, his fingers tented as the last of the black faded from his hair, approached the thickened mess of vines. They grew and parted around him, respectful as he brushed a curly lock from my face again, tucking it behind my ear. A thorn, sharp as my knives, dug into my neck and threatened to slide across my throat.

"You're going to leave me here, like this?" I asked.

"You'll escape. There is magic within you too, Kiera." The vines sprouted blue and violet roses as he mentioned my name. "You felt it in the mountain pass, when you collapsed it. You can tap into the artefact's power, as I can. I can teach you how to become stronger."

"You're out of control. You just can't see it." Tears streamed down my cheeks. "This can't be who you really are."

"Once I have the Tablet, Dominique will no longer be a problem for you. Keegan can return to his old self. The Frostfires can rest frozen in their desert wasteland. If you wish to remain here, you can. You have people to manage. Justice to dole out with the magic I'm going to leave you. But I will find the Tablet. I owe it to you. This is how I will free you. And myself."

The thorn dug into the side of my neck as I struggled. "I won't let you touch it. I'll...I'll find it first. And then I'll destroy it."

"You can't destroy an artefact, Kiera, especially not Keegan's salvation. But because I love you, I will not stop you from trying." He squeezed his hands and the growth halted. I was immobilized and at his mercy. "However, I will stop you from succeeding. Goodbye, Violet Fox."

Conal turned his back to me and strode down the immense hallway alone. He did not look back.

"Don't leave!" I shouted after him.

His body became one with the shadows, so dark not even I could discern the two. Only the Silver Spear, glowing faintly on the floor, gave me light. He had left me with it, I realized. The symbol of our people—and a way to locate the Tablet.

Just as he'd taken the artefact he'd always coveted, the Orb of Dashiell.

The vines did not let up. I counted seconds at first. Then minutes. The guards, the ones who had been knocked unconscious in the fight, would wake soon. Perhaps they would cut me down. Permanently. By the time they discovered Leszek Frostfire was dead and Boris—or Dominique—assumed command of the East and the North, Conal would be several steps ahead of them. He would not stop until he found the Tablet. Once he did, he'd come back for the Spear and the Cloth.

Then it wouldn't matter who ruled what province or what title they held. Magic had corrupted him, and it corrupted all it touched. People were going to die.

Movement to my left. A knife sawed at the magical vines close to my ear. Keegan, looking more determined than I'd ever seen him, cut through the twisting green plants with the knife I'd abandoned. The plant withered beneath the steel, the faint blue glow of the magic fading as the vine died.

"You came back for me," I whispered. "Why?"

"That man...he tried to hurt you. Trapped you here. It didn't seem right."

He'd seen. He was soaked through—he had found a way outside—but he'd returned. For me.

My throat tightened. "I hurt someone and you were afraid."

"You were defending yourself. And...me." He threw a tentative gaze to where my father had disappeared. "I may not know who I am. But I know that is not the kind of person I want to be."

I nodded, remembering my conversation with Bidelia from the cave. My father had always been this way. Yet, he was still my father. I could not distance myself from that, no matter how hard I tried.

Keegan finished cutting the vines and I managed to untangle the rest. I stepped out, thorns scraping my bare legs as the vines lay dead at our feet.

"You said you knew who I was," he continued, looking hopeful.

Despite everything, I smiled. "Yes, Keegan. I mean—your name. It's Keegan. And you're a prince. But don't let that go to your head."

"I don't see how it could. I don't feel like a prince." His three-fingered hand reached around to his back as he rubbed it tenderly. I wondered what the Emerald Cloth had done to his scars. "Do you know who did this to me?"

My voice trembled. "Yeah. That's a long story."

His gaze held mine, the question blooming there before it passed his scarred lips. "Are you really someone important to me?"

My thumbnails dug into my palms as I squeezed my fingers into fists. The cloth around my forefinger had never felt more tangible.

I could hand him over to Bidelia. He could hide with the other Freetors underground. He might not be accepted, but he would be safe, and virtually unreachable as Laoise, Monju, and

I figured out how to wake the other cursed with the Emerald Cloth. Conal wouldn't dare hurt him. He would have the life I had. He would truly understand me.

He would never remember me or say my name with love again. He would never have what he'd always wanted, what we had promised to work toward: a harmonious, united realm.

"All I want is for you to be happy," I said finally.

His eyebrows knitted together, as if he had expected a different answer. He stepped back, touching the stump of his forefinger, and then pointed to my cloth ring.

"My finger had the same wrapping," he said.

I held out my hand before him, choking back a sob. How could I explain the significance to him, tell him what it meant to me, when it couldn't possibly mean anything to him anymore? What if it scared him away—forever?

"It did."

"I didn't mean to upset you," he said quietly. "I only want to know the truth."

The Tablet would bring him truth. I had to find it.

"I'm not upset," I said, wiping my eyes and steeling myself. The Violet Fox did not cry. Only Kiera did. "We...I...should be going. Before the Frostfires—the people who are after me—return with reinforcements." I turned away.

"The man with the blue sphere, was he a Frostfire?"

"No." I didn't want to think about Conal right now. About what I had to do to stop him.

"I'd like to go with you," Keegan said, catching me by the arm. "If you promise to tell me truthfully everything about who I am, what my place is, and how I ended up here."

I glanced down at his three-fingered hand. He removed it immediately, apologetically, which only made me hurt worse.

"Your full name is Keegan Tramore," I said. "You're the rightful prince of this world. You were cursed by an object called the Silver Spear. Part of that was my fault. I didn't..." I closed my eyes. I was getting off track. "Me and my friends came to rescue you. There are other families who have seized power, invaded your home, killed many of our people. If our people see that you are alive, that I am fighting with you...we might have a chance."

He stared at me for a long moment. "I believe you."

"You do?"

"I do." He looked serious. "But I don't know if I can be much help. Not until I get my memories back. You said I was cursed. Can it be removed?" His voice was growing more confident. He was my prince in every way, except one.

The Tablet was the fabled genesis of all magic in the world. Destroying it might eliminate magic—saving my ambitious father from himself—and freeing my people from persecution. At the cost of never returning Keegan, the rightful ruler, to his old self.

I glanced at the Spear. Regardless, I had to beat Conal Driscoll at his own game. With the help of my friends, I would find the Midnight Tablet.

I would free our people—and those I loved above all— from magic.

Stay tuned as Kiera Driscoll's adventures continue in...

THE VIOLET FOX SERIES #4

Rise.
That's what my heart tells me.
But to fight our many enemies
And finally unite my people,
I must destroy what I've become.

COMING SOON

Acknowledgements

Many thanks to Mum and Dad for their continuing support, to Jessie for all her help and ingenuity, and Marie and Joe, for allowing me to stay. Kate and Leif, for driving me around the province, helping out, and generally being nice friends!

Very special thank you to Best Friend Sam, who edited this book and got really excited about Keegan and endured all seventy mentions of the word *lips*. Do not be surprised if there are a thousand more Violet Fox books because of her. Her support means the world to me.

And of course, Dave, who makes my covers, loads the car, drives me to cons, hangs my banners, buys me ice cream and popcorn, and loves me even though I keep filling his place with more and more book boxes. But then I sell them so it's fine!

- THE AUTHOR -

CLARE C. MARSHALL grew up in rural Nova Scotia with very little television and dial-up internet, and yet she turned out okay. Her YA sci-fi novel *Dreams In Her Head* was nominated for the 2014 Creation of Stories award. She is a full-time freelance editor, book designer, and web manager. She is the co-host with S. M. Beiko of Business BFFs, a podcast for creative entrepreneurs. If there's time left in the day, she devotes it to Faery Ink Press, her publishing imprint. When she's not writing or fiddling up a storm, she enjoys computer games and making silly noises at cats.

Photo Credit: Terence Yung

Website: FaeryInkPress.com
Facebook: Facebook.com/faeryinkpress
Twitter: @ClareMarshall13